Acclaim for John Tho[...]
A Hundred Fires in [...]

"Thorndike is a talented, experienced writer, and Clare and Camilo especially are fully developed, attractive characters.... A highly recommended rendering of a love affair and mysterious slice of Cuban history." —*Kirkus Reviews* (*starred review*)

"The prose is elegantly crafted....*A Hundred Fires in Cuba* is a sophisticated historical novel that effectively deploys a love triangle to capture the essence of a remarkable figure and the historic period that produced him, laying bare the yearnings of the heart." —*Foreword Reviews*

"Thorndike gives us a unique lens into Camilo's life through his fictional affair with American photographer, Clare Miller. Thorndike dissects the torrid-but-thorny attraction between Clare and Camilo along with Cienfuego's inner conflict between idealism and the allure of power.... Every page of *A Hundred Fires in Cuba* breathes with life." —Raul Ramos y Sanchez, author of the Class H Trilogy and *The Skinny Years*

"In *A Hundred Fires in Cuba*, John Thorndike has done something remarkable: written a compelling (and thrilling) love story set in the middle of a revolution. Thorndike's prose is both lyrical and sharp as he navigates a country and a couple in the midst of turmoil and transition. I haven't enjoyed reading a book this much in a long time." —Robert Wilder, author of *Nickel* and *Daddy Needs a Drink*

"With *A Hundred Fires in Cuba*, Thorndike explores his great themes: the mother in extremis, the intrigue of a foreign lover (or two), the beloved child, aging men unmoored, and the complications of passion, passion, passion." —Ted Conover, author of *Rolling Nowhere, Coyotes,* and *Newjack: Guarding Sing Sing*

"Thorndike weaves a complex love affair into one of the hemisphere's great dramas, the Cuban Revolution. Evocative prose, timeless conflicts, and an intimate story full of surprises." —Natalie Goldberg, author of *Wild Mind* and *Let The Whole Thundering World Come Home*

"Thorndike's characters know Havana, New York, and Miami well, and his Caribbean story abounds with righteousness, sex, and love. —Tom Miller, author of *Trading with the Enemy: A Yankee Travels through Castro's Cuba* and *Cuba, Hot and Cold*

John Thorndike brings a resonant emotional sensibility to the days of Clare Miller and her baby girl, Alameda. Thorndike knows that to become a father or mother is a revolution in itself, and projects this against the big screen of political revolution, with its savage and often tragic logic. –Paul Kafka-Gibbons, author of *Love [Enter]*, *Dupont Circle,* and *The Last Murder*

"I would like to go to Cuba. Now, with *A Hundred Fires in Cuba*, I've had my chance through John Thorndike's literary rumba of love and passion amidst the Cuban Revolution.... The dance is easy, intricate, flowing, and sensual, with the tantalizing, wry wisdom that always accompanies John Thorndike's writing." – Lady Borton, author of *Sensing the Enemy* and *After Sorrow*

What you've got here is a mystery and a love story about one of Cuba's favorite revolutionaries. –Nancy Stout, author of *One Day in December*: *Celia Sánchez and the Cuban Revolution*

"Thorndike weaves the novel from two interesting threads – a romance rich with passion and sex, and a crucial moment of history starring Fidel Castro and his cohort. We breathe Cuba's hot humid air, taste Cuba's culture, gain insights into what it means to be Cuban, and more, what it means to be human." –Ray Ring, author of *Arizona Kiss* and *Telluride Smile*

"After two nonfiction books, it is a delight to have a new novel from John Thorndike. *A Hundred Fires in Cuba* takes us through a rich story of 1959 revolutionary Cuba where its characters are tested by their own desires and the obstacles of circumstance and history. It clarifies and celebrates the complications of life rather than offering simplistic answers." —Eddie Lewis, author of *Ray Had an Idea About Love*

"For anyone interested in how Cubans experienced their revolution, or simply a good read, *A Hundred Fires in Cuba* is just the ticket. As its subject, John Thorndike has imagined the relationship of Camilo Cienfuegos, the revolution's most charismatic figure after Fidel Castro, with a young American photographer named Clare Miller. (Thorndike's depiction of their sex life is among the best I've read on this always-dicey topic.) Their story takes place within a vivid recreation of old Havana in the midst of revolutionary change. Although the mystery of Camilo's disappearance while flying from Camaguey to join the triumphant Castro brothers in Havana has never been solved, *A Hundred Fires in Cuba* provides a plausible, satisfying solution. John Thorndike's intimate familiarity with his subject is evident on every page of this compelling, well-written novel." — Ralph Keyes, author of *The Hidden History of Coined Words*

A Hundred Fires
in Cuba

John Thorndike

Beck & Branch Publishers

Love must wait; it must break one's bones.

−James Salter

1

ELISEO wore the old face of Cuba, constrained and still. He was a small man whose right hand had been amputated above the wrist, and he drove Domingo's Chevrolet with deliberation, using his stump to work the column shift. All day he'd chauffeured Clare through the small towns west of Havana so she could photograph the colonial churches. Now, as they drove back into the city, he glided to a stop under some palm trees across from a slatted wooden storefront.

"*Aquí venden cigarros*," Eliseo said, and would she like one?

Some women smoked cigars in Cuba, though rarely on the street. "*El tabaco me mata*," Clare said. Tobacco killed her. She had tried a cigarette when she was twelve, and never again.

Eliseo laughed—a rare sound, but so natural that Clare wondered if it was only rare to her. She had sat up front today for the first time. Domingo always rode in back and liked her to do the same, but she'd had enough of that.

Eliseo crossed the street on foot at his usual measured pace. He drove slowly and walked slowly. Fast driving, dancing, drinking and arguing —these were the expressions of youth, indulgences he had left behind. Not cigars, though. He loved a good cigar. Clare settled down for a wait, knowing how long it could take in Cuba to choose the right tobacco and the right wrap. If it took an hour, that would be fine with her. In Domingo's big house, with his maid and cook and gardener, she rarely had the chance to sit alone and think.

Already the day had cooled. Flocks of parrots streaked past the white-washed trunks of the palms, as the fronds clacked above. Domingo and

Alameda would be home by now. Domingo, who was trying to meet a deadline at his magazine, had told Clare that if she'd shoot all the churches today he would take her daughter to the zoo. Ala, now two, had perked up to hear it. "*¡Quiero fantes!*" she cried. She'd been to the zoo before and she loved the *elefantes*.

Sometimes Clare imagined living in a little house, even a little room, on her own with her daughter. How peaceful that would be. But then, of course, she would want a man and a job and help with Alameda—everything she had now. No matter, it would be lovely to have an hour a day on her own. Twenty minutes would be good.

Alone and idle in Domingo's Impala, she clicked on the radio. The tubes warmed up and a woman's voice rose through the speaker, describing in elegant clear Spanish the rebel offensive underway in Las Villas province, where Ernesto Guevara had led his column into the city of Santa Clara. Soon the forces of the people would deliver a final blow to the despot Fulgencio Batista, restore the Constitution of 1940 and guarantee justice for every citizen.

The rhetoric was elevated, but Clare bent forward to listen. In the newspapers and on television—all controlled by Batista—there was little news of the rebellion, and the government troops were always winning.

Eliseo surprised her, returning after only ten minutes with a small package of cigars wrapped in newsprint. He got into the car and cocked his head at the radio, then at Clare.

"Who is talking?" she asked.

"Violeta Casals. She is an actress and a communist. She is speaking from the Sierra on *Radio Rebelde*."

Of course, Clare should have guessed, it was Castro's rebel station. Violeta continued in her thrilling, educated voice, exhorting the people to hold firm. In the cities, she said, in the towns, in all corners of the nation, the time had come for every citizen to support the M-26 movement and counter the monumental perfidy of the Batista government.

Clare reached out and turned the radio off, then on again. "Is this the station that Domingo listens to?"

"It's the station I listen to."

Eliseo's blunt look was unlike any she had seen him give his boss. She was about to ask him outright what he thought of Castro's rebellion when Violeta paused. "Now for news of the Second Column, which is also fighting in Las Villas. The leader of the column, Camilo Cienfuegos—"

Clare lurched toward the dash.

"—with three hundred men, has now surrounded an army garrison of four hundred in the town of Yaguajáy. Within weeks, perhaps even days —"

Clare turned down the volume. "He's alive," she said.

"Camilo? He was wounded last year but now he's fine. He and the Argentinian have taken over Las Villas. They have trucks and bazookas and are making armored vehicles. They control the roads, the train lines and the airports, and it is only a matter of time."

In spite of Eliseo's animation, she stopped him. "Please, what can you tell me about Camilo Cienfuegos?"

"Señora, I know little about him. Only that he is a *comandante* and very brave. That is always how they speak of him on the radio."

"Did he come with Fidel on the *Granma*?"

Eliseo watched her. "You know about the *Granma*."

"It's a famous boat. Even the *Diario de la Marina* has mentioned it. I also read the *Prensa Libre*, but I've never seen the name Camilo Cienfuegos."

"The newspapers cannot be trusted. It is only on this broadcast that you hear the truth. Or, there is one other place—" He stopped, reached across with his left hand and said, "Please, give me a quarter."

He took the coin she gave him, got out of the Chevrolet, dodged a couple of cars he would normally have waited for, entered the little store and came out a minute later carrying a magazine, holding it high in his hand. He crossed the street almost smiling, almost dancing.

It was a copy of *Bohemia*, a magazine she'd never seen in Domingo's house. Eliseo's thumb was between two pages, and as he handed her the magazine it opened to a photo of Camilo.

With a single glance she drank him in. The beauty of him, the power and assurance. He stood in a clearing in the woods wearing a white T-shirt, his rifle slung over his shoulder. She shut her eyes. Her heart was writhing. She looked again. He wore a full beard and long hair under a battered cowboy hat and stared directly at the camera, wearing the same amused look as on the first day she took his photo in New York.

She stared at him too long, then paged forward through the photos of other long-haired and bearded rebels, their names printed below: Raúl Castro, Ernesto Guevara, Juan Almeida, Huber Matos. For two years she'd been convinced that Camilo was dead. Now she saw that if she'd looked for him she might have found him.

"I have to go back to Domingo's."

Eliseo nodded. He said nothing. This was the usual Eliseo, the respectful driver—but she knew how watchful he was. As they drove into the city he glanced at her several times. Beyond the flat streets of Vedado lay the white-capped sea. She should not have shown him how interested she was in Camilo. As they turned onto Domingo's shaded street Eliseo asked, "*¿Quisiera llevar la revista?*"

No, she did not want to take the magazine inside. He was being sly. She pushed it back across the seat until it hit his leg. "Eliseo," she began. "When you and Domingo drive around..."

She stopped. Her Spanish had fled. It shamed her to ask, and all she could do was stare at him across the broad front seat of the Chevrolet. He parked in Domingo's circular drive, reached through the steering wheel with his left hand to turn off the ignition, and held his stump to his chest. He said, with his usual reserve, "I have worked for Domingo for twenty years. We never argue, and there are many things we do not talk about."

She wanted to hug him. Instead, she held her left hand in the air until he reached out with his own, and they shook. They had never touched before. She picked up her camera bag and tripod from the floor, said "Thank you, Eliseo," and got out of the car.

Now she had to go into the house to see her husband and Alameda, and pretend that nothing had changed.

2

No, it was impossible, she could not face Domingo with her body in such a roar. She stood outside the house and rummaged through her bag, pretending to arrange her cameras and lenses. She had to think this through, on her own, in some quiet place—and she had no place. She would have to have a migraine.

She had them often enough. Sometimes once a month, occasionally twice, but only once before had she faked one with Domingo. It was to escape a weekend with his mother, a woman who believed in quiet children. Alameda often ran around laughing, even shrieking, and Clare didn't like to make her stop.

To adjust her face, she imagined the start of one of her headaches: the deep thud at the back of her neck, the pain rising into the right side of her head. Then she stopped, afraid she might conjure up an actual migraine. Please God, no.

"*¡Mamá, Mamá!*" Ala squirmed out of Domingo's arms and ran up to her as she set her camera bag on the floor. "*¡Vimos los elefantes!*"

Clare picked her up. "Did you see the elephants?" she asked in English.

"*Elefantes*," the girl insisted.

She was going to learn Spanish first, that was clear. Clare often spoke English to her, and Domingo as well, but the language of the house and the city around it was Spanish. Ala knew the difference and now resisted most words in English.

"Did it go well?" Domingo asked. He embraced Clare with one hand, resting his other on Ala's shoulder. Of all men, Domingo was the most considerate. He gave Ala plenty of attention, and she, entirely on her own, had begun to call him *Papá*. No one had corrected her.

"It did," Clare said. "The light was good, with lots of big clouds. But Domingo, I'm getting a migraine. The flashes and aura have already started."

"My dear, I'm sorry. Yes, I can see it in your face."

Could he? Or was he lying too? "I won't eat dinner," she told him, "I'd just puke it up."

"Puke?"

He was rarely stumped by an English word. "Throw up," she said, "*Vomitar*. I'm going up to my room to take some codeine, then I'll lie around a little with Ala. I won't feel like it later."

"I would rub your head and your beautiful neck, but I know that doesn't help."

With a real migraine she could not be touched. With the worst of them she lay in the dark with the shades drawn and her eyes and ears covered. Now she carried her chattering daughter upstairs to the room Clare had insisted on when she moved into Domingo's house. Though she often slept in his room down the hall, she was glad to have her own.

"*¡Elefante-camellos!*" Alameda cried. "*¡Elefante-camellos—y un oso!*" She held her hands wide apart: a *big* bear.

Clare lowered her to the bed but the girl sprang up, wanting to be held.

"Wait," Clare said. "*Mamá* has a headache."

Now she was lying to her daughter. She had vowed not to tell Alameda the kind of lies she heard from other parents. If there was candy in the house, she did not tell Ala there wasn't any. If a decision had already been made, one that Ala wouldn't like, she didn't tell her they would talk about it later. But now she claimed to have a headache when she did not. Migraines were tricky. Clare was never sure where they came from, but sometimes wondered if her own tension brought them on. Several times she had convinced herself that some falsehood she'd spoken, or was living with, had triggered the headache, and in desperation vowed never again to lie to anyone about anything. In the middle of a migraine she might swear to that and a good deal more. Later, after the migraine lifted, her vows didn't last.

In the bathroom she opened her bottle of codeine and poured some down the drain. She could get more any time, it was sold in pharmacies in small brown bottles with twist-off aluminum caps. But she'd noticed how many things Domingo kept track of, and the level of codeine in her bottle might be one of them. A flush of resentment overtook her as she stared at her face in the bathroom mirror. She didn't like what she saw: the darkened look of a hider. While there was much she didn't feel she had to tell Domingo, now she was hiding something huge, something he would hate to hear: that the father of her child was alive.

"Shall I tell you a story" she asked Ala, and the girl slipped into her arms. Clare began one in Spanish about a little girl and a clumsy bear who liked to dance the rumba, a made-up story that Ala could not have understood completely. No matter, she lay in the crook of her mother's arm, growing still, her small chest rising and falling as she kneaded Clare's hip with her toes. Finally the two of them lay in silence, Ala's eyes focused on the ceiling or somewhere far away, her limbs at rest, her skin glowing.

Clare stretched out her legs but could not relax. She was thinking of the lie she'd told Domingo the night they met. She told him that Ala's father was Puerto Rican, a drifter who'd passed through New York. It was a revenge of sorts on Camilo, to portray him as shiftless. It wasn't his fault that he'd been deported, but he could have written and never did.

Domingo, inquisitive about so many things, had never pressed her about Ala's father. He took care of the girl as naturally as he took care of Clare. And Ala, unlike her mother, accepted what he gave without a thought. She was too young to owe him anything, whereas Clare was always conscious of how much Domingo had done for her.

She met him in the fall of 1957, when Ala was less than a year old. *Life* had offered Clare an assignment, Alameda's godmother had offered to take care of her for five days, and one cold autumn Sunday Clare flew out of New York into the soft air and warmth of Havana. From her first hour she loved the city. In the streets the people were black and white and every shade of brown. The sidewalks were busy, men played dominoes under the streetlights, and though her Spanish was barely a year old, everyone seemed happy to talk to her.

The next morning she roamed through the city, shooting in color with her wide-angle lens, slowing down the shutter speed, looking for a softer focus. She photographed the pastel stucco buildings and the crowds of slow-moving shoppers, women and men with the same relaxed posture as Camilo's. The city seemed a neighborhood, and all day long she felt oddly at home.

On her second night in Havana, as soon as she entered the Deauville casino with her letter of introduction, she saw what Camilo would have hated: the flamboyant wealth of the place, the muscle that kept the rich in and the poor out, the army of waiters and servants, the expensive and tasteful prostitutes.

She wandered at first without her cameras, to block out spaces and compositions. She wore flat shoes and her best midnight-blue dress. She accepted a rum and Coca Cola—they were offered constantly on silver trays held by waiters in white gloves—and took a few sips. Strong, she thought, and put it down. She talked to some gamblers in both English and Spanish.

Later that evening, with her Leica around her neck and her Pentax hanging from a shoulder, she watched a small drama unfold around a couple betting at a roulette table. They were Cuban-Americans from Tampa who had drunk too many mojitos. A second man, handsome, dark, with a round full face and hair gray at the temples, stood behind them. His suit was a deep blue, almost the color of Clare's dress, and stood out against his cloud-white shirt. He looked on, he made jokes, he quietly signaled the waiter: *No more drinks.* But the couple's mood, originally festive, had now turned grim, and they resisted his attempts to pry them away from the table. They were determined to make good their losses. They'd stopped betting on odd or even and fastened on the number 17.

"Enough, *amigo*," the man behind them said, clapping his friend on the shoulder.

"*Domingo, coño, no jodes.*"

This Domingo pulled his friend away from the table—and the man went, but only two steps. Domingo snapped his fingers at a waiter: "*Dos cafecitos, ya.*" But getting the man away did no good, for the woman simply picked up the chips and continued to deposit them, five with every spin, on number 17. It was clear that Domingo could not clap his arm around *her* shoulder and move her away from the table. She gave him a hard look and said, in English, "Keep away from the chips."

Everyone at the table, including the croupier, ignored her stinging tone. Her husband, after burning his lips on a tiny cup of coffee, shook Domingo off and sat down again at the table.

Clare looked up from the green felt to find Domingo staring at her chest. From someone so presentable, so well-dressed, it seemed a blatant look. He glanced at her face, raised his eyelids slightly, then looked back at her breasts. She didn't understand until, standing behind the couple, he lifted his hands to his own chest as if holding an invisible camera, and pointed his chin toward the two gamblers.

Clare's usual mode was to stay invisible, to let people get used to her and forget she even had a camera. But a camera could be a weapon and she used it now, zeroing in on the couple. Each time the woman reached out with more chips, Clare took her picture. Then she switched from her rangefinder Leica, a quiet camera, to her single-lens reflex Pentax, which made a *clack* with every exposure. The closer she approached, the more the couple ignored her. They kept their heads down, kept betting—but could no longer ignore the sound of the camera. They grew self-conscious. They'd lost a lot of money. Finally, with a sharp look at Clare, the woman leaned back. She had come to her senses. Her husband gathered up what chips remained, and Clare was still shooting as Domingo hooked his arms through the elbows of both man and woman and steered them away over a deep red carpet, the two of them looking more sober by the second.

Thirty minutes later Domingo found her in the bar, where she sat with her reloaded cameras and a daiquiri. He approached her with a slight bow. "I want to thank you, señorita." His English was accented, but not strongly. "I didn't know what to do with those two. I couldn't stop them."

"And I shouldn't have. I'm a photographer, not a lifeguard." What she'd done was unprofessional—yet her photos of the couple, she was sure, would be the best of the night.

"Do you work for someone?" Domingo asked.

"For *Life*."

He was impressed. "I'm always looking for good photographers. I run a magazine myself."

What a pick-up line, Clare thought. But she let him invite her to a late steak at the casino's restaurant. Over dinner she told him about her

daughter and her life in New York. When she glanced at his wedding ring
he said "Yes, I am married. I have two children in college, in Miami and
Boston. I've had a good marriage, but Solana is dying of stomach cancer.
She has been dying for a year."

"I'm sorry."

"Everyone is sorry. I, my children, the doctors, the nurses, all are sorry.
Solana is angry. She is only forty-one."

"How old are you?"

"Forty-six."

He didn't ask how old Clare was: almost twenty years younger. It was a
cliché, she thought. He was old, he was rich, he was handsome—but she
liked him, and two nights later joined him at a restaurant and nightclub
overlooking the sea, a place even more luxurious than the Deauville. A
small conjunto played, and a woman sang the songs of Machito and Beny
Moré, the most romantic Cuban songs. Some were songs that Camilo
had played for her on her phonograph in New York. She hadn't come to
Havana with any illusions about finding Camilo. She believed by then
that he was dead, most likely killed during Castro's invasion of the island,
when almost all the rebels had died.

Still, she loved being in the city where Camilo grew up, where he'd gone
to school and sewn shirts in his parents' shop, and been shot in the leg
at a student protest. This restaurant, she knew, was not the kind of place
that Camilo would have chosen. It was too formal and expensive. But
it smelled of the sea, the songs were evocative, and she was glad she had
come.

After dinner, as Domingo walked her on a promenade above the water,
he kissed her, pressing his palms to the small of her back and his hips to
her own. She was aroused, but then he stopped. He lowered his arms and
said, "I can't."

He could, that was perfectly clear.

"Solana has asked one thing of me, and I have promised not to make
love with anyone else as long as she's alive."

Clare crossed her arms over her chest. "So why invite me to dinner?
Why start kissing me?"

"You are angry with me."

"I'm confused. Okay, also angry."

"Clare, I'm sorry. I am attracted to you. It is selfish of me, I know."

He had a response for everything. She stared at the curving Malecón, Havana's seawall promenade, its lights yellowish in the warm mist. "What would happen if you didn't tell her?"

"She would know."

Of course. Because they'd been married for so long, because they had children, because they were the same age. At least, Clare told herself, she wouldn't be stabbing some woman in the back as she died of cancer. But that wasn't much comfort, because only minutes earlier she'd been willing to do just that. Still, she didn't want to let Domingo off the hook. He'd led her on and aroused her. When it was a woman who did that, the man sometimes thought he could take what he wanted. Clare couldn't take anything from Domingo, but now she wanted to make him suffer. "Maybe she'll know that you invited me to dinner, then kissed me on the Malecón."

"She is sensitive to betrayal," Domingo said, "but she is not clairvoyant."

Clare stepped back. He was too sure of himself, and she wanted to make him doubt. "Maybe I should tell her myself."

His head jerked, but he said nothing. Good, she'd finally gotten through to him. "It was unfair of you," she said, "to excite me and then have no courage."

She meant to insult him, but it only made him smile. He looked her up and down, slowly, with evident pleasure. "I like everything about you," he said.

No, she could not outtalk him. And while nothing would happen between them, something had happened to her. She'd been aroused by a man for the first time in a year and a half. Domingo was still smiling, still watching her, and slowly she relaxed with that.

At the end of the night, in front of Clare's hotel under a pair of arched lamps, he kissed her once on the mouth, then took a step back. "It's not just that I like you," he said. "I could fall in love with you." Without waiting for her response he walked to his car, got in and drove away.

Fall in love, she thought. She had done that once. Now she loved her daughter—and after four days in Cuba she thought she might come to love this country. But another man? She'd only been hoping for an adventure.

Domingo stepped into Clare's room. Ala let him pick her up, and wrapped herself around his neck. He reached for Clare's hand, kissed it and left, his heels striking the tile floor. Clare felt small, a cheat and a liar. Some day she would tell Domingo the truth about Alameda's father —but not before she talked to Camilo. And how was she going to do that?

She lay in her canopied four-poster bed, the most formal in the house. It was the bed Domingo's parents used to sleep in when they came for a visit, when his father was still alive. Airy white drapes tied back to the posts made it feel like a ship. Like much of Domingo's life, it was extravagant, but she liked it. Domingo paid her what *Life* had—a huge salary in Cuba—to shoot vacation homes and romantic beaches, churches and small colonial towns. This was the world of *Ojo*, Domingo's magazine for the wealthy.

How proper he was—to Clare, to his wife who'd died, to everyone. Far more proper than she, who kept secrets from him, secrets that had now grown larger.

Hearing a low rumble, she sat up in bed. An explosion, she thought. All month in Havana there had been bombings, with an occasional short blackout, but the real fighting was in the east. Camilo was in the east, somewhere near Santa Clara, and now she knew: she had to go there.

3

"No, you cannot take my Impala into a battle zone. Why do you want to do this?"

"I'm a photographer, and this is news."

"You are not that kind of photographer."

This annoyed her. "I've shot all kinds of stories."

Domingo did not reply. He would look after her daughter—or Rosa the part-time nanny would—but he refused to lend her his car.

"I shot Albert Anastasia's killing in a barbershop," Clare said. "All right, the aftermath. It was a bloody mess."

She wanted to say she was tired of photographing beautiful gardens and the interiors of resplendent homes. Domingo had made his job offer and she had accepted it, but now he was standing in her way.

When Domingo didn't understand something, he waited and said little. But he was not going to figure this out, Clare thought. He believed that without his car she wouldn't go. *Couldn't* go, because what Eliseo had said was true, the rebel troops had put up a ring of barricades around Santa Clara, and no trains or buses were getting in.

"You're so protective of your car," she told Domingo. It had annoyed her before that he wouldn't let her drive it, that she could only take it out with Eliseo at the wheel. "I've been driving since I was fifteen."

"I'm sure you are an excellent driver."

She wanted to grab his shirt and shake him. She wanted to knock him off stride—and how easy that would be. All she had to do was tell him the truth about Camilo. But that wouldn't get her to Santa Clara.

She left at dawn the next morning. Through Eliseo she'd found a guy with a '48 Mercury he sometimes used as a taxi, and for the fortune of forty pesos he agreed to drive her to the rebel barricades, though not into Santa Clara. In the earliest light the country east of Havana showed no signs of unrest. The sun rose over pastures and green palms, and save for a few local buses and farm trucks there was no traffic. They passed an occasional ox cart. Now and then a solitary policeman, with no car or motorcycle, stood at an empty crossroads. When Clare asked her driver if things seemed quieter than usual, Paco only shrugged. Mile after mile they drove in silence.

It was true: she was not that kind of photographer. Certainly she'd never been close to a battle. When the Korean War started she was nine-teen years old, working for the *Columbus Dispatch* and taking evening classes at Ohio State. Her idols were Margaret Bourke-White and Robert Capa, both of whom had photographed war up close. They'd both sur-vived World War II—though Capa, in 1954, had stepped on a landmine in Indochina, blown off his leg and died before he reached a hospital. Clare had read his book. She had imagined meeting him. After he died she called in sick at the *Dispatch* and sat alone in her apartment, stunned by her own grief. War, she knew then, was not her shoot.

Yet here she was, headed for Santa Clara where some kind of battle was raging. Or so she'd heard on the radio. In print there was little news, and she had no idea of how she might find Camilo. By now everyone had disappeared along the National Highway. There was no one selling coffee or fruit or *fritatas* from little stands, and Paco was clearly worried. It did seem ominous how all traffic had vanished, how no children played outdoors, how no one stood in front of their houses or tended the gardens behind. At the turnoff to Santa Clara, nothing. The open-air restaurants stood empty in the unnatural silence. Clare made out the top of a church and the city's few tall buildings that rose above the royal palms. The road narrowed to a city street running between one-story houses, then the bar-ricade appeared: a string of cars and trucks, civilian vehicles pressed into service with ten or twenty men spread out behind them, all staring at Paco's Mercury. He pulled over a hundred yards short and said, "I will go no farther."

"They're not going to take your car."

In fact, she had no idea what the soldiers would do—if they were soldiers. Most were dressed in civilian clothes. Clare took her Leica from her bag and got out. Her camera was comforting and gave her a kind of strength. It let her go anywhere.

"Wait," Paco said, and jumped out from behind the wheel. Over the top of the car he said, "Pay me the rest of what you owe."

Before they left Havana she'd given him twenty pesos. "When we get back," she said now. "You agreed to all day."

"It's too dangerous here. Pay me the rest."

Clare came around the car and faced him. "Don't play the idiot. If I pay you now, what are the chances you're going to be here waiting for me?"

"I'll be here."

"Good, and I'll pay you as we agreed, the second half on return. Stick with our agreement and stay with the car. *No seas cabrón.*" Don't be an asshole.

She turned and walked away. Either he would be here when she came back or he wouldn't. She couldn't think about that now. She headed for the line of Dodges, Packards and Fords and the rebels who stood behind them, all wearing the red and black armbands of Castro's movement, the M-26.

Clare squeezed between two cars and addressed the soldier who faced her, a young man wearing a scraggly beard, her first *barbudo*.

"Good afternoon," she said. "And this barricade, why is it here?"

"Here the army cannot pass with reinforcements. Here we stand firm."

He was trying to look determined, she could see. But with his rifle pressed hard to his chest he looked nothing like the confident photos of Camilo and other rebels in the Sierra. The men here wore a combination of steel hats, cloth army caps, loose shirts, pleated trousers and polished black shoes. Their arms looked just as irregular, from shotguns and rifles to pistols, some of them little snub-nosed handbag guns. No one looked like the veteran of a battle.

"And in the center of town?" Clare asked.

"They are fighting."

As if to confirm what he said, the sound of distant gunfire reached them, first some faint staccato pops, then something larger, making a dent in the air. By now, seeing the camera around her neck, the men behind the barricade had all assumed their postures of defense. Such posing made for bad photos, but Clare took some anyway, just to relax them. She snapped them off, no need for a light meter at midday. She'd taken ten thousand photos on sunny days like this. At 100 ASA, f11 and a hundredth of a second, they would all come out. She shot the barricade and the men lining it, then turned back to the first soldier.

"I would like to speak with Camilo Cienfuegos."

"Camilo has gone. He was here yesterday, talking to Che, but now he has left for Yaguajáy."

"Can I drive there?"

"All traffic is closed through the city, and the fighting in Yaguajáy is worse than it is here. It would be dangerous to go close."

If she still worked for *Life* this would all have been easier, because someone in New York would have come up with a contact who could lead her to the rebels. Here, Clare was not about to tell anyone she worked for *Ojo*, that magazine for rich Cubans. After a long silence she said to the bearded soldier, "I'm going to take a look at the center of town. Could a couple of these men go with me?"

"Señorita, it is a bad idea. Shooting could start anytime, and my men must stay here. We have our orders from Che."

Maybe it was a bad idea, but Clare could not just turn around and go home. She didn't want to face Domingo and admit that he was right, that she was not cut out for dangerous work. Nor could she get back in Paco's car after fifteen minutes at the barricade. She saw him in the distance, leaning against the Mercury's hood. She'd be lucky if the guy didn't drive off with her twenty pesos and leave her stranded.

She took some photos from outside the barricade, but it was hopeless. The soldiers, stiff and intent, stared out as if Batista himself were about to attack them. Capa said that if your photos weren't good enough, you weren't close enough. Sometimes that was true, but here Clare worked as close as she liked and it only led to more preening. The men gripped their guns, they had cast their lot with the M-26, they were battling the tyranny.

She threaded her way through the barricade and began to walk. She would go a few blocks, maybe farther, maybe all the way into town. She might find this Che Guevara and ask him about Camilo. The street, with not a parked car on it, was lined with yardless houses and a few small stores, all closed. Her soldier called out from behind her with the same message, "*Es mala idea.*" Clare waved back cheerfully, as if she'd misunderstood him, and walked on into the silence. No one stood outside their doors or even at their windows. Far down the next block a man carried a bicycle into a house. Once a woman called and whistled for a dog, but no dog came. The woman watched as Clare approached, and just when Clare was going to ask her a question she stepped inside and closed the door.

Santa Clara—what saint was that? Whoever it was, she and Clare were *tocayas*, they had the same name. Perhaps destiny was at work, she thought.

She walked faster, to shake off all foolishness. Camilo had no idea she was here, he knew nothing about Alameda, and for him Clare was probably just someone he'd had an affair with long ago. Did he ever think of her? Had he ever done so, from the day Immigration took him away? Clare had thought of him throughout her pregnancy, during her labor, two minutes after Ala was born and every day since. Looking at her daughter's high forehead and sturdy little body, she saw Camilo. He was always with them, a phantom third party.

Alerted by something she couldn't see, she stopped in the middle of the street. Her eyes ranged down the next block and the block after that, but nothing moved. Glancing behind her, she could still make out the men at the barricade—but something had lifted the hair on her forearms. It was a sound and she heard it now, faint and intermittent. Not gunfire, she thought, but some bolus of uneasy noise. It came from the city, reverberating off the stone and stucco fronts of the buildings, pressing faintly against her chest. Finally she saw it, a vehicle coming fast from the center of town, kicking up a plume of dust. She stepped up on the sidewalk and put her back to the wall of a house. It was an army truck full of men, all

wearing helmets and each with a gun. They were Batista's soldiers, leaning over the cab and the sides, and they paid her no attention. Dropping
to one knee, she snapped pictures as fast as she could, trying to keep the
truck in focus, the film inside her Leica passing from spool to spool with
a dense mechanical grip she felt halfway up her arm. Shots rang out, the
truck roared past, and as the dust rolled up a bullet smashed into the wall
above her, dropping plaster onto her head and shoulders. Her fear, instead of driving her to the ground, lifted her to her feet, and a moment
later she was sprinting after the truck, taking dust-filled photos on the
run. Hopeless photos, but she had to get closer.

With no way around the barricade, the truck never slowed. It plowed
into a small gap between two cars, veered, jerked and ground to a stop.
In back, the soldiers were thrown into a pile. In front, the rebels poured
bullets into the cab. As Clare ran up from behind, one of the army regulars
got to his feet, ripped off his shirt, ripped off his undershirt and waved
it in the air. All the recruits who still held their guns threw them down.
They swept off their helmets, lifted their hands and screamed *"Don't shoot!
Don't shoot!"*

Ten more seconds and the fighting was over. The rebels, guns pointed,
circled the back of the truck. *"Get down,"* they cried, looking fierce. The
recruits were young, their hair a quarter of an inch long. Clare finished
one roll on her Leica, dropped in another, threaded it and kept shooting.

The truck's radiator steamed. Three men had been killed: the driver,
another soldier in the cab, and one of the rebels. Clare took their photos
where they lay on the pavement, the three of them lined up side by side,
their loyalties ignored. She'd seen dead bodies before—many of them,
in a New Jersey morgue where she'd once been hired to photograph the
corpses. But this was different. Only minutes earlier these men had been
alive. Her hands, firm throughout the skirmish, had begun to shake.

The recruits stood in a clump, half of them shirtless, guarded by a
rebel with a shotgun. He was an older man wearing a sporty white cap.
He stepped up to one of the recruits, a kid who barely looked eighteen,
slapped him lightly on the shoulder and said "Relax, *compadre*, we're not
going to shoot you. That's what the army does to us, not what we do to
you."

The kid did not relax, did not respond to the man's smile, never glanced at Clare. No one did. They paid her no attention at all. Her eyes, and her camera, kept going back to the three dead men on the ground. Her heart still thumped in her chest. She felt as if someone else had been taking the photos, that she'd barely had a hand in it.

The drive back to Havana was long and slow. Paco was in a stew about the danger to his car. Clare paid him his second twenty pesos and didn't talk to him. She let her fingertips rest on her treasure, the four aluminum cylinders tucked safely in her pocket. Instead of having them developed here, she'd send them straight to Black Star in New York. For a while, in silence, she called up the details of the fight: the bullet hitting the wall above her, the truck slamming into the barricade, the panicked recruits. Then, as if waking from a trance, she sat up stiff on her seat. *What the hell was I doing? I have a daughter.*

The car rolled on and Clare sank back. Yes, she'd been foolhardy, but she was glad to be taking pictures of something that mattered. It didn't have to be war, but she wanted to photograph people, not buildings. She liked taking portraits and she liked a story. If only she'd gone up into the Sierra on her first trip to Cuba, instead of to the Deauville Casino. Okay, that was crazy, Ala wasn't a year old and Clare could not have left her to follow Castro and his men as they fought in ravines and little mountain towns. Still, if she'd gone she would have found Camilo. After this single brush with the Cuban Revolution, Domingo's wealth and her work at *Ojo* felt like the wrong side of history. She wanted to shoot the rebellion, and the victory that was sure to come.

Now she had to laugh, for sounding like the woman on Castro's radio station. No matter, for everything was making her happy. She was glad she'd argued with Paco, glad she didn't have to talk to him, glad for the long drive home and the chance to think of Camilo.

The day she met him she was shooting a feature on the Waldorf Astoria kitchen for *La Cuisine*, black-and-white photos of the executive chef, the sous-chef, the line cooks and their assistants, all at work in the big whirling room. Camilo stood at a stainless steel table grating ginger and dicing red peppers. He was slight, fair-skinned, perhaps an inch taller than she was, with lush dark hair and thick eyebrows. He watched as she took her first pictures of him, then went back to work as if unaware of her. She circled around him, shot him from every angle, reloaded, drifted away to film the rotisseur and the patissier. But Camilo, with his tall forehead, deep waist and faintly sway-backed posture, was the one she wanted.

Leaning forward, he glanced down the line and said, "Alberto, give me your hat one minute."

Everyone had noticed, she was sure, how she'd taken dozens of photos of the rest of them, but a hundred of Camilo. Alberto set his tall white toque on Camilo's head and stepped back. He said something in Spanish, and a couple of the men laughed softly.

Camilo ignored them. He stood at the ready, his knife in the air. "You will take one for my family, please, with the big hat." And just before she did, he rolled his hips as if on a dance floor and gave her a smile.

She took many more photos as he went back to work, slicing avocados now, separating the green flesh from its leathery brown skin. His momentary flirtation was gone. From time to time he fixed her with his gaze, holding his look until she lowered her camera. A direct stare didn't make for the photos she needed. She wanted him wrapped up in his job, and now he looked like someone taking *her* picture. His gaze settled on her mouth.

Her attraction to him was visceral, a cord tugged through her body. It shamed her for the other men to make comments in Spanish in their low lilting voices, but the embarrassment didn't stop her from circling Camilo. He rolled his hips again, barely noticeable now, as if a faint rumba had begun to play in his head. It was subtle but continuous, and as long as she filmed him he kept it up.

Clare was twenty-four, small-breasted, tall and thin. Only two months before she'd been living in Louisville, Kentucky, taking photos for the *Courier-Journal* of the mayor and local politicians, of car wrecks and baseball teams. Now, after a month in her parents' Brooklyn apartment, she lived in Manhattan with a roommate, two Leicas and a key to a darkroom. That's where she would go when she finished at the Waldorf Astoria, to develop her film, put the rolls on contact sheets and blow up the best of them. Before she left the hotel kitchen she wrote her telephone number on a torn-off slip of butcher paper and handed it to Camilo.

"Call me with your address," she said casually. "I'll send you copies of some photos for your family."

He studied the paper, folded it twice and slipped it into a tiny pocket on the front of his hip. "*Usted es tan amable*," he said, and in English, "You are so nice."

"So are you," she said. "Extremely nice." Then, embarrassed, she left the room.

Two days later he called and gave her, in clear but hesitant English, his address on East Fourth, near Avenue D. But she didn't want to mail the photos to him, she wanted to see him. She told him she could bring the prints to his apartment.

There was a pause. For a moment she thought the line had gone dead. "It is a bad neighborhood," he said finally. "Better I come to your apartment. I will be your *compañero* and take you here. You will meet my friends."

He came at ten on a Tuesday morning, his one day off. He rang the buzzer downstairs, she let him into the building, he climbed the three sets of stairs but would not come in from the hall. "I will wait for you," he said.

She grabbed her purse, which already held the prints and her black-and-white Leica, and closed the door behind her. Camilo wore a coat and a pair of loose pleated trousers. Clare wore a full-length coat as well, and under it, though the morning was cool, a summer dress. From the doorway of her building she glanced west toward the Hudson, blue in the morning light—but Camilo turned her, with a touch at her elbow, toward Broadway and the IRT.

In the subway he folded into himself and didn't talk, letting the shell of his concentration protect him from the tepid air and the moist steel poles they clung to. But once up the stairs and into the light, as they strolled through the lower East Side, his face opened up. He smiled, he asked about her family, he touched her a second time, the lightest brush against the small of her back as they stepped onto Avenue B. She floated along beside him down the stained sidewalk of the cross street, its garbage cans chained to iron fences, a few lonely sweet gums struggling to grow out of circles in the concrete, the gutters dotted with trash and dog shit. She didn't care about any of that. They were close to the same height, and she matched her stride to his. Pervading the ugliness of the city was a pure brilliant sunlight.

"Excuse me," she said, "but I don't know your last name."

He stopped and formally extended his hand. "Camilo Cienfuegos. You would say in English for my name, a hundred fires. And you?"

"Clare Miller."

They shook hands. "I am very happy," he said.

"And are you from—where?"

"I am from Cuba. My family is there. We are the enemies of Batista."

"Batista. Is he the president?"

"He is killing my country. But this will end."

Clare knew nothing about Cuba. She was not political and had never voted. She was a girl awash in her own body—but the thrill of the city was learning about everything.

Camilo shared his apartment with four other Cubans. They were all waiters or kitchen help, and at eleven in the morning they were all at home. Camilo introduced them: Carlos, León, Neto and Macario. They were all polite, and no one looked her up and down. Taped to the refrigerator was the scrap of butcher paper she'd given Camilo. The apartment was a railroad flat with a bathtub in the kitchen, the whole place clean and tidy. She couldn't believe five men could keep an apartment in such order. Though two of them wore wedding rings, there were no signs of any women.

Neto, who spoke the best English, welcomed her and invited her to sit down at the square kitchen table. There was a plastic tablecloth and only four chairs. She and Camilo were seated across from each other, Neto and Carlos joined them, and the others served them cups of dark sweet coffee. The aroma filled the room. Clare caught herself staring at Camilo's white teeth. She wanted him to bite her.

To distract herself she took the eight-by-ten photos out of their manila envelope and passed them around. Everyone loved the portrait of Camilo with the big white hat, holding his knife in the air.

She drank her coffee and was served another. Behind her camera, Clare was fearless. She had started taking photos at twelve, and sold her first picture to the *Dispatch* at fourteen. She could photograph pumpkin farms and towboats on the Ohio, conniving politicians, jazz clubs in the Village or the cast of a famous restaurant—but she was not a reporter and not that good at asking questions. She wanted to know how these men had come to live in an apartment with no curtains, no phone, almost no furniture, with a pair of white shirts on hangers drying over the bathtub. She wanted to ask if they were here legally, and how long they would stay. How long would Camilo stay?

Instead, she pointed to a pair of framed photos on the wall in front of her, one of a pockmarked building, some kind of fortress, the other of a young man dressed in white, addressing a crowd. "Who is that?" she asked.

"That is Fidel," Camilo said. "The one who will save Cuba."

"He seems so young."

"Like us," said Neto.

"And the building?"

Neto stood up and handed down the photos. "The barracks of Moncada," he said, "after the attack three years ago. Many heroes died that day, but we have given our warning to Fulgencio Batista."

She glanced at Camilo. "The one who is killing your country."

"That's right," Camilo said, and the others nodded their agreement.

"And this Fidel, is he in Cuba?"

"Fidel is in Mexico."

With that a silence fell over the room. Neto explained, "Cuba is not safe for any of us."

"There," said León, "we will all be in jail."

"Everyone," said Camilo, spreading his hands to include the others, "has been in jail in Cuba."

Neto said no more as he rehung the photos. Clare watched the faces of the men, some as light-skinned as Camilo, some smoother and darker. She took out her camera with a rare hesitation, wondering if they would object, wondering if they would want to be seen together. But when she asked if she could take some photos they were glad to stand together, posing stiffly against the plaster wall. She would make prints for their families, she told them. After a time, Neto asked for the camera and stood her beside Camilo next to the framed picture of Fidel Castro. "Closer," he said, gesturing with his palm. At the last instant she felt Camilo's arm slide around her waist, and in the photo it's clear that he's pulling her toward him.

4

O N the first day of 1959, Clare was late to rise and a little hung over. She'd spent New Year's Eve with Domingo, his brother and several cousins, drinking and dancing until one in the morning. Now she swore, *two* glasses of champagne, never more than two. Two glasses of wine, two rum and Cokes, two of anything was plenty. She lay in bed with Ala, listening for sounds from the city. Normally Havana was fully awake by six, and last night had been noisy with car horns and fireworks, but this morning all was still. At eight she got up, slipped on a dress, changed and dressed Ala, then lifted her to the bathroom tap so she could splash her own hands and face.

Downstairs, Domingo was nowhere to be seen. Though always an early riser, he was not in the living room and not in his study. From the kitchen came the high-pitched sound of Lavinia's radio, and when Clare walked in she found Domingo and the cook staring at it, both listening intently. They hardly glanced at her as Violeta Casals announced in Spanish, "From Santiago, the Commander Fidel Castro has called for a general strike. He assures the nation that there is no reason to worry, the transition of power will take place smoothly."

Clare, watching her husband and his cook listen to *Radio Rebelde* together, imagined that in the space of hours a new equality had been achieved between boss and worker, *patrón y obrera*. But no. When Clare asked what had happened, Domingo told Lavinia to get some breakfast on the table and guided Clare and Ala back to the living room. He was on edge, she could see.

"Batista has fled the country. He flew out at three this morning with his family, some generals and probably a lot of money. It is over."

"Will Castro become president?"

"He will do whatever he likes. On the radio they treat him like a god on his throne."

Clare started to object. That wasn't what she'd heard in the voice of Violeta Casals, who'd sounded calm and authoritative. "Isn't this what you wanted? You never liked Batista."

"I wanted an end to his corruption."

"And now we have it."

"Or we may have a new kind of corruption, an ideology that will be all wrong for Cuba."

Ala was tugging at the hem of Clare's dress. "Wait," she said. She crossed the room, picked up Ala's carton of alphabet blocks and set it on the floor so the girl could play with them. "Where is Castro now?"

"In Santiago, at the eastern end of the country. He is sending someone here to take over the army. It might be that Argentinian, Guevara."

"A foreigner would be head of the Cuban Army?"

That slipped out, and Clare was sorry to have said it. Because if it wasn't Che Guevara, it might be the head of the other column, Camilo Cienfuegos. Since returning from Santa Clara she had tried not to mention his name. When Domingo grilled her about the trip, she'd done her best to keep all excitement out of her voice—but Domingo had heard it, she was sure. He knew something had stirred her up, but didn't know what.

"The true head of the army and everything else," he said, "will be Castro. There will be no limit to his power, because he will share it with no one. He has brushed aside ex-President Prio and undermined the Student Directorate."

There was a crash, and Ala's lettered blocks flew around their feet. Clare had barely noticed how the girl had built a tower not two feet away from them. Now Ala lifted her eyes toward them, her message clear: *You see what I can do? Stop all that talk and play with me.*

Clare knelt briefly, started the girl on another tower and stood up. Domingo went on as if never interrupted: "I think he's something of a maniac. He was a thug at the university, then he led that futile attack on the Moncada barracks where so many died."

"Yet Batista has been saying for months that Castro is finished, even that he's dead—and now it is Batista who has fled the country."

There was another small crash at their feet. "You and I," Domingo said, "have never had a political disagreement in this house, and I do not want to start."

This kind of argument, it was true, was new to them. Clare stared back at him, but his look was so serious she felt like laughing. "Getting to know you—" she said, then paused before singing the next line, "—*getting to know all about you.*"

"What is that?" Domingo, usually curious about anything in English he didn't recognize, was now annoyed.

"It's from a Broadway musical. They made a movie of it."

"A movie?"

"*The King and I.*" But what had led her, in the middle of an argument, to start singing? "It was a great show," she said.

Now all her words seemed false. Her lips felt rubbery, the way they did when she told a lie. Domingo stared at her and she stared back. After a few seconds she let her eyes go out of focus so she could look straight at him and not see him.

Domingo swept a hand through the air as if to brush the topic aside, then walked off saying, "I must call my brother and talk to him about the mill."

His abrupt departure was meant as an affront, Clare was sure. But she didn't care, she was glad to be out from under his gaze. She knelt beside her daughter on the tile floor, stacking up blocks so Ala could knock them down. Arguments were new between her and Domingo. He didn't like them and neither did she, and until recently no disagreement had lasted more than a few minutes.

How calm he had always been, and how persuasive. She thought of the letters he'd sent after the first time she came to Havana, handsome cream-colored letters written in a formal and slightly florid English. One day he wrote that his wife was in the hospital, and a month later that she had died. After the funeral he wrote, "Now my children are back in the States, and I am alone in my house. Half the day I am suffused by grief, and half I'm amazed at how the sun and stars keep turning. I would be very happy to see you again some day."

Suffused by grief. She knew he often sat down at night with a dictionary and some American book or magazine, intent on improving his English. When he offered to fly north for a visit, a few months later, Clare declined but continued the correspondence. Finally, in June, she told him she would see him if he came to New York. He took a room at the Plaza Hotel overlooking Central Park, and it was there she slept with him. Domingo was not impetuous, and it was only on the second night, when she was splayed out over his bed with her breath coming short, that he pulled out a rubber and put it on. "Better safe than sorry," he said. "I believe that's the expression in English."

That he would make a joke at such a moment helped her relax. It made her think he wouldn't lose his head over her, or demand too much from her later on.

The next day she brought Ala and met him in Central Park. Sitting on an iron bench, as Ala ran laughing after the pigeons, Domingo made her a business proposition. Or so he called it. If she wished to come to Cuba for a longer visit, he said, he would pay her to take photographs for his magazine.

"I will pay for your hotel, as well. I have an uncle who owns a little place, it's very pleasant. You could set your own hours, my chauffeur could drive you around, you would have all the freedom you have here in New York."

She laughed at this. "I would live in your hotel, I would be driven in your car—but I'd be free, there would be no strings."

"Exactly."

"Domingo, there are always strings. I'm not saying no. I'm not saying it isn't a wonderful offer. I'm just saying it can be a problem to mix business and friendship. Not to mention sex."

Domingo smiled. "I think we would have a great time, all three of us."

When she didn't answer he bought pretzels from a cart, then an ice cream sandwich he shared with Ala. He let Clare think about his offer— and a few weeks later she wrote him that yes, she would go to live and work with him in Havana.

The hotel did not work out, and after a couple of weeks she moved into Domingo's house. Those were lovely days. She had a steady job, she had endless help with Ala, and she was living with a good man who was clearly in love with her. Her flush of happiness was so great that when Domingo asked her to marry him, she said yes. The wedding was small—tiny, really, with only a few of his family members and none of her own.

In his study, Domingo was talking to his brother about the family sugar mill in Remedios. Though they owned the *central* together, it was Felipe who managed the operation. Domingo spoke, was quiet, then spoke again. In his tone Clare caught a hint of exasperation, plus an overtone of guidance. He might have been a father talking to his son. Felipe was not exactly wayward, but he'd had three wives, he had not looked after his children, and he drank too much. Last night at their New Year's Eve party he'd picked up the small Christmas tree and hugged it, pretending it was his partner in a sensual, stumbling dance that sent a dozen ornaments crashing to the floor.

Domingo finished his call, made another and came out to breakfast, which was now on the table. Sitting across from Clare he announced, "Felipe and I must fly to Remedios tonight, before the strike begins. He is afraid that in celebration the workers might burn or damage the mill. I am sorry to leave you and Ala in Havana. I would take you with me, but it could be dangerous."

"I'm sure we'll be fine."

"I fear we are entering a time of chaos. I want you to go to the Hotel Nacional for a few days. I have called them and made a reservation in my name. I think it would be best if you stayed in your room. The food is good, they will bring you meals, and I want you to be safe."

Clare pushed away her omelet, half eaten. Every day, it seemed, Domingo was growing more authoritarian. Was it Cuba's instability, or was it her secret, somehow radiating from her? "You're not making sense," she said. "You talk to Felipe, then you start thinking like him. Listen to the city, it's completely quiet. Do you hear any bombs or gunshots?"

"Batista has abandoned the country, but this battle may not be over. There are many who will resist Castro and his ideas."

"Will you?"

"Of course not. I am no fool."

"I'm sure we'll be safe in your house."

"No, I don't want to worry about you. You must go to the Nacional."

"We *must* go?" Clare sat up straight on her chair. "You must shut up."

To her *shut up* was an insult, words never spoken in her house when she was a child. She stood and glared at Domingo, as Ala scrambled to her feet on the chair beside her. "You should remember what you told me in Central Park. *No strings.* What that means now is that you don't make some reservation without asking me, and you don't tell me what to do. And if you make a mistake, you apologize."

Domingo pushed his chair back and stood up, facing her across the table. His face was dark and his shoulders hunched. When, Clare wondered, was the last time someone had told him what to do? Never in this house, that she had heard.

It cost him, but he said it. "Clare, I am sorry."

She thanked him, even as she rejoiced in secret that he'd made this mistake. He had overstepped, which let her insist on her freedom, now when she wanted it most.

5

THE following morning Clare rose in the dark and let herself out of Domingo's house. Because of the general strike no taxis or buses were running, so she walked down the middle of the street, coatless and chilled as the streetlights flickered off. The eastern sky turned lemon, the sun came up and poured its warmth across her back, and other walkers soon appeared on the streets, some greeting her with a cheerful *Buen dia*, some smiling at the sky like young children. Hope was coming back to Cuba.

Last night on the radio she'd heard Fidel tell the nation that Camilo would be the first rebel commander to enter Havana, where he would take control of the Cuban Army at Camp Columbia. She'd arranged for Rosa to come and look after Ala, and with Domingo out at his sugar mill she was on her own. In part, she felt the way people looked: happy and expectant. At the same time she worried. What if she got through to Camilo, only to have him shrug her off?

A hundred yards short of the camp she stopped, took her Leica from its bag and attached her LIFE pin to the lapel of her blouse. It came from the days when she worked for the magazine, and it had smoothed her way before. Usually just picking up a camera made her feel confident, but not today. At the last moment she slipped off her wedding ring and stashed it in her bag.

At the gate three bearded sentries, full *barbudos* from the hills, stood guard in their ragged fatigues, their rifles held loosely as they stepped forward to block her way. "*Señorita*," said the first.

Clare reached out and shook their hands, one after the other: "*Buenos dias, buenos dias compadres.*"

Could they be of some help? the soldier asked.

"I would like to speak to Camilo Cienfuegos."

This brought a burst of laughter. "You see how fast it starts?" one of the other men said. "We've been here for *six hours* and already a woman wants to meet Camilo!"

"No," Clare said. "I'm a photographer. I work for a magazine." She lifted her lapel, unsure if these men would even know about *Life*.

"It is lamentable," said the first soldier, "but we have our orders. No civilians today, and no journalists."

"Listen, I know Camilo. We are friends."

"Of course. Everyone wants to be friends with *el chico lindo*." The beautiful boy.

This was followed by another ripple of laughter. Was this how it was, that women followed him around? Clare pulled back her shoulders. "No," she told the sentry, "I have known him for years."

"Of course. I'm sure it is so."

Clare lifted a manila envelope out of her camera bag, unwound the stringed clasp and pulled out a glossy black and white photo. It showed a young woman in a summer dress and a man with his arm around her waist, a smooth-shaven Camilo in a white shirt.

This interested them. They hitched their guns over their shoulders and studied the photo, each in turn—and it was true, here was their leader without his beard. "Camilo," one said with a grin, "that shaved dog." The soldier held the photo up to Clare's face, to compare them. Yes, they could see it was her.

"I knew him in New York," she told them. "Before the Sierra, before the *Granma*, before he ever fired a gun. He will want to see me."

This was the speech she had prepared—though in fact she was not at all sure what Camilo would want. Her voice was turning brittle, she could hear it herself. She peered into the compound at the boxy white buildings and wide parade grounds lined with palm trees. Some soldiers from the regular army, all neatly shaved and none with a rifle, stood around in their pressed uniforms.

Beside her, the first of the bearded sentries took another look at her photo, then slipped it back into its envelope. "And if he is not happy to see you?"

"He will be happy."

Her insistence was a shield against Camilo's disregard, against the fact that in the last two years, almost three, she hadn't heard a word from him. The sentry rewound the clasp and held the envelope out to her in his slender fingers. She didn't take it. Instead, she put her hands behind her back and assured him, "He will want to see it."

The sentry didn't know what to do with the envelope. Finally he passed it to one of the other men and the four of them stood in silence. They were turning her away.

She'd been polite long enough. Stepping around the men, she headed for the gate. She was half way through before the first *barbudo* caught up with her and grabbed her arm.

"*No me toque*," she said. Don't touch me. A couple of other bearded soldiers walked over, both with their guns. "I'm a photographer," she announced to all of them, "and a friend of Camilo's. What are you afraid of?"

"Let me see your bag," the sentry said.

She didn't like people handling her cameras, but then she understood: she might have a gun, a knife, a grenade.

Instead of handing over the bag immediately, she said "What do you think, that I am dangerous? All right, go ahead and search me." Doing her best to look reluctant, she passed her bag to the sentry, then lifted her arms in the air as if they'd demanded to pat her down. No one was going to do that, but the other *barbudos* bent forward as the sentry opened the camera bag and held up each article he found: a wide-angle lens, an 85mm, a flash attachment, an exposure meter and eight rolls of film. No guns, no grenades, everyone could see that the bag held nothing dangerous. The sentry nestled everything back inside, including the photo, closed the bag and passed it back to her. In his most official tone he said, "You will follow me, please."

Camilo stood behind a desk, half-turned away, his broad felt hat pushed back on his forehead. His beard was full and his hair fell to his shoulders. How skinny he was.

"Camilo."

He turned at her voice, and for five dreadful seconds stared at her in silence. Clare waited, miserable. Didn't he know her? Would he keep looking at her as if they'd never met?

Finally, "It's *you*!"

He stepped toward her, put his arm around her, then leaned back to look her over. He stared at her face, at her shoulders and chest. He waved his other hand at the half-dozen men in his office: "Leave us, leave us for a moment," and they all filed out. But the door remained open, with two guards just outside and soldiers passing by.

"How can this be?" he said in English. "On this perfect day, on this first day of the Revolution you are here! You are in Cuba!"

"I've been here for months. I'm taking photos for Black Star, and for a Cuban magazine." She was aware, as she spoke, of Camilo's hand moving slowly across the small of her back. He smelled of sweat and soil and clothes slept in for weeks at a time. The odor up close was overwhelming, and seeing her hold back, he laughed.

"*Que olór, ¿no?* I must bathe," he said. "I must sleep, but there is no time. I must smoke a cigar, I must dance in celebration, and still there is no time. And you come without telling me!"

"How could I have told you?"

On the desk beside him lay his submachine gun, its wooden stock stained and dark, its barrel pointed toward the door. His beard was a jungle, and in it bits of something, perhaps bread, were caught beside his mouth. His hat was tattered and his cuffs frayed. He was a *comandante,* but looked the same as any of the bearded soldiers. More beautiful, though. What caution Clare had was dropping away like a skirt off her hips.

She said in Spanish, "I hear you're in charge of Batista's army."

"Incredible, isn't it? I have three hundred men, half of them so new I hardly know them. Here in the camp there are thousands of soldiers, and everywhere I go—they salute me!" He lifted his hand to his forehead, mocking the traditional gesture. By nightfall, he told her, Che and his troops would also reach the city. "But everything is in the air. Now we must guarantee the Revolution, and to relax is impossible."

Camilo seemed shorter to her, until she realized he was standing in his socks. His dilapidated boots with their unraveled laces lay in a corner of the room. He noticed her looking at them, and laughed. "Boots!" he yelled to the sentries at the door. "Go through the base and find out where the boots are. New boots for every *barbudo*!"

One of the sentries walked off, and Camilo grew more serious. "Clare, I want to see you—but what a busy time this is." He lowered his voice. "And you know how Fidel feels about the United States."

"He's angry that the U.S. gave Batista those tanks and airplanes."

"And those bombs that burn, that Batista dropped on the people."

"Camilo, I am not my government."

"No, but now I am *my* government."

She wanted to say that had nothing to do with the two of them. But here in his office, surrounded by rebel soldiers and the Cuban Army, their own history was shrinking to a distant idyll. "If you are your government," she said in English, "can't you do what you like?"

"As long as it is in service to the Revolution."

"Now you sound like *Radio Rebelde*. All that inflated language they use." She saw from his look that he didn't understand. "*Hinchado*. Like a politician, and you were never one of those."

"I am a soldier, nothing more. But a soldier present at one of the great moments in Cuban history."

She looked at his socks, a toe sticking out of each. Could she still talk to him? Was he going to speak like this from now on, as if she were part of an audience? Well, she had insulted him. Maybe it was all language he'd picked up from Fidel. Maybe you couldn't have a revolution without those lofty phrases. But it was jarring, because no matter the beard and uniform and tattered hat, she had seen the Camilo she remembered, exuberant and candid. She imagined putting her fingers to his chest and telling him, *We have a daughter*. That would get his attention. But then what? How simple it would be for him to have her escorted out of the camp. No, she had to know more about how he felt before telling him about Alameda.

He stood in front of her with his shirt pockets stuffed with papers, looking both exalted and worn out. Clare herself felt overwhelmed. Against his power and beauty she had only one card, Alameda, and for now she held it.

"What about Fidel?" she asked. "Is he coming to Havana?"

"Slowly. He will come by road from Santiago, making a caravan from town to town."

"Like a victory lap," Clare said.

When he didn't understand she moved her finger in a circle, pointing down. "*Haciendo el circuito después de la victoria.*"

"*Pero querida*, I love your Spanish!"

"I took lessons from a woman in my building. For two years and more."

This was a veiled complaint, about how long she had waited to hear from him. If Camilo understood, he ignored it. He tilted his head, glanced past Clare toward the hall, leaned forward and kissed her.

She was surprised, and just as quickly annoyed. She put her knuckles to his chest and pushed. "If you want to kiss me, Camilo, don't look around first to make sure no one will see."

"*No no, mi amor, tú sabes que te quiero.*"

In New York he had told her many times how much he loved her. But his Spanish had been flowery on the topic: *Tú eres la luz de mi vida*, he said, and *Que milagro eres*, and *Te quiero como la luna*. What did that mean, that he loved her like the moon? She had bathed in those phrases when he translated them, but later, after he disappeared, she had doubted them all.

She said, "Tell me what happened."

"What happened when?"

"In New York, when they took you away."

"Clare, I am sorry. I was in bed one morning, I was going to see you that day, I was so happy. Then a bang on the door. Macario opens it and there was *la migra*. They took us to New Jersey, to a jail, a terrible place, for thirty-nine days. And then"—he snapped his fingers—"a plane to Cuba."

"You could have written, once you were here."

"I'm sorry," he said again. "It is true, I must to have done that." He did look sorry, but only for a moment. "Soon I went to Mexico to find Fidel, and everything was a secret. No telephone, no letters, we could talk with no one, not even with a Mexican girl, never."

Clare felt like she'd been slapped. What did Mexican girls have to do with this? "I see. I see that what we had was just a fling to you."

"I am sorry, what is this—*fling?*"

"Something you soon forget, with someone who doesn't matter."

"I have never forgotten. I remember everything! In the Sierra I went to sleep remembering what you said, everything you did."

Was this true? It was what she wanted to hear. "Okay," she said. "What song was playing the first time you took me to the Palladium?"

"That is easy! "*Sabroso Mambo* by Tito Rodriguez."

"And what did I say when we walked in?"

"You said you could not dance because it was too fast."

"And you said?"

"I said nothing! I took you onto the floor and put a hand on your hip and we began. You are—what do you Americans say? A fast learner."

"I was never very good, compared to all the others." Clare took a small step back. "And I suppose, now that you're so important, that everything has changed for you. You must have a dozen girlfriends by now."

"A dozen, two dozen, I can no longer count!"

Was he serious?

"*Clarita,*" he said, "two days ago I was fighting in the streets of Yaguajáy. I have no *novia.* I was living in the mountains with many men who smell as bad as me."

But he wasn't in the mountains now. He was in a city filled with lush Cuban women, and from how the sentries had talked she didn't believe him. Her chest gave a pull and she felt sick. What was this? In New York, in the midst of their affair, she had never once been jealous.

She lifted her bag and held it between them. "I only came to take some photos."

Camilo stepped toward her and lifted his hand. For an instant she thought he was going to touch her chest. Instead he tapped the bag. "Fidel will be happy," he said in Spanish, then explained how Fidel wanted pictures of everything. Maybe not pictures of the two of them, but pho-tos of the rebel troops here in the camp of Batista. Camilo took a piece of paper from his shirt pocket, wrote in Spanish, *Admit this woman every-where*, and added his signature below. Then he asked for Clare's telephone number.

"I don't have a number," she said—though of course she did.

"Where are you staying?"

"In the city. In a house."

"Someone's house."

She admitted it was so.

"Take some pictures," Camilo said. "But then come back to see me."

Carrying the piece of paper with his name on it, she wandered through Camp Columbia. Next to the soldiers of the regular army the bearded fighters stood out unkempt, looking like beatniks or the saints of old. Ev-ery *barbudo* had a rifle or submachine gun, either dangling from his hand or tucked behind a shoulder. If there was another woman in the camp, Clare had yet to see her. The same for photographers and journalists: none so far, and she was glad to have the only camera in sight. She didn't like how Camilo, at the end, had brushed her aside, but she was glad to be here in the camp where Barquín and the other generals had handed themselves over to Castro's Revolution. She fingered Camilo's piece of paper. One sentence from him and she could go anywhere. She loved that.

She found the room full of boots, where soldiers from the regular army were filling up duffels with footwear of all sizes. She found a barber shop where two bearded rebels sat in the red leather chairs telling stories about their battles in the Sierra to some clean-faced soldiers. Everywhere she found good photos, and she was now utterly sure that she could not go back to taking static pictures of upper-class Cuban life—if there was going to *be* any upper-class life.

In the basement she found rooms where Batista's prisoners had been tortured. Clare showed her note from Camilo, and an army sergeant opened the doors for her. She saw beds and chairs with cuffs, blindfolds and hoods, cigarette lighters, and an electrical machine with a hand crank and black wires to which nails had been taped. It was just as Camilo had told her years before, and now she shot it all in black and white, using a flash in the darkened rooms.

On the parade grounds Batista's men stood about with little to do. It was the rebel soldiers who were friendly, who smiled and opened doors for her, who asked to see the photo of the beardless Camilo. And they were the ones she wanted to photograph, with their country hats and torn uniforms, a few with bandages tinged with blood, some with great manes of hair and each, always, with his gun held close, as if at any moment a skirmish might break out.

Clare shot five rolls of thirty-six exposures. Then, in a huge mess hall, she ate a late breakfast of rice, beans and bread off a metal plate, and talked with a dozen soldiers. Their Spanish, from all over the island, was sometimes a trial. There were men who spoke as clearly as Violeta Casals on the radio, enunciating every syllable, and others who talked like auctioneers, far too fast for Clare to understand.

She stayed away from Camilo's office. She walked out to the airfield where Fulgencio Batista, after his New Years' Eve party at the camp, had boarded a plane with his money, his family and some of his generals, and taken off for Santo Domingo, fleeing the country he'd held in an iron grip for most of the last decade.

Returning to the parade grounds, Clare sat down on a shaded bench. All morning she'd been immersed in Camilo's world, and now she needed time to think it over.

The last time she'd seen him he was a cook in a New York restaurant. Now, at twenty-seven, he was one of Cuba's new leaders. She loved his attention, but couldn't guess how long it would last. At some point in the years ahead she would have to tell Ala that her father was not Domingo, he was Camilo Cienfuegos. But when? When she was three? When she was ten? Each day was another step into deception. Also, when was she going to tell Domingo the truth—and how much of the truth?

She understood what she had done with her memories of Camilo. Because of how it ended, she had created a love affair with no imperfections.

Their days in New York, their dates, were the opposite of most couples'. First came hours of sex. Then, in the late afternoon, they put their clothes on and went for a walk in Riverside Park, went for a stroll on Amsterdam, took the bus downtown and ate in some small Cuban restaurant. Over dinner Camilo taught her those boyish romantic phrases in Spanish, *You are the light of my life,* and *What a miracle you are.* In English they talked about Cuba and politics and photography. For Camilo that wasn't always easy—but after dinner he took her dancing, where he shone. He took her to El Cubanacán, to the Gloria Palace and the Palladium, upstairs on 53rd where Tito Puente played. In those big lit ballrooms, on their shining wooden floors, the best Latin dancers in the city came to perform their intricate steps. It was not that crowded on Tuesdays, for which Clare was thankful. She was a poor dancer, then not very good, then passable. This didn't worry Camilo, who put a firm hand on her hip or the small of her back, held his left hand to her right with a feathery touch, and smiled without stop from the moment they stepped onto the floor.

Sometimes she sent him out to dance with one of the experts, some girl in a tight-hipped, flare-skirted dress. A girl with pushed-up breasts, bright red lipstick, towering hair and stiletto heels that would have pitched Clare to the ground in ten seconds. But how those girls could dance! To mambos, merengues, cumbias and rumbas, to the *danzón* and the *son cubano.* At the end of the dance, shining with pleasure, Camilo gave the woman a small bow, or kissed her hand and delivered her back to where he'd found her. He loved women, he loved to dance, and he always came back to Clare. He was going to leave her, she knew that early on—but not for some woman. He would leave her for Fidel.

At night, at one in the morning when they returned to her door, Camilo would not come in. He would not spend the night with her there, and never met her roommate. It was always an empty moment for Clare when he gave her a last kiss, turned away from her and disappeared down the hall.

On Saturday morning or on Sunday, before he went to work, he called her from a pay phone on Avenue D. It was always brief, a three-minute call, but enough for her to know that he would come again on Tuesday. Always, after he called, her roommate Debbie grilled her. Did they really spend all day in bed? Did they do it over and over? Was it good every time? Clare said yes and yes and yes, but would not elaborate. She didn't want to expose Camilo's innocence, or her own greed in bed.

One weekend he didn't call. Not on Saturday and not on Sunday. But he would show up on Tuesday, she was sure. That morning she bathed and put on a light top and short skirt, made a cup of coffee and waited. He always came at eight-thirty, never after nine. An hour passed as Clare tried to read the paper. She painted her toenails, like the girls at the Palladium in their high-heeled sandals. At ten she could no longer stand it and walked out the door wearing a pair of sneakers and a coat pulled over her seductive clothes, carrying only her purse.

Men stared. It was an unnerving ride on the subway, avoiding the gaze of everyone on the car, and once out on the sidewalks of the lower East Side she remembered what Camilo had said: it was a bad neighborhood. The whole way to his squat decaying building she felt afraid, then more so as she went inside, her legs exposed in the dark stairwell.

She knocked on his door, waited and knocked again. A third time, louder, fearful now of those who lived in the other apartments. Finally a creak behind her. Clare jumped, put her back to Camilo's door and held her purse in front of her. From the opposite apartment a young woman peered out, wearing a T-shirt and a baggy pair of shorts, her hair uncombed. "There is no one," she said, in a deep accent. "They came and took them."

"Who?"

"*La migra.*"

"The who?"

"The immigration. It was last week. Already they will be in Cuba."

After that, New York to Clare felt dirty and senseless. She couldn't work. She tried to avoid her roommate, then broke down sobbing and told her everything. It helped for an hour, but the next morning nothing had changed. Clare feigned sleep until Debbie left for work, then got up, dressed and walked up to Broadway. She drank a cup of coffee in a shop, which didn't help. People looked strange to her, they hardly looked human. An old man opened the door for a woman, saying, "After you, madame." They looked like idiots with their foolish little smiles. Why did anyone live in this terrible city? Why did people so old bother to live at all? When the man and woman sat down together, Clare realized they were married, or at least friends. It made no difference. They could have been a pair of beetles.

Her chest felt bruised. It felt as if someone had taken her heart, thrown it against a wall and stuffed it back inside her. She had been in love with Camilo, she knew that now. It had only been ten weeks—ten days, really —but that was enough time. It was plenty of time.

No matter that it wasn't Camilo's fault, no matter that Immigration had swept in and grabbed him, she felt abandoned. Her mother and father called, as they did every Sunday, and urged her to come out to Brooklyn to visit. She didn't want to go to Brooklyn. She thought only of Camilo, and of finding him. She called Immigration and Naturalization, who claimed they had no record of him.

"Could he have lived here under another name?" she asked. "There were five Cubans, it was an apartment on East Fourth."

"I'm sorry, we can't comment on any arrests."

He could be in jail, or already in Cuba, as the girl in his building said. Clare sat at home. She had lost her drive, her belief that things would turn out for the best. Time slowed and the days wouldn't pass.

They did, of course—and it wasn't long before she began to suspect that she was pregnant.

At first she told no one about it, but after throwing up into the bathroom sink on three straight mornings, she was confronted by her roommate. Clare went to a clinic and had the rabbit test. Yes, she was pregnant. The word *abortion* barely crossed her mind, and never her lips. It was Camilo's child, and she would have it.

For three months she was miserable from both the nausea and Camilo's absence. In the second trimester her spirits lifted. She looked around the battered city and found something that still interested her. It was everything Cuban, everything Latin. She ate dinner in Cuban restaurants, she took her Leicas to the Palladium and shot a photo essay of one of Tito Puente's rehearsals. Because she was going to need money, she went back to work with a vengeance. Untouched by any seasickness, she took pictures of sailboats for *Yachting*. She did a couple of weddings, some bar and bat mitzvahs. She commuted to Newark two days a week to take photos of the corpses in the city morgue, including some gruesome autopsies. The dead bodies never slowed her down: in a few months she would be giving birth.

She wrangled an assignment at Aqueduct, shooting the trotters. She photographed half the campus of Columbia for a guy in the admissions department who was drawn to her, no matter that she was five months pregnant. She liked him well enough, but couldn't stand how he smelled. It was a meaty smell, like beef in an outdoor stall. "No," she told him, "I'm sorry, we must keep this to business." Besides, he was not Camilo, and Camilo was the only one she wanted.

Now she loved her swelling body, loved how everyone gave way before her, paid her tribute, wanted to touch her arm or shoulder. In the mirror, her face glowed. Her days of nausea were forgotten. Pregnancy was easy, it was a breeze on a summer day.

An editor at *Life* called, Asa Bottomwell, who had seen her Aqueduct photos. He asked her to come in with her portfolio, then offered her an essay on Saratoga with its lavish racetrack and wealthy crowd of gamblers. There she shot in both color and black and white, and Asa was impressed. He liked her sly portraits of the socialites, the photos of elegant women with coiffed hair and broad confident mouths, and he ran those beside shots of the muddy trainers and assistants, the men and women who mucked out the stalls of thoroughbreds as famous as movie stars. *Life* was conservative, it sought not to offend, but Asa was an old New Englander with a socialist streak. He was the one who insisted on a double spread, in several black and white photos, of a jockey in torn silks, thrown during his sixth race of the day, limping back to the stable over the chewed-up track.

Life sent her to Nantucket to photograph the survivors of the *Andrea Doria*, and to the steel strike in Pittsburgh. Clare sold one of her Leicas, bought a new Pentax and set aside more money. By October she'd grown heavy and was moving slower. Her brief months of euphoria had passed, and she began to worry about the future. Her roommate seemed enthusiastic about the child and felt they could all live together, but Clare wondered if that was going to work. Debbie could be intransigent about how the apartment was kept. It was her apartment, and Clare the one who shared it.

By November she was eight months pregnant. Debbie was going home to Connecticut for Thanksgiving, so Clare said yes to her parents' entreaties, and took the subway to Brooklyn to see them. It was cloudy, the streets cold and quiet, and she climbed the steps to their building with a sense of foreboding.

Her parents knew that the baby's father was Cuban, and that Immigration had taken him away. The topic of abortion had never come up, because Clare was four months pregnant before she told them. They did suggest she might have the child and give it away, but after they spoke of that once, she told them not to bring it up again, and they didn't. Really, they'd been decent about it. Still, her father had grown distant, and she thought it was because of the child. Sometimes, on a call, her mother handed him the phone and he had nothing to say. Clare spoke and he did not respond. He was there, she heard him breathing or even asking her mother some question, but to Clare he was silent. He was a pianist who taught at the Brooklyn Conservatory. He had long been absent-minded, even thoughtless at times, but now she took his silence as judgment. Today, at least, face to face with her, he would see that this baby was coming soon. It was not something he could ignore in person.

The apartment was rich with the smell of turkey, and her mother beamed to see her. She hugged Clare from the side, placing her own slender stomach next to Clare's and resting her palm, with the lightest touch, on top of her massive belly. "I remember how it was," Lena said. "I could walk, but I couldn't bend over. You are good to have come. Did the subway shake you around?"

"It's the turnstile that's difficult. And Dad?"

"He's here. *Henry*," she yelled into the living room, "it's Clare."

But Henry didn't come. They found him beside the baby grand, a pile of scores spread out on its closed top. He was looking for something but couldn't find it.

"Henry, our daughter is here."

He straightened up. He looked at Clare quizzically and said, "Hello then." He paid no attention to her stomach. "And where have you come from today?"

"From my apartment."

"In the city?"

"In Manhattan, on 92nd. The one you helped me move into."

"Yes, of course."

"I've brought someone with me," Clare said. "It's your grandchild." She said it lightly, as if joking, but circled her hands under the baby and lifted, her navel sticking out like a little thumb.

"You're having a baby?" He put down the scores he'd been holding, stepped closer, looked Clare up and down, then stuck out his hands and laid them on her stomach. Next he was pressing her hard.

"*Dad, stop.*"

"Be gentle, Henry," Lena said. "You must be gentle. Babies are delicate. Oh, you men." She gave a little laugh. Then, to Clare, "They don't know anything, do they?"

Lena had always been Henry's protector. She'd been smoothing his way for as long as Clare could remember—but this was too much. "Please, Dad, don't do that again. That's my baby in there, and it's delicate."

He stepped back, cowed. "Yes, I understand, I must be more gentle. I will, I will." His eyes drifted off. "Perhaps you could help me find something. It's a score, I had it here somewhere. It's by—by a composer I respect. I was going to play it for you."

"After dinner, Henry. First we're going to have Thanksgiving dinner."

"Yes, of course. How can I help?" He sounded relieved, even cheerful. He searched for his glasses, found them in his pocket and put them on. He'd lost some weight. Both her parents were now trim, but Henry's hair was too long and he was not a good shaver. He'd missed some patches on his face. Missed them for two or three days, Clare thought.

Her parents were older, they'd been forty when she was born. They sat down to Lena's meal in the dining room of their large handsome apartment, a brownstone from the twenties. Amidst the gravy smells, the turkey and creamed onions, Clare caught the odor of her mother's lavender powder.

"Any word from David?"

"Every month."

Clare's brother had moved to Osaka and never returned. His orderly typed letters described Japanese culture and his job with an American insurance company. He'd married a Japanese woman, smooth as a stone, who spoke only primitive English. He sent photos of their two children, but he did not come back to visit. Clare wrote him herself, sometimes on the topic of their parents, but he let her know that the letters he sent were meant for the whole family. It was like getting a newsletter. He was eight years older than Clare, and they had not been close since she was a young girl.

In the other room, the Steinway gleamed. Pianos made Clare anxious, because she didn't like to fail, and she had failed at the piano. "And your students?" she asked her father.

"I have a girl who's very good. If she keeps at it she could perform, I'm sure of it."

Clare had not kept at it. But her father didn't seem to be rubbing that in, or even reminding her about it. He bent to his dinner plate fully absorbed, like a man over a workbench. Clare could not eat much and finished before him. She ate six times a day, because large meals didn't fit. She glanced at her mother, then watched her father and the meticulous way he addressed what was on his plate. She wanted his attention, wanted to see if he could give it to her. She said, in her lightest tone, "You know I'm going to keep this child."

Henry raised his eyebrows, then appeared to focus, his eyes settling on the top of her belly. "Who is the father of this baby?"

"His name is Camilo."

"Camel?"

"Camilo. It's pronounced *Ca-mee-lo.*"

"Where is he from?"

"He's from Cuba."

"And where is he now? Shouldn't he be here?"

Lena reached across with her fork and tapped Henry's plate, as if calling a child to attention. "He disappeared, Henry. You know this. And I want you to be nice to Clare. She has come to see us for Thanksgiving."

"All right, all right, I'll be nice. That's what your mother says sometimes, that I've forgotten how to be nice. And maybe I have. I'll make it
up to you by doing the dishes."

"He likes to do the dishes," Lena said. "He likes to figure out where
everything goes."

Her parents lived in an insular world. They'd never made friends in
New York as they had in Ohio. Something was off kilter here—but it had
long been so. Lena, who for decades had taught piano herself, had now
stopped. She'd become Henry's caretaker.

He excused himself to use the bathroom, and as soon as he left the
room Lena spoke up. "I'm worried about him."

"I see why."

"He's so forgetful. Do you know he got lost the other day, walking
home from the Conservatory? It's eight blocks away. He called me from
a telephone booth and I had to go get him. Then, when he got home, he
was fine."

"Mom, what's wrong with him?"

Lena looked exhausted. "I don't know."

When Henry came back they cleared the table and set about the dishes,
Lena washing and Clare drying and Henry putting everything away. Except he made mistakes. He placed some spoons among the knives. He
hesitated with a drinking glass, then laid it in a bowl. Clare moved the
spoons, she moved the glass, and Lena kept washing. There were other
mistakes, but it was an easy time together with everyone pitching in. It
made Clare feel like she was eight years old, when they all washed up after
dinner. But then Henry stopped. He stared at Clare's stomach as if he'd
never seen it. "What is that?" he said.

"That's my baby."

"Oh, your baby! Let me see!" He came toward her, his hands stretched
out. Clare held a plate between them, like a shield. He curled his fingers
over the top and swept it out of her hands onto the floor, where it smashed.
Immediately Lena stepped between them. "*Henry*, go to the piano. Play
something. We'd like to hear you play something."

Clare stared at her mother, but Lena wouldn't look at her. With her
foot, Lena pushed the larger shards of the plate out of the way, then took

off her apron and tossed it on the counter. "Come," she said, "this always calms him down."

Henry, subdued, let himself be guided into the living room, where he opened the top of the Steinway and sat down on the bench. "I have the score somewhere," he said—but then, without it, he began to play. Clare recognized the piece from the first five notes, Mussorgsky's *Pictures at an Exhibition*. It was a lyrical, then brooding, then deranged piece of music, long one of Henry's favorites, and he sat more and more upright as the composition came apart. It sounded as if the misery of the composer were giving way to madness.

Her father, Clare thought, was turning senile. Not right now, as he played the piano, but in everything else he did. Something was wrong with his mind, and without Lena he'd be lost. Clare pulled her chair closer to her mother's and the two of them listened together. It was not a short piece of music nor an easy one, and Clare could hardly believe her father had it by memory. He could not remember where a spoon went, but never missed a note in this complex suite. He played on. There were reprieves, and at times the music grew lighter.

Outside, dusk was coming down over the brownstones across the street. Henry came to the end, the last notes echoed through the room, and in the silence that followed no one looked at anyone else. The music was a help, and with it Henry had put his confusion aside. But forty minutes later, going home on the subway, Clare curled her arms around her baby and thought, *I can't let him get too close.*

At noon a whistle sounded in Camp Columbia, and Clare returned to Camilo's office. She found him with his boots still off and his feet on the desk beside his gun, smiling broadly at a man who faced him from a second chair, a tightly groomed man wearing a gray suit and dark tie.

"Miss Miller," Camilo said in English, "I introduce to you Earl Smith, the Honorable Ambassador of the United States."

Ambassador Smith stood up, shook her hand, looked at the pin on her blouse and said, "You got here fast."

"Seven this morning," she said brightly.

"I am telling to the ambassador how *la migra* arrested me in New York and put me—*en esposas*."

"In handcuffs," Clare said.

"And how helpful that was, because after that I went to Mexico and found Fidel. The ambassador is afraid that Fidel is not a friend of his country. But I think perhaps we can all be friends together. Mister Ambassador, I invite you to my office at any time. Day or night, any time. Is that good?"

"That's fine," the ambassador said, but he did not look happy.

"Please, Miss Miller, take a photo of this agreement, a photo for history." The two men rose, the ambassador more slowly, and when he accepted Camilo's handshake Clare took a picture, then another. They were good, she knew it as soon as she took them. They were just what the Associated Press would want: the bearded rebel leader in his sock feet, broad-brimmed hat and giant toothy smile shaking hands with the somber U.S. ambassador. Sometimes it worked like this, and the perfect shot fell into her lap. It helped to have a subject like Camilo, someone completely unafraid of the camera.

When they were alone he sat back down. "Please," he said, extending his hand, and she sat down in the ambassador's chair. The room was warm, and Camilo stopped to roll up his sleeves. He looked exhausted.

"What you need," Clare said, "is a siesta."

"No, I cannot do that."

"How much sleep have you had? How much last night?"

He admitted to a total, over the last three days, of five or six hours. He'd drunk a lot of coffee, and two empty cups sat on his desk.

"Lie down," Clare said. "Lie down on the floor."

No, that was impossible.

"Here, take this chair, you can face away from the door. A ten-minute nap and no one will know."

"*Clarita*, I can't." But she stood up, took him by the arm and traded chairs with him. He let out a sigh, and thirty seconds later he was nodding.

"Put your head back," she said, but he wouldn't. Instead, his chin sank toward his chest, and in another minute he was dead asleep.

Clare pulled her own chair closer and watched his face soften. When a soldier came through the door she raised a finger to her lips. He peered around the chair, saw his chief sleeping and withdrew.

She watched Camilo sleep, and while staring at his long tranquil face, all she could see was trouble. He was going to ruin everything. She should stand up right now and walk out of the camp, leaving him to the girl-friends he made jokes about.

In New York, she was sure, he had never been unfaithful. But that was in the U.S., where Camilo had been a foreigner without papers, an assistant cook who lived in a small apartment with four other Cubans. His pay was low and his plans unsure. Their romance took place in her world, and Clare had imagined herself as the one with ambitions and a future.

Leaning closer to him, she took his shirt between thumb and forefinger, bent her nose to the rank smell and inhaled. There was a hole burned on one of his cuffs and a tear on the other sleeve. She was less fearful of war now, but the war was over. Now she was afraid of Camilo. He would tell her he loved her, as he often had before, then do as he pleased. He was too famous now, too powerful. She stood up, determined to leave—but as she did, Camilo opened his eyes.

"Don't go," he said.

"I have to get these photos to New York."

"Come back and see me."

"Perhaps I will."

"Come on Sunday. No, I have to fly to Camagüey on Sunday, to make plans with Fidel. Come on Monday."

"Perhaps I can make it."

Of course she could come on Monday, and of course she would. She didn't fool herself about that, and she could see on Camilo's face that she didn't fool him, either. He was smiling again, that smile that no one could resist.

6

CLARE walked home through the city. She wanted to get back to Ala, to hold her and stare at her face and figure out all over again how much of Camilo was in her. But by now Domingo might have returned from his trip to the mill, and she wasn't ready to talk to him.

Havana, which had woken slowly, was now fully alive. As she walked back toward the center of town the streets grew crowded. Neighbors chatted and called out to each other, and in spite of the strike some of the bars and restaurants had opened their doors so people could sit and talk, listen to music, go out on the sidewalk and dance. A few cars moved through the streets. Taxis too, but there was no way to flag one down because they were all filled with people waving Cuban flags, calling out and singing *La Bayamesa*. Clare took some celebration photos, then put her camera away and walked among the crowds completely at ease, as safe as she had ever felt in Cuba.

Even before coming to Havana the first time she'd been told not to walk the streets alone, that it was dangerous for a young woman. Engracia, the white-haired grandmother who had taught her Spanish and Cuban cooking, had insisted that a woman was at risk on the streets, that Cuban men had no respect. She was remembering, Clare thought, her girlhood in the early part of the century, and surely things had changed since then. But when Clare first came to live in Havana she heard too many stories of rape and torture, and of young men and women who disappeared and were never seen again. Clare also stood out from the crowd, which had its dangers. She was a tall slender American with brown hair, blue eyes and an angular walk unlike the easy glide of most Cuban women. There had

been times she felt nervous on the street, times she would have preferred
to walk but found a taxi instead.

Then, last fall, had come a proclamation from the Sierra. All rape, Fidel
Castro announced, was punishable by death. Men had already been shot
for it, including two of his own soldiers. In Havana it was understood
that under Fidel there would be no gambling or prostitution, and that
rapists would be shot. The job would be done summarily, by his soldiers,
with their rifles.

After that everything felt different. Only last night Clare had walked
through the streets of Vedado with Ala, past families standing quietly on
their doorsteps or on the sidewalk. Many had smiled or waved, and there
were no hissy calls for her attention. Instead, young men in pairs patrolled
the streets, unbearded and without uniforms. Some carried an old rifle
or pistol, and there had been no signs of looting or unrest. All wore the
black and red armbands of the M-26, and Clare felt protected.

Behind her, on a block already crowded with people, a noisy city bus
turned onto the avenue. Over the destination window someone had taped
a paper sign, *¡Viva la Revolución, No Mas Mierda!* Long Live the Revolution, No More Shit! The crowd on board was laughing, waving and
singing. The driver, half dancing in his seat to a radio *danzón*, drove so
slowly that people got on and off without the bus ever stopping.

"*¡Vamos, señorita!*" someone cried from inside. "*¡Vente, ¡mi yanquita!*"

Both men and women hung out the windows. *Come* they said, get on
the bus!

Beside Clare on the sidewalk stood a woman in a long skirt and sandals,
wearing a hopeful look. A young woman from the country, Clare thought.
Catching Clare's eye, she gestured toward the bus and said, "What do you
think?"

"Let's go!"

Clare slid an arm around the woman's waist and the two of them
stepped forward as the bus poked by, three different people helping them
up the stairs and into the laughing chaos inside. Almost immediately
they were separated, as the woman was swept down the aisle. Arms en-
circled Clare's shoulders, then her waist—but they were women's arms as

well as men's, and no one was feeling her up. Everyone talked and sang, and Clare joined in, trying to follow the quick Cuban Spanish with its half-swallowed vowels and missing consonants. She knew the words to the national anthem and *Guantanamera*, and before long she was hanging out a window herself, laughing and shouting at those on the street as the bus wound back and forth through the delirious city.

How she loved this. How she loved it when they called her *compañera*. No one cared now that she was a foreigner, that she didn't look or walk like a Cuban. She belonged to the city and was one of the people—more so than she had ever felt in Columbus, Ohio or New York City. It was intoxicating. It was like falling in love.

If only, she thought, it could be as simple as this with Camilo. But that was madness. A few moments with him and she'd forgotten about her husband. It wasn't the streets of Havana that were dangerous, it was her own mind, her own desires. Whatever happened would be her fault.

Leaving the commercial streets behind, she walked through Domingo's tranquil neighborhood, the houses silent and the sidewalks empty. Already she missed her ride on the bus—but in Domingo's drive she found Eliseo, sitting in the Chevrolet and smoking a cigar. His dark face lit up to see her.

"*Eliseo,*" she said, "*¿que pasa?*"

"*Buenas tardes, señora.*" He was there under Domingo's orders, he told her, to protect the house from looters. From his lap he lifted a pistol in a leather holster.

"And Domingo?"

"He returns tomorrow. Only Rosa is here with your daughter. The cook has gone to her family, and the maid as well."

Clare walked around the Chevy, opened the passenger door and sat down. She set her camera bag on the seat and leaned back against the door. "All down La Rampa," she said, "they're dancing in the streets." They could hear it: faint music and shouts, an occasional high-pitched car horn. A couple of minutes passed without either of them saying anything.

"Is it possible, Eliseo, that you could do me a favor?"

"With all pleasure, señora."

"First, please call me Clara."

"That will be fine."

"I have to get to the airport. I have some film that must go to New York, but there are no taxis, no buses, no way to get out there. Could you drive me?"

Eliseo looked pained. He cupped his hand behind his ear. "You can hear the danger yourself. As you can imagine, Domingo would not want me to drive two blocks with the city in this mood. I'm sorry, I cannot."

"We could take the back streets. Look how quiet it is right here."

"Please, señora, there is no knowing what the Cuban will do. And you have seen how Domingo treats his car."

"I've seen him lend it to you."

"But never on such a day. If something happened I could lose my job."

She had been too insistent. "I'm sorry, Eliseo, I should not have asked."

If only Domingo had trusted her with the car. It was one of his annoying habits, to treat her like royalty, like someone incapable. She gestured at the gun in Eliseo's lap. "Do you think you will need that? Everyone seems so happy with this rebel victory."

"Most people, it's true."

"And you?"

Eliseo took another puff on his cigar. He raised his stump for a moment and looked at it—which gave Clare a chance to do the same, something she had never done in good light. The flesh had been sewn up neatly over the bone, but the knob still made her uneasy.

"I lost this in nineteen sixteen, when I was twenty. I was working at the Preston Mill, feeding cane into the mouth of the crusher. That's how it was done in those days, everything by hand and no thought for safety. They took me to the hospital and the company paid for the amputation. When I went back to the mill they gave me some money and fired me. Fifty pesos, about the same as fifty dollars. For a long time I couldn't find any work. I came to Havana because I had a cousin here who rolled cigars. I could read, and got the job of reading the newspaper out loud to the men who rolled. I was lucky, because out in the country there was little I could do. But today, with Fidel, things are going to be better for the most isolated *guajiros*. Everyone will have a job, everyone will have a doctor, and every child will go to school. So that is what I think. I think this Revolution is going to be good for Cuba."

From the tight-lipped Eliseo this was a very long speech. "And Domingo?" Clare asked. "Will it be good for him?"

"Domingo hated the corruption of Batista. Like many others, both rich and poor, he hopes for a change."

"The rich," Clare said. "Am I one of the rich?"

"You came with only two suitcases. But you are from over there, where everyone has money. Isn't that so?"

"Not really. But compared to Cuba, yes. There is much poverty here."

Eliseo nodded. He smoked. "Year after year that has never changed. But now—you have read the news, what do *you* think of Fidel?"

"I love Fidel."

Clare laughed at herself. Where had that come from? Perhaps it was Fidel's edict about shooting rapists, or maybe it was from riding around the streets in a bus full of singing people.

Eliseo took another pull on his cigar, then stubbed it into the ashtray. "Do you have your film with you?"

Clare patted the bag at her side.

"If you wish, we will go to the airport."

First she went inside to get Ala, who ran into her arms and clung to her, unwilling to let go. This was unusual. It was the near-emptiness of the house, Clare thought, with only Rosa to talk to all day. With Clare, Rosa was deferential. Clare had tried to relax her, Domingo had tried himself, but she only seemed to let herself go with Ala, singing songs and acting out little stories. Clare had never seen this herself, but others had told her it was so. Now the girl chattered away, holding onto Clare's collar and telling her about a *dog* and a *bug*. There were no dogs in Domingo's house, and a bug, once discovered, did not live long, but for some reason Ala had locked onto the two English words. "*Quiero al dog, y quiero al bug.*"

My favorite surrealist, Domingo sometimes called her.

"*You're* the one I love," Clare said.

"*¡No! ¡Habla español!*"

"*Te quiero, te quiero, y vamos al aeropuerto.*"

Clare thanked Rosa, told her to take the night off and the next day as well, and gave her ten pesos, a week's salary for a *niñera* in Cuba. She grabbed a couple of diapers, two bananas and a mango, and carried Ala out to the Chevrolet. Eliseo frowned, but Clare told him not to worry, that she'd seen lots of kids out on the streets.

They drove west, staying on the quieter side of town, then south toward the Rancho Boyeros airport. Ala sat on Clare's lap as Eliseo did twenty-five miles an hour down a broad street with hardly any traffic.

"This revolution," Clare said. "Is it something you talk about with Domingo?"

"Almost never. It is not like this, you know." He gestured with his stump, back and forth between them. "Domingo is the boss and I am the worker, and that's how it is in Cuba."

"But won't that all change with Fidel?"

Eliseo's left hand fluttered in the so-so gesture. "We will see. We've had revolutions before."

"What will Domingo say when he hears you took me to the airport?"

He turned onto a four-lane avenue, still without traffic, and sped up to thirty. The afternoon sun lit up the pavement and the small houses beside it, some gardens of cabbage and squash. "That is nothing he will hear from me."

"But if he asks?"

A horse grazed in the strip between the lanes, and Ala jumped up to watch it. Eliseo's eyes never left the road. "You know how Domingo is."

"I'm not sure I do."

Another long pause. A car passed them with young men hanging out every window. Eliseo let them pull away. "Domingo likes to be in charge."

Clare knew this was so. He was heedful, calm, occasionally mournful —but he maneuvered constantly to stay in control. She had watched him run his magazine, his household, and her.

"On the surface," said Eliseo, "he remains calm. But underneath, when things don't go his way, he can be angry."

"Have you seen him like that?"

"I only tell you this so you can be careful."

Clare wanted to hear more, but Eliseo had said his piece. *Boss* and *worker*, she thought. It was the worker who knew the boss, far more than the other way around. Clare herself had no idea where Eliseo lived. His wife had died some years ago, he had a grown son, that's all she knew. But now she saw that she had more faith in Castro's rebellion than he did. She believed it was going to change everything. She'd been prepared for this long ago by Camilo's descriptions of a ruthless Batista. Now the tide had turned with a rush, and she worried about Domingo. She was a little afraid of him, yet wanted to protect him.

The airport looked chaotic, starting with the taxis. Though there had been few on the streets, here were half a hundred of them angling for somewhere to park. Men passed among them, unloading trunks and suitcases as the women and children waited nearby.

Eliseo refused to drop her off. This tiny one-armed man didn't want her to negotiate her own way through the terminal, even though she had twice sent film to New York on the late-night plane. A hundred yards away, Eliseo found a place to park. He locked the Chevy and gave some coins to a man dressed in a stained jacket and brimless cap, something like a uniform. Paying someone to keep an eye on a parked car was common practice in Havana.

Inside, the central lobby was a tumult of piled-up luggage, loud talk, well-dressed women and many children. The kids were having no fun, for their mothers kept them close and quiet. At the Eastern counter Clare found a clerk she knew, was given a canvas pouch for her film, filled out the address and tipped the man five pesos, her money now pouring out freely. By four in the morning the AP labs would have her film.

Alameda, upright in Clare's arms as she was carried back through the lobby, twisted around to watch. She could sense the tension in the room, Clare was sure. Clare stopped in the midst of it and asked Eliseo, "Why are so many people here?"

"These are the men who know they will be shot."

"Who's going to shoot them?"

"You see that skinny one with his hair slicked back? He is a famous corrupt politician. Everyone knows him, they say he has killed twenty men and raped as many women. We call him *el chacal de Marianao*."

He didn't look like a jackal, he looked like a worried father. His wife held onto his children, four subdued, good-looking girls.

"And he *should* be shot," Eliseo said. "I wouldn't weep to see it."

"You have a gun yourself," Clare reminded him.

"I have never pulled its trigger. But if someone showed up here— the husband, perhaps, of one of those violated women—there could be trouble. You see that there are no policemen. They are probably afraid themselves. Let's go, for nothing good can happen here."

Nothing did. Half way back to Domingo's car they saw the damage: the rearview mirror lying on the ground and the vent window smashed. The driver's door was dented, and of the man Eliseo had paid to keep an eye on the car, no trace.

"*Why?*" Clare said. "Why would they do this?"

Eliseo looked miserable. He walked up to the car with his body stiff, his mouth pinched, his good arm giving little jerks. He pried at the door, asked for Clare's help, and together they wrenched the door open. Eliseo looked under the seat but came up empty-handed. "The pistol," he said. "I thought I left it hidden."

Clare apologized. She should never have asked him to bring her here. She apologized a second time, trying to get him to look at her, but Eliseo said nothing. He picked up the rearview mirror, brushed the broken glass off the seat and drove them home in silence.

7

CAMILO rose in the dark, massaged his aching calf and pulled on his clothes and new boots. It was the second night in a row, but the first time in years, that he'd slept without his pants, on sheets and a pillow. It was a miracle, but he wasn't sure he liked it. He was used to war.

The end of it had come as a surprise. Just at midnight on New Year's Eve the army commander in Yaguajáy had sent him a note, agreeing to a surrender. They signed a paper, then someone passed around a bottle of rum to celebrate both the signing and the New Year, and Camilo went to bed at four. An hour later he was awakened by Fidel, calling from Santiago: "Batista has fled, get on the road, the army will be waiting for you at Camp Columbia."

Now, after gulping two hot coffees and a sweet roll, he stepped outside to find Che already on the parade grounds, chatting with some aides as the first bands of light lifted off the eastern horizon. "*Hola, gaucho,*" Camilo said, "you got here early."

"The trick is not to go to bed. Is the plane ready?"

"They tell me. But they told me last night we were going to have lobster for dinner, and it was only rice and beans with bits of something. There's a DC-3 on the camp's runway."

"Let's go then. I miss Fidel, the old mule."

Camilo, excited as a ten-year-old, stared out the window as they took off. He'd only been on three planes in his life: once up to the U.S., once back, then the flight to Mexico. This was a noisy, throbbing plane, and the two engines roared at different pitches. Already Che had his nose in a book, probably something by a Russian, maybe a Frenchman. Camilo tapped the open page and pointed out the window. "Look at all the cows down there. This could be the pampas."

Che glanced past him. "This is nothing like the pampas. You think there's sugar cane in the pampas?"

"They say we're headed for a big fiesta. The whole island wants to see Fidel."

"We're going to a meeting. We're going to discuss the future of the Revolution. You can have a fiesta later—with an orchestra if you want."

"*Gaucho obstinado*. Once things settle down I'm going to take you out dancing."

"You know I don't dance."

"I'll get Aleida to come. Then you'll dance!"

Aleida was Che's new girlfriend. His wife was in Peru, but it was all over for the wife. Che was smitten with this new girl. It was the closest to drunk that Camilo had ever seen him.

"I'm surrounded by a bunch of professors," Camilo said. "You and Fidel and Huber. All you do is read."

"You didn't bring your Martí? I've seen you read his poems, even memorize them."

"As soon as we get back to Havana I'm going to buy a copy of *Versos Sencillos*."

"A good book," Che said, and went back to his own. The noise of the plane subsided as it leveled off from its climb.

"But *damn*," Camilo said, "I just remembered! Books cost money. I haven't had a peso of my own in years."

"You will go to a library. This book is from a library."

Camilo reached over and took it from Che's hands. It was *El Origen de la Familia, la Propriedad Privada y el Estado*, by Friedrich Engels, and it belonged to the library of Santa Clara. "Didn't you blow that building apart?"

"Only one room. I'll send it back when I finish it."

"Professors," Camilo said again. "In the middle of a battle you stop to pick up a book."

"It's a very good habit. Now give it back and let me read."

"Very stubborn people, you professors."

At the Camagüey airport some soldiers put them in a jeep, then jumped into a truck and escorted them out of town on the national road headed east. The two vehicles sped down the empty two lanes past cattle, rice fields, bananas, malanga and sugar cane. Gradually a few people appeared at the side of the road, some men cheering and waving their hats as the jeep passed. The convoy was headed in the wrong direction, but that didn't matter, everyone was happy to see some *barbudos*. A couple of *barbudos*, anyway. Their driver and most of the soldiers in the truck looked like what they were, teenagers who'd missed out on the war. Some of the veteran rebels affected a disdain for these soldiers who'd never seen battle. Not Camilo. They reminded him of himself when he was younger, when he'd burned with anger at Batista but had no idea of what he was going to do with his life. It still felt like a miracle that he had landed *here*, with Fidel.

The farther they went, the more people lined the road. The campesinos had come in carts, on bicycles and on foot, walking down out of the hills. *Radio Bemba* had been at work: lip radio, the grapevine.

When Camilo and Che met up with Fidel he was riding in the back of an old personnel carrier, standing behind the cab with Celia Sánchez, Huber Matos, Juan Almeida and other companions from the Sierra. Camilo jumped out before his jeep came to a stop, slipped his gun behind his shoulder and climbed up over the sideboards of the truck, many hands grasping him as he jumped down into the crowd. Che climbed in the back, also beaming. It was the reunion they had promised themselves when they left the mountains four months ago with their columns of thirty and forty men.

"Here you are!" said Fidel, grinning as he embraced them both. "You have broken the back of the tyranny. Come, let's get out and walk."

They were quickly surrounded. Fidel pushed ahead through the crowd, shaking hands, smiling, letting old women take his face in their hands. He gestured for Camilo to join him. "Stay beside me," he said, "and don't let anyone with a gun come close. There could always be some maniac."

Everyone wanted to touch him. He might have been the Pope, Camilo thought, or Benny Moré after a show at the *Gran Teatro*.

Walking along the smooth national road felt strange. Victory felt strange. Only three months ago, a few kilometers to the north, Camilo's column had marched through the hills exhausted, wet and out of food, eating their horses one by one—and when those gave out they ate *jutillas*, a rodent not much bigger than a rat. In those days they could only move by night, whereas now, at ten on a sunny morning, people brought them flowers and rum in little glasses. On a tray! Both Camilo and Huber took a drink, but after a scowl from Fidel they waved off the rest.

Camilo laughed to see Fidel's boots. Here was the new leader of Cuba with a hole in both toes. "*Oye, jefe*," Camilo said, and clapped him around the shoulders. "I should have brought you some boots. I have a thousand pairs, courtesy of Fulgencio Batista."

"*Ese cabrón de mierda*," Fidel said. That piece of shit.

"But such good boots!"

"They're not Batista's boots, they belong to the people."

"Yes, and the people are wearing them." Camilo thumped the pavement to show Fidel how solid they were. "I'd give you these if they'd fit, but with those big whompers of yours you're out of luck."

"And that jerk, Cantillo," Fidel said. "He should have stopped Batista instead of letting him escape with his millions. I'd like to shoot them both."

"Fulgencio will be eating Dominican bananas now. We could drop over there and give him a different diet."

"In time," Fidel said. "Perhaps in time. Are you so eager to keep fighting?"

"I like fighting. Fighting and winning!"

Che reported to Fidel about the unions, the old-line communists and the Student Directorate. He had heard that the students wanted to keep their guns, many of them stashed at the university.

"What do they need guns for?" Fidel threw his arms around as if in front of a camera. "If they'd sent them up to the Sierra we'd have put them to use. No guns for them now. Either they study something useful, or they work."

"This could be bad," Camilo said with a laugh. "We might not have any more lawyers."

"Lawyers will be unnecessary in the new Cuba. You, Camilo, what would you need a lawyer for?"

"To protect me from other lawyers, of course."

The joke was that Fidel himself had been a lawyer. "What we need," he said, "are scientists, teachers and doctors. Che, do you want to take over the Department of Health?"

"What I want is more revolutions. I want one in Argentina."

"Some day. But we will have much to do in the coming year. The wealthy will resist us, and already we have started a larger battle, with the United States. They will not be happy when we begin our reforms. They will want to strangle us, and we must prove our autonomy." Even to his closest friends, Fidel sometimes spoke as if giving a speech.

They stopped to eat beside the road in a bower made of bamboo poles and palm fronds, a dozen *barbudos* at each table. Celia Sánchez, Fidel's companion in the Sierra, sat at his side. They talked for an hour—mainly Fidel talked—about constitutional reforms, about the choice of Urrutia for President, about those who must be arrested and killed at once. Fidel wanted revenge on those in Batista's regime who had tortured and killed. Raúl, he said, agreed with him. Che too seemed to agree. They all did.

Camilo didn't like the idea of revenge. He loved the Revolution because it was going to help the most impoverished Cubans: those who suffered from hunger, those who couldn't read, those who died from untreated diseases. All this he had come to believe years ago after reading Fidel's own speeches, so it surprised him now, as cups of coffee were passed around and Fidel lit up a cigar, to hear that while everyone would get a trial, "the worst of the culprits must die, and die now."

Camilo drank his tiny cup of coffee, gritty and sweet. Everyone here liked him, he was sure. They all laughed at his jokes. He had proved himself in battle, and been one of the first to be made *comandante*. Yet there were times he felt that he came from another world. His father and mother were tailors. After the eighth grade he'd gone to work, at first in their shop, later in a clothing store. The other leaders of the M-26 had all studied at some university. Che was a doctor and Huber a professor. Even Juan Almeida, who'd started as a bricklayer, had gone on to study law. Yet now only Camilo would challenge *el jefe*. "With all respect," he said, looking at Fidel across the table, "why is this revenge so important? Don't we have a hundred other things to do? I quote from your Moncada speech, in which you said that for your dead comrades you claimed no vengeance. You said, 'It is not with blood that we can pay for their lives.' Why has that changed now?"

Fidel glared at him. Their table fell quiet, then the tables to either side. Fidel sat rigidly on his bench. He lifted one hand and pointed a blunt finger. "The problem, Camilo, is your innocence. You do not understand evil. In killing these men we will be guided not by vengeance, but the desire for protection. We must protect the Revolution from the acts of the evil and ruthless. The Revolution is still a delicate flower, and we must not allow these traitors to trample it. Do you understand me?"

"The Revolution is a delicate flower?"

A couple of men laughed, but a look from Fidel silenced them. "The flower, *hermano*, is a metaphor, to remind us of how fragile our victory is, and how we must defend it."

Camilo wasn't sure about metaphors, and said nothing. But he did not look away.

"Will you follow my commands?" Fidel asked.

"Every one. You will lead, and I will follow."

"Then let me punish the worst of Batista's men, and any traitors to the Revolution."

"*Jefe*," Camilo said, "you take care of the metaphors and I'll keep my gun close by. Also, I'll make sure you get a better pair of boots."

Now they all laughed, Fidel included. Talk started up again at the long tables, more coffee appeared and they drank, cup after cup.

In the early afternoon Camilo and Che flew back to Havana. Soon after takeoff Che fell asleep, snoring under the deep rumble of the engines, his legs spilling into the aisle. Camilo, solitary and at rest for the first time in months, let his mind drift off—and his thoughts went straight to Clare and the day they met.

How serious she had looked, walking into the Waldorf Astoria kitchen. At first Camilo thought she'd mistaken him for one of the head cooks, then he saw that she just wanted to take his picture. She took it over and over. They were dressed almost the same, both wearing black pants and a white shirt, though his was the double-breasted shirt of a chef. She had hair the color of dark chocolate and surprising light blue eyes. She was elegant, the kind of woman who passed him on the sidewalk without a glance. But she was glancing now. More than glancing, she stared at him through her camera, lifting it to her face again and again.

Alberto, after Camilo asked to borrow his hat, leaned over and whispered, loud enough for others to hear, "*Tu la puedes, hermano*." You can do this one, brother. Several men laughed, and Camilo turned away. He wanted to tell this graceful woman that the kitchen was full of Columbians and Puerto Ricans with no culture, and she should pay them no attention. But even though she was the only woman in the room, she didn't seem upset. She did tell him once, "Don't look at the camera." It was a cool command from a woman with a job to do. But then she gave him her telephone number. As she left the room he set down his knife and rested his palms on the butcher block in front of him. A woman he had never met! What a country this was.

In fact, he had loved the United States. Who would not, after ten weeks with Clare Miller? It was true that *la migra* had put him in jail, in a crowded room where they never turned off the lights. But before that he'd been happy in New York. He liked Americans and could have stayed longer. Now Fidel spoke of *los Estados* as the source of all evil, and it would not go well if he discovered that Camilo had an American girlfriend. He might forbid it, or try to. Yet Fidel, who was always telling his men to be faithful to their wives and girlfriends, was not so *fidel* himself. He had carried on a romance with a doctor's wife and had a child with her. Celia Sánchez was surely his *novia* now, but any pretty girl could catch his eye. So what would Camilo tell Fidel, the one he never lied to, about Clare?

He would tell him nothing. "*En boca cerrada*," his mother used to say, "*no entra mosca*." Close your mouth and the flies won't get in. Besides, what did it mean that Clare had come to see him at Camp Columbia? Though she didn't want to say so, she must be living with some man. A woman that beautiful would always have someone. It didn't calm him to remember that Clare had chosen *him*—and chosen him when he was no one.

He had told her the truth, pretty much. For two years he'd been living hard in the Sierra, with rarely a woman to talk to. He'd huddled against the rain, slept on the ground and eaten whatever was in the pot: one night slabs of beef, the next night *moros y cristianos* with the rice burned and the beans undercooked. In the flush of victory it was good to have new boots and a bed, but the rebels were not going to live like Batista. Che, Fidel, Raúl—they were all clear about that. Camilo himself had no taste for luxury. He wanted justice, health care and education for every Cuban.

Clare was right, that was how Fidel talked. But it was true. Like so many in the M-26, Camilo had left his old life behind when he flew to Mexico and joined the rebels. He didn't write Clare because what could come of it? He didn't write anyone. Would she now resist the changes that were coming to Cuba? If so, too bad. Now he lived in Havana, and soon he'd be surrounded by women. If he wanted, he probably *could* have a dozen of them.

8

CLARE was on the floor with Ala, playing with a small wooden train that had belonged to Domingo as a child, when he returned from Remedios. The girl glanced up, then ignored him. She was funny like that. Sometimes she jumped up and ran to him with her arms out, other times she acted as if she'd never seen him before. Clare stood up and said without preface, "Domingo, I'm sorry about your car."

"Oh, the car." He dismissed the topic and set his briefcase down. "What's important is that you're safe, that no one was hurt."

"I'm fine. I had some photos I had to send to New York. The car was all my fault, not Eliseo's. I made him take me to the airport."

"And there, what happened?"

She should have talked this over with Eliseo. She wanted to take the blame, but didn't want to contradict what he might already have told Domingo. She described where they'd parked, the lobby full of families, then their return to the vandalized car.

Domingo watched her with an unconcerned look on his round handsome face. But she knew how much he loved his waxed and precious Chevrolet. And she remembered what Eliseo had said about the reactions he didn't show.

"How is your mill?" she asked.

"In a moment. You never saw who attacked the car?"

"No. We came back and it was done."

"And Eliseo—why didn't he stay with the Impala?"

"I asked him to come inside with me."

She said this so Eliseo would not be blamed. But what if Eliseo had said the opposite, that he'd insisted on going in with her? Of course, she thought now, that *was* what he would say, because it was the truth. But having started the lie, she continued. "I was glad he was there. The lobby was crowded and you could feel the desperation."

"I wish you and Ala had gone to the Hotel Nacional. These are lawless days, and you're still new to Cuba."

"Eliseo was right about taking the car. He knew the city would be dangerous. It was my fault, I admit it."

Domingo considered this. He said "Darling, the car is no problem. It can be fixed and will look as good as new, so let us forget about it. Tell me about your photographs."

Darling was not a word he used in the bedroom. He said it at times like this, as a kind of reassurance—so Clare answered him directly. "I talked my way into Camp Columbia. There were three hundred rebel soldiers there and thousands of the regular army. That commander was there, Camilo Cienfuegos, and I took his picture. I got a good one of him and the U.S. ambassador."

"Ah!" said Domingo, his face lighting up. "So this is yours." He opened his briefcase and pulled out a copy of the *Diario de la Marina*. There was the photo she had taken of Camilo and Earl Smith. Top left on the front page! The credit was only to The Associated Press, but the photo had probably gone out on the wire to newspapers around the world. She had captured Camilo's big smile, and the ambassador's grudging handshake showed what the U.S. thought of the rebel victory. It made Clare want to pick up her camera and run out into the street to take more photos. Not pictures of landscaped homes and their owners, but photos like this that everyone wanted to see. She laid the paper on the table and smoothed it out, then showed it to Ala, who'd come over to investigate. The girl stared at the paper. Was it mad, Clare wondered, to think that she looked at the photo so closely because she could see herself in it? Yes, that was crazy, no two-year-old could see such a thing. Ala lifted her arms and Domingo picked her up.

Clare wanted to slow down and read the story, and to bask in the front-page photo, but Domingo had other questions. She explained dutifully what she had seen at Camp Columbia: the bearded soldiers, the rooms of torture in the basement, the large number of silent troops.

"And did the rebels treat you with respect?"

"Completely. You know, to a photographer, men with big beards and holes in their shoes are much more interesting than soldiers of the regular army."

"Yes, of course."

Standing with Ala in his arms, Domingo looked completely relaxed. Too relaxed, she thought, too still. She could not stop thinking, *He knows. Somehow he knows.*

"Now," she said after a pause, "tell me about the mill."

After Ala scrambled down, Domingo folded the newspaper and put it back in his briefcase. Was he going to study it later for clues? No, her mind was running away with her.

"Everything is fine so far," he said. "My brother feared they might burn the mill, or burn the cane as they have done in Oriente. I didn't think so, but it was good that we went and stayed a couple of days. You know what we say in Cuba. *El ojo del dueño engorda la vaca.*"

"How is that? The eye of the owner fattens the cow?"

"It's the owner's attention, the fact that he is watching. It's why Felipe goes out to the mill every week, even in the dead season before the cutting starts. Of course this time it was different. Half the men were drunk and there might have been trouble. Still, I don't think they will do anything crazy. The mill is their life, and now they believe that some day it will be theirs, that Castro will give it to them. A dozen men told me what a great day it was for Cuba—men I didn't know, men who embraced me and called me *compañero*. It was probably the rum."

"Do you think Castro would do that? Take your mill away?"

"The land, more likely. All his talk about agrarian reform makes me think they could do it. But that is not going to work in Cuba."

Domingo stopped to open a bottle of wine, then stepped toward the kitchen and called for Lavinia: would she fix some soup for the girl, please, and see if she would eat it. Ala, who sometimes refused everything on her plate, ran off toward the kitchen, crying "*¡La sopa! ¡La sopa!*"

Clare and Domingo drank their wine in the dining room, sitting on a pair of chairs turned out from the table. Now that the conversation had moved away from Camilo and Camp Columbia, she started to relax. "And your brother," she asked, "what does he think of Fidel?"

A ripple of annoyance passed over Domingo's face. *I shouldn't call him Fidel,* Clare thought. *I should call him Castro.*

"Felipe thinks he is the Antichrist, come to destroy us. He has always been more conservative than I, and at the mill he works within an ancient system. Sometimes he asks for my opinion—but then he does what he pleases. That's fine with me. He's in charge out there and he knows the men. My own troubles will come with the magazine."

"Hasn't the new government promised a free press?"

"That won't last long. You know *Ojo,* it has no political content. But it's a magazine for people with money, and Castro won't like it. I am not a criminal, I have stolen nothing and killed no one, yet I may be in danger. You saw all those people trying to leave the country. I saw them myself at the airport just an hour ago, fighting for tickets. A man wanted us to fly his family to Miami in Felipe's plane. It would have taken two trips, but he offered American dollars. He had them in his suitcase. He couldn't believe we had a plane and weren't leaving ourselves. And perhaps that man was right. The truth is, I worry about Castro's inflexibility. All is politics to him, and I'm afraid we'll discover that he cannot be satisfied. But Clare, you have now come closer to this rebellion than I have. What was your sense of that fellow Cienfuegos? Did he seem a bloodthirsty type, as some people have said?"

"Bloodthirsty!"

She could not control herself. She wanted to say, *He's funny.* She wanted to say, *He would make you laugh.* "Maybe he was bloodthirsty up in the Sierra, or at the battles in Las Villas, but all I found was a guy at a desk with dirty socks and his pockets stuffed with papers."

"Dirty socks?"

Stop it, Clare told herself. *Stop telling Domingo anything.* "You can see them in the photo. The one I took."

Domingo opened his briefcase and took another look. "Yes, you are right."

She would not be able to keep this up for long. She'd only managed it so far because she had so little to hide. There was nothing overt, for almost nothing had happened. It was all inside her.

Domingo watched her without saying anything. It was only for two or three seconds, but she noticed. Already, in this new marriage, she had registered his habits, his timing. The pause meant something, but she wasn't sure what. Could he guess what *she* was thinking?

She had never caught Domingo in a lie. He seemed not to lie, though maybe she just couldn't tell. She had lied a lot. She'd lied about her headaches, lied about Ala's father, even about insignificant details—what she'd eaten for lunch, what she'd written to her parents in her latest letter—to see if Domingo could read her. As far as she knew, he had no suspicions. But now she was lying about something more serious. Just thinking about Camilo felt like cheating on her husband.

Domingo tapped a finger twice against the back of his other hand. He was not a man of extraneous gestures, and the tapping, like the pause in his speech, put Clare on alert. He let the silence stretch out, then said, "Tell me, Clare, are you bored here in Cuba?"

"Not at all. Could anyone be bored in Havana right now?"

"I meant—before this, with your job. *Ojo* must seem tame after *Life*. Perhaps you can go on selling to *Life*, or to that agency, what is the name of it?"

"Black Star. This might be a good time for that, now that the whole world is watching Cuba. But what they want, I'm sure, is photos of Fidel Castro."

"Would you say you are a fan of his?"

"I think you mean supporter. Fans are for Beny Moré, or Roy Campanella. With Castro I'd say *supporter,* or *follower.*"

Domingo ignored this little English lesson. "People are cheering him like fans," he said. "Like fanatics. Have you seen him on television?"

"I did, last night."

From Domingo, another three-second pause. "Follower, then. Are you a follower?"

"I think I am."

He nodded. He seemed to have no response. Clare thought, not for the first time, that there was no battle she could win against him. She could correct his English, but that wasn't winning. What she could do was hurt him, and she didn't want to.

On Monday morning after Domingo left for his office, Clare returned to Camp Columbia, where they let her in with smiles all around. Camilo wore new boots and a clean army shirt with a star on one epaulet. Many papers lay on his desk, arranged in piles under a massive paperweight, his gun. He embraced Clare in front of the other soldiers, then waved them out. He smelled better. He smiled, he laughed, he was the Camilo she knew. "Look at all this," he said, pointing at his desk. "I work in an office. I'm like a banker with longer hours. I have to sign all these papers!"

His big felt cowboy hat also lay on his desk, and his thick beard and long hair looked freshly washed. They were his banner, they showed how long he'd been part of the struggle. Some of the rebel soldiers wore little beards only half an inch long.

Camilo held out one of the papers. *On behalf of the FAR*, it said at the bottom, followed by his signature. "Is *this* what the head of an army does?"

Standing beside her and holding out the document, he ran his other hand down her back onto her hip. It was only for a moment, as soldiers came and went in the corridor outside, but it was long enough for her body to light up. She had come with no more fixed intention than the last time, and with just as little resistance. When he touched her, she wanted more.

She asked about his trip to Camagüey, and who was there?

Fidel, he told her, and Che and Huber Matos. Celia Sánchez, too.

"That's—Fidel's girlfriend?"

"It is Celia who makes him organized. Perhaps his girlfriend, yes, but he does not talk of such things. She was with us in the Sierra for a year."

"So it was not just bad-smelling men in the Sierra. There were women, too."

"At the start only Celia and Vilma Espín. She is Raúl's *novia*, I think now they will marry."

Like Camilo, Clare thought, these women had gone up into the Sierra and entered history. She could not have done that—she had Alameda—but she was sorry now to have missed it.

Camilo called for two cups of coffee, and an orderly brought them. The coffee was a jolt, muddy and sweet. Clare asked what he'd talked about with Fidel.

"The march," he said in Spanish, "and plans for his arrival in Havana. But mostly the reforms. We cannot have so many huge farms and no land for the people. The land must be shared, and we are trying to decide how much land a family may own."

"How much will it be?" She had never asked Domingo how big his farm was.

"If Che decides, only a few *hectareas*. Fidel says more than that, but we must put an end to the most oppressive owners."

"And what about those who own the sugar mills?"

A soldier came in with a paper and laid it on Camilo's desk. He glanced at it. "*Clara*," he said, "I know I told you to come today, but now, right now, I have a meeting with General Barquín. Tonight I eat dinner with Che. Could I meet you somewhere tomorrow? Tomorrow night?"

"Not at night. I could do it in the afternoon."

"Where?"

"I don't know. On the Malecón?"

"Name a restaurant or something. In case I'm a little late."

"Okay," she said, "the Café Flor. At one o'clock."

"I will see you there at one."

With that they were finished—and how quickly she'd been dismissed. She left the camp and walked out into the streets of the city. She was angry at herself, at Camilo, at everyone. This would never work, she thought. He was far too busy for her. Still, he was Alameda's father, and one day she would tell him that. She started walking home. She walked all the way to the Almendares River and crossed into Vedado, feeling her legs ache, feeling the jar of her heels on the pavement. What if she took Ala with her to the Café Flor?

No, none of them was ready for that.

9

WHEN she walked into the café, right on time, Fidel was on the television, his face filling a small set which sat on a stand against the far wall. He was speaking in the plaza of some town, and after he finished, the noisy talk in the café was all about his march to Havana.

Clare sipped her coffee, called for a second cup and waited. Surely Camilo would come—but how would they ever talk in here? One step inside and he'd be surrounded, everyone trying to get his attention.

By one-thirty she had almost given up hope. Was there some other Café Flor? The waiter said no, this was the one and all Havana knew it. She could only wait.

Where would they be now, she wondered, if Immigration had never picked up Camilo and his roommates? Would he have gone off to Mexico to join Fidel, knowing she was pregnant? Probably so. Or at least that's how it looked from here, now that he was one of the Revolution's heroes. Would he ever have fit in her tiny New York life? She couldn't imagine it. Especially not after Ala was born and Clare could hardly think of anything else. No, she couldn't imagine him sharing in those days, in those weeks when she did nothing but lie around with her daughter, nursing her and staring at her face, touching her tiny arms and legs as they probed the air. When hungry she cried, but never for long. Clare put her to one of her breasts, Ala latched on tight, and the world could have ended right there without either of them caring.

For a month they didn't leave the apartment. Clare could walk well enough, her episiotomy had healed, but she didn't want to expose Ala to the cold wind that blew in off the Hudson. Her roommate, who'd been doing the shopping on her way back from work, came home one early evening and set some groceries down with a thump. Ala jerked, turned away from Clare's breast and began to cry.

"Damn," Debbie said, "I come in the room and she starts crying."

"The noise surprised her."

"Everything surprises her."

Not everything, Clare wanted to say. Hardly anything. But loud noises, yes. Sometimes, it was true, she cried for no reason that Clare could figure out, and occasionally at night she could not be comforted. Clare would wake, try to feed her, try to quiet her down in bed, then give up and take her into the living room where she could pace. Sometimes there were sounds from Debbie's bedroom. Something thrown? When Clare was pregnant, Debbie had been helpful. She'd often jumped up to bring Clare a bagel or a cup of tea. She said, "We're going to have a baby in our apartment. What an adventure this is going to be!" But now she was tired of the adventure. "Babies are too loud. I don't see how you stand it."

"It's a small price to pay for having *her*. Look, she's calming down already."

"It's all you can think about, isn't it?"

Debbie didn't like how Clare had lost all interest in the stories and gossip they used to exchange as they ate dinner. Now Clare was happy just sitting in a chair with Ala, smoothing her eyebrows, taking her little ears between two fingers, watching her expression change. She knew that Debbie thought her mind had turned to mush, but she didn't care. Debbie put away the milk and eggs, making more noise than she had to. Clare reminded her to write down how much she had spent, so she could pay her back.

"It's not the money. Just—how long am I going to have to do this?"

Clare came to as if she'd been slapped. Though usually observant, she hadn't been paying attention. "I don't know how long. What is it you want?"

"I don't think this is going to work."

From one instant to the next she was alone in a cold city. She had let go of Camilo, but now his absence shocked her. He should have been here to protect her. She still had money, because she'd worked nonstop through much of her pregnancy. But the money would run out and how was she going to make more? Since Ala's birth, photography had barely crossed her mind. At some point she would have to go back into the world with her cameras, but she couldn't do that now. With her father going senile she couldn't live with her parents, and she was not going to plead with Debbie. In one sentence it was done: this wasn't going to work.

Within a week she found another place to live. It was a studio apartment, dark but snug, just down the block on the other side of 92nd. Through the rest of January, Debbie held her tongue and spent little time at home. On the first of February Clare hired the super's son and his friend, two wiry teenage boys, to carry all she owned from one apartment to the next: her bed, her desk, her dishes and clothes. In two hours it was done.

That same day, standing in front of her new building with Alameda bundled against the cold, she met Engracia, an older woman, stout and white-haired, who spoke with traces of an accent and lived on the floor above Clare's. When she heard that Ala's father was Cuban, she exploded with a smile. She was Cuban herself, though she'd lived in New York for forty years. That night she invited Clare up to her apartment for dinner and instantly began to teach her how to prepare a coconut flan. Clare liked how effusive she was, and how generous. It didn't matter that forty minutes later, when Ala started crying and wouldn't stop, Engracia stepped back and said, "*Feed her, please.* Just feed her." It didn't matter because Clare could now retreat to her own apartment.

She imagined that Engracia would turn out to be as ill-at-ease with an infant as Debbie was, but the next morning the older woman knocked on her door holding a plate covered by a paper napkin. "I am sorry about *anoche*," she said. "I see that I am getting old. I raised two *niñas* myself, but now it seems that I have forgotten that babies cry. Here is a Cuban breakfast tortilla."

Engracia loved to cook and to talk. She peppered her speech with words in Spanish as she told Clare about her childhood in Havana and how she first came to New York. She spoke of Cuba as a lost paradise—though each year, when she went back, she only stayed for two weeks. She visited with her sister, then scooted back to New York.

"Why don't you live there?" Clare asked. "I can hear how much you love it."

"No, I have my apartment here. My Benito died here, and I have the rent control. I have a daughter in New Jersey, even a granddaughter. I just go to Havana for a visit. I love it there, but with that pig Batista it's not safe anymore."

Soon it was decided that she would teach Clare both Spanish and Cuban cooking, and three afternoons a week, after Ala dropped off to sleep, Clare carried her and the required ingredients upstairs. There she and Engracia had a long session in the kitchen, preparing *lechon asado*, *pollo en cazuela* and *camarones a la crema*, with lots of conversational Spanish. After a couple of weeks, Engracia showed her the little shrine in her bedroom, half Catholic saints—San Lazarus and Santa Teresa— and half deities she didn't want to offend, like Changó and Yemayá. "Don't worry," she said with a laugh, "I don't sacrifice any chickens in my apartment. No cigar smoke, either. I hate cigars. I made Benito stop years ago, and still he died of lung cancer, the little *cabrón*." She said this while holding Benito's photo against her ample bosom. Engracia's long straight hair was pure white, and she never put on a pair of pants. It was a dress every day, often in colors that belied her age, floral greens and yellows. After showing Clare how to cook her beans to perfection, Engracia gathered the long strands of Clare's dark hair and pinned them high off her neck.

From the start, Engracia wanted to hear everything about Camilo. When she learned that his parents, like her own, had emigrated to Cuba from Santander in northern Spain, she was convinced that Clare would see him again. She said, "You will walk with him again one day, beneath the stars. I am sure of this. Oshun will look after you."

"Oshun?"

"The goddess of love, the protector. Oh, I know it's African and crazy. But I've seen it before. You are destined to meet again."

"Where?"

"If not here, in Cuba."

"How is that going to happen?"

Most days of the week, Engracia read the *Post*. But on Sundays she walked up to Broadway and bought a copy of the *Times*, and one Sunday in late February she appeared at Clare's door holding the first section of the paper. "You must read this," she said.

At the top of the first page was an article by Herbert Matthews about the rebel Fidel Castro and his small army in Cuba's Sierra Maestra. It described how Castro, with a force of eighty-two men, had left Mexico on the yacht *Granma*, how they'd landed in Cuba on December 2nd and been attacked by Batista's troops. Of the eighty-two men only a dozen survived. Fidel and his brother Raúl were among them, but no other names were given.

Clare read the article in her doorway. Her hope drained away as her eyes darted through the article—for Camilo must have been on that yacht. That had been his plan, to go to Mexico and join up with Fidel. If most of the men had died, what were Camilo's chances? She'd never been able to imagine him with a gun. He was committed to Fidel, but he was no soldier. He was a cook, a dancer, a guy who liked to laugh and make jokes. Now, she was sure, Batista's men had killed him.

Her heart sinking, her voice unsteady, she explained all that to Engracia —who was not convinced. "You don't even know if he was on the boat."

Clare was on the edge of tears. Camilo had been taken from her, and now she was sure he was dead. "He never called and he never wrote," she told Engracia, not for the first time. She let the older woman put her arm around her shoulders and guide her to the kitchen table.

"It's what men do," Engracia said . "It's in the blood."

"That's right, they get a girl pregnant and then they leave, it's no concern of theirs. They do what they feel like."

"Maybe if he had known."

"*He should have asked.* He could have written, but not once." Now she was weeping openly. Engracia put her soft Cuban arms around her, but it did no good. Clare's chest shook, the sobs pouring out in waves. Engracia let her cry. She said nothing, for which Clare was grateful. But here in this tiny apartment, whose only window faced another window, she now felt trapped. New York was no place for a mother, and gone were the days when she could stare at Alameda for hours, thinking of nothing. She wiped her eyes, then looked at Engracia. "And you're going to tell me that some god or saint will bring us together?"

The older woman took back her hands.

"Engracia, I'm sorry, I shouldn't have said that. Maybe Oshun *could* help me—I just can't imagine how that would happen."

At this Ala woke with a cry—but it was Engracia who stepped to the crib and picked her up. "Let me do it," she said. "Let me try. I've done it a thousand times, ten thousand times."

She held Ala as she had held Clare. She rocked the baby, looking down at her tenderly, carrying her about the room. But Ala cried with a rising desolation.

"She's hungry," Clare said. "There is only one solution, and I am it."

She took her child and lifted her shirt. She had never fed Ala in front of anyone except Debbie, who'd never been at ease with the sight. But Engracia watched them fondly. "That is more like it," she said. "I love them like that, when they're quiet and happy."

Clare understood that Engracia was making fun of herself. And with Ala latched onto her breast and the milk coursing through her, Clare was calming down. This was the time she loved most. She didn't want to nurse and talk, she didn't want to nurse and think about Camilo. She wanted to lie back and close her eyes and feel the tug of her child at her breast, and watch her downturned eyes, her absolute attention to the job. "Engracia, I will come up this evening. For now I need to be quiet."

Engracia nodded and headed for the door. Clare hoped she hadn't insulted her, but couldn't think of that now. Already she was floating down a river with Alameda, on a trip they both knew well.

Waiting in the Café Flor, avoiding the gaze of those around her, how easily she remembered those quiet moments with Ala. What she could not remember was making love with Camilo. Lying there with him yes, but not the sex itself. This made no sense, for they'd had plenty of it. She remembered all kinds of details from their time together: the two of them dancing naked in the living room to that tango from *Damn Yankees*, and the mouse that had scurried under Camilo's feet one time when they were sitting at the dining room table, how he jumped up and put his pants on. She remembered kissing him when they first got into bed, and in a bus going down Broadway, and on the Staten Island Ferry. But the unruly passion between them had somehow disappeared. It was like a dream half-remembered in the morning, still powerful but the details beyond her grasp.

She waited until two o'clock. Then she was done. The big hero had papers to sign and meetings with army generals, and fuck him. She called for her bill, paid it, and was about to stand up when the café grew silent. Two bearded soldiers entered the room, holding their rifles upright by the stocks, careful not to bang anything as they approached Clare's table. Would she please follow them out to the street—and there, waiting at the curb a few yards down the block, sat a black Ford with tinted windows. It looked like one of Batista's cars, but in the backseat Camilo sat grinning. "Do you see how we travel now? In ease and comfort!"

They drove through the noisy streets, the two soldiers in front, Camilo holding her hand but saying nothing. He didn't apologize for his delay, and if this was a date it included a pair of bodyguards.

"Where are we going?"

"You will see."

"I'm sure I will. But where is it?"

"It's just ahead. Soon we'll be there."

Back in New York, if she asked Camilo a question he answered it. Now he didn't feel he had to. She drew back her hand and watched the city flow by, until the car turned under an arch of pink concrete. Behind the arch was a compound with a row of pink doors, a *posada*. Clare had heard about these love hotels, had even been curious about them, but now she felt insulted. What did Camilo think, that he could decide such a thing without asking her? Still, when he picked up his gun and opened the car door, she followed him to one of the rooms. She didn't want to challenge him out on the pavement where anyone could see them. Camilo opened the room with a key.

"Where'd you get that?"

"Those two stopped by before." Already the two soldiers were walking out to the street.

"Where are they going?"

"Maybe they will meet someone. People want to shake their hands, give them a meal, hear stories of the Sierra. Women all want them—and the *barbudo* pays nothing!"

She had heard this was true. A man who had fought in the Sierra could not pay for a bed, for a dinner, for a willing girl. In several windows Clare had seen the handwritten sign, *Fidel, esta es tu casa*, this is your house.

Clare stepped into the plain little room. Usually she knew what she wanted, but now she had no idea. Camilo lay his submachine gun on the black and white floor tiles beside the bed, where its dangerous barrel shone, dark and potent. This was no pistol in a holster. "Camilo, would you put that somewhere else."

"I'm sorry, my Thompson stays close. I have slept beside it every night for years."

"But here in Havana? In this city where everyone loves you?"

"Not everyone, I promise you. Come, we can sit over here."

She let him lead her to the other side of the bed, where he pulled back the cover. The sheets were clean and crisp, but a faint smell of perfume hung in the air, perhaps the residue of earlier occupants. It might have been the smell, or the strong afternoon light, or Camilo's cool assumptions about what would happen next, but all desire had left her. The *posada* was clean and impersonal. There were no photos, no paintings, no calendars on the wall, not even a portrait of Jesus with a crown of thorns and a glowing heart. Just a bed, a lamp, a door to the bathroom, a wooden table and a pair of chairs beside the frosted slats of the window.

At Camp Columbia, Camilo had thrilled her: his voice, his laughter, the rise and fall of his chest. Now he looked like a stranger. He put his hand around her waist and pulled her to him, but his smell had changed again. It was the starch in his new uniform, a light sweat in the warm afternoon, a whiff of cigar and gun oil.

"Talk to me," she said.

"Talk! I talk all day."

"Not to me."

"Talk about what?"

"Have you seen your parents?"

"Not yet. You see how busy I am? Instead I have come here with you."

"They must be happy that you're safe."

"And that we have triumphed. They are mad for Fidel. They have nothing, just the same little shop where I grew up and the same old pair of sewing machines."

"And your brother, Osmany?"

"Now that the fighting is over, he will come back from Mexico."

"He didn't want to go to the Sierra?"

"He is more of a thinker."

"Do you get along well?"

"¡Clarita, mi amor! We are on a bed after all these years. Don't you want to kiss me?"

"I want to ask you again why you never wrote me."

Camilo's shoulders drooped. He almost squirmed, which she was glad to see. She was tired of being in thrall to him.

He began slowly. "I thought that for us there was no future. La migra came and then I was with Fidel. For a year I wrote no one. Also, I could not talk about you. Especially not to Fidel, who did not like American girlfriends, or American anything except for money and guns."

"I thought you were dead. One postcard and I would have known better."

Camilo looked down. "I see that now. I am sorry."

Was he sorry? She watched him and couldn't tell.

"Clarita," he said, "I am the same Camilo. If you kiss me you will see."

She didn't think he was the same, but she let him start. His lips were as smooth as she remembered, but his beard brushed against her cheeks. She loved his thick dark hair. With her nose close to the opening of his shirt she caught the smell she remembered from long ago, an odor like new-sawn planks. But once he started he moved too fast. His agile fingers unbuttoned her blouse, unzipped her slacks and pulled them off, then slid down her underpants. Just as quickly he got out of his own clothes. He was intent, and hard against her leg. They had barely begun and he was ready to go in.

She put her hand to his chest, but he didn't seem to notice. "*Camilo.*"

She had to say it twice before he responded, before he looked at her eye to eye. She stared at him in the room's frosted light. "We have to be careful," she said.

"Yes, I will be careful."

"No. We have to be really careful. I'm going to put in my diaphragm."

She had taken it this morning from her bathroom at Domingo's. She could see he didn't know the word. "*Una diaframa,*" she said, and still he didn't know. "I'll show you."

Incredible to her now, they had used no birth control in New York. She did remember that. At the most dangerous times she'd made sure that Camilo pulled out—but that was how she got pregnant. Though embarrassed now, she stood up from the bed and rummaged in her purse. She could have gone into the bathroom to put it in—that's what she did with Domingo—but now, with Camilo, everything had to be different. She wanted him to see what it took to be responsible.

Sitting down on the bed beside him, she lifted the disk out of its plastic case. He stared at it. "I have heard of this," he said.

"This is how I don't get pregnant."

"But it's—too big."

"It folds."

She bent the diaphragm back upon itself, to show him. As he watched, his slender muscled body pulled back. He kept his eyes on her face as she wiped cream over the diaphragm, then inserted it.

"That's it," she said, wiping her hands on the sheet. "Gentlemen, start your engines."

It was a joke, but Camilo didn't get it. She put her hand on his knee. "I mean that now it's safe, and we can go ahead."

His next touches were hesitant, as if the diaphragm had made her fragile. That was fine. She lay back as he grazed her shoulders, her neck, her breasts. *Yes*, she thought, *keep going*. But his hand moved no lower than her waist. She opened her legs, she made it easy for him—but already he was easing her down onto a pillow and starting to climb on top of her. She shook her head, and this time put both hands to his chest. "You have to go slower."

Restrained by her palms, he looked as if he were suffering, as if his arousal pained him. He pressed himself against her leg. He beseeched her with wide tormented eyes.

"No," she said, and raised her chest toward him. "Kiss me here."

Hesitant and unsure, he did as he was told. Though self-conscious, she closed her eyes and bathed in her arousal. He was learning, she thought, because he kept at it until she ached, until she was wet, until she lifted her hips toward him—and in an instant he was inside her, surging up and down, pounding her. "*Wait*," she said, but couldn't stop him. He rode her with his head bent to the side and his arms gripping her shoulders, and only seconds later came in a flurry, then collapsed.

If she hadn't been so aroused it wouldn't have mattered. But now she was breathing hard. Her flywheel was turning while Camilo's had slowed, had almost stopped. He lay on top of her, growing heavier, settling in, his breaths coming slower and slower, until his hips twitched.

"*Camilo*," she said. "Don't go to sleep on me."

He raised his head, blinking. He lifted himself up and rested his weight on his elbows, and she pulled her hips away from him. In the insistent light from the window he looked baffled and cautious. "Did I hurt you?"

"No, you didn't hurt me."

She didn't want to explain what was wrong. He should be explaining to *her* why he was so backward. Sliding out from under him, she got up and pulled on her underwear, then stood beside the frosted louvers of the window with her arms folded over her breasts. In New York she had slowed him down by lying in bed all day, by making love over and over. She remembered that now.

"A woman wants to go slower," she said. "*I* want to go slower. I told you but you didn't listen. And afterward you went to sleep, which makes me want to stab you."

"*¿Estab?* What is this?"

"With a knife. I want to stick it in your neck."

Camilo jerked, then glanced at his clothes on the floor.

"Okay, I'm not going to stab you. But you came too fast. Do you understand that, to come?"

"*Acabar*," he said. "*El orgasmo.*"

"Yes."

She wanted to tell him that orgasms weren't easy for her. She could have them on her own, but with someone else they were elusive. "You have to slow down," she said. "You have to touch and kiss a woman all over." At this her face flushed hard. "When you think only of yourself, I want to stab you."

Camilo didn't shrink from this. "Before today," he said, "no one complains."

"Before today, who were you with?"

For a moment he said nothing. Then, "In all last year, only two. There was one girl in the Sierra, a *guajira* with no education. I taught her to read, and she was happy for that, but then her father sent her away."

"And the other?"

"A woman from Yaguajáy. She was older, I could not stop her, she got into my jeep! But she was no *novia,* it was just one time."

"Was it quick? Was it over in ten minutes?"

"Maybe five!"

"You're a dog."

Even at that he couldn't keep a smile off his face. Clare stepped toward the bed and lifted her fist as if holding a knife, and Camilo, instead of defending himself, turned his head away and offered his neck. She plunged the imaginary blade into him, a second time and a third, softer each time as he put up no resistance.

She hated hearing about his other women, but couldn't stop herself from asking, "With those two, did you think about birth control?"

"No," he admitted, "there was no control."

"So next year you might have a little Camilo running around in Yaguajáy. How would that be?"

"*Clarita*, why do you torture me like this?"

If she kept this up, he would figure out what she was hinting at—that *she* had gotten pregnant with him. Instead of telling him this, she wanted him to guess it, but already another smile was playing at the corners of his mouth. "I understand," he said, "and I know I have much to learn about love. I think soon I must have another lesson."

He was ready to laugh and make a joke of her resistance. But maybe she could trust him, because he'd listened to her. He wasn't afraid of her and never had been. Already his hips had begun to move as if he were ready to dance, and he was humming. At first she thought it was something Cuban, some mambo or bolero—then realized it was that tango that Gwen Verdon had been singing on the radio that spring in New York, *Whatever Lola Wants, Lola Gets.*

An hour later they lay in bed as Clare inspected his wounds. The first she knew well, two knurls on the back of his calf, a bullet in and out. He'd been shot before she met him, attending a protest against Batista. On his buttocks were two new scars, and on his side another, with the exit wound on his upper back. This was his miracle wound, he told her. The bullet had passed through without touching any vital organs.

"In a month I was fighting again, and that's when I started to believe that I could not be killed by a gun. Yes, yes, I know. Since that time I have seen several bodies of men who believed the same."

Clare massaged his scars. She kept glancing at his face, hoping to surprise a look there that would tell her how he felt. He'd been glad to take her to bed—but what did that mean to him? What did it mean to any man? He got up and used the bathroom, a noisy splashy creature like the rest of them. He came back naked, lay down beside her, took her left hand in his and tapped her wedding ring. She had left it on today and it hadn't slowed him down, but now he said, "Tell me about this."

"I got married."

"To a Cuban."

"Yes."

"To the one who owns a house."

"Yes."

"What is his name?"

"I don't know if I should tell you."

"Of course you will tell me."

She was going to, but the *of course* annoyed her, so she said nothing.

"How did you meet him?"

"I met him here, on a photo shoot."

"The way you met me," Camilo said. "How old is he?"

"Older."

"And he has money?"

Clare nodded. She pulled the sheet over her legs, then over her chest. She didn't want to offer anything, she wanted Camilo to pry the story out of her.

"Where is his house?"

"In Vedado."

"And when was the wedding?"

"In October."

"This October? Only three months ago?"

"I came to Cuba and then I got married."

Camilo lay beside her, his head propped up by one hand and his hair, almost as long as hers, falling to the sheet. He reverted to Spanish. "In October I was crossing the swamps of Las Tunas with not enough men and not enough guns and everyone wet all the time—and you were getting married."

"The party was at the Hotel Nacional, on the patio."

"It is clear this man has a lot of money."

She nodded.

Camilo watched her. He rested a palm on her hip. It was like the old days, when all his attention was on her. He asked, "Are you happy?"

That was a question she couldn't answer. If she were happy with Domingo, why would she be here? She'd been happy enough until she heard that Camilo was alive. After that, happiness seemed too small.

"My husband's name is Domingo Cantorro Beltrán. I met him when I came down on assignment for *Life*. He owns a magazine himself, and I take photographs for it."

"What magazine?"

"*Ojo.*"

"Yes, I know it. I used to see it in the kiosks when I was young. Even one time in the Sierra there was a copy. No one read it but it served its purpose. Not very well though, because the paper was too smooth."

She could not remember him ever being sarcastic. "Do you hate the rich?"

"The rich are finished. There will no longer be room for great wealth in Cuba."

If this was a battle, she was losing it. She wanted him to be upset about Domingo, to be jealous. "He also owns a sugar mill."

With that Camilo stood up. He pulled on his army underwear and T-shirt. "He owns a *central*?"

"With his brother."

"So that is why you asked me about the owners of the mills."

"I wanted to know what the government will do. I still want to know."

Camilo paced the room, but slowly. "We are trying to decide these things. How many tons of sugar does it make?"

"I have no idea."

"It may depend on that. For now I cannot say. This Domingo—"

A car door slammed outside. Camilo grabbed his gun off the floor and in two seconds stood poised beside the window. He cranked the louvers an inch, then relaxed. "It is only another couple." He set his Thompson back on the floor, pulled on his pants and sat down on one of the chairs. "Perhaps this Domingo is the type that Raúl will shoot."

Clare sat up. "What are you saying?"

"No, *querida*, I am kidding. Some men will be in danger, but not because they own a magazine, or even a *central*."

"Is it true that men will be shot?"

"The worst of them, yes. The murderers, and perhaps some who have stolen. You should tell this Domingo to do nothing foolish."

Clare got up and pulled on her own pants. "You and Fidel, how powerful you are. But you know what they say about power, and absolute power."

This brought Camilo to his feet again. "We will *never* be corrupted. We have done everything to *stop* corruption."

"But what will it be like now that everyone wants you? You know, all those girls who will do anything for a *barbudo*? How much can you get now with a snap of your fingers?"

She was immediately sorry to have said this. She had tried to hide her jealousy, but she was no good at this kind of chess match. What drew her to him would draw any woman: how beautiful he was, and how victorious. His voice was usually full of humor and assurance. Even now his smile was returning. "What can I do?" he said in English. "Everyone is so friendly, after we won."

Clare searched the room for something to throw, something to tear apart. Other than her purse there was only his gun. She walked around the bed, picked it up, took it into the bathroom and stuck it barrel-down into the toilet, making lots of noise. When she turned around, Camilo was at the door, watching her. She put both hands to his chest and pushed him back toward the bed, then onto it. He was grinning again, and tried to pull her down on top of him, but she stepped back.

"I have to go home," she said.

10

HAVANA, by ten in the morning, was noisy with anticipation. Fidel's caravan was approaching the city, though no one knew when it would arrive. Cars honked, church bells rang, sirens and fog horns blared from ships in the harbor. Camilo, following a call from Fidel, had his men drive him out to Cotorro, east of the capital.

There, inside the town's municipal building, he found Fidelito, Fidel's nine-year-old son who'd flown down from New York with his mother the day before. Alone now, he sat at a wooden table in the courtyard. As Camilo watched from the entrance, a soldier brought him a glass of juice. It looked like mamey, which was delicious to adults but not always to children. Fidelito took a single taste, then pushed it aside.

Camilo walked up, set his Thompson on a chair and sat down across from the boy. "Would you like something else?" he asked in Spanish. "Some other drink?"

Fidelito hesitated, then asked, "*¿Habrá una Coca-Cola?*"

Camilo relayed the order, and in less than a minute a frosted bottle appeared from a nearby restaurant, the cap removed. No money was asked for, and Camilo still had none.

Outside, visible through the entrance, people had gathered in the square. There were women on rooftops, men in the trees, families by the curb with baskets of fruit and candied peanuts to offer the rebels when they came. Camilo by now was used to the hubbub, but Fidelito looked wary.

"How's your English?" Camilo asked, in English.

Immediately the boy perked up. "All my friends speak English."

"You live in New York, right?"

"In Queens."

"I lived in New York. I worked there in a famous hotel, the Waldorf Astoria. Do you know it?"

The boy shook his head. Why, Camilo wondered, was he sitting here alone? Fidelito sipped his Coca-Cola. He wore blue jeans and what looked like a little army shirt. He stared out past a couple of soldiers on guard at the vaulted opening, and at the crowd beyond. Then he glanced at Camilo and asked, "Where is this?"

"You mean this town? It's Cotorro."

Fidelito just looked at him. Camilo searched through his pockets, found an envelope and unfolded it, then pulled his chair around and sat down next to the boy. Using a pen, he drew a primitive map of Cuba, putting Santiago in the east, then Camagüey and Santa Clara in the middle, then Havana and Cotorro, a half inch apart. "Right here," he said.

The boy studied the little map. It lay on the table in front of him. He sat up straight on his chair and glanced around the room. He didn't look happy.

"Is your mother here?"

"No."

"She didn't bring you?"

The boy shook his head. "I didn't see her today." He sounded sad and unsure.

"How did you get here?"

"Some soldiers. I don't know them."

Camilo hunched his chair closer. "Pretty soon your father will come. I know he'll be happy to see you, because he is talking about you all the time."

Fidel had only mentioned his son a few times in the Sierra, and always in anger at Mirta, the boy's mother. Still, Camilo's small lie seemed to work, and Fidelito looked less worried.

"We're going to have a good time," Camilo said. "We'll all get on a truck, or even on top of a tank, and we'll drive from here to Havana. You see all those people outside? They're waiting for your *papá*."

"I know."

Fidelito drank more of his Coca-Cola. He looked around the high-ceilinged room, more observant now, his brown eyes as long-lashed as a girl's. He was a good-looking kid, and his mother a famous beauty. He asked, "Is there a bathroom here?"

"I'm sure there is. Let's go find it."

Camilo stood outside while the boy used the room. It took a long time, so long that Camilo called out, "Are you okay in there?"

"Yeah," came the answer. His English was pure yanqui.

"You don't need any help?"

No response. Of course he didn't need any help, he was nine years old. Then the sound of the toilet flushing, and Fidelito came out with his hands wet, drying them on his shirt. "I'll be all right," he said.

This made Camilo even sadder. Where was Mirta, anyway?

Fidel jumped out of his jeep, overjoyed at the sight of his son. He snatched him up, hugged and kissed him, put him on his shoulders and carried him up to a balcony above the plaza, where the people cheered the two of them wildly. With Fidelito at his side he gave a twenty-minute speech in which he mentioned the boy's name a half dozen times.

Finally they were ready to go. Fidel sat his son in the back of an over-sized jeep along with some soldiers and told him he'd be safe there. He stood above the cab and called Camilo and Huber Matos to ride beside him, their guns at the ready.

"And Fidelito?" Camilo said after a few kilometers. "Don't you want to let him ride up here with us?"

"Too dangerous," Fidel said. He did not look back, had not glanced around since they left Cotorro. "Of all the times someone could shoot me, this would be the day. Plenty of people want to, you know. We will soon find out how many enemies we have. Just stay alert—and if anyone points a gun at me, shoot him. You hear that, Huber? Both of you, keep your eyes open."

The crowds grew thicker as they approached Havana. There were two or three men for every woman, but the women were the best dressed, some in heels, almost all in skirts, some groups standing arm-in-arm. Old men approached the truck and reached up to touch the soldiers in back. Young girls tossed candies and pastries wrapped in leaves. The poor and the wealthy stood side by side beneath waving, hand-drawn signs: ¡Viva Fidel! and ¡Viva la Revolución! A few small children stood close to their parents' knees. Camilo saw some scattered pistols and shotguns, but no barrel was ever pointed at the truck.

Surprising him, there was Clare on the steps of a church, wearing a cool white shirt with her hair pulled back. She held her camera to her eye, then lowered it and gave him a smile. When Fidel looked the other way, Camilo waved. Clare waved back, then stepped into the street behind the truck and took pictures of those in back. Camilo watched her as she dropped behind. He leaned out past the body of the truck, staring back at her until Fidel jabbed his ribs. "Pay attention, coño. Don't forget your job. Think of this as a battle. Every moment you must be alert."

"Claro, Fidel, don't worry."

He watched the crowd ahead and tried to pay attention, but this was no battle. Everyone wanted to get close to Fidel—but to touch him, not kill him. Camilo turned his head from side to side as if awake to all dangers, while his mind drifted back to the posada, with Clare stretched out naked on the bed. In New York she had never been so passionate, nor so demanding. Where had this come from?

He reeled at the obvious answer. She had learned it from someone else, from some man, maybe lots of men. Maybe from that rich Domingo.

He wanted to sit down. He wanted to slip into the back of the truck with Fidelito and the other soldiers and ride along with no duties. But he could not, for his place was in the vanguard, at the head of every column. It had always been so. Huber, to Fidel's left, looked vigilant and focused, but Camilo's legs felt wobbly. He held his gun hard against his chest, the safety off. He scanned the crowd but hardly saw it. "Buena en la cama," he had heard men say about women: how good they were in bed. It was a phrase that came with a knowing look but never any details. You were supposed to understand, but he didn't. The peasant girl he told Clare about had done nothing but lie in silence beneath him. Good in bed meant wild, he thought. It meant that the woman had no inhibitions —and that was Clare. He loved this but it scared him. Under his feet the truck dropped into its lowest gear and moved deeper into the city. They passed banks of cheering people, men with guitars, women blowing kisses, paper streamers floating down to the ground amidst a sea of Cuban flags.

Slower and slower, impeded by the crowds, the caravan passed by Old Havana beside the bay, headed for the *Granma*. Someone had brought the cabin cruiser around the island after its disastrous landing on the south shore, and now the boat lay moored against the seawall with five sailors in white standing guard beside it. How squat and small it looked. Camilo remembered what Universo Sánchez had asked upon first seeing it: "Where is the mother ship?" But there had been no mother ship. Eighty-two men had boarded the yacht with their guns and ammunition, along with food and water and two dozen jerry cans full of diesel fuel. Looking at the boat now, it didn't seem possible.

Fidel lifted his son down from the truck and led him across the gangplank. Camilo and Huber followed, and the four of them explored the pilot's cabin, the cramped bunkrooms and the pair of engines in the hold. "Eighty-two of us," Fidel said, looking at his son, "and only twelve survived our first battle. It is something to remember when things don't go well. There is always hope. You must do your best, because the rest of the world may depend on you."

Camilo, feeling the faintest motion beneath his feet, remembered how seasick he'd been on the first day of the voyage. Almost everyone got sick. Only an hour out of Tuxpán, soon after the swells rose up beneath them, the men started vomiting. Some threw up overboard, some into buckets, some were packed so tightly they couldn't move and puked where they sat, spattering those around them. The stench enveloped them all. Camilo himself sat wedged between two men, unable to lie down, feeling like death. For two days no one ate. There were men who shit in their pants and sat in it. Finally, half way through the trip, the sea calmed down and Fidel sent everyone who could swim into the water. "Take off your clothes," he yelled. "Wash everything. There's no soap, just rub it all clean."

Now, in Havana Bay, Fidel scrambled up onto the cabin and gestured down at Camilo. "You remember?" he said. "How you almost didn't make the trip?"

"Because you didn't want to take me."

"It's true. You were nobody then!"

Eighty, Fidel had said, eighty men could go. But a hundred and forty had come to Tuxpán, all trained at Fidel's Mexican camps, all hoping to get on the boat. At two in the morning they stood beneath a single shore lamp. Twenty men were loaded, then twenty more and twenty more, as Raúl kept track of the number. Though Camilo had been one of the last to join up in Mexico, he was sure Fidel would take him. The captain, Onelio Pino, stood at the wheel, shaking his head. The boat was top-heavy, he told Fidel, it was already overloaded. Camilo expanded his narrow chest, trying to catch Fidel's eye, but Fidel never looked at him. "*You*," he said, tapping another man on the chest, "and *you*," and with that Raúl announced, "Eighty, that's it."

Camilo could not believe it. He was going to be left behind.

One of the remaining men stepped directly in front of Fidel. "*I must go with you*," he said. He was a man they all knew, his brother had been killed at the attack on Moncada. Fidel looked him over in silence. He put his hand on the man's shoulder. "Yes," he said finally, "you must come. But you are the last, number eighty-one. Let me hear no more about it."

He lifted his hand to those who remained. "You are the most honorable of men, the flower of Cuba. I thank you for how hard you have trained, and I wish I could take you all. The fault is mine, that I could not find a larger boat. If you can make your way to Cuba we will welcome you in our struggle. Goodbye, and think only of the motherland."

As he turned to climb on board, Camilo grabbed the sleeve of his shirt. Fidel spun around fast. "*Take me*," Camilo said. He raised his arms as if gripping a rifle. "Because I can shoot."

Fidel glared at him. Fidel was huge for a Cuban, the tallest man among them. "Don't you listen? I said *let me hear no more*."

"Take me because I'm skinny and I'll fit."

Fidel put a finger to Camilo's chest and poked him hard, but said nothing. A mist was rising from the river, the only sounds were the slap of water against the hull and the murmur of an idling diesel. Another ten seconds and Fidel's look softened. "It is true, you are a good shot. I see also that you can make a joke, and that you are not afraid. Very well, I need some foolhardy men. Go ahead and squeeze in somewhere."

Camilo, slapped on the back, stepped up the gangplank grinning, the last of eighty-two men. A week later most of them would die in a cane-field, surrounded by Batista's army. Some disappeared, some surrendered and were executed. Fifteen made their way up into the Sierra—though Fidel liked to say it was twelve. Twelve had a ring to it, like the number of disciples. Today, two years later, Camilo still thought it a miracle that he, Fidel, Raúl and Che had been among the few who survived.

On the wharf in Havana, Fidel crouched in front of his son. "Fidelito, I am going on to Camp Columbia. But it will be a long day, and I think you need a rest. A couple of men will take you to a house where you can eat and have a siesta. Tonight they will bring you to the camp where I will give a speech, and after the speech we'll have dinner."

"But *Papá*—"

"No complaints. You must set an example for the youth of the nation. All of us have sacrificed for the Revolution and now you must do your part. We will see each other soon." He turned and gestured. "Nuñez, Luis, make sure he gets a siesta, because he'll be up late tonight."

With that the boy was gone. Camilo watched him get into a waiting car, his shoulders collapsing forward as he disappeared behind the tinted windows.

There were still people everywhere, but they had calmed down. They'd grown almost silent as Fidel spoke to his son. Across the harbor the huge Christ of white marble raised its arms toward them. "You know," said Camilo, "I think he misses his mother."

"*Enough of that.*" Fidel was instantly angry. "Don't talk to me about his mother. She is the worst of a bourgeois family, a family that has fought us at every step."

"Still, he's only nine."

"*Enough*! Are you going to contradict me about my own son?" He stood face to face with Camilo, but several inches taller. "*Are you?*"

Camilo did not back down. He never backed down, with Fidel or any man. "I only spoke because I like the boy."

"He is my son, and I know what is best for him."

"I'm sure you do, *comandante*. But have you become so rigid that a friend can say nothing to you?"

Fidel scowled, his hand going reflexively to the pistol at his belt. Camilo waited him out, and twenty seconds later Fidel gave his shoulder a ritual punch. "Look at us," he said. "We are having another argument, right where we had the last one."

That wasn't true. They'd had their last argument a few months ago in the Sierra, not two years ago while boarding the *Granma*. But Camilo let it pass. He didn't need to be right when talking to Fidel. Even so, the boy's story tugged at him. He couldn't stop thinking of how subdued Fidelito had looked, how defeated, as he followed his father's commands.

In the officers' lounge at Camp Columbia they talked with men and women from the urban resistance movement, with union leaders, with the army generals who had smoothed the surrender after Batista's escape. Too much talk for Camilo, who was still sleeping only four or five hours a night. He perked up when Celia Sánchez crossed the room to stand beside him in her olive green fatigues, the same clothes all the rebels wore. She was lean, dark, somewhat austere—not a woman with any interest in rambling conversations.

"You and I," she told Camilo. "We're the only ones who will challenge Fidel."

"*You* can challenge him! He pays attention to you, but to me he won't listen."

"More than he lets on, I assure you. But like you, I have worried about Fidelito."

"Is he with his mother?"

"No, he will not be seeing Mirta again."

Camilo stared at Celia. Was this some kind of joke? "Of course he will see her again. She's his mother."

"All the same. You heard Fidel about her family. I don't know why she brought him down from New York. Perhaps even she could not resist this triumph, this happiness. But now that Fidel has him, he must grow up to be a revolutionary, and Mirta can have no part in that. I think Fidel will put him in a school."

"This is not human. I know Fidel can be hard, but the boy must see his mother. Where is he now?"

Celia cocked her head. "Do you want to storm the place and rescue him?"

"Of course not. But I can't believe this."

"Perhaps you will bring up the topic with Fidel again this evening?"

He would not. He had watched Fidel outmaneuver politicians, reporters, past presidents of the nation and a dozen enemy officers in the field, and he was not going to go against him. It seemed unfair, but Fidelito and his mother would have to fend for themselves.

"I think," said Celia, "that all of us will have troubles like this. They are the troubles of a domestic life, which we have avoided for years. We've been at war so long we don't know what to do with husbands and wives and children, or with tranquility of any kind."

"Perhaps you are right," Camilo said. He had no wife, and he had no children. But there was Clare, and what was he going to do about her?

On the parade grounds, extra lights had been set up around the podium, the television cameras were in place and the microphones arrayed. The people stretched out before them, a vast noisy crowd that would not let Fidel start speaking. For ten minutes their chant continued: *¡Fidel! ¡Fidel! ¡Fidel! ¡Fidel!* On the podium, Camilo stood where Fidel had placed him, slightly behind and to the right. The crowd went on chanting. Camilo didn't think Fidel was still angry with him, but he could not be sure.

Finally, with his arms in the air, Fidel quieted the chanters and began to speak. He spoke of how far they had come. He told again the story of Moncada, the story of the *Granma*, of their first small battles in the Sierra. Years of struggle, he told the crowd, had led to this moment, which was the end of a war but the start of something much larger. Now the poorest among them would prosper, and the people would govern themselves. Soldiers here at the Camp, though they had served under Batista, were welcome to continue in their jobs, provided they hadn't killed civilians or stolen from them. The Revolution could be lenient—*wanted* to be lenient

—but assassins would meet the same fate they had decided for others. Above all there would be justice, and the people would determine it.

At this Fidel turned to Camilo beside him and asked so all could hear, "*¿Voy bien, Camilo?*" Am I on the right path?

"*Vas bien, Fidel,*" and the crowd roared.

Fidel could hold a grudge. If someone crossed him and betrayed the Revolution, that man was finished. He would be removed, sometimes shot. Fidel's anger at Mirta, Camilo was sure, was not so much personal as political. She came from a wealthy family, none of whom had supported Fidel, so they were banished and could play no part in Cuba's future. But his anger at Camilo, a merely personal anger, hadn't lasted. His question, asked as all Cuba listened, showed that Camilo stood not only in Fidel's good graces but at his right hand.

Even this was a ploy, Camilo knew, because Fidel's truest advisor was Che. Camilo had been chosen to take over Camp Columbia because Fidel didn't want to expose how important a foreigner was to him. Camilo didn't care. He'd decided long ago that in all things he would support Fidel.

Three white doves pulled him back to the moment, flapping up into the air from the crowd in front of the podium. One of them, after swinging back and forth, landed on Fidel's shoulder, gripped his shirt with its talons and peered about. Fidel turned his head to look at the bird, only inches from his cheek, then continued his speech, his tone and gestures unchanged. The crowd roared, and Fidel's anointment was complete.

11

DOMINGO'S shoes were shined and his pants pressed, but the front of his guayabera showed streaks of dirt from the red clay pots he'd brought home, each with a seedling coffee tree from his mother's garden in Cabañas. He was not a man who paced—but he paced now, back and forth in front of Clare on the sofa.

"I've never seen her so nervous," he said of his mother. "So agitated. I know she has some Parkinson's, but it's more than that. She has convinced herself that under Castro we are going to lose everything. She imagines herself an old woman living in a room with no money, no food, no children or grandchildren. She thinks the rest of us will move to Miami and abandon her. She cannot leave Cuba, she says. She's too old for that."

"You're not going to Miami, are you?"

"Not me. I'm like her, I belong here."

"And surely you're not going to lose everything."

"I hope not. But I see why Castro worries her. We watched his speech last night on the television. The people must have this, the people must have that—but where is it all going to come from? He is full of wild promises."

"But what a speaker," Clare said.

"Did you watch him?"

"I was there."

Domingo came to a stop. "You went? What did you think?"

"I love how slowly he talks. I understood every word he said, which in Cuba is a miracle."

"And his ideas?"

"It's hard to argue against everyone having a doctor, and everyone learning to read and write. Don't you think?"

"I'm afraid he will go too far. Already you can see it, how he stirs up the crowd and feeds off their adulation. He believes he can do anything."

"After last night, he probably can."

Domingo gave her a sharp look. "Can you see the danger in a man like this?"

"Perhaps it is different for me. I'm not Cuban and I don't vote, I only went as a photographer."

"It is not a question of voting. There will be no more voting."

"He did promise that soon there would be elections."

"He also promised freedom of the press, but I don't think we'll have it. Criticism will not be allowed, and he will say it is the will of the people. No, my mother is not all wrong about what will happen."

Clare told him how she'd tried to get close to the podium, how hard it was because the crowd was packed so tight. When they swayed, she swayed, and she could barely raise her arms to use her camera. "Luckily I took my eighty-five millimeter lens, which was like standing right in front of him."

Though she told no lies, everything she said felt false. If she were truthful she'd be telling Domingo how happy she'd been the whole night. She'd gone to take photos, but when Fidel began his speech she entered the same trance as everyone else.

"What about that bird," Domingo said. "That was a trick, right?"

"I don't think so. Three were released and one landed on him."

"In that huge crowd it chose him? I can't believe that."

"Domingo, I was there. He was up on the podium, and you know how tall he is. The dove was looking for a perch."

"It was a pigeon. It must have been trained, or maybe it was held by a string."

Clare laughed. "You hate him, don't you?"

Domingo, looking down at his shirt, brushed off the soil from the pots. "I don't hate Castro. You know I wanted a change. The one I hated was Batista."

What led them to argue, she thought, was her secret, trying to work its way into the open. The delirium of last night's crowd, mixed up with her stay at the love hotel, made her say things she should have kept to herself. Even now she wanted to say more: that Fidel had thrilled her, that she loved the Cuban people and their Revolution. Also, that Domingo was part of the old order and she wanted to join the new. That she *had* joined it.

She said none of that. She sat on the living room sofa until rescued by Alameda, who ran into the room in her leather-soled sandals, entranced by the sound of her own heels. She came to a stop, eyes flashing, and stomped her feet against the floor, easily making herself the center of attention. She was a dark-eyed, dark-haired girl who passed for Cuban every day. Who *was* half Cuban and becoming more so. Domingo bent down and lifted her up, but she squirmed against him. He set her down on the floor, where she wrapped her arms around one of his knees and held on tight.

"Going over there," Clare said, "so many people were headed for the camp that I couldn't find a taxi. The buses were filled and wouldn't stop —so I wound up hitchhiking."

"What do you mean?"

"I was walking out Linea and flapped my hand the way people do here, and a minute later someone picked me up."

Domingo looked alarmed. "They could have thought you were a woman for sale."

"No, all that is finished. I rode over with a man and his two sisters and their mother. We had to park ten blocks away, and from there the streets were filled. It was perfectly safe."

"I can't believe this. You *hitchhiked* across Havana? On your own?"

"Domingo, the world is changing. The men are more respectful. They don't want to get shot! You know what Castro has said about rapists."

"Do you think that's going to change the way men are?"

"I don't know if it will last, but for now the streets are safe."

"Clare, you must not do this."

"I *must* not? What I must do is what I feel like doing."

"*No.*"

It was Ala, looking up at the two of them. First she pushed against Domingo's leg, then Clare's.

"*¿No que?*" Clare asked. Ala couldn't say it, but what she meant was clear: *Stop arguing.*

That night, with Ala bathed and read to, with a last sip of water granted but a dish of flan denied, with each of her toes pulled—*este cerdito fue al mercado,* and this little piggy stayed home—and her eyelids kissed twice, then a final time, Clare slipped out of her room and went back downstairs, where Domingo was waiting with two glasses of wine. It was a red wine they had drunk before, but which Clare now resisted. A glass of wine before dinner was an invitation to talk. A glass of wine after Ala's bedtime was Domingo's code for *Let's have a drink and go up to my bed.* And right now she didn't want to go upstairs with her husband.

Wine made Domingo amorous, and Clare didn't know how to slow him down. In public he was not an affectionate man, but in private, yes. He began by pushing the gold circles of her earrings back and forth, then tracing her neck with the soft pad of his finger. He was an attentive lover, at least until passion overwhelmed him. He was a better lover than Camilo—older, slower, and more solicitous. His hands were now drifting onto her chest, but before any sex with Domingo she had to see Camilo again and introduce him to Alameda. She had to know if he would turn and run.

She placed her palm against Domingo's chest. It was their sign, and he understood. But he looked at her for an explanation, and she couldn't give one. She could not, for the second time in two weeks, use a migraine as an excuse.

Domingo pulled back. He set down his wine glass, took hers and set that one down too. "I don't understand."

Everything she said was going to be a lie. "There's nothing to understand. Just—not tonight."

"We *are* married," Domingo said.

"You cannot have forgotten our agreement *again.* That there would be no strings."

He looked at the floor. Of course he had not forgotten.

She'd been happy with Domingo. She'd married him, and Ala had claimed him as her father—but now Clare didn't want him to touch her. It was nothing she'd decided, the feeling just came over her. Going to bed with him would only leave her more confused, and her body said *Don't do it.*

She lay, twenty minutes later, in her ship of a bed on the top floor of his house, the airy drapes swaying in the faint breeze, the city growing quiet outside. If only he'd wait, she thought. Of course that was selfish and unfair—but couldn't he leave her alone for a while? She wanted Camilo, and she didn't want to give up Domingo. She wanted to tell her husband, *Just give me a month. Let me see what happens.*

That was crazy. She was lying in the bed of Domingo's parents, the moonlight pouring in through the window, and she was losing her mind. It was the Revolution, she thought, with its cheering crowds, noisy promises of change and a white dove that had alighted on Fidel's shoulder. The whole country had been turned upside down—but not so much that Domingo was going to let her run free with another man. Not for a month, not for ten minutes.

The next morning she had Ala choose her clothes for the day. A dress rejected, long pants rejected, a pair of shorts accepted without enthusiasm. On her own, the girl would never have worn any clothes at all. Clare slipped the shorts on her and swiftly, before she could complain, a blue T-shirt. "How would you like to live in the jungle and forget about clothes?"

"¡Sí, con los elefantes!"

Clare kissed her face and neck as Ala laughed and jumped around. Yes, Clare thought, that would be good, to live in a jungle with no other people. No confusion. No scary meetings at Camp Columbia.

Domingo had already left with Eliseo, headed for work at his magazine. Clare fed Ala some Wheaties. Domingo had spent so much time in the U.S. he kept boxes of cereal in the pantry and often ate an American breakfast. The Wheaties were followed by slices of mango, which Ala ate with her hands. She wiped her hands on her shirt, and Clare swapped it for a clean one of the same color.

In the street she found a taxi. Ala liked the wind in her face, so Clare sat her on her lap as they drove. They passed stores selling dresses, phonographs and kitchen stoves. Lottery sellers called out their numbers as shoppers mingled with the peanut vendors and coconut ice carts. People buying and people selling. Commerce ruled Havana, it was an unending passion. Twice the taxi driver stopped to talk to someone he knew, offering for sale some used tires and an almost-new, eight-cylinder block out of an Oldsmobile.

"*Estóy de prisa*," Clare told him, though it wasn't really true. She was in no hurry to get to Camp Columbia, she just didn't like the idea that the cab driver was ignoring her. This would not have happened if Domingo had been in the car. Or God knows, Camilo.

At the gate, when she asked if Camilo were there, the sentries gave her the Cuban shrug. It was hard to say, someone else might know, they would escort her in.

Ala wouldn't walk. Shy now, she clung to Clare's neck and watched the soldiers. Clare had said nothing to prepare her. What could she explain to a girl of two?

Camilo sat writing at his desk, his gun to one side. The sentry said, "*Comandante...*"

His smile started, then stopped. He stood up. Alameda lifted her head from Clare's neck and stared at him. From the corridor behind them came the impenetrable murmur of army Spanish. In the room, no one spoke. Clare felt herself lifting away from her body, leaving it behind. She could see everything and do nothing. Camilo and Ala went on staring at each other. Finally he asked, "Is she yours?"

"Yes."

Clare felt Ala breathe, the small rise and fall of her chest. The ceiling fan stirred the ends of her hair.

"What is her name?"

"Alameda. Ala, usually."

"How old is she?"

"She turned two in November."

The calculation was elemental. He nodded, the faintest bow of his head, then reached for a chair, pulled it toward the desk and turned it around. "Please, sit down."

"No."

"Clare, please."

She didn't move. If Camilo didn't want his daughter, she would walk out of the room and not come back.

Ala looked around. She looked at the fan, she looked out the door, she looked back at Camilo. She didn't fidget, but her quiet spell wouldn't last long.

Camilo took two steps toward them. "Let me hold her."

Ala, watchful and silent, allowed him to take her. She held her neck upright and leaned slightly away from him. Could she know? She was rarely so somber. A decision was being made, Clare thought, that Ala had no say in. If she were told that she must change her *papá*, that's how it would be.

Camilo carried her back to his chair and sat down. Ala twisted around to look at Clare, but said nothing. She didn't try to squirm away, and Camilo took his time. He sat and looked at her, ignoring all else. After a moment she slipped her hand into his beard. She took a handful of it and wrapped it up in her fist. Then her eyes went to the star on one of his epaulets. She released his beard, reached out to the star and pulled at it.

"Do you like the star?" Camilo stood her on his chair so he could use both hands to free it. Gently, he pinned it to her shoulder, as it had been pinned to his. Today he wore a star on both shoulders, and when she reached for the other one he moved that as well. She wriggled her shoulders, touched both stars with her fingers and gave Clare a sly smile: *Look what I have.* She stared down at one of her shoulders, then the other, and her smile grew wider.

Clare sat down. Camilo had been good with Ala so far, and he seemed to like her. But one thing had to be said out loud. "She's mine, and she's yours."

"I understand."

Ala watched them. She was never more alert than when she sensed some tension or argument. Her eyes went from Clare to Camilo and back again.

"What do you think of her?"

"I think she is a beautiful girl. Also, one who knows what she wants."

"Like her father," Clare said.

"Like her mother," he said with a laugh.

A bearded soldier came into the room, set some papers on Camilo's desk and withdrew without a word.

"I watch this Revolution," she said, "and I wonder. Will it always come before personal life?"

"I have wondered the same recently, about Fidel and his son."

"And for you?"

He stood up, then leaned back against his desk, leaving Ala on his chair. "I hope for many changes in Cuba," he said, " changes that will help every family. But this will take time."

If he didn't want to help with Ala, she thought, how easy it would be for him, at any moment, to invoke his duty to the nation. It was a mistake to press him, she knew, but even now she hoped for some offer from him. She wanted him to say, *I will help you take care of her. I will be her father.* But of course she would not be hearing that. No man was going to decide something like that in fifteen minutes. And how much time did they have?

Perhaps it had been a mistake to bring Ala to this stark little room, where there was nothing for a child to do. Better to have met at a park or beach—though Camilo, she thought, would not have agreed to that. "I wish that you knew her from the start. That you hadn't missed those years."

"Yes," he said.

Instead of drawing him into her history with Ala, she was making him nervous. *Stop offering anything*, she thought. *Leave it up to him.*

"Is she always so quiet?"

"Not always. Sometimes she talks and doesn't stop."

He touched the girl's shoulder with a fingertip. "*¿Alameda, tu hablas español?* Or do you like English better?"

She understood him, Clare was sure. But she said nothing, and Clare felt a rush of love for her childish ways. When she didn't want to say anything, she didn't.

"Tell me about your mother. Is she a good mother?"

Ala only watched him. The question was a mistake, Clare knew. It was not something a two-year-old child could answer.

"These things take time," Clare said.

"Yes, I see."

"It might be easier to do something with her, something she likes. Perhaps some day you could take her for a drive in your car."

Camilo looked at her as if he didn't understand. Or as if she had lost her mind.

"You could take her to the zoo, she likes that. Or to a beach with little waves."

Now she was playing the fool. Camilo could not do any of those things unless Clare came along—which was why she suggested them. She had vowed to make no more offers, but apparently couldn't stop. *Will you love her?* she wanted to ask. If she could only know that.

By now Ala was growing restless. She reached out toward Camilo's desk, then started to climb up on it. He didn't stop her. She spilled some papers on the floor, and he didn't seem to worry. But when she reached for his gun he got to her faster than Clare. He lifted her away, and immediately she burst into tears, her sobs filling the room. Soldiers peered in at them through the slatted windows. Clare took her back, but she would not stop crying. Camilo didn't look annoyed, the way some men did around crying children, but he didn't look sympathetic, either. Clare had turned her single card, and it was not enough to find out what kind of father he would be. No, she had known it all along: the only way to truly discover that was to throw over the rest of her life. Ala kept wailing and Clare said, "I have to go."

"Give me your phone number so I can reach you."

"Not now."

"Clare—"

He made a move to hold her, perhaps to kiss her, but she turned away. She left the room, then the camp, with her daughter crying the whole way, an incongruous sound amidst the soldiers. Outside the gate, after Ala finally settled down, she found a cab. She climbed in back and held her daughter close, all the way home.

12

A long afternoon, a day without rest. Domingo had bought a stroller and Clare took it out to the Malecón with Ala sitting upright and observant. The Malecón was overrated. There was nowhere for a child to play, no beach, no sand. Just cars in the street, a wide sidewalk and the thump of waves against a rock wall. The sea was azure and Clare unconsoled. She could not escape her own doubts.

The night before, after Ala went to sleep, Domingo had again poured two glasses of wine. He didn't make a fuss about it, just passed a glass to Clare and sat down in his usual chair. She knew what he wanted, but was unsure of what she wanted herself. She'd heard nothing from Camilo in the last ten days. Of course not, because she hadn't given him her number. He could probably have found her, but she didn't expect him to, and didn't want him to show up at Domingo's door. Because what kind of future could she have with Camilo? With Domingo she would know an orderly life and his complete devotion. He sat looking at her, a long stare as he swirled the wine in his glass, slowly, repeatedly. That swirl was a message, she was sure: that once she was naked he would submit her body to the same kind of slow, circular touch.

It wasn't arousal that led her to say yes, it was caution. If she kept saying no to her husband, she was afraid it would look suspicious. So she resigned herself. She would go upstairs with Domingo. How bad could it be?

It wasn't bad at all. After she inserted her diaphragm in the bathroom, he stood her beside his bed and with many caresses removed her clothes. Her mistake was thinking she could keep her distance as she went through the act. By the time he stretched her out on the bed she was eager for his attention—and Domingo was an unselfish lover. Even after he entered her he held himself back, hardly moving, rocking her in the faintest rhythm until she wound up clinging to him and saying "*Sí, sí.*"

Later that's what upset her. All today she had thought about it. She could sleep with two men, she discovered. She could be unfaithful and lie about it. What she couldn't bear was the confusion of being aroused by both of them.

Now, after her trip to the Malecón, she sat in Domingo's high-ceilinged living room in a stiff-backed chair, the cold remains of a cup of coffee beside her. On the floor, Ala played with the wooden train from Domingo's childhood. She ran it across the tiles, a steam engine and three little carts filled with matchstick sugar cane. She had on her shirt with the stars. Clare had put it at the bottom of a drawer, but today Ala had remembered it and demanded to wear it. Every so often she stopped what she was doing, looked down at one of her shoulders, then the other, and beamed a smile at her mother.

Domingo would notice the stars right away. Clare still didn't know what she was going to tell him. She had tried to practice but nothing came.

The light at the windows was beginning to fade. The color had drained from the formal oil portraits on the walls, generations of stiff-necked Cantorros and Beltráns. The room was long and tall. Each morning and afternoon the floors were mopped with wet rags and the ceilings swept for cobwebs. Clare, opening her eyes after a thirty-second upright nap, found that Ala had also fallen asleep, had put her cheek to the floor and conked out without a word. It was a bad time of day for her to take a nap, because if she slept now she'd want to stay up late. If Clare picked her up immediately she'd be fine after a bit of fuss, but if left for ten minutes she would drop into the cave of sleep and not wake up for an hour. Clare let her sink. She left her chair and crouched above her still daughter, watching her face, her smooth cheeks and translucent eyelids. Breathing, breathing, in the rhythm of the sea but twice as fast. By the time Clare picked her up and laid her on the sofa, her body was slack.

In the cathedral silence of the house, with Alameda asleep, Clare could finally think. All logic told her to stay where she was. Domingo loved her, he loved Ala, he was older and stable, he had money and she liked him. Loved him, in a way. She had come to this marriage on the wave of his intent, and it had made both of them happy. And what could she expect from Camilo? He had no money, his job was the Revolution, and for lovemaking they'd snuck off to a *posada* where they would not be seen. She could not imagine a domestic life with him, in the ways that mattered when you had a young daughter. Yet Camilo was the one she wanted.

Outside, a car door closed with a *whump*. Thirty seconds later Domingo entered the house, wearing a suit and tie and carrying his briefcase. He turned on a light and Clare stood up. "*She's sleeping,*" she said, holding a finger to her lips and glancing down at Ala.

Domingo set his briefcase on the floor, gave Clare a kiss and bent over the girl on the sofa. Did he notice the stars? He said nothing about them, but it no longer mattered. The time had come.

"You were sitting in the dark," he said.

"Yes."

"Would you like me to carry her upstairs?"

"No, she's fine."

"And you?" he asked. He leaned toward her, his weight on the balls of his feet. Though bulky, he was always poised. He didn't like surprises.

"Domingo, I'm sorry. I have to move out of your house."

He jerked, his eyes flew open and panic overwhelmed his face. Immediately he composed himself, but half a minute passed before he said, "There is no reason."

"Yes, there's a reason. I want to be part of this Revolution."

"That cannot be. You're an American and these are violent Cuban socialists, even communists. Clare, you don't have to leave my house. Whatever you believe, it's fine. We are married. I want you to stay."

"I can't."

What she couldn't do was carry on an affair with Camilo while she lived with her husband. She watched his face harden. He wasn't used to losing. He had lost his wife, but that was to cancer, a fate beyond his control. He was not a man to beg, either, and now he clamped his jaw shut, a ridge of muscle tightening below his cheek. He stared at her. He said, "Now you must tell me the truth."

"Yes."

"It's a man, isn't it?"

"I should have told you before. Ala's father is Camilo Cienfuegos. Until three weeks ago I didn't know he was alive."

Her deception was now clear, all the way back to her first lie about Ala's Puerto Rican father. Domingo stood still. Not a finger moved. "So that is why you went to Santa Clara."

"I didn't see him there."

"Where?"

"At Camp Columbia. When I took that photo of him and the ambassador."

"Where else?"

She was not going to tell him about the *posada*. But she didn't want to lie, either, to this man who had never deceived her. She said, "We are lovers."

She wasn't sure it was true. She should have said, *I went to bed with him*. She should have said, *I want him*. But the blade had passed between Domingo's ribs. He said, in a voice like gravel, "He will never make you happy. Even I have heard that above all else he loves women and a party."

She hated this, because she feared it was true.

Domingo pointed a finger at her, stabbing the air in a gesture she had never seen him make. "He would be no father to Ala. No, you cannot do this."

She was instantly enraged. This had happened before, when Domingo told her what she could or couldn't do. She stepped closer to him. "He *is* her father, and I'll do what's best for us."

At this, though Clare hadn't raised her voice, Ala woke up on the sofa. It was uncanny, Clare thought. Even when asleep she knew an argument had started. Clare bent to pick her up, as Domingo walked off down the hall. She should not have begun this with him while Ala was in the room, asleep or not.

He came back with Lavinia, but Ala wouldn't leave with the cook. Not even the promise of a coconut flan persuaded her, so Clare carried her to the kitchen and stayed until the flan was set on the table. Ala looked suspicious. She held back, but in the end the creamy dessert won out.

In the living room Domingo's face seemed to have swollen, and his body shrunk. He was shorter than she was. Of course—he always had been. But now she was attentive to everything about him. She watched his eyes as they darted back and forth, how his shoulders drew forward and his chest sank. She had never feared him, not once, yet now imagined him walking to his study and coming back with a gun—a second gun she didn't know about—and shooting her in the chest.

"You lied to me," he said.

She nodded. It was true.

"I told you about my wife, about her cancer, about everything, and you couldn't tell me who Ala's father was?"

"I thought he was dead."

"And now what? He's alive so you have to fuck him?"

"Shut up, Domingo."

"Tell me about him, because I have to know."

Clare shook her head.

"You owe me this, just tell me. Is it because he is so important? Is it the sex?"

"I'm not going to talk about that."

"Yes you are. You are going to tell me."

He was hissing now, and scaring her with every word. "I have to leave," she said. "I have to find my own place."

Domingo turned, his face contorted. He picked up his briefcase from the floor and flung it the length of the room. "You want to fuck him? *¿Tu quieres pisar a esa pinga hueputa?* Go on then. Go over to Camp Columbia and start fucking him. Throw the other women out and strip off your clothes and try to make him happy. *Go on. Go. Go out the door. Find a taxi and get out of here.*"

Half-crazed now, he was bellying up to her, threatening to push her toward the door. She took two steps back and put up her hands. "Don't do this."

"*Just go. Go.*"

"My daughter is in your kitchen."

"That's too bad. She is better off here."

Clare tried to go around him, but he stopped her. He didn't use his hands, just put his body in front of her. She pushed him hard, as far as the hall, and there he stopped. "You're not going to my kitchen. You don't deserve her."

At that she flew against him. She beat on his chest, she battered his face with her hands, then her fists, and put a hard elbow to his ribs. He stumbled, and in an instant she was past him, running down the hall, just as Ala and Lavinia came out of the kitchen. Clare scooped up her daughter and headed back to the living room.

Domingo retreated before her, all the way to the front door.

"Lavinia," he said, "Please call Eliseo and tell him to come at once." He rubbed the side of his face and tucked his shirt back into his pants. "Clare, I'm sorry. I am very sorry. I wasn't thinking well. I didn't mean what I said."

"But you said it. You *thought* it."

"Eliseo will come, he can take you to the Hotel Nacional. I will call them. I'll pay for the room."

Clare was still breathing hard. She said nothing.

"Tomorrow you can come back and get what you want. I won't be here, I'll go to my office. Please let Eliseo help you. I am truly sorry. Perhaps you can understand what a blow this is."

As he spoke, Ala began to cry. Softly at first, then louder. Clare took her to the sofa and sat down. Domingo came half way toward them. "Ala," he said in Spanish, "it will all be well. Please do not worry."

Clare held her. Would all talks now lead to Ala's tears? Eliseo had warned her about Domingo, and clearly it was true, that he could do things she could never have imagined. He had calmed down, she no longer feared him—but now she had to find her own place and start living alone with her daughter. It was clear to her that she could no longer be married, or supported, or controlled.

13

AT eight the next morning, Eliseo came to their room at the Hotel Nacional. He wore a neutral face, but he was clearly not averse to helping them find a place to live. "Don Domingo has told me to give you the whole day, as long as it takes."

This was gracious of Domingo. Of course, if Eliseo helped her find a place, Domingo would know where it was.

"Sit down, Eliseo. Would you like some breakfast?"

"Thank you, I have eaten."

"Let me show you some ads in the paper. I circled them."

He scanned them without sitting down. He shook his head. "Too much money," he said.

"I don't want—a dark place with not enough light." Clare had seen how the poor of Havana lived.

"Don't worry, we'll find a good apartment."

In the Chevrolet she rode up front with Ala between them. The girl stared openly at Eliseo's stump, then climbed onto Clare's lap and watched the rows of stuccoed buildings pass by, the motorcycles and bakery trucks, groups of children gathered outside their schools, puffs of diesel exhaust and the warm winter sun that flooded the streets. Clare felt that before, in spite of how their trip to the airport had ended, she had shared a certain bond with Eliseo. Yet she'd never been comfortable with having him drive her. She was an American, she could have driven herself. Domingo's world of servants was sometimes oppressive to her—which now let her feel what she wanted to feel, that she was doing the right thing to go off and live on her own.

That worked for a mile or two. But she knew the truth and it soon seeped back: her egalitarian principles were not that strong. She didn't want to be poor, and she liked living in a beautiful house. She loved having help from Lavinia and Rosa. And in spite of herself, she responded to wealthy or powerful men. She was drawn to Fidel as he spoke to thousands at Camp Columbia. It was true that she'd loved Camilo in New York when he had nothing—but he thrilled her even more when Fidel turned to him and asked, "¿*Voy bien, Camilo?*" and tens of thousands roared in approval. No, she was not as humble nor as democratic as she liked to think.

Eliseo glanced down at the newspaper and groaned again at the prices. "No," he said, "we will talk to some people I know."

They spent the morning dropping in on store owners, restaurant managers, Eliseo's aunt, a plumber and a lawyer. Eliseo knew many people. He was poor but drove for someone rich. They toured a cramped apartment with a low ceiling, and another accessed through the owner's house. "No," Eliseo said.

Just before noon they found a small airy apartment above a dress store, two rooms with their own entrance up a half-enclosed set of stairs, all facing a small park. The apartment came with a miniature kitchen and a pair of single bed frames. The buxom landlord, Natalia, owned the store below. She was taller and darker than Eliseo, with a broad African face and a pile of tangled hair. Upon settling the deal she shook hands with Clare—no paperwork, she just slid the first month's rent into her cash register and handed over the keys. She sealed the deal with a big hug for Clare, another for Eliseo and a squeeze for Alameda, who had stayed in her mother's arms.

"She won't cry too much during the day," Natalia said, "will she?"

"Oh no," Clare said.

"I close the store at seven, so at night it's always peaceful here. She's a beautiful girl."

Smiles, thanks, another handshake and off they drove, with Natalia waving goodbye from the sidewalk. How quickly it had all been settled. Clare had the advantage of being a yanqui, and everyone knew that yanquis had money. Natalia owned and tended the store downstairs, so she must be responsible. She'd looked stylish, even somewhat risqué, in a knee-length dress and white high heels. Maybe this was part of the new Cuba, to make a deal in ten minutes, with the Revolution smoothing out race and money.

Eliseo grinned as he drove. "And that's how you find an apartment," he said. His relish at their success was great—but his smile, Clare guessed, was the afterburn from Natalia's voluptuous hug. "Now you need mattresses," he said, "and a lamp, and you can tell me what else."

Ala fell asleep in the car. Clare left her with Rosa at Domingo's, then spent a couple of hours shopping with Eliseo. They returned to the apartment with two mattresses tied to the roof of the car and Clare's domestic purchases—sheets, pillows, towels, some pots and pans—laid out on the backseat. Natalia, in her high heels, helped them lug the mattresses upstairs, and as dusk fell the three of them stood in silence on the shallow balcony overlooking the street, watching the brilliant green parrots flash past. In the park a man and woman held hands as they strolled behind their two boys, and the sight of them made Clare uneasy. An instant before she'd been happy with her new place, but a single glance at this family made her doubt everything. She had just destroyed her own family, in an act as impulsive as the one that had brought her to Cuba. If Camilo were true to his past he could easily abandon her, and she'd wind up alone with Alameda in this foreign country. She had a new apartment, but neither the park, the parrots nor the soft approach of night could calm her.

The next morning, fully moved in, with the beds made and her clothes hung in the closet, Clare's desperation lifted. On her way with Ala to buy some food for their empty kitchen, they stepped into the store downstairs. Natalia was leaning over her counter, staring at a new copy of *Bohemia* with Camilo on the cover. He stood smiling at the camera, somewhere in Havana but with his gun in his hands. Natalia smoothed the magazine with her palm. "Aren't you glad our *muchachos* have come to town?"

"You mean, do I support the Revolution?"

"Exactly."

Clare quoted Eliseo, a bit primly: "I think this Revolution is going to be good for Cuba."

"That Batista was such a *cabrón*. But I knew Fidel would win. For two years I listened to him on *Radio Rebelde*. The whole country was waiting for him, we just couldn't show it. You would not believe how much money I paid to Batista's men just to keep my store open. You paid in money or you paid with your body. Pigs, all of them."

At this unlikely moment, Ala reached out and thrust herself toward Natalia, who received her with a smile, a blaze of perfect teeth.

"She likes you," Clare said.

"They all do! All children like me."

"Do you have any of your own?"

"Not a one. I don't think I can, because so many times it might have happened and didn't. When I was younger, you understand, when I was your age. And this one, tell me her name again?"

"Alameda."

"What a beautiful name. Is her father the man you came with?"

Clare smiled to think that Eliseo might be taken for her husband. It was not so impossible in Cuba, where the races were more mixed, the young and old as well. Still, Eliseo was in his sixties. "No," she said, "he is a friend."

"You have other friends, I'm sure."

Clare shrugged: maybe she did, maybe not. Ala started wiggling, and Natalia set her on the floor. Clare said, "If you let her loose, you never know what she'll tear apart."

"If she pulls something down, we'll pick it up. *Tan querida que es.*"

As Ala looked around the store, stuck her head into one of the dressing rooms and wandered beneath the hanging clothes, Natalia laid a finger on the magazine's cover. In a low smiling voice she said, "How about this one? What woman would not want to take this white boy between her legs?"

Clare thought with alarm, *This is how it's going to be.* All over Havana women were dreaming of how they could get Camilo into bed. She stared at his photo, kept staring until Natalia picked up the magazine. "Oh yes," she said, and batted Clare's arm with it. "Tell me you do not find him handsome!"

"*Es algo guapo*," Clare admitted. A fairly good-looking guy. "He looks kind of primitive with all that hair."

Natalia, though large and heavy-breasted, pranced like a girl in her heels and magenta dress. Turning the pages of the magazine, she showed Clare the photos of Fidel, of Raúl, of Che and Ramiro Valdés. "And here is *mi negrito*, Juan Almeida. If I came across him I would light him like a match. Still, Camilo tops my list. They say he's the only one who likes a glass of rum, and who likes to dance. He's one of us, you know. His father is a tailor here in Havana, but *¡que hombre mas rico!*" With a hard click of her heels on the floor, she gave a turn that sent her dress swirling.

Clare tried to imagine what Natalia might say to the news that not long before, Camilo had *been* between her legs. "Perhaps it is only a fantasy," she said, "but I have the feeling I might stand a chance with him. I know I don't have the hips, I don't have the ass—"

"Nor the tits!" Natalia said in an exaggerated whisper, as she pushed up her own. "But you need not be ashamed, you are a graceful girl. You have the neck of a swan, and one of these boys could lose his head over you, I've seen it happen a hundred times. I'd hire some skinny girl and everyone would tell me I was crazy, but she would always do some business."

"You mean—here in the store?"

"No no, in my old business. I ran a house of women and the whole world knows it. But you see how smart I was."

"I—I guess so."

"I not only knew that Fidel would win, I listened to him and believed him. I understood that I was in the wrong business, and that with Fidel there would be no more houses of beautiful women, and mine would be worth nothing. So I sold it to a client from the old days, a banker—and now he is desperate! Half his girls have already left him, but they still buy dresses from me. A woman cannot live without a good dress. *Chica*, you could use one yourself. Those old pants of yours, the same today as yesterday. To speak sincerely, how will you find a boyfriend in Havana?"

"I suppose I should think about that."

"What you need is something sexy, something that shows off your waist."

"My *waist*! Is that all I have?" But yes, that was already understood.

"If I had your waist and *these*," Natalia said, "I would have my pick of the comrades." She spanked the magazine with the back of her hand.

Clare picked it up and tried to look casual as she leafed through it, then set it down on the counter. "I understand," she said, "that the casinos have all been closed, and that gambling in Cuba is no longer permitted. But perhaps we could make a small bet."

"What kind of bet?"

"That I will take one of these boys between my legs before you do."

"*Done*! Girl, you are going to lose some money."

"Ten dollars American," Clare suggested.

"*¡Dios mío!* But no, I cannot take candy from a baby. If I win, you give me ten dollars. If you win, I give you free rent for a month. Even this is unfair, because I know what Cuban men like. I'm sorry, but they want a big ass. That's just how it is."

Natalia was having fun, and Clare as well. How she wanted to tell someone about Camilo. She bought a dress, the price cut in half. It was knit, short and ice blue, and she could not imagine when she was going to wear it.

14

FIDEL was a nightbird, he slept at odd hours and never for long. Camilo, Che and Ramiro Valdés had been meeting with him to discuss the structure of the new government. They met two or three times a week, late at night, sometimes talking until almost dawn. Fidel, in the middle of the discussion, might slip away, lie down on a sofa and sleep for an hour, but when he was ready to continue, everyone else had to be ready as well. They met across the bay at Che's La Cabaña house, in Cojímar on the coast, and on the 23rd floor of the Hilton, now renamed the Habana Libre. They talked about banks and agrarian reform, about the nickel mines and the utility companies. They talked about those who would try to derail the Revolution.

Camilo knew nothing about the nickel mines, but Fidel and Che had decided they should belong to the Cuban people. The financial world was even more complex, and Fidel was going to make Che the head of Cuban banking. *Not a job for me*, Camilo thought. He'd cooked at the Waldorf Astoria, he'd become a soldier, he was neither capitalist nor communist. He was sure of only one thing: wherever the Revolution headed, he would remain a *Fidelista*.

Still, he hated it when Fidel told him, "I need you to help Che in overseeing the tribunals."

Banking would be easier, Camilo thought. In the Sierra he'd seen men shot for treason. He had condemned some himself, but there, at least, he knew the facts: that the culprit had stolen a rifle from the rebel troops or had raped someone's daughter. The rules were strict but clear. Here at the trials in Havana were prisoners Camilo had never met or heard of, accused

of crimes that took place during Batista's rule. Witnesses told their stories
of murder, rape and thievery, evidence was presented and the decisions
made. Some men were absolved, most were not.

A guilty man, if condemned to death, was taken directly from the trial
to an execution yard, stood against a wall and shot. During the first day
of trials Camilo didn't watch the executions, but that night Fidel spoke
to him. "You are head of the army, Camilo, so you must be present. You
don't have to pull the trigger, but you have to be there. Anything less
dishonors our system of justice."

"You tell me to go, and I will go."

Ever since boarding the *Granma* he had followed Fidel's orders, but he
wasn't happy about this one. He hated everything about the trials: the
stifling makeshift courtroom, a terrified man accused of crimes against
the state, the shrill accusations, the sobbing witnesses—almost always a
mother or sister—who attested to the man's good character. If the accused
had worked under Batista, no one but his family dared speak up for him.

The next morning, the first defendant was a captain in the army. There
were official papers, even photographs of him and the men he had tortured. Here at La Cabaña and over at Camp Columbia, members of the
M-26 were poring over the records, and this man was one of hundreds
who stood no chance. The judges did not take long, and Camilo followed the prisoner out of the hall and downstairs into an ancient moat
that surrounded the Cabaña castle. There five rebel soldiers stood waiting, their faces blank. The man was placed against a bruised white wall—
el paredón—already flecked with dried blood, its plaster pocked by bullets that had passed through the bodies of other men. The prisoner stood
unmasked, he raised his hand, he said "*Viva Cuba—*"

"*¡Fuego!*" barked the head of the squad. The soldiers fired and the prisoner slammed back against the wall. Someone came forward with a country wheelbarrow, the dead man's body was lifted over its worn wooden
sides and carted away, the steel wheel beneath him clanking against the
paving stones.

Camilo went back inside. It was ten in the morning. He wanted to
rinse out his mouth with a glass of rum, but the next trial had already
begun. There was no swearing in, no delay. The tribunal moved from one

case to the next. The new defendant, having heard the shots outside, had broken into an obscene sweat. This man, witnesses claimed, had stolen several houses by evicting the families at gunpoint. When two young men resisted him, he had them arrested and put in the back of his jeep, and they were never seen again. By all accounts the man was a sodomist, but neither the sodomy nor the death of the two young men could be proved, and the judges gave him ten years. The relatives of the missing youths were unhappy. They wanted the man shot and began to chant, *¡Paredón! ¡Paredón!* They were silenced, the man was marched away and the next trial began.

After ten days the press of trials eased. Still, the late-night meetings with Fidel continued, and one day after lunch Camilo began to doze off in his Camp Columbia office. He told his sentry to let no one in, took off his boots, put their toes under his head and lay down on the floor. But then he didn't sleep. He started thinking, as he had every day, about the girl Clare had brought to his office. Alameda, his daughter. He didn't doubt that she was his. The timing was right, and she looked like the photos of his mother as a child: the same full mouth, with a pronounced drop at the center of her upper lip. She was a Gorriarán, a Cienfuegos— but what could he do about that? He liked kids well enough, but knew nothing about little children. Though Clare aroused him as much as she had in New York, he didn't want a daughter who crawled across his desk, knocked his papers to the floor and cried when he picked her up. He was much too busy to be responsible for a child. Night and day, he was busy with the Revolution. He had judged Fidel about how he treated his son —but now Camilo saw that he didn't want to spend any more time with a child than *el jefe* did. He thought he should be better than Fidel, a better parent. Instead, he would have to get away from Clare somehow.

Perhaps none of this mattered. She hadn't written him in two weeks, and maybe she'd had enough. Maybe she could tell how he felt about children. He had a thousand jobs to do, and Clare would have to raise her daughter on her own. What she wanted was impossible. He could not get involved. Slowly, as it all became inevitable, he settled down and went to sleep.

When he woke he was given a note on a folded piece of paper.

> I've moved to my own apartment, upstairs at 215 Calle de las
> Moradas. I'll be there tonight. No midnight visits, please,
> but if you come early you can stay late.
>
> —Clare.

All his resolutions vanished. She had written him! She had her own place!
Alameda was not his job, and she'd probably be asleep anyway. He would
leave the camp after dinner, before some message could call him to another
meeting. All he could think about was Clare's smooth body, naked from
the waist up, as she knocked the barrel of his gun around in the *posada*
toilet. He would have to punish her for that! He would punish her with
kisses all over, as long and slow as she liked.

He found her standing on a narrow balcony above a store. She pointed
to the stairs at the side of the building, and he started across the street,
leaving his Thompson behind. His driver called out, *"Jefe, tu arma,"* but
Camilo waved him off. He had his pistol, he'd be fine.

Clare met him at the door and let him into a modest room laid with
common red tile, the kitchen on one side and a bed on the other. Ala was
asleep in a second room, its door half open. Camilo stepped in to look at
her, lying without a sheet, wearing only a diaper, her face turned toward
him. Yes, the resemblance to his mother was strong. He thought again,
I should leave. It would be simpler now than later. But turning back into
the main room he found Clare just behind him, standing on her toes,
wearing a black dress that clung to her hips. He could not walk out on
this.

Clare closed the bedroom door and he whispered, "Will she sleep?"

Clare laughed. She said out loud, "Once she goes down she sleeps like
a stone. For three or four hours a freight train wouldn't wake her. In the
middle of the night that changes, and sometimes she comes in and lies
down with me."

Camilo glanced around at the apartment. It surprised him, how small
it was. Not small for Cuba, but for an American. "There is no other
room?"

"The bathroom," she said, gesturing at a door.

"But—you have no maid?"

"A maid? That's for people like Domingo. Do *you* have a maid?"

"I have soldiers," he said. When she laughed at this he added, "Che has a maid."

"He does?"

"Fidel, too, so Celia doesn't have to spend time cleaning. They live in houses. Me, I sleep on a narrow bed in the barracks. I am the one who embodies the Revolution. Even Fidel says this." Except, he thought, that he had a yanqui girlfriend and a daughter no one knew about.

"You didn't bring your machine gun," Clare said.

He tapped the butt of his pistol. "I have only this. I am almost naked."

Floating in on the night air, through the open balcony door, came the sounds of a *son cubano*. The two soldiers in his car had turned on the radio. Clare went to the balcony and looked down. "Are they going to stay? Right there?"

"Yes, it is a good idea."

She looked from the car to Camilo. "Does it seem to you that we need a chaperone?"

"You don't want them here?"

"I'm sure it will be fine, Camilo, if you just want to sit and talk."

All right, he'd tell them to go. He leaned over the railing and gave a whistle between two fingers. Instantly the men scrambled out of the car with their rifles.

"*Tranquilos,*" he said, with his hands in the air. They could leave, he told them, and he'd drive himself back to the camp later when all was quiet. "You can throw me the keys."

They looked doubtful, but Camilo held out a hand. They turned off the radio, locked the car, tossed up the keys and walked off down the street.

Then he wasn't sure what to do. Did he have to slow down now, as well? Did she mean all the time? He had to talk to her, he remembered that—though looking at her, all he wanted was to kiss her and take off her clothes. He held back, searching her face for clues until she laughed, until she came to him and pressed her breasts against him and let him know she was ready.

Late at night they lay in bed, the hum of the city drifting into the room. Camilo, after sleeping in the woods for two years, was alert to every sound: the grind of a truck on Neptuno, a ship's horn out in the harbor, a rumba on someone's radio. While in Clare's arms, kissing her neck, her eyelids, her teeth, he'd been oblivious to the city. He'd even forgotten about Alameda, asleep in the next room. Now he glanced at the door and asked, "Will she come in?"

"Not yet. She's good for another couple of hours." Clare stretched out naked beside him, her head propped on her palm. "So now we can talk," she said.

"Okay."

"I want to hear about these tribunals. Are you part of them?"

Camilo drew back. Not far, for there wasn't much room on the single bed. "I am part of everything, so yes, I am part of that."

"The executions too?"

He closed his eyes. Already he'd seen forty men stood against the *paredón* and shot.

"Camilo, I'm not the *Prensa Libre*, I'm just curious. Do you think the trials are fair?"

"They are quick. But yes, I think they are fair."

"How quick?"

"Thirty minutes, perhaps an hour."

"*Thirty minutes*? Then they are shot?"

"Some of them. There are many who must be tried, many who were killing and stealing. Batista did nothing to stop it."

He hated the trials, yet found himself defending them. Clare stood up and pulled the bedsheet around her. "I thought a revolutionary's job was to fight for justice everywhere. These trials don't sound fair at all."

"The U.S. ambassador also makes his complaints."

Clare watched him. Her apartment was orderly. Every plate was washed and put away. She had placed his boots by the door, and his pistol in its holster lay at the foot of the bed. After she'd stared at him for a full minute, he rose and pulled on his pants.

"All right," he said, "I do not like these executions. I know the trials are short, but I do not think that innocent men are being punished. All the same, I find it difficult."

"Why?"

"In battle I have killed many men. Once a soldier of Batista ran into me in the woods and I shot him in the chest. He was so close I caught his gun before it fell. I *had* to kill that man, because he would kill me. But these executions—"

She waited. Clearly, she wasn't going to help him.

"They are cold blood and I hate them."

"So why do you go?"

"I was told I must."

"Told by who?"

He glared at her. Of course she knew who it was.

"What if you said no?"

He gave a little laugh, almost a bark at her innocence. "I cannot say no to Fidel. No one can do that. If you're part of the Revolution, you don't say no to *el jefe*."

She considered this. Then she stood, dropped her sheet and walked naked to her tiny kitchen. She took a towel and a pair of mangos, brought them back to the bed and gestured for him to sit down. Face to face, they ate the fruit in silence, the juice running over their hands, her breasts standing out from her chest. After they finished the mangos she cleaned her own hands with the towel, cleaned his, dropped the towel on the floor and gave him another long look. "Do you understand what I have done?"

He was lost, he understood nothing.

"I have left my husband."

That was what he'd wanted, when she first told him about Domingo. But now it made him nervous. He stood up, then sat down again. Did he have to be more responsible, now that she'd left Domingo?

"You're not going back to his house?"

"No."

"Good," he managed to say. But he saw, in her watchful face, that she read his doubts. She waited him out until he gave his excuse. "I have no money. I have nothing."

"The money is not important."

He did not believe this. He was not like Che, who thought money should play no part in romance, fatherhood or family life. "What *is* important?"

"You and me. And Alameda."

"So I can come here again to see you?"

"Yes, that's what I want."

"Good," he said again, and this time he meant it. He would think about Alameda later.

Clare gave him a quick smile, picked up the towel and walked across the room on her toes. She put the towel and the mango pits in the kitchen sink, washed her hands, took a blouse from her closet and put it on. She pulled one of her chairs close to the bed and sat down on it. The bottom of her blouse fell onto her thighs, and he caught a glimpse of the hair between her legs. He wanted to stare at it, but made himself watch her face.

"What *I* want to do next," she said, "is to take the kind of photos that interest me. Especially portraits. I'd like to take some of Fidel."

"That you must do on your own."

"Don't worry, I'm not asking for your help."

Of course she was, he thought. And the more sex they had, the more demands she would make of him. He could see it coming. He thought of their old life in New York, the long hours when they lay in bed laughing and kissing. Now there was Alameda, asleep in the next room, and the Revolution, and many people watching him.

"That day when Fidel came to Havana," Clare said, "was that his son in the back of the truck?"

"Yes, that was Fidelito."

"Tell me about him."

Too much English tired Camilo out, so he explained about the boy in Spanish. He described the scene at the *Granma*, and the argument that followed.

"You liked Fidelito," she said. "Because he was a boy?"

"I wanted to protect him. I do not dislike children."

"Yet Alameda makes you nervous."

"*You* make me nervous." It was a joke but she didn't laugh. "I am no father," he said. "You must know that."

"But in fact, you *are* a father."

The refrigerator hummed. The girl slept. Clare sat on her chair in front of him. He said, "I mean that I would be no good at it."

She watched him, her face rinsed of emotion.

"Does Domingo know you are here?" he asked.

"He loaned me his car and driver to find this place, so I'm sure he does."

"He doesn't care that you leave?"

"He cares a lot. But he restrains himself. That has always been how he gets what he wants."

Camilo could not believe this. No man would help a woman like Clare leave his house.

"He'll show up here some day," she said. "I just don't know when."

"And Ala?"

"She misses him. She calls him *Papá.*"

None of this would be easy, Camilo thought. It was too soon after his years in the Sierra, years in which he rarely spoke to a woman save for Celia Sánchez, Vilma Espín and the girl he taught to read. He didn't know how to defend himself.

Clare put her hands on her thighs, smoothing them slowly. Her long slender toes lay flat on the floor. "Tell me," she said. "Does Fidel know anything about me?"

"No, I cannot tell him."

"Does anyone know?"

"My men. Some day, when things are calmer, I will tell Fidel."

Clare's mouth tightened. "Don't say things to make me happy, Camilo. If you don't want to tell anyone, just say so. We're in my bedroom, we're not fighting some battle. Don't be a *comandante* when you come to see me."

"Of course not," he said. But what he thought was, *No soy rival para ella*—that he could not keep up with her. Not when it came to talk, and to these conflicts. Because they *were* fighting a battle.

Still, it was Clare who stopped asking questions, who stared at him, who told him to lie still on the bed as she rubbed herself all over his chest and mouth. It was Clare who said, when he came into her a second time, *I have to have you*, the words coming out in a rush as if against her will. After that she said nothing more, but was *muy muy buena en la cama*.

15

OCCASIONALLY, when Natalia had to go to the bank or the post office, she asked Clare to look after her shop for an hour. Clare liked to do it, and Ala had learned not to go out onto the sidewalk, but that inside she could wander freely. Clare was behind the register one afternoon, and Ala playing with some small metal cars—she preferred them to dolls, and liked to send them spinning across the glossy floor tiles—when Domingo's Impala pulled up and parked across the street. Clare stepped behind a rack of dresses and let him climb the outside stairs. She listened to his feet on the treads, then his knock on the door in that familiar American rhythm, *shave-and-a-haircut, two bits.*

She didn't want to talk to Domingo, but didn't like hiding from him, so when he came back down the stairs she stepped out onto the sidewalk. Ala followed her, and when she saw Domingo she ran to him, her arms lifted.

Domingo scooped her up. He kissed her and let her snuggle against his neck. To Clare he was polite. In the tone of an old friend he said, "It's good to see you. I've missed you."

In the silence that followed, a hummingbird darted up and hovered beside their heads. Ala watched it for a moment, then reached for it, at which the bird tilted and vanished.

"*Un colibrí,*" Domingo told her.

'*Coliba,*' Ala said, unable to get her mouth around the word.

Domingo laughed. "That's close enough."

How easily he slid back into their lives. He held onto Ala, who tugged at his hair. She loved him, of course. Clare's heart sank. *What have I done?*

Half smiling, Domingo said, "It seems that Castro and I have something in common, that birds are drawn to us. Of course the bird at his speech was much larger—but that is only right for the maximum leader."

This was the old Domingo, ironic and relaxed. All right, she thought, they could talk.

They talked about Eliseo, about Natalia and the dress shop, about the course of the Revolution. Ala, soon bored, shimmied down to the pavement from Domingo's arms, then leaned against his legs. "My dear, let me suggest something. I would pay you well, and it is truly a job without strings."

"What kind of job?"

"I'm planning another article, and I know you would take the best photos."

"You're going to keep printing *Ojo?*"

"Until they stop me. I want to do an article about the cane, about the land and the mills and how sugar is made. The harvest is underway in Remedios, and cane is the essence of rural Cuban life. I think it would interest you."

"Is this so they won't take your mill?"

Domingo gave her a steady look, his brows smooth. "I have no control over such reforms."

Clare missed working, and missed her salary. The AP had sent her a check for $400, payment for two of her photos they'd sold around the world: the one of Camilo shaking the ambassador's hand, and one of Fidel with the dove on his shoulder. She could live for months in Cuba on $400, but opportunities like that did not come every day. Black Star had also taken some of her photos from the first dramatic days of Castro's return, but by now the jubilation had passed and the city had settled down.

"Would the article make it look like I'm taking sides with the landowners, or that I'm against the Revolution? Because I'm not."

"You can take whatever photos you wish, and I will choose from what you give me. I'm sure you will see the beauty of the land—but also the life of the workers, which is often hard. Photograph anything. If you like, take only photos that Castro would approve of. From me, no restrictions of any kind."

"I'd have to take Ala with me. Would Eliseo drive us?"

"I would drive us."

She studied him. All this would be easier if she were more sure about Camilo. Making love with him, she had everything she wanted. Then he left, the morning came and she had no idea when she would see him again.

"Clare, I know I have made you uncomfortable before. I am sorry about that. I regret what I said that night."

She wondered if Camilo could offer so simple an apology. Or if she could.

"We could take Rosa with us," he said. "She misses Alameda."

Rosa had come to Havana after working for Domingo's mother. She had come still grieving the loss of her own child, a boy of four who'd flown out of her arms when they were riding in the back of a pickup that was hit by another truck. That had happened two years before, and Clare was sure it had much to do with how tenderly Rosa cared for Ala, played with her, carried her around the house, gave her a subdued but extravagant attention. Clare, ashamed now of her selfishness, had thought little about Rosa since leaving Domingo's house, had not stopped to consider the new grief that Rosa must be feeling. She told Domingo that yes, she would do the shoot.

They drove east through a rich land, green with cattle pastures and clumps of trees. Clare and Domingo sat up front, and a happy Alameda rode in back with Rosa. The wide fields were broken by side roads that led to the distant hills. Occasional houses dotted the landscape, all small and tidy, made from the curved slats of palm trees. From the slightest distance their simplicity looked appealing, but Clare had long ago vowed not to take pictures that made poverty attractive.

They stopped to buy chirimoyas, nances and zapotes, sold from fruit stands beside the road. There were pie-like pastries and sweet dark coffee served in little screws of paper. Clare drank three in a row, got back in the car and felt like she was growing taller on the seat.

On into cane country, past fields already cut and others dense with stalks twice as tall as a man, three times as tall. Railroad tracks diverged

from the main line, curving off toward distant haciendas and the towering smokestacks of sugar mills. The harvest, which had started in December, was now in full swing, and the roads were littered with fallen cane,
dropped from trucks and oxcarts piled high with stalks.

"I grew up in country like this," Domingo said.

As a boy he'd ridden horses, climbed the palm trees and swum in the
rivers. An idyllic childhood except for his father, who drank. At eleven
he'd been sent off to school in Havana. "Actually, the same school Castro
went to, a school for families with money, the *Colegio de Belén*."

"But not at the same time."

"My dear, he's fifteen years younger."

She still liked how at ease Domingo was with himself, with his body and
his age. They passed through Remedios and drove on to La Voluntad, the
Cantorro family mill. Outside the ancestral house, with its whitewashed
walls and red shutters, Clare loaded her Pentax with color, her Leica with
black and white, and walked straight to a field where men were cutting
cane. They nodded to her. Some tipped their hats, then went back to
work. In the hard heat of the late afternoon they wore boots, gloves,
heavy pants and long-sleeved shirts, and still there were lines of blood
on their wrists and necks from the sharp-edged leaves of the cane. The
harvest was a dance, more like a waltz than a rumba: slash the stalk close
to the ground, trim the leaves, lift and cut it at midpoint and throw both
pieces on a pile. It was repetitive, interminable, back-breaking work, and
Clare discovered the best cutters as quickly as she would have found the
best swimmers in a pool. Some struggled and looked tired, others flowed
with the job and made it look easy. She shot and shot.

At the Cantorro house the cook had a meal ready, a roast duck with
ginger and cabbage. Delicious, but Clare ate fast. Darkness was falling
and she could see the flickering lights from the *central*. Tomorrow, in the
daylight, she would photograph the crusher, but she wanted to shoot the
furnaces at dusk with her fast 400 film.

Domingo introduced her to the foreman. The workers, stripped to the
waist in the high heat, fed the flames a constant stream of bagasse, the
squeezed-out stalks of cane. Everywhere Clare went, Domingo followed,
explaining how the *guarapo*, the first light juice, was growing thicker and

darker inside the boilers, where eventually it would turn into molasses. "They bring the bagasse straight from the rollers. The mill never stops, because if there's any delay the sugar content drops and—"

"*Domingo*, would you leave?"

"Why? What's wrong?"

"Can't you see it? As long as you're here I'll never get a natural look out of anyone. You're the *patrón*, and everyone is aware of every step you take."

"I'm sure they're also aware of you, my dear."

"Just go outside and let me do my job."

The next morning she rose early, loaded her cameras in the first light and walked from the hacienda to the mill. Inside, where the boilers had been running day and night for weeks, a wave of heat rolled over her. A different foreman, a skinny black man with two gold incisors, told her how the huge centrifugal baskets, whirring at the far end of the building, were separating the sugar crystals from the mother liquor. Clare set up her tripod on one spot, then another, as a different crew from the night before sang out snippets of Spanish, all too colloquial or singsong for her to understand. Unloaded by tractors with mechanical claws, then propelled on beds of steel rollers, a living river of cane poured into the mouth of the crushers. Larger grooved rollers mashed the cane, the dark green *guarapo* gushed into a tube that led to the boilers, and the bagasse was ejected beyond. Clare photographed the foreman, the men feeding the cane and those at the controls. She photographed the women sweeping up the remnants of stalks that littered the floor. The noise was constant, and the heat grew until Clare's blouse stuck to her back and chest. She didn't care. She loved a shoot in which everything was new.

At noon, returning to Domingo's house, she found Rosa and Ala outside, lying on some machete-trimmed grass. "*Alameda*," Clare called from a distance, and the girl turned toward her. She came at a run, smiling, laughing, beautiful.

With Ala's arms around her neck, Clare thanked Rosa for looking after her. "You are so good with her," she said.

Rosa's round tranquil eyes were focused on Ala. Her hands, folded together, now opened with her fingers spread, like a dove taking flight. She said, "I love the girl," and Clare knew it was so.

Domingo drank a rare glass of rum before the noon meal. He helped seat Ala at the long table, on top of a Spanish encyclopedia on a chair. But when the girl was presented with a stew of chicken and pork and yucca root, she pushed her plate away. She wouldn't taste the broth or any part of the meal. "*No quiero*," she said. "*No quiero no quiero no quiero.*"

"*Está bien*," Clare said. "Don't eat anything you don't want."

But Ala would not be calmed. She reached out to push the plate again, spilling some of the broth. Clare told her to stop. Instead, she picked up her spoon and dropped it on the floor. It was good silver and rang like a chime. Clare picked it up and set it aside, then took her daughter's hand. She wanted to smack it, something she had never done. She cleaned Ala's fingers with a napkin, which brought new cries of outrage.

These fits came over her sometimes, more often since they'd moved out of Domingo's house. With a look of resolute calm, Domingo stood up from his seat at the end of the table and came around to her. He soaked a piece of bread in her stew, but when he offered it to her she turned away and wouldn't look at it. She said "*Tú, no.*"

"Alameda," Clare said in English. "Don't say that."

In response, Ala grabbed the knife from Clare's setting and banged it on the table in front of her. Clare took it away, but made the mistake of setting it down within reach. Ala, with her eyes locked on her mother's, put the back of her hand to the knife and slowly swept it to the floor. It rang with the same silvery note, and Clare stood up. "Enough," she said and picked up the girl, who flooded the room with her cries.

Outside, Clare set her on the lawn. Ala twisted away from her, wailing. She beat her forehead on the ground, she stood up, she rolled her eyes and dropped limp to the grass. For a moment Clare could have laughed, but the cries continued, interrupted only by Ala's gasps for breath, as if she were dying. Clare took her in her arms and tried to console her, but the girl pushed her away. She cried and screamed like a wounded animal, and Clare was embarrassed to have this heard by everyone in the house. How long could she keep it up? Clare checked her diaper but it was dry, and Ala kept screaming.

Clare looked up to see Rosa standing at a respectful distance. When Clare gave her a desperate look she said, "I could try."

"Please," said Clare, "because I'm lost. She's not wet, she's not cold, I don't think she's hungry. I don't know what's going on."

Rosa picked Ala up, and twenty seconds later the girl quieted down. "I'll take her for a little walk," Rosa said, and headed around the side of the house toward the cane fields beyond, as Ala stared back over her shoulder, quiet and still, a different child—which put a blade through Clare's chest.

Domingo came down the stairs from the house. "Do not feel bad," he said, and laid a gentle hand on her shoulder.

She could not accept his sympathy. She'd left him and could not turn to him now for comfort. From the mill came the high whirr of the centrifuges, as smoke from the chimneys poured into the sky. Clare loved Cuba, but the Cantorro home felt alien to her. She should never have come on this trip, with a man she had deeply insulted.

Domingo had always preferred to speak English with her, and spoke it now. "I cannot stand by," he said, "and watch you suffer as you go down the wrong path. You know what I am talking about."

"No," she said.

"It cannot end well with these *barbudos* of yours."

It was the *patrón* in him that angered her, and his tone of disdain. What *barbudos* of hers? There was only Camilo.

"They are full of ideals," Domingo said, "but as men they are lost. This Castro is a personal disaster. He has a child by another man's wife, Naty Revuelta, do you know that? He has children from before his exile and he pays them no attention. Now he has stolen Fidelito from his mother, and instead of looking after him he sends him away to school. And that Ernesto Guevara—he is married and has a child, but also a new girlfriend. Of course he will abandon his daughter. And Camilo Cienfuegos, do you think he's going to be any different? He's not a family man, he's a boy who loves to drink and dance."

"*Enough*, Domingo. He is Alameda's father, so don't say another word."

"This Revolution, as they call it, this new dictatorship—they want to ruin this country. Destruction is all they care about, the destruction of the old Cuba, of everything that is pure and good."

"Domingo, stop. I'm not going to talk about it."

"Even so, I cannot let this pass. You know I have loved you since the night I met you, but your daughter is suffering, I can see it. I know that you are not a woman who will abandon your child to follow some bearded Casanova."

She put her fist to his chest. "What do you mean *abandon*? Because I let Rosa take her, do you think I'm abandoning my daughter? Do you imagine you're going to steal her?"

"Clare, of course not."

She pressed him harder with her fist. "You tried this once before, *now take us home.* I'm going to get my suitcase, and you get your car. If you won't take us I'll find my own ride."

On the long silent trip back to Havana, what galled her was the fear that Domingo was right about Camilo, that he would never be part of a family. To him the Revolution was everything.

16

CAMILO sent word that he would come at nine. He chose this hour, Clare knew, because by nine Ala would be asleep. But not tonight. That afternoon, instead of letting her take a nap, Clare kept her on the move. They took a bus out along the northern shore to a beach with gently lapping waves, and on the trip back Clare held Ala on her lap and told her fantastic stories about the cows and goats and dogs they saw, keeping her awake until they got home. At dusk she collapsed, and didn't wake up until eight.

Clare was feeding her dinner when Camilo tapped at the door. She rose and let him in. "*Pase, pase*, I'm just giving Ala some croquettes. She didn't go down for a nap until six."

The disappointment was clear on Camilo's face. She had asked him more than once to visit during the day, but no, he could only come at night. Now it was night and his daughter was wide awake.

He stood just inside the door. Clare took his arm and led him to the table. "Are you hungry?" He shook his head. "Perhaps it is better if I come back later."

"Sit down," Clare said. "Help her with her food, and I'll get some plates for us."

The girl would have none of it. When he offered her a spoonful, she turned her head away. "*Mamá*," she said.

Clare ladled rice and croquettes onto two more plates and set them on the table. Before dinner she had brought out Alameda's shirt with the army stars on it. Ala had slipped into it with barely a glance at the stars, but now, next to Camilo, she tugged at one, then the other. "*Quita*," she said.

"You don't like your stars any more?"

"*No inglés. Español.*"

Camilo watched her as she fussed with her stars, then offered to unpin them for her.

No, the girl said, her mother had to do it.

By now Clare was having second thoughts about keeping Ala awake. Camilo looked good. His beard had grown almost as wavy as his hair, and his army shirt was half unbuttoned, showing the white V of his T-shirt. "Let's eat," he said. "Perhaps later she will like me. Some things with children cannot be forced."

Was he going to instruct her on how to raise a child? Clare removed the stars. "Do you think I am forcing her?"

"You guide her, do you not?" He ate, then waved his fork in the air. "This is not only a problem with children. How do you make anyone do what you want?"

"How do you?"

"I remember Fidel and Che in the Sierra, in the early days, trying to persuade the *guajiros.* They listened but did not believe. What convinced them was how we treated them. No one before ever gave them respect."

"And with Ala?"

"We can respect how she wants to ignore me!"

Camilo's first interest, Clare was sure, was to eat his meal in peace. For herself, she wanted everything at once. She wanted nights like their last one in which they made love as Ala slept, ate dinner at midnight and went back to bed for another two hours. At the same time she wanted the three of them to be some kind of family. Over coffee she said, "Why don't you take me to meet your parents? Take me and Alameda."

Camilo sat up straight on his chair. He looked as if she were holding a razor to his throat.

"Isn't this common in Cuba?" she said. "When you have a girlfriend, don't you take her to meet your parents?"

Ala looked back and forth between them. Through the balcony door came the faint sound of traffic, the last of it, and a few lonely bird calls. Finally Camilo leaned back in his chair and said, "All right, I will."

Ramón Cienfuegos and Emilia Gorriarán were a pair of anarchists who had emigrated to Cuba from northern Spain in the twenties. Both were tailors, and when Camilo, Clare and Ala arrived at their house in the Barrio Lawton they were both at work on their Singers. It was a hilly neighborhood in south Havana, far from Camp Columbia, far from the Habana Libre—but not far from the Revolution. The house, already famous to the residents nearby, was bedecked with flags and signs in support of the M-26.

Camilo introduced Clare to his parents as a photographer, the one who had taken the photo of him wearing a chef's toque, the photo he sent them years ago. It hung now on the wall in a frame of plastic flowers. "And this is Alameda," Camilo said, at which his parents cooed and smiled. His mother knelt and held out her hands, but Ala only leaned back against Clare's knees. Just by looking at her, Clare thought, they must have understood that Ala was their granddaughter. But no word was said about that, and no questions asked. The house was small. One of the paired rooms in front held the sewing machines, the other a sofa, two chairs and a rack of customers' clothes: blouses, guayaberas, dresses and men's formal jackets. Camilo asked about his brother, Humberto. "Still driving his bus," Ramón said. Osmany, the only brother who'd studied at the university, had returned from Mexico to work as an architect with the Revolution. Camilo was the youngest.

They settled Ala on the sofa with some pastries and a glass of milk. Ramón, wearing a pair of round Trotsky glasses, looked like a professor. Emilia took Camilo by the arm and didn't let go of him. Their vagrant son now overwhelmed the room with his laughter, his broad gestures, his hat pushed back on his forehead. Clare had left her cameras at home. Outside a crowd gathered, and people now stared in through the open windows, turning to call out to others, *Camilo has come back, he's here!*

Finally, so they could talk in peace, Emilia closed the living room shutters. Clare said, "Camilo tells me that you came from Spain, that you are anarchists."

"Not any more!" Ramón said.

"Now we are *Fidelistas*," Emilia explained, "one hundred per cent."

"He is a good man," Clare offered. "Has there ever been anyone like him?"

Ramón shook his head. "No one. Some say José Martí, but Martí was never practical. He rode his horse into a stream of bullets. It was a kind of suicide, something Fidel would never do. Fidel would be thinking of the people and what would be best for them. No, in Cuba there has never been his equal."

Clare liked this couple. They were older, like her own parents, and in the U.S. they would have been nearing retirement. Clare wanted her daughter, as she grew up, to know all four of her grandparents, but she could not imagine how this might happen. Still, Clare loved the photo albums that Ramón brought out from a closet, large books of soft black paper to which the photos had been glued, with comments below in white ink: *Camilo en el mar, Camilo a los nueve años, Camilo con su amigo Rafael.* She loved most the photos of him as a child, skinny and carefree, his hand on his hip, looking straight into the camera. Had he ever been shy? His mother said no.

They headed home through the narrow streets of the barrio, then out onto the broad avenues, riding in the back of Camilo's Ford with his two guards up front and Ala asleep on Clare's lap. His men spoke no English, Camilo had told her. Though some of his best fighters, they were illiterate, men from the Sierra who could neither read nor write. Though Clare felt awkward in their presence, she asked Camilo, "How is it that the whole world knows how brave you are? It's what everyone says."

"Please pay no attention to that. It is only people talking."

"Is it true?"

"It's something that happens to me when the shooting begins. Afterward I don't remember it."

They passed flowers for sale on wheeled carts, men with sheaves of lottery tickets, women carrying melons and yams. Clare watched the city go by, then turned again to Camilo. "Why is it then, when it comes to me and Alameda, that you have no courage at all. You introduce me to your parents as a photographer."

"In my parents' house, I am sorry, I cannot say you are my *novia.*"

She understood this. In Spanish *novia* meant girlfriend, but also fiancée. "You could call me *compañera*. You could call me *una amiga*. Don't you think your parents understood? Anyone can see how much Ala looks like your mother."

"So now they must know. I took you there, as you asked."

"Then pretended you barely knew me. I felt like stabbing you again."

"No, no more stabbing!"

"I'm serious. Don't make a joke of it."

They drove in silence.

"Sometimes I feel like that girl Psyche," Clare said, "waiting for Cupid in the dark. Do you know that story?"

"She wants to know what he looks like."

"Yes. But he only comes at night and in the dark she can't see him. He might be some kind of monster. A big serpent is what she thinks."

Camilo let his eyebrows rise, and Clare banged her invisible knife into his shoulder. "Don't," she said.

"What happens to them?"

"I can't remember. Everything was a tragedy for the Greeks."

"I will read about this. I will get a book from the library."

"Camilo, I'm glad you took me to meet your parents. I just don't want you to come to my house only late at night. I don't like being someone you hide. From your parents, from Fidel, from anyone."

"Another day when I am free, we will do something together. But I must tell you, it is better if Fidel doesn't know."

"I won't be the one to tell him. When I photograph him, which I am going to do."

A cold look from Camilo. "You should know that if you tell Fidel, this will end."

Clare turned on her seat, Ala still on her lap. "*You would do that?*"

"*He* would do it. He would find a way."

"You are *comemierdas*," Clare said, "the two of you."

Later that night, alone in her bed, her consolation was recalling the look on Camilo's face—the shock, the hurt—after she called him and Fidel a pair of shiteaters.

Each week in *Revolución*, the official newspaper, the martyrs of the struggle were profiled and held up to praise: famous young men like Frank País, murdered on the streets of Santiago, Eddy Chibás who shot himself in the stomach, and Abel Santamaria who died at Moncada. Others less known, as well: Ciro Redondo and René Latour and Roberto Rodriguez, all heroes now.

Clare wondered about their parents. Camilo's family had been lucky, but there were many whose sons had died in battle. The parents of such martyrs, she thought, might be glad of the recognition given to them, might even feel, for a time, that their lives now brimmed with meaning. But what of their misery late at night, when no one was watching?

She took a bus one day out past Matanzas, to visit the parents of José Antonio Echeverría, who had led the failed attack on Batista's palace two years before. She left Ala with a niece of Natalia's, a level-headed girl of sixteen, with Natalia downstairs to keep an eye on both of them.

Fidel had gone to visit the Echeverrías, which was how Clare knew where they lived. They were polite, and welcomed her into their house. They had suffered the worst loss any parent could know, but their sacrifice had not been in vain, and their son lived on in the hearts of the people. Every time Fidel spoke on the television, he gave meaning to their grief.

Through the Echeverrías she met other parents, but not all were so content about the Revolution and the death of their children. Many looked beaten. An article about their son, or occasionally a daughter, was welcome to them, it brought attention and sympathy. But after a few days or weeks the attention died away. They lay down at night and found that nothing could change the bitter truth. Their nightmares returned, they had trouble breathing, they rose at dawn hating every bird that sang. All this they told Clare as she photographed them.

"I care nothing for this Revolution," one woman told her. "The whole country is celebrating, but both my sons died in the Sierra. My daughters are running around like whores, dancing and drinking with men I don't know. Two years ago my husband lost both his legs when his tractor turned over on him. It took him a year to die. Fidel says there will be medical care for everyone in Cuba, but my husband suffered and now he's dead, and my sons are dead, and I hate those who survived. I slap their faces. I shit on them. The only ones I love are my sons, who I will never see."

The woman lifted up her face and wept, directly into the camera.

Clare, who'd found a photo lab where she could develop her own prints, hung them on a string across her room, black and white photos of something more than anguish. They were portraits, but also accusations.

Black Star, she thought, would not be interested in these photos, and the Associated Press less so. What the AP wanted was photos of Fidel and his leaders. Pictures of Camilo would be good, but Clare wasn't going to shoot him as he walked in her door, or lay in her bed late at night.

She wanted Fidel, but hadn't found a way to get near him. Some Cuban photographers had close ties to the Revolution. Korda, who'd been a fashion photographer, now followed the leaders of the M-26 everywhere. Osvaldo and Roberto Salas had access, and their photos in *Revolución* showed Fidel playing basketball, Camilo on horseback riding into Havana, Che gazing over the nickel mines at Moa Bay.

Rosa, one happy afternoon, showed up at Clare's door. Ala jumped straight into her arms, and Rosa explained how Domingo had let her go —and might Clare have need of her here, looking after the girl?

From time to time she would, Clare told her. Indeed, could she stay with Ala right now, this afternoon?

Twenty minutes later she was on her way to the house of Celia Sánchez, who controlled Fidel's schedule. Everyone knew where she lived, and where Fidel often slept, on Calle Once near the western edge of Vedado. Clare took a bus, walked to the sentry post, had her bag searched by a pair of guards and was led into a waiting room where people came and went. There seemed no order to it. From time to time a woman, not Celia, stuck her head into the room, said nothing at all or sometimes just, *Usted*, and the chosen person rose. An hour passed. Another hour, and Clare was never called. The little room emptied out. She sat alone, staring at a photo of the Moncada barracks and its bullet holes. Then Celia herself opened the door and asked bluntly, "¿*Sí?*"

Taken aback, Clare plunged straight into her request. "I would like to photograph Fidel."

"You and everyone else," Celia said, without the least smile.

Clare pulled her two best-known pictures out of an envelope and explained that she had taken them.

Celia glanced at them and looked up. "You are Clare Miller."

Stunned, Clare admitted that she was.

"Come with me."

Celia looked the same as in the pictures Clare had seen of her, wearing a tailored blouse and army pants pulled tight with a belt. She was a plain woman with a fervent look. She offered Clare a seat in her office but remained standing herself. Her desk was covered with papers, manila folders, a pack of Winstons, a full ashtray and a plaster cast of someone's teeth. Her father had been both a doctor and a dental surgeon.

Face to face, under Celia's direct gaze, Clare asked, "How do you know me?"

"You did well with the dove. Also the photo of Camilo with the American ambassador. Fidel pays attention to such things. He is interested in photography, but he is also extremely busy. You must understand, all of Cuba depends on him. He often speaks in public, and I could give you a schedule."

"What I would like is to talk to him in a more personal setting."

Celia stared at her hard for ten seconds, then sat down on the chair behind her desk. She tapped out a cigarette, offered it to Clare, then lit it herself. "Is it an interview you want?"

"I wish to take some portraits, and I think the best photos come after some talk."

"Like the best sex," said Celia.

Clare had not thought this through. She should have considered that Celia, as Fidel's lover, might be suspicious of another woman. Also, since Celia knew her name, she might know about her and Camilo. It might look like she was trying to go from commander to commander.

"I'm a photographer," Clare said. "I'm always looking for subjects. I could show you many other photos I have taken here in Cuba."

Celia smoked. She placed her cigarette next to others in the ashtray. She moved a couple of folders. She was silent for so long that Clare wondered if she had been dismissed. Then, "I'm sure you know that Fidel is a great talker."

Clare nodded.

"He gets started and forgets his schedule, sometimes forgets who he's talking to. He can go on and on."

"That's fine with me. The more invisible I am, the better the photos."

After another moment's silence, Celia picked up a notebook and wrote in it. "I will see if I can get you thirty minutes with him, perhaps next week. After you have talked, once the time is up, I will come and get you. Then, no matter how fascinating the conversation, please say goodbye and accompany me out of the room."

"Of course."

The following week she found a hand-delivered note in her mailbox: Fidel would see her next Monday at four, and would she please bring her recent photos. Not her camera this time, just the photos.

That was disappointing, but it was a door that might open. It was a coup, really. She was going to meet the heroic leader, and she had pulled it off by herself. Now, what was she going to say to persuade him? That she used to work for *Life*? That she used to work for *Ojo*? The closer the day came, the more uncertain she felt.

Again she waited in Celia's anteroom on a wooden bench, more nervous by the minute. Five o'clock came and went. The sky turned rose outside the single small window, and it was almost dark by the time Fidel strode in, cigar in his mouth, several pens in his left flap pocket, no insignia on either cap or shirt. Like Camilo, he wore his pistol on a web belt. He marched past Clare as if he didn't see her, talked to Celia in her office, came back two minutes later and asked Clare to follow him to another room, where he turned and shook her hand. How large he was up close. She had never stood next to a taller Cuban. He looked her up and down, but not like a man would on the street. He scanned her. He asked her to sit down, then sat himself, facing her knee to knee. On his left wrist he wore a pair of watches. He was famous for them—but how odd, Clare thought, for someone known as the least punctual man in Cuba.

"Is it true," he asked in Spanish, "that you have come to photograph the Revolution?"

Don't lie, she thought. If they knew who she was, they might know a lot more. "I came at first to work for a Cuban magazine, *Ojo*. It's run by Domingo Cantorro."

"Do you still work for him?"

"Only on occasion."

"He is not the kind of person who is going to help the Revolution."

"Nor hold it back," she said. "There is nothing political in his magazine."

"Everything is political, especially money. Why do you want to take my picture?"

"Because the world has an endless desire to see you."

Fidel considered this with no hint of self-consciousness. "Doing what?" he asked. "They have photographed everything already. They have taken pictures of me playing baseball, playing ping pong, fishing, holding my gun, eating breakfast, eating dinner, signing papers, even sleeping in a chair. What else can there be?"

"I'm interested in the families of the Revolution. I would like to photograph you and your son, Fidelito."

Fidel's eyes never moved, but his face tilted slightly, as if someone had turned it with a crank. "You know my son?"

"I saw him the day you entered Havana. Here." She reached into her bag and passed him a picture of Fidelito, sitting on the back of the truck that carried both Fidel and Camilo. It was a selected photo in which Fidelito looked fairly cheerful. There were others, taken only moments later, in which he looked tired, even a little sad, propped between two soldiers.

"He is in school," Fidel said. "It is not possible." He stared at her, the topic closed. "Do you have a copy of the dove photo?"

She gave it to him. He inspected it, then asked if he could keep it. Clare nodded yes. "That was a great night," he said, "a momentous night in the history of Cuba. And as we celebrated the purest victory of the people, that dove came out of nowhere! Three of them!"

She didn't tell him that she had seen the man who released the birds from a cage, not far from the podium. She said, "It looked as if it had happened before."

Fidel straightened in his chair. "Do you imply that I *rehearsed* that?"

"Not at all. Just that you were so comfortable with the bird on your shoulder, and went straight on with your speech."

"Well, yes."

This mythic leader of the Revolution, she thought—how much like other men he was. How easily offended, how easily calmed.

"*Bueno*," he said, "show me what else you have. Do you have more recent photos?"

Clare, relaxing under his interest, reached into her manila envelope and passed him the best of her recent work, all parents and relatives of those who had died in the struggle.

Fidel had spoken many times about remembering those who had fallen, those who didn't live to see the changes for which they'd sacrificed their lives. Yet now he went through Clare's prints with increasing speed. Toward the end he barely glanced at the parents, at the grief radiating from their faces, from the very bones of their skulls. He gathered the photos and handed them back. "We don't need more stories of suffering," he said. "That is all in the past. Today we are creating a glorious future for Cuba."

Clare tried to defend herself. "Every parent in those photos lost a son, or a daughter. A few of them lost two. I feel I am honoring the heroes of the Revolution."

Fidel lifted his hand, palm out. "The duty of a revolutionary is to help the Revolution. Are you helping in some way? I hope you will take some other photos, something more uplifting. If you do, show them to Celia and perhaps we can talk again. Now, I have a meeting."

That was it, the interview was over. Clare, shamed and angry, made her way outside into the street. She would take no portraits of Fidel Castro. For days she held tight to her grudge, hating him fiercely.

17

O UT on the street, Camilo was a target. Wherever he went, women approached him. They took his arm, they put their cheeks to his beard, they gave him their names and phone numbers on slips of paper. One of them had added the words, *Mi cama es tu cama*, my bed is yours. While one woman told him how she'd listened to him speak on the radio and left her boyfriend the same night, he felt the delicate fingers of another sliding a note into his pocket, her fingertips lingering on his hip. What man could resist that?

Perhaps, Camilo thought, this was why Fidel always went out with an escort. It wasn't just to protect him from an assassin, but from the women.

Fidel never spoke about his women, not even about Celia, though toward the end of their time in the Sierra he'd shared a little house with her. Now, Camilo had heard, he had a new girlfriend, a German girl only nineteen—which didn't stop him from telling his *comandantes* who they should sleep with and who not. Camilo had heard him grill Che about Aleida March: was she a true revolutionary, or just a bourgeois girl on a fling? If so, he should drop her and go back to his wife. In the end, Che would do what he wished. *Me too*, Camilo thought. In fact, he never had to make a move. Once, parked in the Plaza de la Revolución with his men not twenty meters away, a good-looking black girl had sauntered up to his car. "*Buenos dias, mi comandante*," she said, and an instant later her head was inside the window, then her chest, then her whole body as she wriggled in on top of him, her skirt pulled up and her legs in the air. She did her best to hold and kiss him as he laughed and cried out for help. His bodyguards came running and pulled her out of the car, a job they complained about for days in mock anguish.

One Monday morning Camilo went to the barber at Camp Columbia. "Don't touch the beard," he said, "but give me a haircut."

Later he was sorry. His head felt light and unencumbered, but something was lost. It was his time in the Sierra. Those years were in his hair, and now it was gone.

Long hair or short, the women didn't care. A couple of nights later, after a girl worked her way into his office by claiming to be his sister—everyone knew he had no sister, but she *was* a beauty—he drove her to the Rio Almendares, they stripped off their clothes and he carried her into the warm water, the two of them thrashing in the moonlight like a pair of fish. She was a delectable girl the color of cinnamon, and if Clare had seen them she would have stabbed him for real. Clare had called him a *comemierda*, but he could not resist her. Even while kissing the girl in the river, up to the very moment of orgasm, he was thinking of Clare. He remembered how she had looked on her bed two nights before, her arms flung wide and her legs spread to the corners as she commanded him not to move, just to stand and look at her.

There was much Camilo had not told Clare, and much he'd never told Fidel, especially about his stay in the United States. The worst of it wasn't Clare, it was that before he met her he had enlisted in the U.S. Army. Damn, if Fidel ever found out about that he'd be rabid. Yet there had been a logic to it. He'd been stuck in Tampa, had run out of money, couldn't find a job and figured that in the yanqui army he would learn how to shoot. After he knew enough he could slip away, cross the border into Mexico and join up with Fidel's men who were training for the invasion.

Isabel, the woman he was living with, couldn't believe he had enlisted. She was a Salvadoran nurse, now a U.S. citizen, and she thought he was nuts. "The *army?*" she cried when he told her. "Of the United States? *¿Estás completamente loco?*" He was living in the land of milk and honey, why didn't he forget about shooting people and get his green card instead? If he wanted, he could always marry her and become legal that way.

After knowing her for barely a month? She was the one who was crazy. A week later Macario wrote him with news of a job in New York, and he left the next day on a forty-hour bus ride, the money for the ticket borrowed from Isabel. He did pay her back. But three weeks into his job at the Waldorf Astoria he met Clare and forgot about Isabel. He fell in love and soon forgot the U.S. Army.

Still, he'd signed the papers in Tampa and was now officially a deserter. He doubted the army would ever find him in New York, and they never did, even when *la migra* put him in jail. But now he was afraid that one day, here in Cuba, word might get out that Camilo Cienfuegos, the revolutionary hero, had once signed up to fight for the yanqui army.

Something else he'd never told Fidel was how much he liked the United States, and how much fun he'd had there, especially when he was making good money—*buena plata, dólares en grande*—and making love to a beautiful woman. He would not get far if he tried to explain how none of that had changed his original plan to join the movement. *El jefe* would not want to hear anything good about the U.S., or anything about American girlfriends. He'd view it all as behavior unfit for a revolutionary.

Clare finally had a telephone. For weeks she'd been entreating the telephone company in vain, until Camilo stopped by their offices and put in the request himself. The next day they showed up at her apartment with an old 1930s phone. She left a message for him and the following morning he called her back. Could he come for a visit at eight o'clock tonight? he asked.

She said seven would be better, but okay, come at eight.

He'd found an old Plymouth that didn't call as much attention to itself as the government's black Fords, so he could drive across town on his own —at least at night—without everyone watching. But now, approaching Clare's, he was nervous. Not about Clare but Alameda, who would probably still be awake. Would she ignore him? Would she be upset to see him?

Clare opened the door in her underwear. After a quick glance she said, "Your hair."

"I had it cut."

Ala was sitting at the table and turning the pages of a book, solemnly, as if she could read. She glanced up at him, then went back to her work. Clare turned and stumbled to her bed.

"What's wrong?"

"I have a headache. It's bad, and I left my codeine at Domingo's. Can you get some?"

"At a pharmacy?"

"Make one open up. It's easy for you. Please, I can't talk."

She lay down on her bed, covered her face with a towel and tucked it around her ears. After a glance at Alameda he went out, got in the Plymouth and headed downtown.

Somewhere there would be an open pharmacy—but the ones he passed were all closed. Finally he doubled back, parked in front of the Farmacia Regal and banged on the door. Silence. "*Compañeros*," he yelled, "open the door!" No one stirred. The lights were off inside and the windows protected by a steel grate. He yelled again, as some people gathered on the sidewalk behind him. He turned around. "Is no one here? It's an emergency."

"Is that you?" a man asked. "Really you?"

"Do they live upstairs?"

"No, in back. I'll get them," and the man disappeared down an alley.

Three minutes later Camilo was inside the store with a flustered pharmacist, who poured an amber liquid into a small bottle. "It is an honor," he kept saying. He handed Camilo the bottle and would take no payment for it.

"It's for a friend," Camilo explained.

"Of course, of course."

In the street more people had gathered. He passed through them, avoiding all eyes, got into his car and drove off.

"Thank God," Clare said. She sat up in bed, unscrewed the cap and drank half the bottle. Camilo took it as she collapsed onto her pillow. Beside her, Alameda leaned on the bed with her elbows, staring.

Camilo put his hand over Clare's. Would it help if he rubbed her head?

"*No*, don't touch me. Not my head. Oh, Jesus." She arched her back, then curled up in a ball. "It will be better later. The codeine always saves me. Please, Camilo, will you change Ala's diaper and put her to bed. She's probably wet."

"Change her diaper?"

"You can do it. I have to be quiet."

With the towel over her head, she withdrew into silence. Camilo looked at Ala, who stared back at him. "All right," he said. "Let's see how we do this."

The girl was no help. He asked in a whisper, "Where are the diapers?" but she didn't answer. He found them in a basket in her room. You had to fold a diaper, he knew that—but then what? He made a triangle of the square cloth, but when he turned around Ala was again leaning against her mother's bed, her head only inches from Clare's. He asked her to come, but she ignored him. When he picked her up, she screamed—and as soon as he let her go she flung herself onto the bed, climbing up onto her mother's hips. Clare sat up and pulled away her towel, her eyes dark and bruised. She took Ala's hands and gripped them hard. "*I can't,*" she said. "I have a headache. Do you remember about my headaches?"

Under her mother's brutal gaze, Ala relented. She let Camilo carry her to her room, then sat on her bed looking almost as miserable as Clare. "Help me out," he told her in Spanish. "You know this better than I do."

He got her pants off and unpinned the diaper she had on. It was wet and heavy. He set it on the floor—but then what? Was he supposed to clean her? She was skinny and pale and exposed, but he wiped her with a corner of the diaper. Though she submitted to this, when he spread out the diaper and tried to lower her onto it, she spun away from him. "*¡Pañal no!*" she cried. "*¡No quiero!*" He passed the first pin through one corner of the cloth, but attaching it to the other corner, with Ala's legs pumping and her small torso twisting, seemed dangerous. He didn't want to skewer her. She cried, then screamed. He got up and closed the door, came back, took one of her legs and pinned it under his knee, held down her squirming chest with his forearm, yanked the cloth together and guided the big pin through both ends of the diaper—at which Ala lay back in bed and wailed, as he attached the second pin. He had manhandled her, and now she wouldn't look at him. She curled up like an animal, like her mother, and he covered her with a sheet that she immediately kicked off. He went back into the other room, feeling miserable and inept.

He wanted to take off, to drive out to one of the little bars in Marianao and drink a couple of mojitos. But he could not leave Clare with her headache, and Ala so unhappy. He opened the refrigerator, found some rice and beans and ate them cold. It was comforting. It reminded him of the many unheated meals he'd eaten in the Sierra.

Twenty minutes later he heard sounds from Ala's room: Opening the door, he found her staring at him with a book in her hands. "*Usted*," she said.

Did she want him to read to her?

She did.

He took the book, stretched out gingerly on the bed beside her and pulled the table lamp closer. It was a book he knew, *la Cucaracha Martina*, a book his mother had read him as a child. He remembered the illustrations, the splashes of red and brown. He opened it and began to read, quietly. After a while Ala rested her head against his arm, and her breaths smoothed out. When he came to the end, to the last word, she said "*Otra vez*," and he turned back to the beginning. Slowly, her eyes began to droop. They opened, they closed, her chest rose and fell beside his own, and she slept.

When he thought she wouldn't wake, he turned off the lamp, put his arm around her and drew her close. For an hour he didn't move, just lay in the darkness beside her as she breathed.

Two days later Clare called him at the camp. Her migraine had run its course, she told him. "The world is beautiful when it lifts. Thank you for helping, and for looking after Ala."

"Well, I learned something."

"What?"

He was about to say how much he liked having Ala fall asleep beside him. Instead, "I learned how hard it is to change a diaper when a child isn't willing. I even told Fidel about it."

"You did?"

"Not exactly, not about Ala. We were talking about the people, and how some of them cannot accept the Revolution. I told him we must not go too fast, not simply decree what we want. I said that would be like changing a child's diaper through pure force."

"Hah. What did he say to that?"

"He wanted to know what experience I had with changing diapers."

"And?"

"I asked him what experience he had with agrarian reform. I can always make him laugh. But I have an invitation. José Figueres is going to speak on Monday night at a big labor rally. He was the President of Costa Rica when we were fighting in the Sierra. We never had enough guns, and he sent a plane full of them. If you come, I will take you out to a late dinner."

"Dinner at a restaurant? In public?"

"I can go out to dinner with my friend, the well-known American photographer."

"And with your lover? Can you go out to dinner with your lover?"

She was relentless, she couldn't seem to stop. But he said yes, he could. They would go out to eat like any couple. "I could meet you behind the Presidential Palace. I will take you somewhere nice, and hold your hand."

"I'll see if Natalia will look after Ala. But won't Fidel want you around after the rally?"

"He and Che will stay up half the night with Figueres, but I can slip away. Don't worry, I'll be there."

"I'll wait for thirty minutes."

The rally did not go well for José Figueres. Short and handsome, he was a liberal democrat who had eliminated his country's army in favor of better healthcare and education. He offered some advice to the huge crowd, urging the wealthy to join the Revolution instead of fleeing from it. His great hope was that other countries in the hemisphere would rise up and overthrow their dictators, however they could. His own faith was in representative democracy.

Compared to Fidel, whose speeches were impassioned and often formless, Figueres spoke calmly and to the point. But then, after invoking the dangers of the Cold War, he admonished Cuba that if hostilities should ever break out between Communist Russia and the United States, the democracies of the Western Hemisphere must side with the U.S.

This, Camilo knew, would never fly with Fidel—and even as Figueres spoke, David Salvador, the trade union chief, stood up, pushed Figueres away from the microphones and shouted into them that Cuba would never side with the U.S. in any war, that those days were finished, that the epoch of true Cuban independence had begun.

The crowd, momentarily stunned, came to life when Fidel stepped forward. He explained, in slowly rising tones, that Cuba now faced an international conspiracy and a new enemy. "Yes, this man sent a load of guns when we needed help. But that cannot be weighed against his terrible loyalty to the United States, a country that has no respect for Cuba. This man," he said, turning with a sweep of his hand to indicate a visibly shaken Figueres, "is a bad friend, a bad democrat and a bad revolutionary."

In the cheering that followed Fidel's speech, Camilo left the podium. It pained him how Fidel had treated an old friend of the Revolution, and how no one had objected. Camilo himself had not objected. Who would interrupt Fidel while two hundred thousand people cheered him? Camilo walked to his Plymouth, nodded at a pair of army guards and drove off.

Down the long Malecón he drove, trying to calm himself. Was there something wrong with this Revolution? Could no one even listen to José Figueres, who had done so much for the poor in his own country? A man who, in all the hemisphere, had seemed Cuba's best ally?

The sea air blew through the car. Then—*Clare!* He'd forgotten about their date. *Coño, que idiota.* He sped back to the palace and found her standing behind it with her back to the building, looking stiff in a tight blue dress. She got into his car and sat with her purse on the floor and her palms on her bare knees. She didn't say anything. She let him apologize, then apologize again. She watched him. He started a lie about getting caught up with some people, then stopped before he got in too deep. She tapped her fingers on her knees as he drove, headed down the long curve of the Malecón. An offshore wind had picked up and in some places the waves, beating against the rocks below, sent a fine salt spray across the street.

He parked where it was dry. Or partly dry, because the air was misting around them. For a few minutes neither of them spoke. Then Clare said, "Tell me what happened up there. I thought Fidel liked José Figueres."

"He did. But now Fidel is obsessed with the United States, so much that he cannot tell a friend from an enemy. José Figueres helped us, and now we push him away from the microphone. For the first time I am ashamed of this Revolution."

"Are you, really?"

He was, but his own disloyalty unnerved him. "It was wrong to say he was a bad friend, and a bad democrat."

Camilo tried to keep his eyes on Clare's face, but could not. Her long legs, stretched out in front of her, were lit by the streetlight above them. She asked, "How well do you know President Figueres?"

"I only met him today, at the Habana Libre."

"You could talk to him. You could apologize from the people of Cuba."

"No, I cannot. I cannot go behind Fidel's back."

"But you think he's wrong."

He did think Fidel was wrong, but no matter. "Fidel decides, and I follow. Without him there would be no Revolution."

"Yet always he talks about doing the will of the people."

"You heard him, he has made up his mind. He is done with Figueres."

"It could be a private apology, one man to another."

"Clare, you do not understand."

"I think I do. A good man comes to Cuba and is insulted, and no one will talk to him."

On the Malecón beside them a few cars idled by, the city still settling down. "Do this," Clare said. "Drive me to the hotel and I'll apologize to him myself."

Camilo laughed. She had the nerve to try it, he thought.

"I'm serious."

"I'm sure you are."

Moving without hurry, she picked up her purse, got out of the car and headed across the street. Camilo followed, catching up with her beside the seawall. He took her elbow and she jerked it away, never changing her stride. She looked taller than before. It was her shoes, which had little heels on them. "Clare, please."

"You saw how unhappy Figueres was. I think he'd welcome an apology."

"It's a long way to the hotel."

"You think I can't walk it?"

Already her face and arms were glowing from the mist. A car drove past and honked. *¡Compañeros!* came a call, as the taillights trailed away. Of course she could walk there, her heels and short dress didn't slow her down at all. Camilo kept up beside her but she paid him no attention. She was on her way.

Finally he ran back to his Plymouth, pulled out onto the street and caught up to her. "All right," he said, keeping pace beside her, "I will take you."

She got in without a word. He had already figured out what she was after. An apology to José Figures, he understood, would stand for the apology *she* wanted. Camilo had said he was sorry for making her wait, but she'd ignored that. Instead, she wanted to see him make an apology that did not come easily, that would embarrass him, that could get him in trouble.

Damn, she was clever. What a revolutionary she would have made.

He pulled up in front of the hotel's white columns and they both got out.

"You coming with me?"

"No," he said. "And they won't let you up on your own."

"I think they will." Already she was pulling out her Leica. Of course she had brought her camera, she was rarely without it. She removed the lens cap, and in front of the bellboys, soldiers and some guests waiting for taxis, she began to take photos of him, one after another from different angles as she strode back and forth over the polished floor.

The one thing he didn't want was a photo of him with José Figueres. "He'll have guards. You'll never get to his room."

She stuck out a slender hip. "*Whatever Lola wants, Lola gets...*" She sang it slowly, ignoring everyone around them. "Tell you what. You come with me and I'll leave my camera downstairs."

When he didn't agree she moved in closer. Still shooting, she spoke like an announcer: "*And now I give you the beautiful commander, the hero of Yaguajáy, the wildly famous Camilo Cienfuegos.*"

"Okay," he said, "put away the camera."

She spun around, not bothering to conceal her smile, and walked into the hotel. She slipped the Leica into her purse, handed it to a man behind the desk and asked if President Figueres was in. The man, after a quick glance at Camilo, said yes, he was on the twentieth floor. "Please announce two visitors," Clare said, and set off for the elevator.

A soldier from the lobby went up with them, and in the corridor there was another, who bristled before lowering his gun. "*Camilo*," he said in surprise, then corrected himself: "*Mi comandante*." Camilo waved, then asked which room was that of President Figueres? Better to take charge now, he thought, and rapped twice on the door.

The President was alone inside, standing in his socks. With an evident look of surprise he shook hands with Camilo, then turned to Clare, who said, "*Encantada, señor Presidente*."

"Call me Don Pepe," he said in Spanish. "Everyone does. Or just Pepe is fine."

Behind him a large window looked out over the city, the white and yellow lights fading into the distance. Clare gave Camilo a glance, a slow look with her eyebrows faintly rising. She was giving him his chance, he thought—and he took it. "We have come because of what happened tonight. That David Salvador, who acted so rudely, is no friend of the Revolution. On behalf of the people of Cuba, we wish to apologize for how you were treated at the rally."

Clare, in her clinging blue dress, was smiling widely. Don Pepe looked back and forth between them. "*We?*"

"*Esta visita,*" Clare said, "*es el resultado de un acuerdo internacional.*"

Don Pepe laughed and said in English, "You are from the United States, I believe."

She answered in a tone of mock surprise: "You mean I *still* have an accent?"

"A delightful accent. I have been married to two women, both from the United States. One of them is my wife now, Karen Olson de Figueres, with whom I am very happy. And you two, how did you meet?"

Clare told him about the Waldorf Astoria.

"So all of us," Don Pepe said, "have lived in New York. After MIT I went to Columbia. It is from those days that I have such a fondness for the U.S."

"Fidel has traveled there too," Camilo said in Spanish. "But he can hear nothing good about a country that, in truth, has done much harm to Cuba."

"I understand."

"Still," Clare said, "it is shameful how you were treated tonight."

Don Pepe nodded. "Even at home that has happened—though usually at the hands of some crazy person. I was surprised by Fidel, I admit. Yet it has not diminished my respect for what he has accomplished. My only fear is that he might wind up closer friends with Russia than the United States."

Camilo shook his head. "He will never be friends with the United States. As for Russia, he listens too much to his brother Raúl, who has always been a communist."

Don Pepe considered this. "I saw today that you and Raúl do not get along."

This surprised Camilo. "We didn't say a word today."

"Exactly."

"It is true, I have always been closer to Fidel."

"Very tactful," Don Pepe said. "And Huber Matos, who flew that plane of guns to you—I didn't see him there."

"He is head of the army down in Camagüey. It's a wealthy province filled with big farms, an important post."

"He was very persuasive when he came to Costa Rica. A good man, and I think we see eye to eye. Let us sit down and drink a toast to this country. I've been given a fine bottle of rum, and I am not someone who drinks alone."

They sat and talked, in Spanish and English, with Havana spread out below them: the bright dots of headlights and streetlights, the long yellow bend of the Malecón. Camilo was glad that he and Clare had come.

"Tell me about your wife," she said.

"I'm sure you would like her, and she would love to talk to you, especially about how you moved to Cuba. She felt somewhat lost when she first came to my country. Such a change is never easy, and she was still learning Spanish. But after only five years she plays an important role in the life of the nation. She has worked with the poor and is a member of the National Congress. I think the two of you would find much to talk about."

"She didn't join you on this trip?"

"One of our children is sick. I wish she were here, I would like to explore this beautiful city with her."

"You could come out with us," Clare said.

"Thank you, but no. I'm afraid I have stirred up too much trouble already, and my next step out of the hotel will be onto a plane for home. But some day you must come to visit Costa Rica, both of you."

"One day," Clare said, "Camilo will take me."

For a blazing moment he resented, even hated her. Would she always put him on the spot like this? But she paid him no attention, only asked Don Pepe about his presidency, about dismantling the Costa Rican Army, about giving the women of his country the right to vote.

No matter what she said about power, Camilo thought, she was drawn to it herself. How much she liked talking to someone who'd been the president of a nation. She was easy with this gentle man. She liked him, and liked talking about his wife and family. The three of them went on drinking rum, and by the time Camilo and Clare said goodbye and took the elevator downstairs it was two in the morning. The city was quiet and cool, with almost no one on the streets or sidewalks as he drove her home.

Where, he wondered, would all this lead? Would he wind up married, like Don Pepe? He could see why Clare liked him so much: he was married to an American, they had children and shared a life together. But Camilo could not imagine this for himself, not with Clare or anyone else. His own example of marriage was his parents, two quiet people at work in the same room, year after year. He wanted more than that. He wanted to dance and laugh. He wanted this Revolution to overturn the old Cuba and make it better in every way. He wanted Clare, and other women too.

That never worked, he thought. Or it didn't work when spoken of openly—and Camilo didn't want one of those marriages out of the old days, in which a man had his secrets and kept them. What Clare worried about was surely true: he would not make a good husband. Yet now, right now as he drove her home, she was all he wanted.

18

I$_{\text{N}}$ April the streets were full of dust. The talk was of the rains to come, of agrarian reform, of rent reductions and Fidel's disapproval of private business.

Natalia had been alerted by the neighbors about their famous nighttime visitor, and Clare had won her bet. She tried to refuse her free month's rent, but Natalia insisted. "You won," she said, "fair and square."

"It wasn't fair at all. I'd been in bed with him many times."

"But girl, what a triumph for you! And how you fooled me! I would never have believed my innocent American could catch the greatest of the bearded ones. But you have done it, and one day you will introduce me. No, don't worry, I know how to be polite. And I'm sure you have some exciting stories."

"He is a man like any other."

"That I don't believe."

"But he is. Okay, he knows everyone and he talks to Fidel all the time. But you know how it goes. He comes over, he's hungry, he's upset about something and we have our arguments."

"When you grow tired of him, you send him to me!"

Clare wasn't tired of him, she was putting up a screen. She didn't want to let Natalia see the wave of desire that had enveloped her and Camilo after their evening with Pepe Figueres. They were floating in a sea of arousal, and Clare knew why. In a kind of experiment, she'd decided to let Camilo come and go as he chose, to let him show up after Ala went to sleep, to make no demands on him at all. If she knew he was coming she left the door unlocked so he could walk in and find her naked on her bed, her hips raised, wet from the moment she heard his feet on the stairs. She was coming now like a teenage boy. She came once, sometimes twice before she let him inside her. Camilo did not come, she made sure of that. She held him back. He moved—she made him move—with thrusts as slow as a locomotive gathering steam. If he started to lose control she bit him on the shoulder, and only when ready herself released him to a fierce spasmed ecstasy above her, or beneath her.

Talk, laughter, music, food and sex late into the night. Why did the world do anything but this?

One evening in May, dressed for Camilo in a short skirt and blouse—he'd told her he would show up after dinner—she was surprised by a *shave-and-a-haircut* knock. In a panic she opened the door and there stood Domingo, his hands at his sides, in a blue suit and a white shirt open at the neck.

"How have you been, Clare? May I come in?"

She could not refuse him. She nodded and stepped aside.

"And Alameda?" he asked.

"Asleep."

"May I see her?"

They watched her from the doorway, lying in the band of light from behind them.

"She's bigger," Domingo whispered, and once back in the living room, "I'm sorry not to hear her speak. She must be learning new words every day. I have missed her."

Clare wanted him to leave, but led him to her table beside the balcony. When he sat down, she did too.

"I've missed you as well," he said.

Only once had Clare seen any violence in him. Everything in his world had been achieved through money and persistence. Still, she had left him for someone else, and his reserve now felt dangerous.

He glanced toward her kitchen, said "May I fix some coffee?" and without waiting for an answer crossed the room to her small stove and began to heat up some water.

"I've never seen you in a kitchen," she said. "This must be an effect of the Revolution."

He laughed. "We must all adapt to change. Luckily, I have not yet had to cook my own dinners."

She was aware of her short skirt, her eyeliner, and of the ends of her hair still wet from the shower. Domingo strained the coffee, poured two cups and set them down on the table with a precise hand as if long used to serving. He sat down on his small stiff chair, crossed his legs and made it plain how at ease he was in the cooling air, beside the balcony. He seemed a man at peace, not a rejected husband. "Guess who I have in the car?" he said.

"Eliseo? He's down there waiting?"

"No, it's someone else who has worked for me."

It was a stupid game, and unlike him. Looking down at the Impala, she saw no one.

"It's Rosa," he said. "I stopped by her house and picked her up, so you and I could go out for dinner or a drink."

This was what she disliked about him: his presumption. It was bad enough with her, and worse with those who worked for him. In this country full of change, as Fidel talked daily about the rights of the poor and the landless, about their dignity, about giving them some control over their lives, Domingo could go by the house of a woman who once worked for him and pick her up like a package. Not even bring her to Clare's door, just make her wait in the car until all was convenient.

Of course Rosa had come with him, because she needed the work. What Cuba needed, Clare thought, was more Fidel and more change. She said, "I've already had dinner. I ate with Ala."

Behind every word lay Camilo. Neither of them had named him, but at any moment he would be pulling up outside. He didn't know Domingo's Chevrolet and would come right up the stairs. He'd come up the stairs if he *did* know the car.

Clare went to the cupboard, brought back two coconut flans and set them on the table in their white bowls. It was dessert, meant to point to the end of Domingo's visit. But they had barely started to eat when she heard a car door thump. Domingo, holding his spoon in the air and watching her expression, said, "I wonder who that is."

She stood, opened the door and waited until Camilo appeared. It was the moment that had to come. She'd thought about it many times, yet was not prepared. She looked at Camilo, then back over her shoulder. Domingo stood by the table in his suit and polished, thin-soled shoes. Camilo's clothes had never varied: boots, an olive uniform, his big hat.

She thought they would introduce themselves, as people did in Cuba. Domingo would offer his full name, *Domingo Cantorro Beltrán*, and Camilo would respond in kind, *Camilo Cienfuegos Gorriarán*, at which they'd shake hands and say the usual thing—*¿Que cuenta?* or *¿Como anda la cosa?* But none of that happened now, and after twenty awkward seconds Clare stepped in. "Domingo," she said, "this is Camilo."

"*Tanto gusto*," Domingo said formally, stepping forward and extending his hand.

"*Claro, Señor*," and Camilo shook it. Then no one moved.

"Tell me," Domingo said in Spanish, "it must be fascinating. What is it like to run a country at your age?"

His tone was familiar. *Díme* he said, using the *tú* form. Domingo was no soldier. He had no gun at his waist, the members of his class were fleeing the country every day, and his power was nothing compared to Camilo's. But Clare understood what he was doing. He was a smooth master of authority and control.

Camilo didn't shrink from the question. He eyed Domingo coolly. "President Urrutia, Fidel, Che, Raúl, the Cabinet, there are many who are running the country."

"But you are one of them. I see your face everywhere—in the magazines, on posters, even on the sides of buildings."

Camilo leaned forward into the space between them. There wasn't a man in the country who could intimidate him. "We are making many changes. Do you welcome them?"

"I've heard talk I don't like, about how the government might take my family's mill."

Camilo watched him. He seemed to be memorizing Domingo's jaw line, his nose, the hairs on his head. "*La Voluntad*," he said, "in Remedios. You've had a good harvest this year, more than forty thousand tons so far."

"Forty-three thousand, eight hundred." Domingo inclined his head minutely. "There are a hundred and fifty mills in Cuba. Do you know the production of them all?"

"Of those with the most workers."

"And what do you think? Will my family keep our mill?"

"It is doubtful. You have read the Proclamation of Agrarian Reform, issued from the Sierra. Now we are revising it to give even more land to the people, and to make sure that the biggest mills contribute to the economy of the nation."

Domingo's face, his chest, his legs had all stiffened. Camilo, seeing the breach in his defense, pushed into it. "The harvest is coming to an end, but you are not at your mill, you are here."

"My brother looks after the family land."

"He lives there?"

"He has a little plane and flies out every week, sometimes twice a week."

All his life Domingo and his family had been winners. But Cuba's new winners were younger men wearing beards and army fatigues, all eager to dismantle the old ways. Clare understood how hard this was on Domingo, and was not surprised when he turned away and sat down casually at the table. "Would you like some coffee?" he asked—as if he were the host and Clare would serve it.

She did, to give herself time to think. Something was going to explode, and she didn't want it to be here with Alameda in the next room.

"*Bueno*," she said, when the cups were half drunk. "Who's taking me dancing?"

When neither man spoke, she went out on the little balcony and yelled down to Domingo's car. "Rosa, are you there? Could you come upstairs?"

Fidel's idea of celebration was a speech to hundreds of thousands, but at El Panchín the glossy yellow floor was filled with couples celebrating the Revolution in a more traditional way, dancing to a ten-man Cuban *charanga*, drinking and flirting and paying no attention to the fact that Fidel wanted to close such nightclubs.

The three of them were seated at a table near the dance floor. Camilo had left his hat in the car—too much like a flag, he'd once told Clare—but even so, a ripple soon spread through the crowd: *It's him.* Couples broke off in the middle of dancing, women waved handkerchiefs, a girl sat down smoothly on his lap and kissed him on his bearded cheek. Camilo turned to a pair of waiters hovering nearby. "*Muchachos,*" he said with a laugh, "protect me," and they did.

"Have you been here before?" Clare asked Domingo. She thought it unlikely that he would have frequented a neighborhood such as La Playita, a rundown part of the city filled with bars and cabarets, drunks and loose women. Here, in his dark blue suit, he stood out as much as Camilo in his fatigues. But his answer was yes. "I came once when I was young, as an adventure." He held out his hand. "Would you like to dance?"

She glanced at Camilo. At the Palladium in New York he'd been the one to dance with others. Now, like a pontiff granting an indulgence, he lifted his hand toward them.

Domingo danced well. Though thick in the waist he moved smoothly in his dapper shoes. They danced a rumba, then a slow bolero. Was Camilo even watching? He was talking to a pair of women, so Clare danced another song with Domingo. She caught glimpses of Camilo past the other dancers—glimpses, she understood, that Domingo was allowing, even lining up, as he turned her this way and that on the floor.

"You can see for yourself," he said, "what kind of life he leads."

What she saw were the two women sitting on either side of him, their own chairs pulled close, bending toward him to give him a look at their breasts.

At the end of a cha-cha-cha she stepped away and headed back to their table—where Camilo, without a glance at the women beside him, stood up and took her hand. He turned her as if Domingo were one of the waiters and led her back on the floor, which immediately filled. Camilo's big teeth gleamed. He was light-footed even in his boots and moved her without effort, signaling with his hands. She gave in to him. She loved how he'd left the other women behind, without a glance. She thought,

I should not be so easily won—but she was, and didn't try to hide it. She knew Camilo on the dance floor as she knew him in bed, and let his palm on the small of her back guide her every move. They danced again, and again.

At the table, Domingo sat with three mojitos in three tall glasses. He rose as they came off the floor and tried to do what Camilo had done, take Clare back to the dance floor. But the moment he touched her arm Camilo wedged himself between them. *"Basta, viejo."*

Domingo, the heavier of the two, tried to push past him, but as soon as they touched, Camilo took hold of his jacket, extended his arms, and Domingo slid backward in his light shoes. The orchestra, just beginning a song, stopped.

"Get out," Camilo said, as if dismissing a vendor. "I've had enough of this."

Domingo put his hands to Camilo's chest. With a quick shove and a swing of his right foot, Camilo dropped him to the floor. Chairs flew, the two of them writhed, and five seconds later Camilo had his knee jammed between Domingo's sternum and jaw, choking the wind out of him. Domingo's eyes bulged and he stopped struggling.

That was not the end of it. "You and your brother are finished," Camilo said. "Of course we're going to take your mill. You don't have the decency to live there, you just fly there in your plane. You own a plane! You're much too rich. Your money is made off the backs of those who do the work. I've seen this all my life and we're going to end it. Fidel is going to change this country, and I'm going to help, and you are going to stay away from my woman. Do you understand?"

When Domingo said nothing, Camilo drove down again with his knee, until Domingo slapped the floor with his hand.

"*Say* it."

"I understand."

Camilo stood up, brushing his hands as if he'd touched something unpleasant. It was a Camilo Clare had never seen. He waved at the band. "Play, play, we are fine now. Go out and dance," he told the crowd. From the floor, Domingo rose to his knees, then his feet.

Clare did not feel fine at all, and when Camilo put his hand on her
back and tried to steer her to the dance floor, she stepped away from him.

"I'm not going to dance after that."

"That was nothing. I hope you are not sentimental about such a man."

She was sorry to be wearing a little skirt. She'd have been happier
dressed like Celia Sánchez, in an olive uniform. She was finished with El
Panchín, and with Camilo too. Domingo stood with his back to them,
pulling on the suit coat that had been yanked off his shoulders. Clare
tried to take his arm but he shook her off, his face full of rage and shame.

"Come," she told him. She turned her back on Camilo and led the
way out of the nightclub, trusting Domingo to follow her, which he did.
But on the wide seat of his car they sat far apart. He drove in silence, all
the way back to her apartment, and stopped in front of it with the motor
running.

"Domingo, I'm sorry."

"Get out." His lips were tight and his eyes hooded. "You're a fool, and
you'll be sharing him with every woman in Cuba."

She hated them both. Domingo even more, as he drove off without
another word. Did he even remember about Rosa? In two hours, in two
men, she had seen the worst of Cuba.

19

S HE didn't call Camilo, and he didn't call her. She mourned him. She'd become used to his body, to his skin. She wanted his weight on top of her. She wanted to feel him tremble when she slowed him down and made him hold still, when she opened his shirt and pulled up her dress and straddled him on a chair and they had one of their long conversations about the weather, or what they'd eaten for lunch, insistently bland talk with Camilo forbidden to touch her with even the backs of his hands. *I hear it's going to rain tonight*, she'd say, as she pressed down on him. He was hard, but not allowed to move. *I was listening to the radio and it's going to rain, but tomorrow it's going to be sunny and warm, and the next day the same, with a warm day and the night cool*—all as Camilo went crazy beneath her, struggling to obey her and sit still.

Now instead she was alone at night. She was still angry at him, even as she hated that he didn't call. She'd given too much to him, thought of him too much, paid too little attention to anything else. She had no family here and not enough friends—almost no one except Natalia. There was Domingo, but after that night at El Panchín she thought they'd never talk again. Cuba was falling apart for her, and photography as well. She took her camera into the street, met some people and took some portraits, but when she developed the film every photo was lifeless. The fault was hers, she knew. She had lost all faith and could engage with no one.

Except Ala, of course. They had an easy routine. At home they played games, including Ala's favorite, "No jumping on the bed." Clare lay down and pretended to sleep, telling Ala she could do what she liked, but there was one rule: *She must not jump on the bed*. That was dangerous, Clare explained, it was prohibited absolutely. Ala lay still at her feet. Clare closed her eyes and pretended to drift off, and just as she gave a little snore, Ala jumped up, already laughing, and began to bounce up and down.

"*No, no, no!*" Clare grabbed the wild little animal and held her down. "*What's going on here?*" she asked in Spanish. "Were you jumping on the bed? You *must not* jump on the bed! I need my rest. Oh, I am so tired, I am feeling so sleepy, I'm just going to drift off for a bit." And a moment later all was repeated. It was impossible to play as long as Ala wanted. After thirty minutes, after forty, she was still enthralled by her own disobedience.

"Alameda, please. Don't you want to stop and play some other game?"

"*No!*"

"Don't you want to take a break and sit down with me at the table and we can read the newspaper?"

"*No!* You tell me not to do it!"

"Don't you want to listen to the radio and hear how the Revolution is doing, and what advances have been made in the cultivation of new crops?"

"*No! No! No!*" Ala's hair was in her face, her eyes wide open, her shirt half off. "You have to do what I want!"

Sometimes that was a game in itself, a calmer and longer game. After a morning trip to the market, Clare told her that for the rest of the day she would do anything Ala wanted. There were a few rules: they couldn't go far from Havana, and it couldn't cost a lot of money. Otherwise, Ala got to decide everything.

Being in charge was the thrill. She chose a trip to the zoo, they went to the Malecón, they took the ferry across the bay. But mostly it was small commands: Now you have to give me a coconut water. Now you have to walk behind me. Now you have to be the baby and I'm the mother. Now you have to crawl—you're a *baby*.

They were in the Parque Trillo, and Clare was doing what she was told. She got down on the grass and crawled. She was told to cry, then to cry louder. When two old women passed by and stared, Clare explained, "It's a game." It might have been just a game, but clearly she was a demented yanqui. Besides, such explanations were not allowed by Alameda. "No!" she said, "you're the baby. You can't talk. You have to cry!" Clare cried until she laughed. She was crawling around on a little patch of grass in a Havana park, acting like an infant as her daughter played the tyrant. She laughed, and Ala said *No!* But she couldn't stop and soon Ala joined her. The two of them lay on the ground and stared at each other, making crazy faces and laughing even harder.

One morning, after coming downstairs with Ala, Clare found Natalia counting her money. "*Yes*," she said, as she pulled a rubber band around the bills and slipped them into a zippered envelope, "I am in the right business now!"

The bundle of bills was so thick that Clare couldn't help teasing her. "Don't you worry these days about having a store? Some say that every business will soon belong to the state."

Natalia, of course, had heard this, it was a rumor known to all. "That is not possible. Don't we have to wear clothes? Every woman must have some dresses, so there will always be stores."

"There are those who say there will be no more dresses."

"Close your mouth, girl."

"Some say we'll all be wearing army uniforms, men and women alike."

Natalia, quick and affectionate, spun Clare around and slapped her bottom. "No Cuban man wants a woman in pants. Did you go dancing in a pair of pants?"

Clare had told her about the night at El Panchín—and Natalia was right, every woman there had been wearing a skirt or dress. "But you know," Clare said, keeping her serious look, "sometimes I think it would be easier if we all wore the same thing. Not the boots, perhaps, but we could all wear olive fatigues. That's what Celia Sánchez wears—though I think they're tailored. You could offer a line like that, it might catch on."

Natalia stopped to consider this. "You yanquis," she said, "you do know business. But are *you* going to wear a pair of pants like that?"

Clare picked up Ala, who was tugging at her hand. "Only if *el Caballo* tells me I must." *The Horse* was a name people used for Fidel.

"What Fidel decides is good enough for me," Natalia said. "But not even Fidel can tell us what to wear. This is Cuba, not Russia."

In photography, Clare's interest had long been the same: people whose lives were going astray. She was drawn to the jockey who'd fallen off his horse, to the couple gambling away their savings, to the Cuban parents of those who'd died in the struggle. Black Star, after buying her photos from the Santa Clara barricade, had surprised her by taking a dozen portraits of mourning parents and grandparents. Fidel had turned her down, but to hell with him. Cuba was full of faces from the old days, people she had barely noticed when she first came to Havana. Now, on almost every street, she saw portraits she wanted to take of the elderly and broken down, men and women too old for the hustle of daily life, too old for sex, perhaps too old for the Revolution. Some were decrepit, others encumbered by disease or heartbreak. If they had suffered, Clare wanted to talk to them.

She went out with Ala, whose carefree beauty touched everyone. The more the girl chattered and jumped around, the more Clare's subjects opened up to her about the Revolution, about Fidel, about their families. Slowly, Havana was regaining its charm.

Then there were the days when Clare came home, shut the door behind them, set Ala up with some paper and crayons and curled up on her living room bed. She was fooling herself. She hadn't heard from Camilo, she was not Cuban, she could not become Cuban, and where would all this end?

20

H E went early to Clare's house, at dusk, under a sky the color of a ripe mango. He climbed the stairs holding a bottle of Harvey's Bristol Cream, and over his other arm a white robe embroidered with Claridge's seal. He tapped the bottle against the wooden door, which opened onto Clare's quiet face. She watched him as if from a distance, as if staring out at the ocean. Behind her Alameda looked up at him, more inquisitive.

"*Buenas tardes*," he said.

From Clare, no response at all. Was she going to let him in? He lifted the bottle and the robe. "I brought you something from London."

"London...England?"

"The robe is from the hotel where I stayed. They had a little store."

He held it out but she wouldn't take it. She was still angry, he was sure, after that scene at the nightclub with Domingo. But *coño*, the guy deserved it.

It was Ala who reached out and took the robe in her fist. "*Es mia*," she said, and Camilo let her pull it from his arm onto the floor, where she burrowed under it. Too late, he realized he should have brought something for the girl as well, some kind of gift, even if it was only a Cuban toy or doll. How could he have forgotten that?

Still, Clare's face had softened. Perhaps it was the gifts, or his mention of London—or more likely, the amusing sight of her daughter crawling around under the robe. Of *their* daughter, he reminded himself.

"What were you doing in London?"

"Fidel sent me. I was trying to buy some jets."

"Jet airplanes?"

"He should have sent Che, he's better at such things. But Che is in Egypt talking trade deals, and from there he goes to Japan. We are all becoming businessmen."

"Did you get the planes?"

"I don't think so."

This seemed to soften her even more. At least they were talking now, if only like a pair of acquaintances.

As Ala crawled around on the floor between them, her head popping out then disappearing, he explained how he'd gone to speak with England's Foreign Secretary, Selwyn Lloyd. Fidel wanted to swap five English Sea Furies, a prop plane already purchased by the Cuban Air Force, for some Hawker Hunters, much faster jets.

He reverted to Spanish. "The trouble is, I had to go incognito. Fidel wants the planes, but the yanquis don't want us to have them. Of course they don't, if they're going to invade us. The English want the money, but they're afraid of Eisenhower. Every day I was driven to Selwyn's office, to the back door. I had to smooth down my hair and wear a thick English suit. With a necktie—terrible! But I liked talking with Selwyn. He fought in the big war over there, in France, and he knew all about me. I think he liked me."

"Doesn't everyone?"

"Not really. Not everyone all the time." But he could not help smiling.

"What a life you lead, Camilo. Three years ago you were cutting up vegetables in a New York restaurant, and now you're making deals with England to buy jet planes."

From under the robe Ala was yelling "Find me! Find me!" Camilo bent down and picked up both her and the robe, and she screamed in delight —until her head emerged and she saw who was holding her. Then she kicked her legs in outrage and fought to get back to the floor. He put her down and she scrambled to her feet, watching him, suspicious.

Clare invited him to dinner: "I have plenty of food, it's almost ready."

She spoke as if he were a friend who'd stopped by. He should have brought some dinner with him, he thought, he could have stopped at a restaurant on the way. He had plenty of money now. Fidel, for his trip, had given him a wallet stuffed with pesos and English pounds.

They ate a Cuban meal, rice and beans and pork. "What else did you see in London?"

"Nothing! Fidel didn't want the Americans to know what I was up to, so I couldn't go out in the street. I read *The Old Man and the Sea*—in English—and watched some television. I stayed indoors for five days straight, can you imagine? It was like an expensive prison, with a bed two meters wide. Claridge's is a hotel for the rich, and Fidel would not have been happy. You cannot imagine how the English live."

Alameda got down from her chair and crawled onto her mother's lap. She looked at Clare, looked at Camilo and said, "Don't talk."

"I'm sorry," Clare told her, "but we are going to talk. Adults like to talk. You can talk too, and we'll listen."

Instead, she jumped down and ran into her room.

"Soon a bath," Clare called after her.

"*No.*"

"Oh yes. You love a bath."

"*No.*"

"It's her favorite word," Clare said.

She opened the bottle of Bristol Cream and they drank out of two squat glasses. She had no wineglasses, Camilo saw, and nothing of luxury in her apartment. Nothing of value save for her two cameras. At Camp Columbia his own room was even sparser, but he too had a pair of expensive possessions: his M1 Thompson and his Colt .45 pistol, both excellent American guns. He'd taken off his pistol for the trip to England and had yet to put it back on, but Clare didn't seem to have noticed.

From Ala's room came a rising chant, a moan, then tears. "She's tired," Clare said. "Let me get her bathed. Once she gets into the water she loves it."

Clare carried her across the living room as the girl squealed *No*, she didn't want to take off her clothes, and *No*, she didn't want a bath. Clare closed the two of them into the bathroom, and Camilo was alone. He took off his boots and lay down on Clare's bed, then thought better of it and sat on a chair. Damn, a child was exhausting. As long as she was awake you could not relax. An all-night march was easier.

The squalls in the bathroom turned to shrieks, and finally he had to see what was going on. He opened the door to find the water in the tub running and Ala writhing naked on a floor mat. *No,* she would not get in the tub. She hated baths, she hated water, she hated everything her mother told her she liked. Finally she slowed down enough to consider Camilo. She stood up, stared at him hard with her dark brown eyes— *his* eyes, he saw, not the blue of Clare's—and said in her determined little voice, "*Usted afuera.*" You get out.

"Okay," he said, and went back into the living room, closing the door behind him.

He wanted to get in his car and leave. But even more, he wanted to kiss Clare and take off her dress. How easily she kept her distance—which of course made him want her more. He paced around the room. He stepped onto the balcony and looked out at the blue night. All right, he would wait—and only ten minutes later Clare opened the door and called for him to come. Ala was sitting in the water, absorbed and happy, playing with two little wooden boats.

"She always loves it but never remembers."

"Why not just run the water and put her in? Why argue with her?"

"Weren't you the one who said let her decide? Who told me to let her ignore you?"

"I let her ignore me."

"And I let her get into the tub. If I forced her she'd hate it. She'd fuss all through the bath and never touch her boats. Force is not so simple."

"I'm sure you are right," he said. *Coño,* this was going to drive him crazy.

Clare, once Ala was washed and dried and dressed in a nightshirt, carried her to bed and tucked her under the sheets. "How about telling her a story?" she asked him. "She likes that even more than books." The girl looked up at him, waiting. Yes, that's what she wanted. After all her fussing she wanted to hear a story from him. But he had no stories, or none for little girls. The stories he told were of men and battles and walking by night across half the country.

"Maybe some old Cuban story," Clare suggested. "Something your mother or father told you."

He knelt beside the bed, and at first nothing came. He could barely remember the times when his mother came into his room at night to soothe him, to lie down beside him, to tell him some story. What story? He couldn't remember a one. Then, as if floating to the surface of a well, came the tale of the bossy rooster.

"There was a rooster," he began. Could he remember how it went? "There was a bossy rooster who was on his way to a wedding, when he stopped to pick up some kernels of corn."

Would Ala know what a wedding was? She looked wide awake, so he went on. The rooster, while picking up the corn, got his beak dirty, and he ordered the grass to clean it. The grass refused, so he told a cow to eat the grass. No, it was a goat! A goat had to eat the grass, but the goat refused. The rooster told a stick to beat the goat, and the stick refused. He told a fire to burn the stick, told some water to put out the fire, told the sun to dry up the water. Only the sun agreed—because the sun and the rooster were old friends, they met up every morning. And that's where it ended, with the sun and the rooster happy ever after.

"Another," Ala said.

"Another story? Here we have a very bossy little hen."

"Another one."

"That was good," Clare said, stepping forward from where she'd been listening. She sat down on the bed and took Ala's hands. "I'll do the rest, Camilo. In ten minutes she'll be asleep."

"*No*," Ala said.

He stood outside the door, listening to Clare go through *este cerdito* with Ala's fingers and toes. Then she sang *Aruru mi niña, aruru mi amor.* It was lovely—and lovely that Ala was going to sleep.

Finally, silence in the other room. He lay down again on Clare's bed, but she didn't come out. He waited. Had Clare dropped off herself? He realized, with a kind of panic, that this is what Clare did every night. *Impossible*, he thought.

Celia Sánchez had been right about domestic life. After the simplicity of their years in the Sierra, in which wives and children had been ignored or non-existent, a visit to Clare's apartment was a delicate expedition. He wanted to come and see her—but how unsure he felt.

He was calmer, twenty minutes later, when Clare emerged from Ala's bedroom. She had indeed fallen asleep and now blinked it off, rubbing her face with her palms. At the stove she made two small cups of coffee. Camilo wasn't like Fidel, who could drink three cups and fall asleep the next minute. But some coffee now was fine, he had no plans for sleep. They sat at the small round table, they drank the coffee and some more sherry, and Clare relaxed. He could see it in her limbs. Yes, it was going to be all right.

"Tell me more about England," she said. "How did you get there?"

"In a Cubana plane. A huge Viscount, and I was the only one on it! Just me and the pilots. They let me fly it for a while."

"You went to England and I had no idea."

"It was a secret from everyone. Fidel said that was vital."

"But now you have told me."

"You should not repeat it—though in a two weeks it won't matter. Either they sell us the Hunters or they don't."

He settled back in his chair. Perhaps he should not have put his knee to Domingo's throat. But the incident had passed and now all seemed well. Clare's apartment was still cooling off, the palm fronds outside knocking like blocks in a dance band. The birds had gone to sleep in the trees.

"So there you were, locked up in your hotel room and no one knew you were there. You couldn't even meet any English girls."

"Well..."

He shouldn't tell her, he knew. But it was only a lark, as they said in London. "The English are very strange. You don't think so at first, because they're so formal, but at night someone kept sending girls to my room. They'd knock on my door, carrying an envelope. At first I thought, *It's a menu*. But when I opened the envelope, inside was her name, and already she was taking off her sweater."

"Did you let them stay?"

He looked down. He struggled to arrange his face. "A couple of them. Clare, don't worry, I'll never see them again. Their names—even now I can't remember them."

Clare brought her face closer, slowly. "You liked it."

What could he say? Of course he liked it.

"And here in Havana, where you're the center of so much attention—how many women have you slept with here?"

She seemed curious. She waited for him to answer. "Not that many, *mi amor*. Clarita, they don't mean anything to me. It is you I love."

Her face grew still. She said nothing.

"Clare, I'm sorry."

She stood up. She walked on the balls of her bare feet to the balcony door, open to the night. For several minutes she stared into the dark. Then she closed the door behind her and came back.

"I do not understand men." She pulled her chair closer to his and sat down. "When I make love to you, that's all I want. Sex with someone else doesn't interest me. Why is this different for you?"

"I don't know."

"If I slept with someone else it would mean that I was unhappy with you. Are you unhappy with me?"

"No! I am very happy."

She stared at him. She looked sincerely puzzled.

"*Bueno*," he said. "There are women who might be—easier for me. But I must have you."

"Do you have me now?"

"I don't know."

Her expression changed no faster than a cloud in the sky. But it changed. She looked sad. "Thank you for telling me the truth, Camilo. That is always better than lying to me about it."

He was not convinced it was better. No, he thought, he should never have said a word about the English girls. Clare sat completely still in front of him. She said, "How do you feel about Ala?"

He should not say another word. He felt like one of Batista's men on trial: if he told the truth, they'd take him straight to the *paredón*.

"You might as well tell me," Clare said, "for in the end it can't be hidden."

"I like her. I hope that she will like me. But sometimes—I am afraid of her."

Clare's eyebrows lifted minutely. He tried to explain. She was a *niña muy simpatica*, he said, "but when I'm with her I never know if I'm doing the right thing. I don't know what to say to her."

"It takes time. I'm sure you would learn."

How graceful Clare was as she rose, how smooth and fluid. She stood with her back straight and her hands at her sides. She looked like a girl on a diving board—the girl she had been in high school, the girl in the photos she had shown him.

"I am sure you understand that I do not exist without Ala. If you want me, you get her."

He understood. He just didn't know what to do about it.

"I'm trying not to take your English girls as an insult. As any woman would."

"I never asked for them. They came on their own."

"You mean to say it wasn't your fault."

He lowered his gaze. Of course it was his fault.

"And now that you are home," Clare said, "when the next beautiful Cuban woman offers her body to you, what do you think you will do?"

The firing squad was ready, their barrels pointed at his chest. "I don't know," he said.

Another thirty seconds passed. Clare turned, walked to the door and opened it. The night poured in, cool and heavy, smelling of palm and jacaranda. "Thank you again for being honest. Thank you for the presents, too. The robe I will give to Ala, to play with on these hard floors. You know, Camilo, even if it is difficult you should always tell me the truth. Otherwise, some night I will stab you for sure. Now go home."

She said this as simply as if telling him he should pick up his shirt or lower the volume on the radio. She held the door for him with both hands. As he approached she took a half step back. He hesitated, then went out.

Was it over? He went down to his car, got in and drove away. He thought of going to a bar. He could go back to El Panchín, where all the women loved him. Instead he drove to the Malecón. He got out and sat on the wall above the sea, letting himself be calmed by the smack and retreat of the waves. He sat there long enough for the earth to rotate a few degrees under the Southern Cross. Then he drove back to Camp Columbia, lay down on his cot, and in the glaring light of the overhead bulb searched out two lines from Martí.

Con los pobres de la tierra
Quiero yo mi suerte echar:

Like Martí, he had cast his lot with the poor of the earth. Beyond that he didn't know what to do.

21

HAVANA in July. The sun came up like a boxer, smacking Clare's face as she and Ala walked to a café to drink some fresh juice. Clare liked a little routine, liked chatting to the teenaged girl who skinned and pressed the pineapples, liked walking home through the busy streets as the stores rolled up their clattering steel shutters. The heat and humidity climbed without pause, until an afternoon rainstorm swept in from the sea and cooled the pavement with a hiss. An hour later the streets were dry. Dusk fell, the dense squat buildings radiated their heat deep into the night, and the sun rose again in a cloudless sky.

At ten Clare took Ala to a little half-day school she'd found, only a couple of blocks away. Ala liked it and was learning to play with other children. Sometimes, after dropping her off, Clare went to the darkroom, sometimes she came home and sat on a chair.

Natalia motioned to her one morning as she passed the store. "*Vente, muchacha,* I want to ask you something."

Clare stepped into her affectionate embrace, and the two of them stood in the store's shaded entrance. Natalia's look turned somber. "I am starting to think you were right. I've been listening to Fidel, and I believe he wants to take over all the stores."

"And who could stop him?"

Natalia lowered her voice. "I've been thinking of selling. Even now I have some offers. But I wonder—have you ever talked to your friend about this?"

Clare laughed. "You would like some inside information, but I don't have any. I'm sorry. I haven't talked to Camilo in two weeks."

Natalia's eyebrows lifted. "What's going on?"

"What's going on is that the guy is a dog."

"Of course, it has always been so. Man, dog—there is little difference. What happened?"

"I threw him out. Well, I told him to go." There was a satisfaction in saying this. How good she felt to have *hated* him, if only for a moment.

Natalia spread her hands as if to say, *Is that all?* "When *you* throw *him* out, that's not a problem. But now perhaps you miss him."

"Yes, I miss him—but sometimes I can't stand him. Look at this." She pulled a copy of the latest *Bohemia* from among the avocados and onions in her shopping bag. In it was a photo she had already stared at for ten minutes, a photo taken when Camilo still had long hair, standing next to a woman with an ammunition belt across her chest. It was the woman's look of adoration that Clare hated. She tapped the woman's chest. "This is what he sees every day."

"No, that is nothing." Natalia waved her hand over the photo as if clearing the air of flies. "In the world there will always be other women. Look at this picture. It is the woman who has the eyes of a cow, not your Camilo. Tell me, is my guess correct that Camilo is Alameda's father?"

"Yes, he is. But I don't know what kind of a father he would ever be. He told me he's afraid of her."

Natalia had an easy laugh. She knew the world, she knew Cuba, she knew about fathers. "Please remember my years in the arms of a thousand men," she said. "Some, you know, came only to talk, especially as I grew older. There are men I have known for twenty, even thirty years, we're friends, they tell me about their lives. And believe me, many of them are afraid of both their wives and their children. Camilo could be afraid that Ala won't like him. He could be afraid that he'll feel helpless around her." She stopped and put a hand on Clare's shoulder. "First tell me this. Are you sure you want him?"

"I've been sure up to now."

"Good. Then you must decide whether you can bear it after you find out all that is wrong with him. There is no man who won't make you despair."

To this Clare could only nod. "What about you?" she asked. "Do you have a boyfriend?"

"I think I've had too many. What I have now is a friend who understands me. He says that if we can be friends for five years, he'll marry me. But in five years will I even care? For now, yes, I have a kind of boyfriend. But for you that won't be enough, because of Alameda. First, you must take your time. Even if you are miserable you must not hurry. I've struggled with this myself and am not immune to such feelings. But if you give in and plead with him, even talk to him calmly and ask him to come back, you will regret it. These are the iron laws of romance. You must not show desperation. Even worse, you must not depend on him. You must have your own life."

"That's what's so wrong. When I met Camilo I had money and a job. I was in my own country, I wasn't married, I had no child, everything was simple. But now, in Cuba, with Alameda—I don't know what I'm going to do."

Natalia took a turn past a rack of dresses, her heels sounding on the black and white floor tiles. "Tell me. You are going to stay here, right? You are going to be Cuban."

How could she be Cuban? But at the same time, she didn't want to live anywhere else. "I want to see what happens with the Revolution."

"Me too," Natalia said. "But now I fear that my store will be taken. I don't want to cling to it until it's worthless—and already I have another idea. It is Fidel's idea, really."

"What?"

"You know what he believes, that no one should make more money than anyone else. Well, they say that a third of Cuba's doctors have already left the country. No one stops them, and Fidel says good riddance, let the *gusanos* leave. But because these worms are leaving, Cuba must train more doctors—and among the students, says Fidel, there should be blacks and women. I, of course, am both black and a woman! And *you* are a woman. A very smart woman, and how would you like to be a doctor?"

"But I'm not Cuban."

"That won't matter. He will invite students from other countries, from Mexico, from Venezuela. How Fidel would like to have some yanquis who come here to study medicine!"

"But Natalia, I never finished college. I bought a camera and went to work for a newspaper."

"Do you think I went to a university? I finished my secondary, then it was either become a secretary, or the other. I wanted to make money, so you know what I chose. But now, all who have finished their secondary will be eligible—and the state will pay for everything!"

Natalia stood in front of her, lit up by her plan. A year ago she'd been right, Clare thought, when she sold her house of women. Maybe this too was a good idea.

"Say yes," Natalia urged, with a hand on Clare's arm.

"Let me think about it."

"Don't be so cautious! We'd have a great time at school together."

"My Spanish would have to get better."

"Your Spanish is excellent, you understand everything, and Camilo can smooth our way, he can make sure we are chosen."

"If I'm still talking to him."

"Of course you will be talking to him. I will help, and soon he'll be as attentive as you wish."

At noon a week later, waiting for a light to change, Clare spotted a familiar face at the wheel of a taxi. "Eliseo!" she called.

He stopped the car and leaned across the front seat, his weathered face opening into a wide smile.

"*Lleva me al polo norte,*" she said with a laugh, and got in, "*que hace un calor de diablos.*" It was hot as hell. "Eliseo, how happy I am to see you."

He shook her hand. He held it as he stared at her face, her hair, her legs—until the car behind them honked. Finally he started driving, but slowly. "You look more and more like a Cuban," he said with approval.

She was wearing a rayon dress, bought cheap off a vendor on the street, and carrying a woven bag filled with sweet potatoes, cooking oil and a coconut. "Why are you driving a taxi?" she asked. "Where's Domingo's Chevrolet?"

"I must have a job. Domingo says there are troubles at both the mill and his magazine, and he doesn't have enough money to pay me."

"I don't believe that. Domingo is full of shit."

The phrase in Spanish, *lleno de mierda*, made Elisco laugh. "I was lucky to have a friend," he said, "who owns this DeSoto. It's a good car and we're driving it day and night."

Clare worried that he'd lost his job because of her. "Was Domingo angry because you helped me find my apartment?"

"No, this only happened last month. It may be true about his money, because he let his cook go too. His cousins from Cabañas have all left the country, carrying only their suitcases."

"Come," Clare said, "I invite you to lunch. Can you stop for an hour? Let's go to El Pacífico, I'm paying." She had some money in her pocket, and would give it to him.

They sat at a corner table in the Chinese restaurant, the walls open to the narrow streets of the Barrio Chino. Clare's back was damp from the heat, and her hair had curled. They ate soup, then egg rolls, but it was too hot for more. The waiter brought tea but they couldn't drink it.

"Can you earn a living, driving the taxi?"

Eliseo rested both his hand and his stump on the table. "It's good for now, but I fear it won't last. Che and Raúl want to take over everything, and for them every taxi must belong to the state."

"But Eliseo, you've always been on their side."

"You will see." He pushed his teacup away. He spoke quietly, a line of sweat forming on his brow. "The airlines, the buses and trains, all will be owned by the state. And perhaps that is fair—but they will take the taxis, too, and then it will be restaurants, like this one, and pharmacies and barber shops and hot dog stands. Everything. This is not what they said when they were in the Sierra, but now they are drunk with their ideas. I'm glad Fidel got rid of Batista, but this won't work for me—or for Domingo. He has lost his cane fields, and next he will lose his mill. He wants to stay in Cuba, but many landowners have already left and he may go too."

"You heard him say this?"

"No. But I heard other things."

"Tell me."

Eliseo hesitated. He wiped his forehead with a paper napkin. "He was angry after that night the three of you went dancing."

"He told you about that?"

"He and his brother Felipe were in the car. Sometimes they talk and don't remember I am there. Domingo told him what happened at the club, and how furious he was. I looked just once in the mirror, and his face was twisted. He told Felipe he wanted to go home and get a gun."

"That would have been a mistake."

"A humiliated man is dangerous—and Felipe had his own story of dishonor. When the rebel soldiers came to his mill he tried to defend it with a shotgun. He didn't shoot anyone but they put him in jail. He'd never been inside a jail before, and it was a shock for him to sleep there and eat that food."

The waiter came with two cookies on a straw plate. Clare's cookie said *Long Live the Revolution!* Eliseo's said, *The Fortune of One Is The Fortune of All.*

They lay the slogans on the table and ate the cookies. Above them a ceiling fan turned in slow circles. Eliseo said, "I think Camilo should be careful."

"Do I have to be careful of Domingo?"

"No, because he is in love with you. You left him, but you didn't put your knee on his neck."

They parted awkwardly, their affection derailed by Eliseo's warning and the ungodly heat. He dropped her in front of her house, and it was only after he drove off that she remembered the money she had meant to give him. *Damn* it.

22

AUTUMN arrived, the season of hurricanes, with towering clouds and an occasional break in the heat. All day the city lay bathed in light, and after dark a gusty wind pushed the smell of the sea through the streets. One night after Clare put Ala to bed there was a knock on the door. She opened it and found Camilo. He held a bouquet of flowers and six dinner plates, ringed in gold and tied up with string.

She looked at the plates. "You stole those from some *gusano*'s house."

"I bought them. But with so many people leaving," he admitted, "there is a large black market. Clare, I'm sorry for what happened. May I come in?"

That was his apology and she would get no other. She didn't close the door on him, and he didn't tell her that anything would be different. She let him in, put the flowers in a tall glass jar and the plates in her cupboard, and told him he could have what was left of a plantain omelet. He ate, then they sat on their chairs with Ala asleep in the next room, talking about the cooler weather, about Fidel's five-hour speech at the Plaza Cívica, about the little school that Ala now attended.

Clare slept with him, and the next day she told her confessor how the night had gone. Camilo, at dawn, had risen and dressed in silence. He had hovered over her, kissed her temple as she pretended to be asleep, and stepped quietly out the door.

"Good," said Natalia. "Don't pour your love and tenderness over him. Let him give *you* those kisses. Eventually he will figure out that he needs much more than sex. For now, give him your body and let him become dependent on that. Let his need grow. You're a busy woman. You're a photographer and you might become a doctor. Did you have a good time last night?"

"We were up until three."

"Remember that what drives men wild is *your* pleasure, even more than their own. *Pobrecitos*, they think it is something they are giving you. No, it is yours and you are taking it."

That much, Clare thought, Camilo already knew.

She was speaking with him one night about the Revolution, about Che and Raúl. "What about those two?" she asked. "Do they run around with a bunch of shopgirls?"

That was Clare's word for the women who threw themselves at Camilo: *dependientas*. It was an old-fashioned term, dismissive and elitist, but she didn't care. She wasn't going to call them *compañeras*.

"Che and Raúl," he said, "are family men."

She had heard that. "Do you get along with them?"

"With Che I can laugh, he is not so stiff. When Raúl and I are in the same room, the talk stops. He knows I can't stand him and his politics. He's too extreme, he thinks Russia's communism is impure, that they have allowed too much private initiative. He is too much in Fidel's shadow, like a hungry little kid. He *looks* like a little kid."

Camilo served himself from pots of rice and beans on the stove, then added an avocado. He'd come late, so she let him take care of himself. He did so without the least hesitation, she granted him that. He looked somber tonight. Wistful, Clare thought, as if remembering better days. She had bought some rum and poured half a glass for each of them, then looked in on Alameda. The girl seemed warm, and Clare removed the sheet that covered her, then left the door ajar behind her. It was a warm night and windless, the city almost silent.

They drank the rum. It was clear where they were headed, and Clare was glad. Camilo began by looking at her earrings, two silver pendants she'd bought in the street, most likely the property of someone who'd left for Miami. Camilo inspected them, unhooked them, set them on the table and went back to her ears, tracing his fingertips down her neck and onto her chest.

An hour later she lay with him inside her, his weight on his elbows, his hips barely moving, their eyes locked on each other, her body clenching and releasing. She loved, at moments like this, how everything showed up on his face. She never heard Ala get out of bed. She didn't hear the door open, but there she was, standing just inside the room, saying *Mamá, me duele.*

Clare pushed Camilo out of her, away from her, and jumped out of bed. She knelt and embraced her child. She asked what was wrong, and Ala threw up on her.

In the bathroom she cleaned Ala's hands and face, stepped into the shower, rinsed herself off, then dried them both. She could get nothing from Ala but tears. She changed her diaper, carried her back to her bed and lay down with her. The girl was slightly feverish, and there was still some vomit in her hair. No matter, Clare lay beside her daughter, watching her, on the lookout for other symptoms. She hoped it was no more than stomach trouble.

She was still awake but drifting off when she heard Camilo at the door. She'd forgotten him, or almost, and didn't want to think about him now. He stood there, naked in the semi-dark. After a moment he asked, "Are you coming back?"

"Go to sleep," she said. "Or go home, whatever you want. I must stay with Alameda."

"But Clare..." He didn't complete the sentence, but went on standing in the doorway.

"Don't play crazy," she said. Did he think she was going to go back to her bed and continue making love to him? She turned back to Ala and watched her. At some point she dropped off, and in the morning Camilo was gone.

Two days later she read in the paper that the Ministry of Defense, under the leadership of Camilo Cienfuegos, had been replaced by the Ministry of Armed Forces, led by Raúl Castro. The same day, after leaving Ala at school, she found Camilo talking to Natalia in her store.

"Since you weren't here," Natalia explained, "I have introduced myself, and I've been asking him some questions."

"She is a great supporter of the Revolution!" he said. "I think she knows more about Fidel's plans than I do."

This was not the Natalia who had imagined taking Camilo between her thighs. Polite and intent, she plied him with questions about agricultural land and the utility companies. Camilo, as he answered, was full of enthusiasm about the changes being made for the poor of Cuba, for those who'd never owned anything, for those who'd never had a doctor.

"Is it true," Natalia asked, "that the government may regulate private businesses? That it might close them all down?"

Camilo woke up to what she was asking, and took a step back. "Fidel and Che and Raúl are the ones who talk about that." He looked around the store, at the racks of dresses, the tall narrow mirrors and the cash register. "In spite of what they say, señorita, I cannot imagine the end of stores and private businesses. My own parents own a business. They have run the same shop in their home since before I was born, and I cannot believe we will take that away from them."

"Fidel took his father's lands and gave them to the state."

"He had to, or he could not take land from anyone else. It's true that some people have too much—but a small store like this? No, it cannot be."

"And what of your job with the army?" Natalia asked.

Camilo sagged. "That's why I came." He turned to Clare. "Can we go for a drive?"

Natalia saw them out to Camilo's Plymouth. "Don't worry about Alameda," she said. "I will pick her up at two, and my niece can look after her, or I will call Rosa. Give no care to the hour. Go for as long as you like."

Clare thanked her with a hug—during which Natalia gave her ass a hidden, suggestive pinch. Perhaps she thought they were headed off to some *posada*.

Camilo said little as they left the city. They drove through the tunnel under the bay, emerging into the sunlight beyond. His shirt pockets were empty, his hair and beard trimmed, and after some miles he tossed his hat into the back seat. "This is what I need," he said. "To get into the country more often."

It was a peaceful day in the middle of the week, an unremarkable day, a Tuesday. They drove east along the coast past a few small towns, past seaside farms, then back into the hills and out again beside the blue water. It was a day in which Camilo could travel almost incognito. Some farmers watched the car as they drove past, but no one waved or seemed to recognize him. Clare remembered Natalia's advice about holding back —but when they got somewhere, anywhere, she would unbutton his shirt and put her hands on his chest. She was about to do it now, as they drove, when he asked, "Did you read the paper this morning?"

"I read that Raúl is taking over the army."

"The little shit. So now I am no one. Worse than that, I came back from the Escambray yesterday and found all my men gone. Men I fought with in the Sierra, the bravest of men, Orestes Guerra and Arsenio Carbonell and Walfrido Pérez and a dozen others. Raúl has separated them and sent them all to distant regiments, far from Havana."

At this he took an abrupt left turn down a dirt road. The ocean gleamed before them, and when the dirt turned to sand he parked and faced her. "I have no command. My men are all in little outposts, split up as if they were part of some cabal, as if together we might be dangerous."

"No one can doubt your loyalty to Fidel."

"Worse, more insulting, Raúl brought in a barber and had the men shaved, and if their hair was long he had it cut. They all have clean faces now. He has made them nobodies, as if they never fought in the Sierra."

"Have you talked to him?"

"I went straight to him! I walked into his office and called him a *comemierda*. Soon both of us were screaming, and the little filly pulled his pistol on me. He aimed it right at my chest. He would never have the nerve to shoot me. I tore the gun out of his hand and threw it on the floor. I tell you, it is going to come down to him or me."

"But he's Fidel's brother."

"I cannot bear to be under his command."

"What does Fidel say?"

"Only that we must look forward, not back. Come, let's walk."

Barefoot over the fine sand they mashed their way down the beach. There was no one in sight: not a fisherman, no children digging in the sand, no lone strollers. A string of pelicans glided by, their wingtips only inches above the water, but Camilo didn't seem to notice them. "Raúl wants all the power, and he can have it. Sometimes I think I've been too busy with this Revolution. I've been faithful to it but I have no other life. Why *shouldn't* I have an American girlfriend?"

Clare thought of what her father used to say about negotiations of any kind: *The next one who speaks loses.* She let the pelicans fly past, let the curling waves wash up on the shore, let Camilo find his way.

"Do you know," he said, "that Raúl's wife went to school in Boston?"

"I didn't."

"And that Fidel's old girlfriend, Naty Revuelta, used to work for the U.S. Embassy? She went to school in Philadelphia, then worked for Esso. When it's Fidel and Raúl, they do what they like."

Clare did not remind him that both these women were Cubans, and both had risked their lives many times for the Revolution.

"Here," he said, "let's lie down."

She let him kiss her. He opened her shirt. He rolled over her with his elbows and knees on the sand, and kept kissing her as he lowered his hips, pressing against her so she could feel how hard he was. Still fully dressed, he rocked slowly above her, pushed aside her skirt and ran his hand up her thighs. Her hips rose, for she too wanted it.

"No," she said, "we can't."

"There is no one. The beach is deserted."

"We can't because I don't have my diaphragm."

The mention of this seemed to make him more urgent. "I have to be inside you."

"No."

"It's because I love you."

"We're not going to do that."

"Yes, this time we will. I'll be careful."

When his fingers slipped beneath the elastic of her underwear, she reached down and took his wrist. "*No.*"

In his eyes a tiny flicker, through his body a pulse. She knew what it was: the thought that here, on this isolated beach, where no one would see or hear, he could take what he wanted. For a long frozen moment his eyes locked on hers. Then he breathed again and pulled back his hand. His face lost its foreign look, but his cock was still insistent. She sat up, pushed him down on the sand, opened his pants and took care of him with her hand. It didn't take long.

They lay on the beach half undressed, side by side. By race he was pure Galician, light-skinned, almost pale. He sat up and turned his back to the sun. His hat was in the car and they had no lotion. "*¿No te vas a quemar?*" he asked.

"I don't burn that easily."

As she spoke he was staring at her mouth. Gently, with a delicate fingernail, he pushed up her lip and tapped one of her two front teeth. "What is this?" He bent closer. "These two, they are a different color."

She sat up beside him. "You can see that?"

"In the sunlight, yes."

"Those are my false teeth."

"No."

She laughed. "You think I 'd make this up? I lost the real ones when I was seventeen, on the bottom of a swimming pool. You know I was a diver."

In her next-to-last year in high school she'd finished second at the Ohio Junior Championships. But the following year, on a practice dive off the three-meter board at the same tournament, her face hit the bottom of the concrete pool. "I swam up and spit everything into my hand. It looked like a pile of bloody Chiclets."

Camilo put his arm around her.

"My mother came and took me home. The pain was horrible, and no one gave me so much as an aspirin."

"I can't believe I never saw the difference."

"You're not supposed to. Come, let's go in the water."

Naked, slippery, they floated up and down as the waves pushed past them onto the sand.

"You and Raúl—" she said. "Have you ever gotten along?"

"Not from the start. He didn't want me on the *Granma*, and it was no better in the Sierra. We are nothing alike. He can't tell a joke or laugh at one, and he thinks music and rum are common vices. All he can talk about now is socialism and communism. It's the same with Che. He's a doctor, but he will never practice. He wants to run the mines and the National Bank. Fidel tells him he's too extreme, that he must not speak about politics outside Cuba. He doesn't listen. He wants a big stage."

"What do *you* want?"

Camilo turned and gazed out over the water, at the pelicans and the waves. "I believe in the Revolution and want it to work—but I hate how Fidel has taken the army away from me. Have you heard the news about my friend Huber Matos?"

"It's been in the paper."

"Huber is a good man, one of the early *comandantes*. He risked his life to bring that plane full of guns from Costa Rica, and we have fought side by side many times. But he hates communism. He doesn't like where the Revolution is going and wants to give up his post. This, Fidel will not allow. He takes it as an insult."

"President Urrutia resigned."

"Yes, and look what happened to him. He was afraid of being shot, and had to sneak into the Venezuelan Embassy dressed as a milkman. I've been friends with Huber since the early days, and I've tried to talk to him, but he has no restraint. I told him he must not resign, and a week later he writes Fidel a public letter saying that he wants to give up his commission. He says he will not resist arrest, that he believes in Cuba, that he has the strength to do twenty years in prison—and I'm afraid he will, if Raúl doesn't convince Fidel to shoot him. Raúl's heart is cold. He thinks the Revolution would do better without Huber, and better without me. If he could get away with it, I'm sure he'd shoot me himself."

"I can't believe you're in any danger. After Fidel, you're the most-loved man in Cuba."

"Not by Raúl."

Headed back to the city, Camilo hunched over the steering wheel and stared at the road ahead. Clare could feel his tension growing. He parked his car in front of her apartment, they climbed the outside stairs and there, taped to the door, was an envelope with black and red stripes, the colors of the M-26. Camilo's name was on the front. Inside was a folded sheet of paper with more stripes and a note in Fidel's orderly cursive: *Where are you, coño? There are troubles with Matos. I need you right away. F*

Camilo folded the letter, then opened it and read it again. "Huber is too blunt. He follows no one blindly, and Fidel won't stand for it. To Fidel you're either faithful to the Revolution or you're the enemy. I have to go."

"Camilo." Clare grabbed his arm, holding him back before he went down the stairs. "Will Fidel be faithful to *you*?"

He paused. "Probably not as long as I am faithful to him."

23

THREE days later she heard someone climbing her stairs. Natalia, she thought, but when she opened the door she found Domingo in a white guayabera, holding some children's books and a tub of ice cream from Carmelo's Café.

"Coconut" he said, holding it out. It was Ala's favorite.

The girl, who had followed Clare to the door, now jumped out from behind her skirts and cried, "*¡Helado, helado!*"

Domingo offered her the carton, which she wouldn't take. He showed her the books, but she held back from those as well. He let her warm up at her own speed, and eventually she said, "*Helado en una copa*"—and Domingo had to serve it. She grabbed hold of his shirt and pulled him toward the kitchen.

The ice cream was a ploy, but no matter. After their ugly parting the last time, Clare was glad to find him relaxed. She set three bowls on the table and let Domingo fill them.

"And your room?" he asked Ala in Spanish, "which is it?"

"That one." She waved a hand toward it. "I have a new pillow."

"How well she is talking," Domingo said.

Clare watched him as they ate their ice cream. He had come for some reason, she was sure, but he would not be hurried. He finished his bowl and had another. He asked Ala if she liked her school—how did he know she was going to school?—and had she made any friends? He folded his hands in his lap, then looked directly at Clare.

"I have some news. This may surprise you after what I said before, but I am leaving Cuba. Like so many others, I'm going to Miami."

Clare tried to keep the relief out of her face. She was ashamed to feel glad, but Havana would be simpler without Domingo. Walking through the streets, she would no longer worry about running into him.

"I didn't want to leave, but perhaps it was inevitable. My son and daughter are in the U.S. and tensions keep growing between the two countries. Here, the family land is gone, they have left us only the house and a few hectares. Felipe is convinced we will lose the mill as well, most likely before the next harvest. He has sent his daughters ahead, our cousins have gone—even my mother has given in. I put her on a plane last week."

"What about your magazine?"

"The final edition is in the kiosks. The government didn't have to intervene, because all the advertisers pulled out. No one believes that a graceful life can survive under Castro. I've had my fun with the last of the articles, describing the wonderful new resorts that the government is going to build for the people. From cover to cover I've used the most uplifting socialist prose. But *Ojo* is finished. All that remains is to see how much money I can get out of the country in dollars. Luckily, I have an account in Miami."

"And your house?"

"They will take it. It's almost empty, but they take everything. Felipe is living with me. All he has left is his plane."

"Are you cooking your own dinners?"

"Every night. Don't tell Eliseo, but I'm going to leave him my car. I don't want Castro to have it, so perhaps that beautiful Chevrolet will become a taxi. Now, I must go." He turned in his seat. "*Alameda, ¿me quieres dar un abrazo?*"

The girl stared at him. No, she didn't want to give him a hug. She looked cautious, and Domingo's eyes were starting to water up. She came no closer, nor did he move toward her. "*Hay un gato en el parque,*" she said. There's a cat in the park.

Domingo saw nothing strange in this announcement. "Do you like that cat?"

Ala nodded, her head bobbing over her small chest.

He held out a hand and waited. Now his eyes were wet. Perhaps that was what convinced Ala, for she went to him and buried her head against his chest. She could do what Clare could not. Clare had feared Domingo might try to work his way into Ala's bedtime, using the books he'd brought. But his bribery stopped with the ice cream, and Clare was stricken to think that this was the end, that Ala was unlikely to ever again see the man she had called *Papá*, a man she would not remember when she was older.

Domingo stood up. He walked to the door, opened it, and paused. "You know I miss you, Clare. But I also wish you the best. It seems I can't help it." And without a look back he went down the stairs.

It was quick, like a heart attack. Clare went to the balcony and watched the lights of his Impala as it nosed into the street, then slowly cruised away. That he'd been honorable, tonight the same as always, only made it worse.

Then, an hour later, she found a surprise in her silverware drawer. It was an envelope thick with Cuban bills, more than a thousand pesos in hundreds, fifties and twenties. Domingo had always bound her to him with money, but this did seem a gift without strings. She pinned the envelope into the sleeve of a dress she rarely wore, and hung the dress in her closet. She would not tell Camilo about it, or Natalia, or anyone else —by which she understood how ashamed she was that he'd given her the money. Both ashamed and grateful, for she was likely to need it. She needed it now, just to go on living in Havana.

The weekend passed with no word from Camilo. In *Revolución,* the daily paper, she read that Fidel had sent him to Camagüey to arrest Huber Matos, and that Matos was now in the El Morro Castle jail.

Camilo showed up at noon on Monday, wearing his *guajiro* straw hat with the Cuban flag sewn onto the upturned brim. He couldn't stay, he told her. He paced the apartment and would not sit down. He told her about the Matos disaster. He was doing his duty, but hated it. "At four I must speak to the nation from the balcony of the Presidential Palace. Fidel wants me to stir up the crowd—but why? So that even before his trial the people will condemn Huber? So they will call out to send him to the *paredón*? I don't know what to do. Either I'm a traitor to the nation or a traitor to my friend."

Clare got him onto a chair and rubbed his shoulders. His muscles felt like bands of copper, but slowly they warmed to her hands. She told him to take off his shirt, and for twenty minutes she massaged him in silence. Then, still working on his clavicles, she said "The Revolution will continue long after this Matos affair is settled. His ship is sinking and you cannot save him. Just talk to the people about the good that the Revolution is doing."

Camilo was grunting now in affirmation, his head lolling from side to side. Natalia would not approve of this attention to him, Clare thought. But by now her body, her mind, the very tips of her fingers had given in to him. All calculation was finished, and if it ended badly, so be it. She could not resist him. She would give him what he needed. "If you want to come over later, after the speeches, I will be here. It doesn't matter how late. Come whenever you can."

Later that afternoon she picked up Ala from school, and from there they walked to the palace, as the sidewalks, then the streets filled with people. The crowd carried signs in support of the Revolution, and there were occasional cries of ¡Paredón! ¡Paredón! In the plaza Clare hung back with Ala, afraid of the tightly–pressed crowd as it pushed and swayed. The first to take the microphone was David Salvador, the one who'd insulted Pepe Figueres. Next came the new President of Cuba, Osvaldo Dorticós, a cautious and sober speaker compared to Fidel. Of course, everyone was.

Introduced by Dorticós, Camilo stood on the balcony in his cowboy hat, his hands at his sides, waiting through a long ovation, letting the people cheer. He didn't interrupt them, he didn't wave to them, he stood until the cries, whistles and rhythmic shouts diminished slightly. Then he bent toward the mike. He began by praising the Revolution—this movement that would never die—and the unbreakable will of the Cuban people. He spoke of how treason must be resisted, yet never mentioned Huber Matos. His speech was short, he was done in five minutes, and the crowd roared for as long.

After Camilo came Che, who would not finish quickly, Clare was sure. Nor Raúl, who would follow, nor the long-winded Fidel, who might speak for hours. Already Ala was fidgeting, so Clare turned and slipped away from the crowd. She went home and made dinner for the two of them, hoping that Camilo would come that night.

He didn't.

24

How Fidel loved a crowd. After Che and Raúl spoke, Fidel went on for three hours, his speech broken only by waves of applause. Camilo had been up late the night before and now, protected by the stone railing of the balcony, he was going to sleep in his chair. Fidel bewailed the treachery of the United States and the treason of men like Huber Matos—and twice Camilo's head slumped forward before snapping back to attention. The second time he woke to hear Fidel asking the crowd if they thought that traitors like Huber Matos should be executed by firing squad. The crowd roared ¡Sí! ¡Paredón! ¡Paredón!

Camilo shrank from this. The Revolution was the future of Cuba, and Huber a fool to resist it. But shoot him? This was surely the work of Raúl, who loved an execution. Just as Fidel had demanded that Camilo make the arrest, next he would insist that Camilo testify against his friend. In the trial, Camilo would be the main witness. Fidel had already told him that he must return to Camagüey to root out any lingering anti-Revolutionary sentiments. Camilo objected, he said the city was calm, but Fidel insisted.

The rally closed with Fidel's usual exhortations to either conquer or die, and as soon as he could, Camilo slipped away. He found his parents and his brother Osmany—people he could relax with, people who spoke in a normal language about normal lives—and they walked to La Bodeguita del Medio to eat some fried plantains. Sometimes at rallies and meetings the Revolution's rhetoric—even his own—exhausted him. But he loved how his parents, a pair of anarchists who had hated all government, had now found one they believed in. They and his brother were happy. They drank, they talked, Camilo drove them in his Plymouth up and down the Malecón, and it was well past midnight before he got to bed.

Two days later he slept on the plane going down to Camagüey. Some turbulence in the air woke him, but he slumped in his seat pretending to still be asleep, so he wouldn't have to talk to anyone. That night, if he got back to Havana in time, he'd go over to Clare's and read Alameda a story, perhaps fall asleep as Clare cooked him dinner. This lack of sleep was getting serious! Instead of looking forward to Clare's kisses, he was dreaming of a nap.

Camagüey was peaceful, just as he had assured Fidel. He appointed Agustín Méndez Sierra as interim head of the province. He stopped by the Agrarian Reform offices, he went to the radio station and spoke on the air about the importance of this wealthy cattle province and of its duty to the nation. He picked up a box of papers for Maria Luisa, Huber's wife. Then he was done and ready to go home. But his plane, he found, was no longer in Camagüey. Raúl had insisted that the pilot fly on to Santiago and deliver a captain to his regiment. This was pure Raúl, secretive and unpredictable, asserting his control where he could.

Late in the afternoon, Camilo went to sleep at the army camp in a padded chair. Moments later a sergeant woke him, handing him a telephone at the end of a long cord. It was Fidel, and he was angry. "¿*Una siesta?*" he cried. "¿*Que coño estás tomando siesta en esta hora?*" If he'd finished his work, why wasn't he on his way back to the capital? Didn't he understand this was a perilous moment for the Revolution, that Huber Matos was a threat and Camilo should be in Havana?

"*No seas—*" Camilo was about to say *Don't be an idiot*, but Fidel was inflamed and his temper renowned. So he only said, "You're the one who sent me down here, and against my advice. It was that brother of yours who sent my pilot to Santiago. I'll head back as soon as he picks me up."

But Fidel had run off the edge of reason. "*Get some other plane!*" he yelled. "Get on a train, find a car, however you want but get back here! I need you to help form the tribunal for that *cabrón* Matos. I don't care how you come but *get moving.*"

"Okay, Fidel. I'm coming."

Sometimes it was easier to agree with Fidel than argue with him. Luciano, the pilot, was due back at five with his Cessna. Camilo would get on it and they'd be in Havana that evening. He wasn't going to drive through the night, or get on a train for ten hours. What was Fidel talking about?

It worried him, because Fidel was no fool. He was an endlessly calculating tactician, and now he was talking nonsense. Camilo paced around the regiment headquarters, he answered some questions from Méndez Sierra on the phone, and finally dismissed him. "Enough," he said. "Do the best you can."

It was Raúl who made him nervous, for he was the one who'd set up this delay with his plane. Something was going on, and Camilo couldn't figure out what it was. Ever since Fidel put his brother in charge of the army, Camilo felt threatened. He had wondered, even, if after Huber Matos he might be next.

At five-thirty the chief of the airport called to say that Luciano had landed and would soon be refueled. Camilo climbed into a jeep and sped out to the airport, but he could not relax. He felt trapped. At Huber's trial he would have to stand up in court and say what Fidel wanted him to say. He might speak against the death penalty, but Raúl would be eloquent about why it was necessary. Camilo hated all of it. He felt as if he'd been walked to the edge of a cliff with the Castro brothers behind him, pushing him on.

At the airport he found the twin-engined Cessna waiting in front of a hanger. Luciano was inside the terminal, drinking coffee from a tiny cup. He stood up immediately, but Camilo signaled for a pair of shots for himself, and downed them hot as he stood beside the counter. Within a minute he felt the first pure liquor of animation. "The time has come," he said. "Let's get out of here."

Luciano had already done the pre-flight inspection. They settled into their seats, the pilot checked his instruments and called the tower for clearance, and at one minute after six the Cessna took off into the softened light of dusk.

25

CLARE waited. She was paying the price, Natalia would have said, for trampling the laws of romance. She had withheld nothing from Camilo, and now didn't know when she'd hear from him again. Wednesday passed, Thursday, she was a fool for having told him to come at any hour, because once he heard that he didn't come at all.

On Friday morning as she and Ala were eating breakfast, she heard a faint knock on the door. She opened it to find a young girl she knew from the neighborhood, a girl of twelve who'd always been eager for a glimpse of Camilo. Now she stood folded into herself, her face contorted.

"What is it?"

The girl lifted her right hand, in which she clutched a newspaper. Its large black headline read *DESAPARECE CAMILO.* Clare grabbed the paper as the girl slumped to the floor. On Wednesday the 28th, Camilo and his pilot had taken off from Camagüey at six in the evening, bound for Havana. The plane had disappeared—*two days ago*—and a search was now underway between the two cities and over the sea as well. "If he is alive in this nation," Fidel was quoted, "we will find him. Every citizen will help, every resource will be applied, and nothing will be withheld."

Clare dropped to her knees as if hit by a plank. She toppled onto the floor beside the moaning girl. From the first instant she knew that Camilo was dead, and that Fidel had killed him. She gasped. She took her first breaths. She would get to Fidel and kill *him*. She would find Raúl and kill him too. Something stirred beside her, and Clare remembered the girl. She jabbed with her heels until the waif got up and left. Then twisting her head, she spilled a thick pale vomit onto the red floor tiles. It pooled there, the color of flesh against blood.

Ala stood beside her but away from the mess on the floor, pleading with her to get up.

Clare managed to get to her feet, but there was no hope. She never had a minute of it. She stumbled through the days that followed, with Ala hanging from her neck, holding onto her clothes, calling out for her if she took five steps away. Ala's school was closed, businesses were closed, the entire island was paralyzed. Every day Fidel appeared on the radio and television. Every day he flew back and forth over the provinces of Las Villas and Matanzas. He appeared in a photo with Camilo's parents, the three of them staring intently into the sky, as if at any moment the missing plane might fly into view. It was a staged picture that made Clare weep. That *coño cabrón*, that son of a whore Fidel. From Raúl not a word, but the two of them had done it together, she was sure.

On the third day a rumor swept through the city that Camilo had been found alive. People poured into the streets, dancing and setting off fireworks. Clare walked among them, watchful and disbelieving, holding Ala in her arms. There had been no word from Fidel or the government, and the rumor ran unchecked. The next morning, another headline: *UNA BOLA MALDITA*—a terrible rumor. The plane had not been found, Camilo and his pilot remained missing, and only a day later Fidel called off the search.

Clare hadn't realized how many people knew about her and Camilo. Sitting outside in the park with Ala, one woman after another approached her. They wanted to commiserate, they touched her shoulder or hand. Clare let them touch her and say what they liked, but if they wanted her to respond she picked up Ala and left. The girl seemed to understand. She grew less willful, even as she asked for more of Clare's attention. The one person Clare let into their lives was Natalia, who climbed the stairs from her shop three or four times a day, opened the unlocked door and lay down with Clare on her narrow bed. They wept together, and Ala soon joined in, climbing on top of them and adding her high-pitched wails.

For a week Clare ate nothing. She fed Ala what food she had in the house, bought her *fritatas* from a nearby stand, and they went to sleep at the same time every night. At five in the morning Clare woke to the roosters. For a moment she clung to whatever she'd been dreaming, then the truth slammed her again: *He's dead*. She lay waiting for the sunrise, recoiling from the light when it came and from the early sounds of the city. When she got up, her chest ached as if someone had been clubbing her ribs.

Finally, with little food left in the house, she took her shopping bag in one hand, Ala in the other, and went out to the market. They stopped first at the fruit stand, where Clare ordered two glasses of pineapple juice and found she couldn't taste either hers or Ala's. She swished some around in her mouth, but nothing. She smelled the juice and there was no odor. Beside her, Ala drank from her glass. Several other customers stood at the bar or sat at tables, and none of them looked worried or suspicious. Clare asked the bar girl for a banana, peeled it and took a bite. It felt like a banana, it squooshed up in her mouth like a banana, but it could have been wet paper. She spat it out in her hand, walked to the curb and shook it off. She wiped her hand on her pants, paid her bill and took Ala to the market. There she bought plantains and beans, oranges and papayas and some chicken. She felt the rasp of the plantains, felt the dense chicken through its white paper, but could not imagine eating any of it.

That night, after feeding Ala dinner, Clare explored what remained in her cupboards. Vinegar and minced garlic, normally so pungent, smelled like air. An orange had no taste. Salt had no taste. She gave up and lay on her bed, letting Ala go to sleep beside her, the girl's hair and body unwashed after another night without a bath.

She needed to get away from her daughter. She felt guilty but had to do it. She wanted to walk through the city alone, to sink into her worst grief. It lay waiting for her, Clare knew—but she didn't want to scare Alameda. Finally she called Rosa and asked her to come the next morning and stay for a day and night. She didn't know what she'd do or where she'd go— just away.

Lying on her bed, all desire was beyond her reach, as far removed as taste and smell. She couldn't remember sex with Camilo or anyone else. Why had she ever bothered? All she wanted now was to sleep, and sleep wouldn't come. She didn't want to die, she didn't want to live, she didn't want anything.

Ala was glad to see Rosa. The girl could tell, Clare thought, that here was someone whole. Rosa had endured, she'd survived the death of her own child, and Ala turned to her as if to a life raft. Clare, the lost and negligent mother, gave her daughter a hug, grabbed Camilo's straw hat that he'd left behind on his last visit, and walked out the door.

Outside, the alien world had nothing to offer. She walked, she kept going, but every person, every dog and bird and building felt wrong. She sat down finally in a distant park on a wooden bench under a lone magnolia, took off her hat with its Cuban flag and stared down at her legs and her brown arms as if looking at someone else's body.

Walking again, she found no comfort anywhere. She hated the cars on the street, those steel cages with people inside. She hated the racks of bread displayed at the bakery, hated the juice stands and the bees hovering over half-empty glasses. She hated the sky and the hot midday sun that cooked the pavement beneath her feet. Worst of all, she hated the posters of Camilo that now hung from telephone poles and streetlights throughout the city, showing his long-nosed Galician face and the gun in his hands, his Thompson, that she had once stuck down a toilet bowl. Already they were turning him into a martyr, destined to be glorified, not remembered. This was how they would forget him, these sly Cubans with their terrible capacity for happiness. She recoiled from all of them. She watched strolling couples, kids playing soccer, old men hunched over sidewalk games of dominoes, and everyone looked false. She shrank from the pigeons that clapped up into the rosy sunset, from the dusk that fell like a platter, from the windless night that followed. The dark brought no escape from the only truth that mattered.

She walked, sometimes staggered down the middle of streets. Late that night on a quiet block, his name escaped her in a scream: *¡Camilo!* A few people came to their doors but said nothing, only watched her pass by under the streetlights in her sandals and rayon dress and tattered hat. It looked crazy on her, but that's what she wanted. She turned the corner into the next street. *¡Camilo! ¡Camilo Cienfuegos!*

Like anyone in the city, she headed for solace to the Malecón, with its curve of yellow lights and eternal waves slapping in from the dark. She walked for miles. Long after midnight she stumbled onto the portico of a building that faced the sea, and on its bare tiles she lay down and went to sleep—to be wakened in the first light by the scritch of a street sweeper's broom. He was working along the gutter, cleaning out leaves and paper. Clare watched him without raising her head. At the sight of her open eyes he said *Buenos dias*, then continued down the street.

This was how it would be. The city, the whole country would make do without Camilo, and she would be left, hating that he had vanished, hating that everyone else—even she—would go on living.

26

Pain, then nothing.

Pain again, instant and hard. As soon as *he* was here, the pain was here.

Pain again, long enough to know he was lying down. Where? He tried to move but couldn't. The ends of his fingers felt something, maybe cloth. He was on a bed. There were faces above him.

Every breath he took seared his throat. Someone took his hand and squeezed it, but when he tried to squeeze back to show them how much he hurt, they all looked happy. They hovered over him and gave little cries. Why were they happy when the pain was so bad? He closed his eyes and left.

He came back. The pain was the same. The people were women. They were—what? He couldn't remember the word. What was wrong with him? There was a name for them but he couldn't remember it. He had other words. He remembered *cama* and *mano*. He remembered *garganta*, his throat that ached at every breath.

He went away. He came back. They were *enfermeras*, and they were taking care of him. They liked it when he looked around, when he hurt, when he moved his fingers. *Los dedos*. He needed words to think and it was hard to get hold of them.

They asked him how he was. He said, with just his lips, "*Me duele.*" It hurts.

They bent closer. He watched their hair and ears and little caps. Their *gorras*. He had words, but sometimes the pain wouldn't let them come. "*Me duele.*"

They nodded. "We know," they said. But they didn't.

He slept and woke and slept again.

They called him Armando. He didn't think that was his name—but all names had left him. He had parents, but their names were out of reach. Even their faces wouldn't come to him. He knew *plato* now, and *sopa* and *sangre*. He was in a hospital. There were nurses and doctors. Somewhere there was someone he hated. Who was it? There was a woman he wanted to see, but who? She had no name, no face, and even if she were here he couldn't touch her. He couldn't touch anyone, because all touch was pain. Still, when he hurt he learned things.

He had come here from somewhere. He tried to remember, but soon the pain was too much and he left.

The pain was on his left side, on his chest and neck and face and the one place he could see, the back of his left hand, which was bandaged. *Pecho, nuca, cara, mano, vendas.* His back hurt, too, whenever he moved. The nurses told him he was burned.

They held him down. They told him it would hurt but they had to do it. They scraped his pain, they dug at it, they dragged their fingernails across his skin. That's what it felt like. That, or a board full of nails jerked across his burns. He screamed and told them to stop. He told them to let him die, anything but this pain.

Later they did it again. Every day they had to do it, sometimes twice a day.

"We'll help you with the pain," they said, but the pain didn't change. Maybe a little, for a few moments, but then they scraped his raw skin. Every day the cleaning, the debridement. "We have to do it," they said. They feared infection, which could enter through dead skin. With no blood supply, the medicine couldn't reach the wounds. He heard the words and understood them: to fight infections the dead skin had to be removed by raking it with nails.

A doctor came and told him his body was thirty percent burned. This was serious, but they were sure now he'd survive—if they did the cleaning. They'd kept him in a coma for a month, but now he was conscious and they knew the pain was bad, so they were giving him morphine every day. The second-degree burns were the ones that hurt. But he had third-degree burns as well, with skin that wouldn't grow again on its own. They would fix that later, with grafts. His back was burned but the worst of it was in front, and every day they logrolled him back and forth. The cleaning was essential, he would die without it, and they understood how painful it was.

They didn't. They couldn't.

The doctor told him he was responding well. Being young and strong helped, and now his lungs were working fine, even if his throat still ached.

He didn't feel young or strong. He could hardly move, and when he did it was agony. Day and night he lay in bed. He pissed where he lay. He shit where he lay and a nurse cleaned him up. He looked away. None of them spoke when they cleaned his ass, except to coo at the end that it was done.

Who was he?

He was Armando, they said.

How old was he?

They looked at his chart. Twenty-seven, they said.

What happened? How did he get here?

There was a plane crash, that's all they knew.

He remembered a plane, or something about a plane, but no crash.

He woke and found a man sitting on a chair beside the bed. The man seemed to know him, he said "Hello Armando, how are you doing?" Armando still didn't sound right. The man was short and well-dressed, he wore a coat and tie. His name was Pepe. "Here in this country," he said, "everyone calls me Don Pepe."

"Do you know me?"

"We have met," the man said. "It will come back to you. The doctors tell me it will all come back in time."

Instead it was pain that came back, a wave of it that filled the room. He couldn't think anymore, he had to breathe, and breathe, and keep breathing. Without that he would die.

The man called a doctor, and sometime later the pain eased. He floated above it. He could look down at it, look down at his body on the bed, and the pain was in the body but it was separate from him.

The man sat by his bed. Again he called him Armando.

"I don't think that's my name."

"It's what we call you here. I'm going to tell you your name from before, but it would be best not to use it."

"Why?"

"I will explain. Your name was Camilo."

Camilo, of course! He'd forgotten his own name. *Coño*, this was bad.

"Do you remember Cuba, and Fidel Castro?"

"Fidel, I love Fidel. Am I in Havana?"

"You're in San José, Costa Rica. Your plane crashed near the coast six weeks ago."

"And you?"

"They called me because it was a Cuban plane. We brought you here in a helicopter."

It was coming back now, in glimpses. He'd been flying in a plane. "My pilot," Camilo said. "Captain—what is his name?"

"Luciano Fariñas."

"Where is he?"

"I'm sorry, he died in the crash. Again, it would be better if you didn't talk about it to the nurses and doctors."

"Why?"

"The world believes you are dead. All Cuba believes this. You flew here at night, unannounced. In Miami, the exiles say you had trouble with Fidel."

"I don't remember."

"Just in case, I brought you here under a different name, and I had the plane dismantled. We have buried Captain Fariñas. I would like to notify his family, but I can't."

"Why does everyone think I'm dead?"

"Because your plane disappeared."

All of it confused him. He had parents, but could not remember what they looked like. There was a woman, but who was she? He didn't want to ask this stranger about her. "So I am—Armando?"

"Armando Benitez, as long as you like. I have all the papers. If you choose to be Camilo Cienfuegos again, there is no problem. I have only done it to protect you."

Camilo sank back against his pillow, his history a blur. *Six weeks* ago. He could still barely tell when a day came and went. "And you," he said. "Do I know you?"

"You used to." Don Pepe smiled. "We met in the Habana Libre hotel, after Fidel called me a bad democrat and a bad friend."

Camilo said nothing. He remembered nothing.

"You came with a young woman, an American."

"*Clare*," Camilo said, her name coming to him instantly. But not her face, not her body. It was maddening.

"An intelligent woman, and pretty. She reminded me of my wife, who is also from the United States."

Camilo wanted to think about this woman Clare. He closed his eyes and tried to will her back through the pain. She was tall, he thought, but he could not be sure. Had they gone somewhere in a car together? This was agony within agony, not to remember anything, not to know anything.

When he opened his eyes the man was still there. Don Pepe. Once he learned something in the hospital he did not forget it. Don Pepe hadn't moved at all, he'd simply waited. He was a gentle man, Camilo could see.

"How long will I be here? How long until I am better?"

"A long time, I'm afraid. When you are stronger you must start your grafts. The dead skin that has not separated must be removed, and new skin grafted on from other parts of your body. It has to be done."

Just the talk of it sent a wave of fear through his body.

"It prevents infection and limits the scarring, which will be important to you. For those operations you'll be given anesthesia, and you'll have the two best specialists in Costa Rica. Both of them worked at the Burn Unit at Mass General in Boston, and they know what's best."

He couldn't speak. His skin, teeth and entire body ached.. He could not keep back a moan.

Don Pepe disappeared and came back with a nurse. "You can have some morphine now, but there's a limit to it."

The nurse added it to a line that ran into his arm. Don Pepe talked on but Camilo wasn't listening. Already the pain was easing, once again he was floating above it.

He could sit up and feed himself. He could even walk to the bathroom. There was no mirror there, and they wouldn't give him one to look at his face. His chest was horrible when they took off the bandages to clean his skin. It looked as if a lizard had crawled onto him and died. He wanted to see his neck and face, but couldn't. He stared at the back of a soup spoon to catch a reflection, but it was only a blur. He was not allowed to touch his wounds. "Very dangerous," they said. "You must not, absolutely."

"And my face?" he asked one of the nurses. She wasn't one of the young ones, but an older woman he thought might tell him the truth.

"It's not too bad."

"Like my chest?"

"Oh no, your chest is third-degree. The burns aren't as deep on your neck or face. Or on your back. Those are almost healed."

She could be lying about his face. "What about my chest, how do you think that looks?"

"I've seen worse—but pretty bad. The doctors will work on it, they'll make it look better."

"And my neck?"

She wiggled her hand, she didn't want to say. From this he knew that it too was bad. When he moved his head his neck felt crusty and painful. "Second- and third-degree mixed," she said. "That's why it hurts so much."

Young or old, he was glad to be surrounded by these Costa Rican nurses. Some were dark-skinned, some light, some were blacks from the Caribbean coast. Some were thin, some bulged within their uniforms. They walked around in squeaky shoes and starched white dresses, their hair pulled back from their faces. The younger ones were not as assured. They could swab away at his chest or back, and work their way up his neck, but the closer they got to his face the quieter they became. They bent their heads and their mouths tightened. He didn't imagine kissing them. He didn't imagine holding their hands—what could he do with a woman now?—but he hated to see them look afraid.

He tried to remember more about Clare. She had a child, a little girl. They lived in Havana, he thought. Somewhere in Havana.

As the morphine came on, before he forgot everything, he liked to think about this Clare. He had slept with her, he was sure. He remembered lying on her bed, not talking but naked late at night. There was comfort in this vision. Maybe it was the morphine that made him feel so good, but he didn't care.

He asked for news of Cuba, and Don Pepe told him about Huber Matos. Camilo remembered him. He was a friend from the Sierra, they were both *comandantes*.

"You took him from Camagüey to Havana," Don Pepe said. "Castro put him in jail and now they're going to try him."

"For what?"

"Treason. Raúl is calling for his death."

"That's what he always wants."

How did he know this? But he was sure of it, and he remembered Raúl all right. Remembered Raúl pointing a gun at him. Remembered, too, how Raúl had taken over his job as head of the Cuban Army. But what neither Don Pepe nor Camilo could figure out was why he'd flown to Costa Rica. What had happened to make his pilot head so far south?

He had to figure this out, had to remember what brought him here. In his easy moments, as the morphine took hold, he now thought of Huber Matos, of Fidel and Raúl and what happened before the crash. He gave up the pleasure of lying in bed with a woman so he could focus on how he got here.

Slowly, over weeks, some images came back to him.

There was a suitcase. At first it was just the sensation of the suitcase on his lap, not heavy but somehow wrong. It was a small suitcase made of soft red leather. For a long time that was all he could remember. Over days and nights the memory filtered back, until he saw the little suitcase in the plane's luggage compartment. He'd moved his yoke aside and crawled into the back seats, looking for something to eat. Luciano had never seen the suitcase before—but there it was on the plane, and later on his own legs.

Don Pepe brought more news from Cuba. "The country is in an uproar. The trial of Huber Matos has begun, with Fidel claiming that he betrayed the Revolution."

"He only wanted to resign from the army. He wrote Fidel and told him. But Fidel knew he was no communist."

"Neither were you, I believe."

The past tense stung. He was no communist, it was true—but he'd given everything to the Revolution. "Fidel would never put me on trial."

"As it turned out, he didn't have to."

"It's Raúl who hates me."

Don Pepe watched him but said nothing.

Three days later he returned to Camilo's room and announced, "They gave him twenty years."

By then Camilo had reeled in the memory of his two trips to Camagüey and his arrest of Huber Matos. Another day passed in his hospital bed, then another. The suitcase was the key, he was sure. He remembered hauling it over the seat and onto his lap. It wasn't his, he'd brought nothing with him but a briefcase. He remembered trying to open it, flipping the two hasps but finding the lock closed. He remembered sticking the point of his knife in the lock, and breaking the tip. Now, just lying in his Costa Rican bed as he tried to call it all back, he felt nervous. Another day passed. He'd jammed the broken blade under one of the brass latches and pried, enough to get his fingers into the gap. Pulling at the two halves of the suitcase, he worked his way toward the lock in the center. He was sweating and nervous. With a sharp crack the top of the suitcase flew open. *Son of a whore.* Cushioned on some balled-up newsprint were four sticks of dynamite tied together with strips of cloth, and a fat alarm clock, its secondhand slowly revolving behind glass.

Once that dam broke, the rest poured back. Luciano stared down in horror. *"What is it?"*

"It's a bomb."

The pilot's voice rose in panic. *"Can you turn it off?"*

"I don't know."

"Who has done this?"

"That *comemierda* Raúl."

Camilo, beneath his anger, was terrified. His legs began to shake.

He told Don Pepe none of this. First he had to think it through, and he had plenty of time, for the doctors had started the grafts. As Don Pepe had promised, these were carried out under anesthesia. Where the dead skin hadn't sloughed off it had to be removed with a razor, down to the living tissue. In some places they went down to the underlying fat, even to the fascia that covered the muscles. The blood loss was great, and when he emerged from the anesthesia he could hardly move. It was better that he didn't. From other parts of his body—from donor sites on his buttocks and the inside of his thighs—they removed thin sheets of skin to transplant onto the tissue beneath his burns, and those sites were pure pain.

At night they put his hands in paper mittens and bound them to the bed so he wouldn't touch his wounds while he slept.

In these days he thought less of Clare. What sustained him through the grafts was anger. By now he knew he was going to get better, and when he did he'd go back and kill Raúl. But first he had to remember everything.

The suitcase haunted him. It was the feel of it on his lap, with the dense sticks of dynamite and the clock with its deadly secondhand. On his march across the plains of Las Villas he'd had an expert with him, Sergio, and they'd blown up some bridges and once a truck full of gasoline. But Sergio had done all the work with the timers, and now, staring at the bomb, Camilo had no idea how to disarm it.

"I have to throw it out," he told Luciano.

"The door won't open. Not at this speed."

"Then slow down."

"Wait until I tell you."

They rose in a sickening upward lunge. At the top of the arc, with his eyes on his instruments, Luciano said, "Sixty miles an hour. *Open the door.*"

Camilo unlatched it and tried to push it open with his elbow. Air screamed in as he pushed the suitcase away from him, trying to keep it level—but the door wouldn't open far enough. He had no leverage. He turned his face away.

"*Do it now.* We have to have more speed!"

The bomb was going to go off in his lap. He was trembling, and the plane gathering speed.

"*Get it out!*" Luciano cried.

He twisted, lifted a foot to the door and pushed. The crack opened, he turned the suitcase on its side and slid it through, and the door slammed shut. They waited for the explosion but nothing came. Luciano pulled them out of their dive, sweating and cursing, and they flew on over the dark ground below, over the isolated lights of small Cuban towns. Far to the west lay the last red light of day, a thin line between clouds and sea.

Luciano checked his flaps, his rudder controls, his instruments. Wild-eyed, he looked across at Camilo. "What will we tell them in Havana?"

"Are you kidding?" Camilo almost laughed. The bomb was gone and he still had his legs, his balls, everything. "Raúl Castro, the new head of the Cuban Army, just tried to kill us. If we land in Havana he'll have me shot, and since you know everything he'll shoot you too."

"Then where? Back to Camagüey?"

"Luciano, wake up. *They're going to shoot you.* Raúl doesn't care. He's shot hundreds already. To live we must leave the country. As of this minute, we are exiles."

They droned on over a dark Cuba.

"Where can we go?" Luciano asked. "The Dominican Republic?"

"Trujillo would love that. He'd stick us in prison and ask for ransom. Or he'd shoot us himself."

"But you are Camilo Cienfuegos!"

His fall from grace still wasn't clear to the pilot. "I have no command," Camilo said. "Raúl is in charge and all my men from the Sierra have been disbanded. I should have seen where this was going. What's the range of this plane? Can we reach Costa Rica?"

"Florida is closer."

"Not the United States. I am no *gusano.*"

Luciano took out his maps. He measured, he divided some numbers on his pre-flight clipboard and said, "We could reach Nicaragua."

The guy knew nothing. "Somoza would be worse than Trujillo. He'd claim we were invading his country. It has to be Costa Rica."

"Not at this altitude. If we go up near the ceiling, perhaps we can make it. But we have no oxygen and the heater doesn't work. At nineteen thousand feet we'd freeze."

"Go up now. Turn south."

Luciano was right about the cold. There were a pair of jackets in back and Camilo dug them out, but within minutes his fingers were stiff and his breath labored. He felt like Che with his asthma. Finally they leveled out as high as the plane could fly. Stars above, the ocean black below and only once a ship, its dots of light far to the north.

"My wife," Luciano said miserably. "My children."

"This is what happens."

They flew, shivering in their jackets. Their breaths, growing thinner, emerged in wispy clouds. After two hours of cold and darkness, Camilo saw that Luciano was no longer in control of his trembling legs.

"Are we getting close?"

The pilot checked his gauges. He looked at a map but the scale was small. "We're not going to have much fuel. There's an airport in Puerto Limón, but that's too far to the south. I can't find anything between the coast and San José."

"Head for the capital. But we better drop down, it's too cold up here." He didn't want Luciano to pass out.

At three hundred feet the nighttime warmth was delicious. After twenty minutes Luciano said "*Look*, we're going to make it! You see that white streak? That's the beach."

"Can we get to San José?"

"I don't know if we have enough fuel."

"Can we put down on the sand?"

"Bad idea, because if it's soft the plane will flip. We should look for a road."

The beach grew closer, with a whiter line of waves. In a flash they were past it, the land ahead even darker than the ocean.

"Slow down," Camilo said.

"Any slower and we'll stall."

"*There*, what's *that*?"

To their left a paler streak ran parallel to their course. Luciano gave the plane some gas and banked, then dropped lower. "This might work," he said. He banked the other way, straightening out above the road—until they saw the pavement ripple. The pilot cried *"No! It's a river!"* and poured on the gas. Too late, they lifted a few meters, clipped a treetop and slammed into the canopy.

The skin grafts continued. They went on for weeks, a month, another month. The donor sites healed as if they were second-degree burns themselves, after which they were harvested again.

His neck and chin took the longest. They didn't want to excise any flesh there, hoping to preserve more tissue so the scarring wouldn't be as bad. The painful cleanings continued, each session a torture. When the dead skin finally lifted, they applied a mesh of donor skin, holding it down with dressings and adhesive strips. The pain never stopped. He knew it was coming but never got over the fear of it. His life was pain, dreams of revenge, and sometimes as a kind of dessert, a long reverie of Clare.

He pulled her to him late at night, when the hospital was quiet and his pain controlled. In these waking dreams he lay beside her and watched her face. Only that. He didn't kiss or touch her. Touching anyone for pleasure was still nothing he could imagine. He saw her upper lip with the lightest wisp of hair on it, her faintly crooked lower teeth, the delicate folds of her ears and the strands of hair she tucked behind them. She had a tiny scar below one temple, from when she was ten and flew off a bicycle. He had her face now in every detail, and whenever he wanted he could have the rest.

Though he longed to be well, he also thought, *What good will it do?* He could go back to Cuba and kill Raúl—but what could follow after that?

He felt miserable about Luciano's death, and said this one night to Don Pepe. The next morning a priest appeared in his room, speaking about forgiveness and the generosity of Christ. Feelings of guilt helped no one, the young priest said. Besides, there was a larger plan, and Camilo should use the life he'd been granted to do his best for mankind and himself.

Camilo nodded. He thanked the priest for his concern. But he had never been devout, and the priest must have seen it. The two men sat for a time in silence, facing each other in chairs beside the hospital bed. "Sometimes," the priest said, "those who suffer and can see no way out, even through Christ, have escaped their trials by imagining themselves to be in a more peaceful place. In a garden, perhaps, or on a beach, or even inside a church. A place where everything would be easier to bear."

"The most peaceful place is morphine, but they give me less and less."

"I mean a place for your soul, which morphine cannot help."

Camilo had long hated the Cuban church for its craven support of Fulgencio Batista. Still, this priest was not insistent, and suggested something that didn't sound religious at all. So that night he tried it. He imagined himself sitting in the small garden behind his parents' house, where he'd played as a child. He imagined a grassy spot on the Almendares River where they sometimes went on Sundays with a basket of food. He imagined himself stretched out on the beach where he'd gone with Clare, the beach with the pelicans. He tried to *be* a pelican, sweeping over the water in an easy glide. None of it worked. His agitation grew, and the pain was no less.

His only escape was his dream of punishing Raúl. That's how he disappeared from himself and the agony of his skin. He plotted his return. He imagined all the ways he might surprise Raúl: how he would find him alone and knock him to the ground and smash his face with the stock of a rifle, the barrel of a pistol, with his boot, a chair, an iron pan grabbed from a stove. Each fantasy culminated in a beating that ended in death. In all of this Raúl had a chest and arms and legs, but Camilo ignored them. He only beat on Raúl's head and face, on his darting eyes and nearly beardless cheeks. He rained blows on his skull, he broke it apart and spilled gobs of brains on the ground. Then, magically, Raúl healed and could be smashed again.

Camilo was sure that Christ could not help him. God could not help him because God did not exist. When the pain was bad only rage would help, only revenge. He'd given the Revolution everything and it had spat him out. He missed Cuba—and at the same time, with a cold eye, saw how much he missed his life there as a famous revolutionary. He hated being no one, a *fulano de tal.* In this stark little hospital room, living without strength or beauty, he missed his former life like a drug, like his painkillers when they were late in coming.

27

WHY, Camilo asked Don Pepe, had he helped him so much? Don Pepe stood with his back to the window. "I am grateful to you. You were famous for your loyalty to the Revolution, yet in Havana you came to me and apologized for what Fidel said. I am fascinated by Fidel. He went into the Sierra with a dozen men, and in two years he drove Batista out of Cuba. He's a genius, and all who resist him are crushed."

"I've lost my faith in the Revolution," Camilo said." Perhaps it will come back, but I don't see how. I'm less of a man now. I no longer care about Cuba and the poor. I think only of my own pain, and of going back to kill Raúl." He passed his fingers over his neck and chest. "Every day that's what I dream of."

Don Pepe nodded. He was a short, even-tempered man. He came less often now to the hospital, every four or five days, but he still came. Today he'd brought some orchids from his farm at Tarrazú. "I understand your desire," he said. "But if Raúl tried to kill you once, won't he do so again? And how could you get into Cuba without anyone knowing you're there?"

"They all know me with a beard—and they don't know me burned. Don Pepe, let's go for a walk outside. They let me out yesterday for the first time."

The Hospital San Juan de Dios had a cobbled drive in front and a few patches of spiky grass. Camilo thought he could walk a block or two, but soon, breathing hard and afraid he might fall, he leaned on Don Pepe, who led him to a bench. Ashamed of being so weak, he recovered slowly. Fidel Castro, he knew, would have had no interest in anyone so infirm. Don Pepe was a more patient man by far. A better man, Camilo thought.

"In this country," he asked, "can you do anything you wish? Can you give this Armando Benitez, this man you have created, a Costa Rican passport?"

"Very simple. We'd need a good photo, and perhaps it's too soon for that."

"I'm in no hurry. But I've also wondered, after all this surgery, if perhaps these doctors could remake my face a little."

"I suppose."

"My nose has always been too large."

"Cosmetic surgery for the revolutionary hero! Excuse me Camilo, I shouldn't laugh, but there's some humor to this, surely."

"If it's too much money I can go to work, I will repay you."

"There's no need, because health care in Costa Rica is free for everyone."

"Even for this kind of surgery?"

"Don't worry, the doctors are my friends."

"Everyone here is your friend, isn't it so?"

"Like you in Cuba."

"Not anymore," Camilo said. He didn't say it bitterly, but it put a gap in the conversation.

Don Pepe waited it out, unruffled. Camilo liked how he rarely tried to cheer him up, and never assured him that all would be fine with his scars. He'd heard enough of that from the doctors and nurses, and didn't trust them. Don Pepe accepted the disaster, accepted the scars and looked past them.

"What about Clare?" he asked.

"I hope to find her some day."

"In Havana?"

"She loves Cuba, but I don't know if she'll stay. Fidel wasn't friendly to her."

"He was no friend to me!" Don Pepe said. "But I get along fine without him."

A week later Don Pepe's wife, Doña Karen, came to visit. Dressed in a dark skirt and jacket, she entered the room alone, shook Camilo's hand and told him how glad she was that he was doing better. Her accent was pure Costa Rica, her Spanish so good she could have done the news on television. After her first few words she bent down for a good look at his burns, or what could be seen of them above his hospital gown.

"Bad," she announced, "but good that it didn't reach your mouth or eyes. I hear the cleaning is very painful."

"Three bullets have passed through me, and they were nothing compared to this."

She sat on a stiff-backed chair, upright, her eyes on his. He was ashamed of having mentioned his old scars, and of complaining about the new.

"Don Pepe tells me you have a story like our own. That like us, you and your *novia* met in New York."

Camilo told her about his weeks in Manhattan with Clare. Also, how she'd come to see him on his first day back in Havana, a day of delirium.

Doña Karen sat still. She was younger than Don Pepe, but of the same tranquil demeanor. She didn't tap or move her fingers, didn't cross or uncross her legs. "Perhaps your friend would like to visit us here in Costa Rica."

"With me this burned? I don't think so."

"A woman can surprise you."

He sat with this. He wanted to hear it, but didn't believe it.

"Clare has a daughter, three years old, and I am the father." This was something neither he nor Clare had told Don Pepe. "Her name is Alameda, and for the first two years of her life I knew nothing about her. I only met her in Cuba."

"Do you love this girl?"

Doña Karen's look was inquisitive, almost neutral. He said, "I no longer know what I'm capable of. I was not that good at domestic life."

She laughed at that. "I know men often fear it, yet many have harnessed the horse to the cart and found it rewarding. Well, now you can see that I'm talking like a farmer. I've just come back from a tour of Guanacaste, our northern province. I think much depends on what you hope for in life."

"Or what you can get."

He found himself explaining to this young and confident woman that not everything had gone smoothly with Clare. That among other things, he'd been friends with too many women.

"You don't mean friends."

"No."

Doña Karen considered this. "Perhaps now there will be fewer."

There seemed no insult to this terrible statement. It was simply what lay ahead for him. He'd known this for months—that of course there would be fewer women. For the rest of his life there might be none at all.

"You are suffering," Doña Karen said, "but I imagine that Clare is too."

A nurse entered, took three steps into the room and stopped, then started to back out. "*Doña Karen,*" she said.

"Come in, come in, don't mind me."

"Oh, it is such an honor. My sister was at your House of Hope. I have only to take his blood pressure and temperature."

"Every two hours," Camilo explained. "Even in the middle of the night."

After the nurse left, Doña Karen stood up. "When you leave the hospital, Don Pepe and I hope that you'll come to stay with us on the farm. There's a little house you can have, and we could use some help with the rope cooperative. It wouldn't be too strenuous, and I think you'd like to see how we work. We're somewhat like socialists here in Costa Rica. Fidel wouldn't think so, but this is Don Pepe's vision of an enlightened democracy. It's worth seeing."

Camilo thanked her. He didn't tell her that he wouldn't be able to stay for long, that as soon as possible he'd figure out a way to get back to Cuba and take his revenge. Perhaps her husband had already told her about this plan, but Camilo didn't think she'd approve of the idea any more than Don Pepe. As for finding Clare, he'd think about that later. First to come would be Raúl's punishment, then some future he could not imagine.

The name of the Figueres farm was *La Lucha sin Fin,* The Struggle without End. "That's how everything good happens," Don Pepe told Camilo as they drove out to Tarrazú on the day he was released from the hospital. "You have a goal and you keep at it."

"A dictator might say the same."

Don Pepe laughed. "I suppose you're right. I named the place when I was young, and since then many jokes have been made about it. Still, my best ideas have all come to me there on the farm. I hope, Armando—as I will continue to call you, until you correct me—that you will drop the *Don*. In public even my wife calls me Don Pepe, but among friends just Pepe is fine."

His farm was vast. A thousand campesinos grew and processed coffee, as well as the manila they turned into rope. The manila growers were sharecroppers, but free to sell their crop to anyone. Almost all sold to his mill. "Because I pay a fair price," Pepe said. "There's a dairy, and those with children get free milk. Vegetables, too."

The workers lived in small wooden houses, and Camilo's was only distinguished from the others by having an inside bathroom with a toilet and sink. Like the rest, it had a cold-water outdoor shower screened by latticed panels.

"It's not much," Pepe said, as he showed Camilo around. "But there's a bed and a little table where you can work or write letters. This was the house of one of my first managers. When he came to work in the factory he couldn't read or write. And guess where he is now? At the university, studying to become a lawyer. A campesino who will be a lawyer! We're very proud of him here."

Camilo wondered if that's what Pepe hoped for him: a return to school —he'd only made it through the eighth grade—and a move to some new career. He couldn't think about that. He fingered the scar on his neck, then stuck both hands in his pockets. Pepe took him for a walk among the coffee trees, large bushes that flowed over the hills under the shade of larger trees. Underfoot, the soil was dark and soft.

First he learned about making rope. The farm had two large German machines that pulled the manila yarn into strands. The manila was a species of banana known as *abacá*. There were large plantings on the farm's lower elevations, the harvest continued almost year-round, and the three-strand rope that emerged from the machines was strong and sweet-smelling. Over a couple of days Pepe took him everywhere and introduced him to fifty people, too many to keep track of. After a polite first glance, most kept their eyes off his face.

A week later some boys showed up at the door of his little house. They wanted, he guessed, to see the man who'd been burned, and before long one of them, a boy of six or seven, asked him if it hurt.

"It itches. Do you want to see the bad part?"

The boy said nothing, but didn't back away. An older boy answered for him, "Yes, we do," and Camilo opened the buttons of his shirt and let them see his chest. In spite of all the grafts, it still looked terrible.

They stared in silence. He'd shocked them, he thought—but over the next few weeks their curiosity abated and they treated him more naturally. They knew him. He was Armando, the burned guy, *ese hombre quemado*. Don Pepe was training him to be a manager, though everyone must have seen that he knew far less than anyone else on the farm, men and women who'd spent all their lives with coffee and rope.

The adults were slower to relax around him. His own constraint was the problem, he thought. He never got used to his scars, he only forgot them for longer periods: a minute, ten minutes, finally an hour at a time.

In his bathroom was a small square mirror. He wondered how it got there, why it was hanging from a nail the first time he went in. He suspected, from the newness of its frame, that either Pepe or Karen had put it there. He was glad to have it, because buying one for himself would have embarrassed him. On most evenings, in the light of a bare bulb, he took off his shirt and held the little mirror in front of him. No, he would never get used to it. He rubbed a cream into the scars, given to him when he left the hospital, but aside from a little softening he could see no improvement in his banded red skin, the patches of animal hide. "We have done our best," the doctors said, and he knew it was so. He was grateful that where the burns crept up onto his neck and the bottom of his face, it was not so bad.

On the farm he looked away from the young women. He'd always loved a pretty girl, or a woman with a lively spirit. Now he tried not to see them. He thought instead about all the women he'd ignored in the past, the plain and awkward women. If he'd met a woman in Havana with scars like his own, he'd never have thought about kissing her. A burned woman, an old woman, a woman with a limp, an ugly or unattractive woman—he would have turned away from all of them, because there were so many others who were young and beautiful. What, he thought, if Clare had been burned like this? What if her chest and neck looked as bad as his? The answer dismayed him. He wanted a beautiful woman, not one with skin like his.

28

ON a Saturday afternoon, walking home from the Faculty of Medicine, Clare and Natalia talked about their anatomy, biochemistry and musculoskeletal classes. Next week they'd start on the nervous system, and a month later they'd begin the dissection of a cadaver.

"I don't mind blood," Natalia said, "but cutting into a dead body scares me. What about you?"

"I used to take photos in a morgue, so I've seen hundreds of bodies. I got used to it—but somebody else was doing the cutting. I'm not sure. I think I'll be all right."

The streets grew narrower, holding in the exhaust from trucks and badly-tuned cars. After a few blocks they emerged onto a boulevard lined with trees. "What really makes me nervous," Natalia said, "is what that guy from the Ministry of Health said." She glanced around and lowered her voice. "I understand that country people need doctors, and I believe they should have them. But I don't want to go! Do you?"

"Far away from Havana? Not me."

A ministry spokesman had come to describe the many rural hospitals that Cuba was now building. That's where doctors were needed, he explained. The campesinos had never had enough medical care, and many had never seen a doctor in their lives.

"Fidel's theory is fine," said Natalia, "but they could send us to Pinar del Rio or Holguín, and never let us come back."

Clare was less concerned. "That's years away, so for now I don't care. But no, I wouldn't like it. Listen to us. We sound like a couple of almost-counterrevolutionaries."

"*Oiga, muchacha*, do not joke about that. Do not say that even with a laugh."

Clare rested a hand on Natalia's forearm. "I'm sure that after our years of training we will *want* to go to the country and make life better for the *guajiros*. That will be our only goal in life."

"Girl, you're going to get us in trouble."

"No, I know when to keep my mouth shut. I love this program. I'm glad they let me in."

"Me too," Natalia said. "And glad it's Saturday, and that my boyfriend will be coming over tonight."

"The one who's going to marry you after five years."

"*Querida*, he will or he won't. I'm not going to worry about that after I light the candles, and tomorrow I'm going to sleep all day."

"Not me," Clare said. "Ala will have me up by six."

Clare cooked dinner, then took Ala into the park across the street. It was a Cuban Saturday night, the domino players seated at tables under the streetlights that ringed the park, a few aproned women standing with friends, gossiping and calling out to their kids. Clare was exhausted, but at peace. Later that night she might stretch out on her bed and weep. That often happened on a Saturday night. For now she watched her father-less daughter run around laughing, then return to wedge herself between Clare's calves, to gather her confidence and take off again. Her Spanish was flowing freely now, she spoke rivers of it. Last night she'd demanded her dinner of Clare with the casual vocabulary of an adult: "*Tengo hambre, coño, ¿'onde está mi comida?*" Damn I'm hungry, where's my food?

They were living a Cuban life. Clare read a Cuban newspaper, ate Cuban rice and beans, drank her morning coffee from a screw of paper on her way to school. Often on Sundays she and Ala took the ferry across the bay to the Virgen de Regla church, where they sat on a dark wooden pew after the morning services, breathing in the smoke from the incense and votive candles. Later they walked beside the blue water, looking out at the small boats that dotted the bay like toys, and at Havana, gleaming white in the distance.

On this Sunday morning they went shopping. They shared a tamarind juice, then Clare bought some plantains, yams and a piece of pork wrapped in butcher paper. Clare felt calm walking home, even as they passed under a poster of Camilo, then another. The photos no longer upset her. That was another man, the public hero known to everyone. Her own Camilo she had locked up in her chest.

Rounding the corner of her block, she stopped at the sight of a black Ford parked in front of Natalia's store. What would someone from the government be doing here now? Her stomach tightened and she reached for Ala's hand. She wanted to step back around the corner, but already she'd been seen, and a man in fatigues was waving to her, sweeping his fingers toward the ground in the gesture that meant *Come here*. There were two other soldiers as well, and her apprehension grew as she walked toward them. The first soldier was middle-aged and wore a beret like Che's. Though none of them had a rifle, to Clare they looked ominous. The older one stepped forward as she reached the store, took her by the elbow and said, "Let's go upstairs."

One of the others tried to take hold of Ala's hand, but the girl cried out "*No!*" Clare jerked her own arm away. "You don't have to drag us. Just tell me what you want."

"I want you to go upstairs."

They ascended with a soldier in front of them and two in back, as if they might try to flee. They all went inside and the door was closed. "Do you have a suitcase?"

"Why?"

"Please pack it. One suitcase for the two of you. Take anything you want that will fit inside it. You have five minutes."

"What are you talking about?"

"Take what you want. In five minutes I will lead you out the door."

"To where?"

"The time is going by."

"Who has decided this?"

The man was silent.

"It's Raúl, isn't it." She glanced at the other soldiers but they were young, they knew nothing. "Or is it Fidel?"

"I have my orders. You now have four minutes."

It was that shit Raúl. "Do you know I'm a medical student? I'm study-ing to be a doctor, in a government program."

The officer sat down at the table and laid one wrist over the other, exposing his watch.

Angry and helpless, Clare grabbed the larger of her two tan suitcases and opened it on her bed. She dropped some of Ala's clothes and books into it. "Get your duck and monkey," she said, then gathered up some of her own blouses, pants and dresses, making sure to take the dress that held what remained of Domingo's pesos. She took her passport from her top drawer and put it in her camera bag, but the soldier interrupted her. "One suitcase," he said, "nothing more." She placed her passport, both cameras, her lenses and filters into the suitcase, then took a folder of contact sheets from the bottom of a drawer, all her best work, gathered up dozens of rolls of exposed film and tried to add them to the pile inside the suitcase. It didn't all fit. She yanked out some pants, a dress and the books, angrier with each move, then closed the suitcase, leaned on top of it and snapped it shut. A watchful Ala stood at the door of her bedroom, holding her monkey.

"And your duck?"

The girl held out her hands. It was missing. They would have to leave it behind.

"It's time to go, señora." The soldier in the beret took her suitcase, Clare picked up Ala and they all went down to the Ford.

The Castros didn't need laws. They just said something and it was done. Was she never coming back? They all climbed into the car, then headed south out of town. Ala, too overwhelmed to complain, sat on Clare's lap and watched the blazing streets flow by, the July sun now half way up the sky and starting to cook the city.

At the airport they stopped at a metal gate, waited as a pair of soldiers opened it, then drove across the apron directly to a plane. It was a *Cubana de Aviación* with a set of aluminum stairs leading up to the open door, and all four propellers were turning loudly. Clare started up the swaying stairs, holding Ala to her chest. The propellers, only twenty feet off, made her nervous. A soldier followed her, set her suitcase inside the cabin and went down without a word. Clare hesitated. A stewardess and a pilot were saying something to her from inside the plane, and the older soldier below was making the reverse sweeping gesture with the back of his hand: *Go on.*

¡Cretino desgraciado! she wanted to scream. But it was hopeless. The pilot took her arm and she stepped inside. The door closed behind them, the noise diminished and Cuba disappeared. She turned to the pilot and asked, "Where are we going?"

He lifted his palms. Could there be any question? "To Miami."

29

A LAMEDA, through the noise and vibration, seemed oblivious to the
takeoff. She sat her monkey on her lap, she moved his arms and legs
around, she corrected him with *Mono, no se permite,* and *No te vayas a
llorar,* he was not to cry. Though never spanked in her life, she thwacked
the little animal with indignant fervor.

Clare was lost. In thirty minutes she'd gone from living in Havana to—
nothing. Medical school was finished, Natalia gone, the city streets with
their posters of Camilo already far away. She closed her eyes and let Ala
talk to her monkey. She remembered, too late, the things she'd forgotten
to put in her suitcase. A slender volume of Marti's poems, given to her
by Camilo. His straw hat with the Cuban flag on the brim. Her Cuyás
dictionary, worn as an old Bible. Her codeine. At that she felt a moment
of panic—even though, in the months since Camilo's disappearance, she
hadn't suffered a single migraine. Her grief, it seemed, had overwhelmed
her headaches.

Damn it, her 85mm lens. Crowded out of the camera bag by her Leica
and Pentax, she had kept it in her underwear drawer, which she hadn't
opened because of the soldiers. Damn *them,* and damn both Castros.
She was now sure they had killed Camilo. He was no socialist and too
well-liked, which made him a threat, so they shot down his plane and
turned him into a martyr. Now that the furor had died down they were
getting rid of her as well.

Barely an hour later she carried Ala down another set of stairs. The first
ones off the plane, they were led across the pavement to the cold Miami

airport, the air-conditioning a shock inside the glass-walled corridors. Up a level, then another, and Clare presented her passport to Immigration. It carried a page for Alameda, and though they'd been in Cuba for almost two years the man said nothing about it, only "Welcome back to the United States." He stamped the passport and waved them on to Baggage and Customs.

They waited. The suitcase came, Clare opened it on a bench, a man glanced inside and marked it with blue chalk. She was free to go.

But go where? The only person she knew in Miami—she assumed he was here—was Domingo. Ala was hungry. At an airport café they wanted a *dollar* for a ham sandwich. She had no dollars, but dug her pesos out of the suitcase and went to the exchange. For years the peso-to-dollar rate had held steady at one to one. Now it had fallen to forty American cents to the peso, and the teller assured her that the rate was still dropping. She handed over her 300 pesos and was given just under 120 dollars. She bought the sandwich and Ala ate it to the last crumb.

She wished she were in a hotel room, somewhere she could close the curtains, pull the covers over her head and sob as Ala watched television. But a few days of that and she'd have no money at all. Stylish men and women strode past them, their heels ringing on the polished marble floors. There were Latinos here, some of them certainly Cubans, but Havana and the Revolution seemed a hemisphere away. Clare's malaise was now getting through to Ala, who looked tired, perhaps ready to melt.

"Do you want to stretch out and take a nap?"

She did not. She'd stopped looking at other people. It would not be long now.

Clare was adrift in her own country, all her ties long abandoned. She hadn't talked to Engracia in years, nor Asa Bottomwell at *Life*. She knew Ben Chapnick at Black Star, and a couple of people at the AP, but not well enough to call them in distress.

She took Ala's hand, picked up her suitcase, walked to the Eastern counter and—with almost the last of her money—bought two tickets to New York. She would have to go back to her parents.

She didn't let them know she was coming, just walked from the subway through Brooklyn's quiet Sunday streets with Ala beside her, holding on to her monkey. At seven in the evening the girl was wide awake, having slept through most of the flight to LaGuardia.

Clare knew her father was failing. It made no sense, for he was barely seventy. But his memory had been going the last time she saw him, and Lena had probably tailored her reports about him since. She'd written, a few months ago, that he was retired from the Conservatory, that his concentration was a bit worse but they were making do.

Lena's surprise at seeing them was brief, her reproach even less so. Her hands went to her chest, her eyes jumped from Clare to Alameda, and the rest was adoration. "She is so *beautiful.*"

"I should have called," Clare said, "but at ten this morning I had no idea I was leaving Cuba. Castro threw me out. At least I think it was him." She lifted her suitcase into the vestibule. "And Dad?"

"He's in his chair, in the living room. He's going to be so happy!"

Neither happy nor sad, he looked up with a mild curiosity, his eyebrows slightly raised. He was thin, almost emaciated, his hair long and wispy.

"Henry," Lena told him, "Clare has come with her daughter."

Slowly, like an old man, he lifted his hand to shake Clare's. "How do you do?" he said.

She accepted his hand and shook it, but she was close to tears. Didn't he know her?

"And this is Alameda," Lena said. "She's your granddaughter. Isn't she a beautiful girl?" Lena spoke slowly, without raising her voice. "Clare is your daughter, and this is your granddaughter."

Ala, getting over her shyness, now watched everything with her *ojo del inspector*, as Camilo used to call it. Even a three-year-old, Clare thought, could tell that something was wrong in this house.

Lena wanted to hear more about Havana and what had happened. Clare explained, but soon neither of her parents seemed to be listening. What Lena wanted was to stare at her grandchild, and to hold her. Ala let her, briefly, but soon wriggled down to the floor and began her explorations. She looked out the window, then leaned against the piano, pressed two keys, glanced at Clare and pressed two more. Lena brought her a glass of milk, then stared at her as if in prayer. Clare understood. Though Lena had two grandchildren in Japan, those were boys she had never met. Now, standing before her, was a girl who would change everything.

Ala finished her milk and gave the glass to Clare. "We've already eaten," Lena said, "but let me warm up some ravioli. Will she eat that?"

"She'll eat anything. She's still great about food."

In the kitchen, Clare leaned forward and asked, "How is he doing?"

"He has some problems, I'm sure you can see."

"Mom, *he doesn't know me.*"

"I think underneath he does. He just gets nervous sometimes."

"Where's he going?"

Henry had risen from his seat and was headed toward the bedrooms. "I don't have to watch him every minute," Lena said. "He moves around on his own. Sometimes he's hardly confused at all."

A moment later Henry returned, holding a photo in a small black frame. It was Clare when she was little, in a plaid dress, white socks and black shoes, holding a small round cake with four candles. Henry held out the photo, then swung his gaze to Alameda.

"You see!" Lena said. "He *does* remember. He knows you. And Ala is going to be so good for him. He'll remember so many things now."

Lena's enthusiasm for this level of remembrance made Clare even sadder. She sat at the kitchen table as her mother put the ravioli in a pan, heated it up and cut it into little pieces. Ala ate it, wielding her own spoon. "Oh, she is so advanced!"

Henry disappeared again and came back with something else from Clare's childhood. It was a primitive little music box, and when Ala finished eating he handed it to her. She sat on the floor with it, trying to figure it out, and Clare was glad to see that no one rushed to explain it to her. They let her find her way, and eventually she figured out how the metal crank turned a tiny spindle, which plucked the teeth of a steel comb, which played "Amazing Grace." Ala played it over and over as the two women talked quietly in the kitchen.

"He can't teach, can he?"

"No, we had to give that up. He can't remember who's who, or what they worked on the week before. But I've gone back to teaching myself, and some of his old students are mine now. It *is* kind of sad, because he gets everyone confused. Sometimes he thinks I'm his mother, can you imagine? It can be very embarrassing. But you know, he's good when students come over for a lesson. As long as we're playing, even if it's just scales, he never makes a fuss."

"And other times?"

Lena shrugged her shoulders, committing to nothing.

"Is he ever dangerous?"

"Oh, I don't think so."

But on the back of Lena's hand was a livid mark. Clare pointed to it and asked, "What's that?"

"It's nothing. I banged myself trying to help him with his bath. He's not as agile as he used to be."

Her mother, Clare saw, had buried herself in this apartment, taking care of her forgetful husband. She was earning their living, cooking for him, giving him baths and pretending he was doing much better than he was. Clare asked, "Would you leave him alone with a child?"

Lena looked unhappy. "He was never an angry man, so I can't understand it. Most days he's fine. Look how good he is right now. But then, for no reason, he forgets himself. It isn't anger, really, because he stays so calm." She looked back and forth between Henry and Ala, as her eyes teared up. "No, I wouldn't. Maybe for a few minutes, but I wouldn't go to the store and leave them alone."

Henry sat in his recliner with his fingertips in a steeple, tapping them in time to the hymn from the music box. Clare watched him from the kitchen. Ala stopped turning the crank and stood up, still holding the box.

"Come here," Henry said.

Ala, who didn't always do what she was asked, in either English or Spanish, approached his chair.

"What's your name?" he asked.

Though Clare was quite sure she understood, Ala only held out the box, as if he'd asked her for it.

'No," he said, "tell me your name."

She stared up at him with her dark eyes. Calculating, Clare saw. "Alameda," she said.

"And who are you?"

To that the girl had no answer.

"Who are you?" he asked again, a little louder.

"*Me llamo Alameda.*" She stood upright in her blue pants and white T-shirt, her sandals kicked off. She held out the box but Henry didn't take it.

"Tell me in English," he said. "You speak English, don't you?"

"*A mi no me gusta el inglés.*" She didn't like English.

Henry reached out and took her arm. Ala pulled back but he held onto her. Clare was on her feet.

"Why do you talk like that?" he said. "Stop that talk."

"¡*Suéltame!*" Ala cried.

He twisted her arm so hard it wrenched her to the floor, and the next instant Clare was on him, swinging one leg over his chair and driving her fists under his chin. *"You touch her again and I'll kill you. Do you understand me? Do you understand anything? I'll kill you with my hands. You don't touch my daughter."*

Ala lay on the ground, weeping. Lena crouched above her and tried to take her in her arms, but Ala would have none of it. Henry looked terrified, with Clare's fists still pressed to his throat.

"Clare, please, it's not his fault. He doesn't know what he's doing."

He didn't, she could see. He was bewildered, he seemed to have no idea of what he'd done wrong. Clare got off him, picked up Ala and carried her into the kitchen, cradling her, swaying her softly as if she were a baby. "*Querida*, I'm sorry. You're my duck, you're my monkey. I'm sorry. I'm sorry and I'm going to protect you. He doesn't know anything. He's old, he's an idiot. Alameda I love you, I love you and love you."

Ala was a long time quieting down. She stopped crying, and two minutes later started again. Clare kissed her face, she kissed her hands, she promised to hold her forever. The rest of the world meant nothing. Camilo, her father, even her mother—she slapped their faces. The only one she loved was her daughter.

In the morning, with Ala and Henry still asleep, Clare sat with her mother over coffee at the kitchen table. She said, "I have to go somewhere else."

Her mother bent her head. Clare wanted to help her, but couldn't. Ala had changed Lena's life for an hour, but now Clare would take her away.

Lena's kitchen was clean. The dishes were washed, the floor spotless, the African violet on the table a perfection of leaf and flower. The shining Steinway hovered in the living room, a dark ship in a high-ceilinged room. The floors were two-and-a-quarter inch oak, waxed, ancient, the boards as tight as on the day they were laid. A wooden box on the sideboard held David's letters from Japan. None of this, Clare knew, could save her mother. What she wanted was her granddaughter.

"I'm sorry," Clare said. "I'm really sorry, but I need some money. I have nothing. I'll pay you back."

Lena was slow to respond. She slumped in resignation. "All right," she said.

"Can you get it today?"

"I hope you don't need too much—because there isn't that much."

"Can you get five hundred dollars?"

Silence. Then, "I'll go to the bank."

Henry got up. He was cheerful and remembered nothing. Ala would not go near him. Clare dressed her from the small selection of clothes in the suitcase, fed her eggs and toast for breakfast, and the two of them left. In an oversized purse borrowed from her mother, Clare took along a portfolio of her photos.

They took the 7th Avenue Express to Manhattan, roared up the West Side, got off at 96th and walked toward the Hudson. There, long ago on the cool spring grass of Riverside Park, Clare and Camilo had sometimes lain in a blanket and kissed for an hour straight.

Her building on 92nd, a half block from the park, looked familiar but not the same. The wide Hudson still gleamed in the distance, but the building looked darker and less cared for. The tag for her apartment now said Kozlowski, but in 3B Engracia's last names were still there in the same block printing: Trejo Salas. Instead of ringing the bell, Clare entered the building after a tenant walked out, took the elevator to the third floor and carried Ala down the dim corridor. She'd forgotten how narrow it was, forgotten its smell of dust and ammonia and ever-burning light bulbs.

At her knock someone came to the other side of the door and took a look at them through the peephole. A pause, then the door opened, still held by a chain. Instead of Engracia it was a young woman, a dark-haired girl who might have been Cuban save for her jeans and short hair.

"Is Doña Engracia at home?" Clare asked.

"I'm sorry, she isn't here right now." The girl's English was as native as Clare's.

"Will she be home later?"

"Actually, she's away on vacation. She went…to visit her family. I'm her granddaughter."

Clare shifted Ala from one arm to the other. She'd hoped that Engracia could take them in for a couple of weeks and let them sleep in her second bedroom. "I just came from Cuba yesterday."

"Cuba, that's great. And the Revolution, how's that doing?"

Clare wanted to say that the Revolution was a catastrophe—but that's not what she'd been thinking only a couple of days ago. "Many changes," she managed to say. "I knew your grandmother when I lived downstairs in 2C. She taught me Spanish, here in this apartment."

The girl put her hand to the chain. "Would you like to come in?"

"Please," Clare said. All her will had vanished. She was feeling faint and was glad to be offered a seat.

The girl's name was Mary. "It's Maria on my birth certificate, and I wish Abuelita had taught *me* Spanish. She tried, but I never cared about it. Would you like some coffee? Cuban coffee—at least she taught me that."

Thank God for a cup of coffee. Ala got down and explored, which was what she liked to do in any new place. She opened drawers, she opened cupboards and pulled things out, and Mary only laughed. Slowly Clare revived. She explained how Engracia had also taught her to cook: coconut flan, roasts and casseroles. "Do you know when she's coming back?"

"I didn't want to say it, but she doesn't live here anymore. She hasn't for a year. We don't tell anyone, because of the rent control. She moved back to Cuba."

"No."

"She was excited about Fidel. As soon as Batista fled she started making plans."

"I can't believe it. We were there at the same time."

"It didn't last. She went to stay with some relatives, and at first she was in love with Fidel. Then she was not so happy with him, then she said he was just another dictator. Me, I still think he's great. Anyway, she moved to Miami to stay with her sister."

So Clare did know someone in Miami.

With Engracia's address and phone number in her pocket, Clare walked up to Broadway, going slowly so Ala could keep up. Gusts of hot wind came off the river behind them, flapping their clothes and pushing them up the street. On Broadway it shook the awnings over stores and lifted scraps of paper into the air, where they floated briefly, then whipped away. Clare carried Ala into the subway, they took the IRT downtown, then the crosstown shuttle, then walked to the Black Star offices on East 47th. Ben Chapnick was out. He might be back in an hour.

Clare didn't wait, but left the secretary her portfolio, mostly photos of older Cubans. The negatives were in her suitcase. In the old days, without Alameda, she would have waited for Ben to return, but now she was exhausted and they headed back to the subway.

Nothing was working out. Clare wanted Ala and her grandmother to be close, and her mother's longing for that had been clear. How easy it would be, how lovely, if her father hadn't become senile and dangerous. For now, Lena was trapped. She would take care of her husband and miss out on so much else. Maybe that's all anyone could do, Clare thought: take care of one other person. She herself, it seemed, could only take care of Ala. There must be families that worked, in which everyone got along —but she couldn't think of any. Everyone was missing out on something. She felt torn, she felt guilty, but saw no way around it. She would go back to Brooklyn, get some money from her mother and fly to Miami tomorrow.

30

H<small>E</small> owned six shirts, three pairs of pants, some socks and underwear, a pair of boots, a pair of shoes and a light jacket. Every Monday morning a woman came to his house, took whatever clothes he left out for her, washed them and returned them in the late afternoon, folded and smelling of sunlight. Now, after a hot day and a cool shower, he put on his best pants and white shirt, then paused to inspect his face in the small mirror, as he'd done every day since his rhinoplasty. He had two black eyes, but the bruises were fading. The scars were barely visible, and the doctors claimed they would disappear entirely. Compared to his skin grafts, the operation had been a drink of water. Someone who knew him well would not be fooled, he thought—but not that many Cubans knew him from years ago, before he grew his beard. Scarred, shaved and with a smaller nose, he was pretty sure he could walk through a crowd in Havana without anyone guessing it was him. It would help that they all believed him dead.

At the Figueres house Karen thought his new nose a miracle. She had him stand still as she passed back and forth in front of him, viewing his face from all angles. "My own nose..." she said to her husband.

"Is the perfect nose on the perfect face. You must not change a thing."

It was actually kind of large, Camilo thought. *Coño*, what kind of bourgeois madness was this? Would he now start looking at a face as something that could be manipulated and improved? His own nose job was tactical, nothing more. He wasn't trying to look better. His good looks were part of an old story, one that ended more than a year ago.

They talked about the coffee harvest, now almost finished, with the last of the cherries turning a bright glossy red. For three months the harvest had been their focus. Everyone picked, sometimes even Pepe and Camilo, then the beans were raked, dried and hulled, put in burlap bags and trucked to San José. It was an obsession that gripped the entire farm —but Camilo didn't think he'd been invited to dinner to talk about the coffee market. He suspected he'd been asked so Karen could lend her weight to Pepe's plan for him, that he go back to school the way Segundo had, the one who would soon be a lawyer.

He didn't want to go back to school. He hid this from the Figueres, but his discontent had been growing. He wasn't afraid of work, even of something as simple as picking coffee—but what did it amount to? What did it mean? *This* was no revolution, it was just a job he got up for every day and came home from every night. In Cuba his days had been vital, because he was part of a great change in the world. Also vital, he now saw, because everyone knew and loved him. Now he lived a small daily life, hardly different from his parents. It was like living inside a box, and becoming a lawyer wouldn't change that.

The three of them sat down to the meal's first course, bowls of *sopa negra*. Food in the Figueres house was simple and came from the farm. It was a large house with few pretensions beyond its extensive library. It was a working house. As Karen said, it was the home of Costa Rica's social democracy.

Pepe finished his soup and set his bowl aside. "Armando," he said, "I have some news. Remember when I asked for Clare's address? A doctor, a friend of mine, was invited to Havana by the Cuban Ministry of Health, and I asked him to find out what he could. Last year on a Sunday morning, three soldiers came and took away both Clare and her daughter. Not to prison, the neighbors thought, because she was allowed to take a suitcase. We think she has left Cuba."

"We hope you don't feel we are meddling," Karen said.

They *were* meddling—but the news of Clare poured through him: her name, spoken aloud, and the image of her walking down the steps of her apartment, carrying a suitcase.

"Would she go to New York?" Karen asked. "She had family there, didn't she?"

"Her parents live in Brooklyn. I never met them."

"If you like," Pepe said, "I could call and make a polite enquiry."

"No, please."

How stubborn he was, how ungrateful. But he didn't want anyone else involved. "Sometime soon," he said, "I would like to go to the U.S. myself."

On the surface this seemed like a good idea. But there was another reason for him to head to *el norte*, and they all knew it. The easiest way to sneak into Cuba would be through Florida. Miami was full of exiled Cubans all calling for an invasion, and even now Cubans were running boats across the straits, carrying guns for the counterrevolutionaries in the Escambray or picking up relatives who wanted to get off the island. In Key West, Camilo thought, he might find someone who could drop him off, some dark night, near Matanzas on the north coast.

It would be easier to fly to Cuba, either from Costa Rica or Miami, but that seemed a dangerous idea. Some Immigration officer might want to know who this Armando Benitez was, and what business he had in Cuba. What a disaster it would be if some soldier from the old days recognized him and cried out, *¡Camilo!*

"Can we speak openly," Pepe asked, "about those other plans of yours?"

"No."

He didn't want to speak in front of Karen about his desire for revenge. But he could not be cold to either her or Pepe. "Please understand," he told them both, "I owe you everything. I am alive because of you, and now you have given me a job and a place to live. I honor your farm and wish always to be your friend—but I must go to Cuba and carry out my plan, this act that I'm sure you feel is a mistake."

"We do," Karen said.

" Sometimes I go to sleep at night thinking I should forget about what happened, thinking I should just be glad to have survived. But in the morning I wake knowing that if I don't go back I will never rest."

The cook brought a dish of chicken and sweet potatoes and set it on the long wooden table, where Pepe, Karen and Camilo were seated at one end.

"Of course you understand our hope," Pepe said. "That once you see Clare she will knock this train off the tracks."

"I'm glad to know she has left Havana, and I want to find her. But that must come later."

"What of the danger?" Pepe asked. "We've seen how ruthless Fidel can be when threatened. If someone recognizes you it will all be over. One person is all it would take."

"I go in, I take care of Raúl and I get out. After that I will think about the rest of life."

Pepe didn't argue it further. Though he hadn't gotten far with Fidel Castro, he had a gift for discourse, and here in Costa Rica, working slowly and patiently, he had won over sworn enemies and opposition congresses. He was a realist, Camilo thought. He didn't fight battles he couldn't win.

"Do you have enough money for your trip?"

Camilo had saved almost every penny he'd earned. He ate the farm's beans and chickens, he drank the farm's coffee, he lived in the house they gave him. "I'll be fine," he said.

"Perhaps you will fail to reach Cuba," Pepe suggested, with something like humor. "But if you do get into the country, don't tell me about it except in person. I will read the newspapers. Perhaps you could leave your Costa Rican passport behind. It would embarrass my country if it seemed that we sent you."

"When I go to Cuba I'll be just another exile, undocumented."

"Thank you," Pepe said.

They ate for a while in silence, then Karen asked him about his latest trip to the hospital.

"They gave me a new cream. But the doctor admitted that little will change. This is the skin I have, and I must live with it."

"Are you at peace with that?"

"No. I will always hate it."

This couple, who had saved him, were the only ones he could complain to. In the old days he would never have shared such a solemn meal with friends. He'd have made jokes, he'd have poked fun at Pepe's mania about the dried coffee—his recent concern over the traces of parchment skin, a gram in a thousand kilos, that had been found in some hulled beans. But now no jokes came to Camilo, and life rarely seemed funny.

Pepe Figueres wasn't one to give up easily. "I still imagine," he said, "that you might go to the university here and get a degree."

"Pepe, that's not for me. Fidel was a lawyer and even he, who loved to talk and argue for hours, couldn't bear the practice of law."

"I am a lawyer."

"I mean no offense. If I went to school I would rather be a doctor. That is something I believe in—especially after this." He placed his fingertips on his chest.

"I think you would be a great doctor."

"If I could pass the courses."

"You were head of the Cuban Army! You helped run a nation. School might not be as much fun as that, but you could do it."

Camilo only nodded. He would consider all this later, after his mission to Cuba.

That night he lay in bed thinking of Clare. If banished by Fidel, she must be back in New York. He remembered the mornings in her apartment there, mornings full of laughter and sex. He could no longer imagine taking off his shirt in front of her. He couldn't imagine her touching him, or wanting to. In Havana, late at night, she had sometimes run her fingertips, then her lips, over his whole body. She had taken his nipples and sucked on them until he trembled. Now his nipples were little stubs folded into the scars on his chest.

One of his doctors at the hospital had spoken to him on the day he left, thanking him for being so brave. "Now," he said, "you must remember that you are the same person you have always been. If you give other people a chance they will see this too, that you are the same inside."

Camilo did not believe this. He was different in too many ways. At the farm, around the machinery, he was known as a fanatic about safety. He no longer drank, had not once gone out dancing, and had never come close to kissing a woman. He had escaped Cuba and died into this new life, in a country he liked but that would never be his own.

A week later he took the bus to San José to buy some clothes that Pepe insisted on giving him. The store Pepe chose was run by a pair of gringos who imported everything from New York and London, and Camilo was to buy a blazer, some slacks and a pair of good shirts. "When you fly to Miami," Pepe said, "you will look like a businessman on vacation."

The store reminded Camilo of the shop in Claridge's Hotel, with its walls and shelves of dark polished wood. He felt as out of place here as he had in London—even more so, as he'd come today wearing a plain country shirt and pants. The owners of the store were out, but after he presented his letter from Pepe Figueres, a woman came out from a room in back, a stylish woman in her thirties wearing stockings and heels, a straight skirt and a rose-colored blouse. She read the letter and announced, "We will find you something good. And it all goes on Don Pepe's account! We love Don Pepe, he has shopped here for years."

She hadn't noticed his scars, he was sure. Camilo was aware of them every minute. He'd entered the store, as he did whenever he went somewhere new, with a slight turn of his chest and face, so as to present his good side. The woman showed him some blazers, lifted a blue one off its hanger, even helped him on with it before stepping back to look him over. Then she froze. One of her smooth legs was extended, her heel on the floor and her exposed toes pointing up. She pulled her foot back, put her hands behind her and stood stiffly upright, her eyes ranging around the store, steadily avoiding his.

They would all look away, he knew. He took off the jacket and laid it on a counter. His neck itched. He put his hand to it and rubbed, but the itch grew. He wanted to scratch it hard. He felt dizzy. Finally the woman turned and walked toward the shelves of folded shirts, and he followed, though keeping his distance. This was how every woman was going to react, and there was nothing he could do about it.

The woman talked about the shirts, how the cotton came from Egypt. "It's very soft," she said, but still she didn't look at him. She unfolded a shirt, then pulled back her hands.

He picked out two in his size. There was a changing room but he didn't want to use it. He told the woman his waist size, looked at a rack of gray pants, picked out one that looked like the right length, scooped up the shirts and the blazer and pulled them all to his chest. "I'll take these," he said.

"Let me help you. I can fold them and put them in a box."

"No, I'm fine. I'm going. Thank you for your help."

He was glad to leave the woman and the store behind, but once outside he found the streets filled with people. People who looked at him, then looked away. He saw that there was nothing he wanted to do in this city. He didn't want to sit in a restaurant and eat lunch. He didn't want to go to the market, to a park or museum. Instead he walked back to the bus station with his arms full of clothes, climbed on an empty bus and waited for it to fill. He kept his eyes off the women passing by outside. None of them wanted him, and he didn't want them. The only one he wanted was Clare, and of course she would run from him too.

31

ENGRACIA loved two things: Alameda, and complaining about Fidel. Every day she picked Ala up from her nursery school and brought her to Clare's apartment. When Clare returned after class or work she found dinner on the table. As they ate—*moros y cristianos, platanos fritos,* hamburgers or roast chicken—Engracia inveighed against the dictatorship. Fidel was a socialist, he was a communist, he was determined to appropriate every U.S. business in Cuba. Because this topic was Engracia's passion, Clare listened. She had reason to hate Fidel herself, yet she still believed in the Revolution. Engracia was devoted to changing her mind about that, and Clare let her talk. It was the one thing she did for her, and it was little enough. The rest was all Engracia helping her and Alameda.

After dinner, as Clare cleaned up, the girl and Engracia played. They had a kind of mock early bedtime with stories and silly games. Ala lay in Engracia's arms and called her *abuelita.* Engracia wore a look of stunned happiness, a joy she had not expected. Clare was glad to have found her in Miami—but watching her, she thought of how much her mother would have liked to be in her place. Lena's letters from New York described how Henry knew her less and less. Every week, Clare took photos of Ala and sent them to Brooklyn.

One night she asked Engracia if she'd ever had another man, after her husband died.

"You won't believe this, but I made a friend this last time in Cuba. I wasn't going to tell you, because of course he was married. I don't know what I was thinking. We were only kissing and—you know. But I liked him. I let myself dream a little. Then he was gone. He and his wife left the country without a word. From Fidel on down all men are alike. They fool you. They will never make you happy."

"You were happy with Benito."

"Well, that's true. Either they fool you or they die on you. Benito was a man from the old days, he was courteous and proper. Oh, don't listen to me, I'm too old to be talking of such things. I'm happier with a simple life like this. Your daughter is the one I love."

"And Alameda," Clare asked, "what do you think of your *abuelita*?"

"I *like* her," the girl said. She climbed onto Engracia's lap and wrapped her arms around her neck.

Engracia lived with her sister. Clare and Ala had stayed with them when they first flew down from New York, but Flora, though younger than Engracia, was a true old maid, too set in her ways to have a child around for more than a couple of weeks. Clare found her own apartment, then talked to the *Miami Herald* to see if they had any work. They liked her portfolio, but they wanted someone who could travel: all over the Caribbean, but especially to Cuba. They wanted a photographer who could drop down for a day or two to cover Fidel's big rallies and his speeches that went on for hours. Clare explained that in Cuba she was now *persona non grata*. Still, the paper found some work for her filling in on sports and political shoots, and at meetings of the city commission. Also, as in New Jersey, she found a part-time job documenting autopsies at the Morgue Bureau. She needed the money, and after her half semester at Havana's Faculty of Medicine she took a more clinical interest in the procedure.

Her months of classes there carried no weight with the University of Miami. If she wanted to go to med school she had to start with a college degree. It seemed a painfully long road, but she had started. She was taking a class in Latin American History, reading about Simón Bolívar, Toussaint L'Ouverture and Bernardo O'Higgins. The Cuban Revolution did not appear in the syllabus.

Engracia, even as she inveighed against Fidel, now clung to an even greater nostalgia for her homeland. Like many exiles in Miami, she yearned for the country of her youth, for family meals where a dozen people sat down to eat, for the fresh *guarapo* sold during the cane season from carts on the Malecón, for the drumming that spilled into the street from little rumba clubs, for the towering clouds that built up over the ocean at dusk. The same clouds appeared over Miami, but it was the Cuban clouds she missed.

Clare had a car, a 1955 Volkswagen she bought for $600, half of it borrowed from Engracia. Miami was impossible without a car, because when the *Herald* called she had to jump. She drove Ala to school, she drove to the university, she drove to the morgue—and now she was waiting at a garage on 12th Avenue to have a new muffler put on. The old one, after a week of rumbling, had fallen clean off.

In the waiting room she read the *Herald*. She read *U.S. News & World Report*. She looked up at the sound of a little bell mounted on the door and saw a man in a Cuban guayabera enter the room. It was Domingo. He went straight to the desk and asked if they would look at his Chevrolet. It was running rough and he suspected the timing. When he turned to take a seat he found Clare standing behind him. "*Clare!*" he said, and wrapped his arms around her. It was instantaneous, unprepared, and a moment later he stepped back.

She had thought about sneaking out of the room behind him. Indeed, it was only the bell on the door that stopped her. "Hello," she said.

She'd always worried about running into him, and now they were trapped, both waiting for their cars. Domingo looked the same, perhaps a bit thinner, slightly more gray at the temples. He held his arms behind him. "What are you doing here?" he asked.

"Fidel kicked me out."

Domingo shrugged his shoulders. *You see*, he implied. "And how is Alameda?"

"She just turned four. She speaks lots of English now."

"I'm sorry about Camilo. It must have been hard on you."

"It was."

That was brave of him, she thought, to bring up Camilo so directly, and to say he was sorry about the man who'd replaced him. And cowardly of her not to say something more. But slowly she let down her guard. She asked about Domingo's children and his brother. The Revolution had united the family, he explained, and now they all lived in Miami. His mother, however, had died, from her Parkinson's and her grief at leaving Cuba. His son and daughter were well, and both had jobs. Domingo himself was buying houses and renting them out.

The talk stopped. The bell on the door sounded as someone else walked in. The man behind the counter shuffled through a stack of repair orders.

Domingo asked, "Would you like to take a walk?" It was a delicate invitation, politely tendered. "Such a beautiful day," he added, "so sunny and cool."

How good he was at soothing her. This had always been so, and she let him lead her out onto the street and from there toward the river through Henderson Park. Domingo said nothing for so long that Clare finally asked, "Do you miss Cuba?"

"Every day. But the old Cuba is not coming back, and few of the exiles can accept that."

"From everything I hear, they would like Fidel's head on a post."

"It's true, they would assassinate him if they could. Myself, I'm not so bloodthirsty."

It was a word he'd once used about Camilo. Did he remember that? Talking to him was like walking through a minefield. They could speak of his family, of Ala, and mention the death of Camilo Cienfuegos—but after that, what? They walked to the river, then headed back. At the garage her car was ready. Domingo stood back as she paid the bill.

"Well," she said, the keys in her hand.

"Perhaps you would give me your telephone number?"

"Domingo, no. I don't have to explain this, do I?"

"You don't have to do anything."

Driving home, she thought about his request. She regretted sounding so cold. But what else was possible? She thought of the young woman she'd been when she met him in the Deauville Casino. How open she'd been, how ready for an adventure, how beguiled by the romance of Cuba. It seemed a hundred years ago. A hundred years, a hundred fires, and most of them banked. For now, the only people she wanted in her life were Ala and Engracia.

It was always Clare who actually put Ala to bed, but that evening, after dinner and Ala's bath, she asked Engracia if she would take care of the job so afterward they could talk. Clare sat at the kitchen table with her textbook on revolutions, as Engracia settled down beside Ala in the next room. She read her some Dr. Seuss in English. She sang "You Are My Sunshine," then the itsy bitsy spider song, then she checked on all ten of Ala's little piggy toes. Clare came in to finish things off with a hug and a kiss, a promise to be there in the morning, a glass of water, another hug, another kiss, an elaborate adjustment of the sheets and blanket and the pillow under Ala's head, and finally it was done.

Quietly, in the kitchen, she offered Engracia a cup of coffee.

"Oh, I'm such an American now. I cannot drink coffee at night."

"I have some Sanka."

"Then yes."

Clare poured the cups and they drank it black, but sweet. "Guess who I ran into today?"

"Domingo," said Engracia, without the least hesitation.

Was it as inevitable as she seemed to think? Clare described their meeting in the garage, the walk they took and Domingo's request for her phone number. Engracia asked how he looked and how he was doing. How many houses did he own, and had he married no one else?

"Didn't you tell me that men were nothing but trouble? Why are you so interested in Domingo?"

"You *were* married to him."

"The divorce came through before I left Cuba. I treated him badly."

"But he still loves you."

"I don't think so."

"Please, do not pretend such innocence. Without even being there, just *hearing* about him, it's obvious."

"You're not suggesting I should have given him my number?"

Engracia laughed. "If you were my daughter—which in a way you are —I'd be worried about you. You're thirty years old and of course not finished with romance. You might go some years without it. You can put it in a trunk for a while and still be happy. But I'd hate to see it erupt with the wrong person, someone charming but useless. At least you know Domingo. He's someone you can trust."

"Are you suggesting that I go to bed with him? Engracia, you've lost your mind."

"It was only a thought. But when you spoke of him, did I only imagine a bit of longing?"

"I don't long for Domingo or anyone else. Or no one who's alive."

"Be tranquil, *m'ija*. I did not wish to offend you."

Clare stood up, peeked into Ala's room to be certain she was asleep, and returned. She sat down, with her fingertips on the table's edge. "Look what I've already done to Ala. First I married Domingo. He was like a father to her, and she loved him. Then I had to leave him. Okay, I didn't have to, I wanted to. I left with hardly any warning, I was worse than that man you met in Cuba. Ala suffered from what I did, and she was much more cautious with Camilo. Slowly she was warming up to him, and then he disappeared. After that I took her to Brooklyn where my father didn't know who I was and grabbed hold of her so hard I was afraid he'd break her arm. So no, I'm not going to subject Ala to any more sadness and deception."

"I understand." Engracia stood up and cleared the cups to the sink. "Perhaps I was not thinking." She looked calm, even chastised, but not for long. "I didn't mean to suggest that you marry him again, or move into his house. Just that—you might have some fun."

"Engracia, you are much more *picara* than I'd imagined."

"You know what they say in Spanish. *Soy vieja pero no estoy muerta.* I'm old but I'm not dead."

"You're not even that old. You were ready to have an affair in Cuba."

"And what a terrible thing that would have been," Engracia said, though her smile belied her words.

32

D OMINGO opened a bottle of wine and they drank it in bed. On the previous nights—there had been two of them—Clare had felt relaxed after they made love. She had worried before and relaxed after. Her arousal, tamped down for so long, had leapt up and surprised her. Not tonight. She didn't know why, for Domingo had been just as attentive. After thirty minutes, instead of prolonging the act, she'd let him believe she was coming, and ended it. After that she wanted to get up and go for a walk, go for a nighttime swim in the ocean, take a plunge from the high board of some pool. Instead, she asked for the wine.

"It worries me," she said. "That you'll make too much of this."

Domingo offered her a pillow, then placed one behind his own head. "I cannot tell you that I don't love to be with you. I do. But I've said before that there's nothing you have to explain. I think we understand each other. We both remember the road we took to get here."

Usually this would have calmed her, but now she reached for her blouse and buttoned it up over her bare chest, putting at least that barrier between them. She was thinking of a beetle she'd once seen on a Cuban bus, pinned to the blouse of a ten-year-old girl, a beetle painted red and blue and allowed to crawl at the end of a two-inch chain. No, Clare thought, there was no disconnected sex. She could not have a fling with Domingo, because he still loved her and would be drawing the cord tighter, telling her all the while that she could do whatever she liked—until she wound up like that beetle, tethered to the girl's shirt.

Whatever they'd started, she must stop. She drank the rest of her wine, and when Domingo offered more she said yes, please. He filled both their glasses, and as he leaned away to set the bottle back on the bedside table she gave a little hitch and spilled her glass over the two of them, a wide red splatter. "*Damn*," she said. "Domingo, I'm sorry."

She was devious, she was false, and instantly felt better. Domingo jumped out of bed and pulled at the sheets, trying to protect the mattress. "*Get up*," he barked. Then, controlling himself, "Don't worry, don't worry about it. It's only wine and I'll clean it up."

Tugging at the sheets from his side of the bed, he looked both fussy and comical. She'd never seen him so worried about a domestic problem—perhaps because in Miami he lived without servants. He cooked his own dinners and made his own bed. Clare unbuttoned her stained shirt and asked if she could borrow one of his.

"Of course. Give me that one and look in my closet, you'll find several. I'm going to soak everything in water. I'll be right back."

His bedroom was on the second floor of a house south of Calle Ocho. There were ornamental palms outside, a formal yard and an iron gate. Clearly he'd managed to get some money out of Cuba. His walk-in closet was wide and deep and as orderly as the rest of the house. To one side sat his luggage: three different suitcases and an overnight bag. On the back wall hung some dark suits with a tie draped around each collar, and on the right side his shirts and pants. She slid into one of his guayaberas, buttoned it up and put her underpants on. The shirt was too large, but soft and comfortable.

Meticulous in all things, Domingo brought fresh sheets to make the bed. Clare helped, but she was not as careful with the corners as he was. He started to explain his method, then did the job himself, and finally they lay down again, all sex pushed safely aside.

Clare asked him about the news she'd heard from Engracia, that Manuel Artime and his men were preparing to invade Cuba. Artime was an exiled army officer, once a member of Castro's rebel forces.

"An invasion is coming," Domingo said, "we just don't know when. They'll pretend it's all the work of Cuban exiles, but in fact the government here supports them."

"Do you think they'll overthrow Castro?"

"Not unless they have help from the U.S. Navy and Air Force, and I doubt if Kennedy will allow that. To be honest, I fear a disaster."

"What if they managed to get rid of Fidel? Would you go back?"

"They will fail, so I don't think about it. Well, of course I do. Every Cuban in Miami thinks about it. But would Felipe and I get our mill back? Could I start up my magazine again? I think *Ojo* is finished, no matter what happens. Also, my children are happy in the U.S., and this is the country where money flows like water. I've thought about starting another magazine, here."

"Domingo, I never thanked you for the money you gave me. You were very generous and it was a great help. When did you leave for Miami?"

"We flew up—after Christmas."

"In Felipe's plane?"

"Yes."

"How's he doing?"

"He drinks. Our mother's death was a blow to him, and he makes other excuses, but he starts every day with a rum and Coke, then another. I no longer know what to say to him."

"What about his plane?"

"He sold it. He sold it at the Tamiami Airport the day after we got here. He wanted the money, but by now he has probably spent most of it. There is too much rum in the world, and Felipe would like to drink it all."

33

Camilo was in Miami, having sailed through Immigration at the airport. He had a tourist visa, a Costa Rican passport and his new clothes, courtesy of Pepe Figueres.

The Cubans in Miami, still a minority among other Latin Americans, had settled along West Flagler, and only a block away Camilo found a boarding house that served two meals a day at a long table lined with Cuban exiles. There was a doctor now working as a hospital orderly. There was a civil engineer who went five nights a week to English classes, hoping to get a better job than the one he had, supplying cooking oil to Miami restaurants. There was a lawyer who drove a forklift all day. They all hated the Revolution, and they were all rabid on the subject of Fidel Castro. Camilo went with the lawyer one night to attend a *Reunión de la Comunidad* in a rented VFW hall, where the talk was all about how to get rid of the communists. It was clear that the rumors were true, that Manuel Artime and a group of Cuban exiles were in Guatemala, preparing for an invasion. People lowered their voices when they spoke of it, but everyone knew that Artime and his men were being trained by U.S. soldiers. Camilo was glad that Artime himself was not at the meeting, for Manuel was someone who might recognize him. He had joined the rebels in their last year in the Sierra, and twice Camilo had slept in the same tent with him. He was feisty and outspoken, and to Camilo he had seemed sincere—but he'd been quick to grow a beard, and quick to shave it off.

Partly to test his disguise, Camilo stood up at the meeting and asked, now that so many were hopeful about Artime and his brigade, whether there was still room for individual attacks on the regime. That raised a clamor. Oh yes, they said, there were many who'd been rejected by Artime as too old and soft, but they were not going to sit back and wait, they were gathering guns and equipment and hoping to find some boats. "*Hermano*," they told Camilo, "we work on this every day."

No one recognized him, and no one asked about his burns. The Cubans were as polite about it as the yanquis. On the streets of the city, or at a meeting like this, no one seemed to notice his scars. They did, of course, but no one stared and no one knew who he was.

He found a job at a South Beach restaurant, a day job washing dishes. The Raleigh Hotel had the only restaurant in Miami that served true Cuban food, and Camilo worked there as Armando, a Costa Rican with a Cuban mother. He spoke a mixture of quick Cuban lingo and the calmer Spanish of Central America. There were a half dozen Cubans in the kitchen, and as far as Camilo could see, no one suspected anything.

His search for Clare did not go as well. The downtown public library had telephone books for each New York borough, fat books filled with Millers. Camilo ran his finger through the Brooklyn directory, then Manhattan's, but he'd forgotten the names of Clare's parents. If she had a phone number of her own, it might be too recent to appear in the book, so from a pay phone he called the operator. There were two Claire Millers in Brooklyn, both with the wrong spelling. There were three Clare Millers in Manhattan and these he called, feeding dimes into the phone. The first was an old woman. The second was helpful, but she'd never been to Cuba. The last was not at home. He called again, four different times over the next week, then gave up.

He knew that Clare had sold photos to *Life* and to the Associated Press. He found those numbers and called them, but couldn't get past the women who answered the phones. They knew nothing about any Clare Miller. They were sorry, they would ask around the office—but when he called back someone else answered and said the same thing.

Day by day he became more confident that even those who'd seen his photo in Cuba, perhaps dozens of times, were not going to recognize him. At the boarding house his own name sometimes came up in the conversation. Camilo Cienfuegos, he found, was admired. They liked him because, unlike Che and Raúl, he was no communist. There were several theories about what had happened to him. He'd been taken to an airport and killed, someone said. Others were sure that a Cuban Air Force plane had shot him down. Armando offered his own suggestion: perhaps someone had put a bomb on his plane.

"That could be," the doctor said. "I think Castro was afraid of him, the way he was afraid of Huber Matos—and look what they did to him. If only the two of them had joined forces and killed Castro, we could have our country back."

Camilo wanted to say, *Raúl is the one to blame!* He said nothing, but day after day the exiles' hatred of Fidel wore him down. He wanted to get to Cuba and punish the right man.

At the Raleigh Hotel the owner saw that Armando knew his way around a kitchen, and offered to put him on the line at night as assistant cook. Camilo said no, he'd rather stick with his daytime hours and washing dishes. He was busy meeting people at night, and he wanted to work without thinking about the job. He sprayed the plates, glasses and silverware, and fed them into the big conveyor Hobart, and while his hands were busy his mind could wander. Always it was the same: he imagined how he would find Raúl and kill him.

Kill him late at night in his home, with everyone else asleep. That would be the easiest way. Camilo saw him in his study, rising from his chair, slow to realize who it was who'd come back from the dead. Camilo, his gun pointed at Raúl's face, would unbutton his own shirt, exposing his scars and making Raúl look at them. The *puto* would try to make a bargain, of course. He'd pretend to be glad to see him, call it a miracle, make a move toward his telephone. But Camilo, with his pistol, would wave him away. Raúl would be wearing a robe, maybe pajamas. He was the type to wear pajamas to bed. He would try to stay calm, but his desperation would be obvious, and the last moments of his life would be filled with panic. Camilo would say, *Ask for my pardon,* and Raúl would do it. Camilo would say, *That day you had the chance, you should have shot me. But you are a little cabrón without balls, and I'm going to rearrange your face with this pistol.* Or he'd ask him about the bomb in the suitcase. Did Raúl make it himself, or did someone else put it together? And Raúl would lie. He'd say one lie after another, thinking that as long as he was talking Camilo wouldn't shoot him. But he would. He'd shoot him in the mouth. Then, as he lay dying on the floor, another shot to the temple and it would be done.

Camilo understood that these fantasies could not come true. Not as he imagined them, because nothing worked that way, the details never turned out the same. Before coming to Miami he'd imagined staying in a *pensión*, but the boarding house he found looked nothing like the one he'd dreamed up. He'd imagined buying a gun from some secretive guy on a dark street, and found that pistols of all kinds could be bought by anyone in a hardware store. The rule, he was sure, was universal: no battle, no nighttime march, no conversation with Fidel, no visit to Pepe and Karen's house, no trip to a store to buy a bar of soap—*nothing* could happen the way one imagined it beforehand.

It didn't matter, for the details of Raúl's death were infinite, and he swam in them as he worked. The busboys unloaded their trays, the dishes rattled along the belt into the humming dishwasher, and Camilo passed his time in reverie.

At his boarding house, in cafés, even standing at a bus stop, the talk he heard was all about the coming invasion. As soon as Artime and his men landed in Cuba they would be embraced by all who hated Fidel Castro, whose days were numbered. By the end of the year the exiles would be free to go home.

Camilo hid his disdain, sometimes his fury at such talk. How could they hate Fidel, who'd done more for the poor of Cuba than anyone in history? Of course none of these men had been poor. They might be cleaning offices now on the night shift, or manning the pumps at a gas station, but in Cuba they had all been rich. Camilo could hear it in their voices, their stories, their nostalgia. He saw, finally, that he was at odds with every other Cuban in Miami. He listened to them and kept his mouth shut. They were dreaming, and would soon understand that without U.S. forces they were never going to defeat Fidel. Just from reading the *Miami Herald* Camilo could tell that all Cuba was on the alert. Fidel's speeches were defiant. He knew what was coming, he'd passed out arms to ten thousand people and locked up everyone who spoke out against him. He was in his element. He loved battling a powerful foe.

Camilo worried that this might be a dangerous time to sneak into Cuba. The whole country was preparing for an invasion and would be on the alert for assassins. Still, each day he spent around other Cubans reassured him. He stood out—but not in a way that people feared. He stood out because he was burned. Everyone noticed, but then they busily pretended *not* to notice. On the rare occasion that someone asked how it happened, he told them he'd run into his house to save his wife and child, and the roof had collapsed. He told them he'd barely escaped, and his family had died. After that, no one asked another question.

Returning from work, Camilo got off the bus at Flagler. Here there was as much Spanish on the street as in the restaurant kitchen: the same quick and lyrical Spanish he'd learned as a child. Every day more Cubans were landing in Miami. They flew in on Cubana or Pan American, or came north on the ferry that still ran to Tampa. Cuban markets and coffee-houses had sprung up on both Flagler and Calle Ocho, and the backbone of almost every conversation was the same: Castro had ruined Cuba and had to be killed or pushed out.

I could never live in this city, Camilo thought.

Idling along Flagler, he was on the lookout for a man he'd met, no name or phone number yet, who claimed to know another Cuban who owned a boat in Key West, someone who might be willing to make a trip across the straits. Camilo glanced inside the shops and cafés, but no luck. Ahead, a woman walked toward him on the sidewalk. He no longer looked at women on the street, or not in the way he used to. Often he looked away. But something about this woman put him on alert when she was still a half block off. She walked upright, and even for an American she was tall. She glanced at him once as she approached, then not again. He stopped. He stood in the middle of the sidewalk. Without looking at him, she adjusted her stride and passed not five feet away, her neck slender, her skirt swaying, her feet sandaled, going away now but slowing down, her shoulders starting to turn. She came to a stop. Her eyes came around and locked on his, and for twenty seconds neither of them moved. Other people walked around them and between them. She took a step toward him, then another. She looked afraid. She stopped short of him and said, just above a whisper, "Speak to me."

"Hello, Clare."

As if blown by an explosion she flew across the last ten feet, took his shirt in her hands and pulled him to her. She released it, put her palms on his chest, then on his shoulders and arms. She brought her nose close and smelled him. She took a step back, then another. "How? *How?*"

"I've been trying to find you," he said.

She shook her head. She came close and grabbed his shirt again. "How could you find me? You *died*."

"I almost died."

"Camilo—"

"*Please*, do not say my name."

"What's wrong with your name?"

They stood on the sidewalk in front of some shops. It was after work, and a slow stream of people passed by, headed back and forth along Flagler.

"I have a new name."

"What are you talking about? You're killing me all over again. I was lost in Havana *and you weren't even dead*."

"Please, Clare. Could you speak more quietly?"

People were staring. He'd gotten used to his cocoon, in which people glanced at him, then looked away. Now they were all watching. They slowed down, turned their heads, some even looked back over their shoulders. Of course, for Clare was a beautiful woman in anguish, clutching at him.

Her eyes came to rest on his neck. "What *is* this?"

He took hold of her bare elbow. "Let's go around the corner. There are too many people here."

She shook him off. "I'm not going anywhere. Tell me what happened."

He didn't want to talk about it here, but she was planted in front of him. She stood with her eyes locked on his, breathing, waiting, until finally he explained, as quietly as he could. "Someone put a bomb on my plane. I threw it out, but we crashed in Costa Rica."

"What were you doing in Costa Rica?"

"*Clare*, I beg you. Not so loud."

"Just tell me." Then, with her voice finally lowered, "Everyone in Cuba thinks you're dead."

"My pilot was killed and I was badly burned. My chest is the worst."

"I walked all over Havana, screaming your name. I wore your old hat and almost went crazy. The whole time I wanted to kill Fidel. It was him, wasn't it? I never believed him about that search for your plane."

He wanted to tell her no, it wasn't Fidel, it was Raúl. But those two names were like magnets to which all ears on the street would be drawn. Besides, Clare was now moving her head from side to side, looking at him from different angles. "What happened to your nose?"

"I had an operation. I had a lot of help from—you remember Pepe Figueres."

"Of course."

He waited, watching every expression on her face. Once she got a full look at his neck and chest, would she turn and run?

"Come," she said. "I see this is hard on you here." She led him across Flagler, down a side street, then stopped under the trees. "Now tell me everything."

That he could not do. He had plans, and she must not find out about them. He told her, in Spanish, that he was working in a restaurant, that he'd only been here for ten days, that he'd tried to find her number in New York. As he talked he watched her wide-open eyes, her parted mouth, the glistening ends of her teeth. His desire came back in a rush. It was a rich feeling but he wasn't ready for it. He looked away. He asked how she came to be in Miami.

She told him how she'd been run out of Cuba. She told him about her parents, about Engracia, about her jobs. She stopped. "In my heart, you're dead."

He had feared this, he had known it would happen. He looked down, hiding sudden tears.

"No, Camilo, I didn't mean it that way. *No*, no, let me hold you."

She put her arms around him and pulled him close. Her smell was the same, of her perfect clean body and the faintest perspiration. He kept his head down and breathed her in.

"I meant that when you died, I had to live with that forever. I thought it was forever. My heart's still damaged, because in it you're dead. Here you are, alive, but I have to catch up."

He almost said, *I don't understand.* He did understand, but wanted her to keep holding him. He didn't look up until she stopped.

"Come home with me," she said. "It's not far from here."

"Is Alameda there?"

"Yes, and Engracia, who looks after her. I will introduce you."

Again he touched his fingers to her arm. "I must explain to you why I'm no longer Camilo Cienfuegos." He took his passport from his pocket, opened it and showed it to her. "This is who I am now, Armando Benitez, a citizen of Costa Rica."

"But Camilo—why?"

"*Not Camilo.* That is why I hesitate to go to your house."

"What's going on?"

He took back his passport. He wanted to put his arms around her and think of nothing else. "I cannot tell you now."

She looked unhappy with that. "I don't think I can stand any more mysteries."

Camilo stood back under the leafy trees, to let a woman with two young children go by. Instead, the woman kept her distance, leaving the sidewalk and steering her kids over someone's lawn.

"All right," he said, "I'll tell you. But you must tell no one else. If so, it could be bad for me. Can you promise?"

Clare's eyebrows lifted faintly. "Let me guess. You want to go back to Cuba so you can kill Fidel."

"Not Fidel! It's Raúl who put the bomb on my plane. He's the one who hates me."

Clare waved this off. "Do you think that Raúl could have you killed without Fidel's consent? That can't be."

On a hundred nights he'd lain in bed, thinking this through. He knew it wasn't logical, because Fidel controlled everything and no detail escaped him. But Camilo couldn't live with the thought that Fidel had ordered his death. It was true that Fidel had always been ruthless with anyone who stood in the way of the Revolution—but Camilo had never done that. Even when furious at Raúl for scattering his men across Cuba, he hadn't complained. He'd done what was asked of him. No, he thought, Raúl had found a way to put the bomb on the plane himself. Then he'd told his brother about it and Fidel, in defense of the Revolution, had closed ranks with him publicly, if not in private.

"Can you understand?" Camilo said. "Fidel's dreams for Cuba are my dreams, and I will never turn against him."

"We've all seen how dangerous it is to do so. Huber Matos is serving twenty years."

Did she now renounce the Revolution? He didn't want to ask. He said, "I've been through a great deal of pain."

Instantly she softened. "Camilo, I'm sorry."

He didn't mean to use his suffering as an excuse. He meant to say that the agony of his burns and Raúl's punishment were irrevocably bound. He explained, as calmly as he could, the cleaning of his wounds, the months of skin grafts and how thoughts of revenge had kept him alive through the pain.

Clare listened. She dropped her eyes to his chest. "Show me."

He didn't want to, but she waited him out. He unfastened the top two buttons of his shirt, then dropped his hands. She undid the next three buttons herself, pulled his shirt open and stared at the worst of it. She said nothing, but in her stiff posture and drawn face he saw that she struggled. How often he had looked at his own chest with aversion, imagining a moment like this one with his ruined flesh exposed to a woman. To Clare.

Slowly, with her slender fingers, she buttoned him up again. She said, so softly he barely heard her, "It will be all right." She put both palms on his chest and kept them there, motionless, for half a minute. Then, "Come, let's go back to my house."

"Do you think Alameda will know me?"

"It's possible. But you look so different, and she's only four."

Ala stared at him hard, but said nothing. He couldn't tell if she knew him or not.

The white-haired woman, Engracia, showed no sign of recognizing him, but she did look surprised. Was it that Clare had brought home a man, or that the man was burned? Camilo chatted with her, he asked about her recent stay in Cuba and what she thought of Fidel. She'd been disappointed, she told him, and Camilo let her talk. She was part of this Miami nest of vipers, all of whom complained about Fidel's betrayal and his secret communism. In the U.S., Camilo thought, communists had taken the place of the devil.

After only ten minutes Engracia announced that she couldn't stay for dinner, and left. It was clear from the table, which she'd already set for three, that she'd planned to eat there. Camilo wasn't sure if she liked or disliked him. Perhaps she'd appraised him and seen no danger. The meal was already prepared, and he sat down to eat it with Clare and Ala, who still stared at him—though when he glanced at her she looked away. She was thinner and taller, a growing girl.

After dinner, as Clare carried off the plates, Alameda stood beside him, staring again. He looked away, he held still, and finally she pointed at his face and asked, "What's that?"

"*Es quemadura.*"

"Not in Spanish."

Camilo laughed. "Now there's a change. It's a burn. Have you burned yourself one time?"

Alameda nodded solemnly and opened her palm to him.

"On the stove," Clare said. "She remembers that."

He reached for her hand to take a look, but she pulled it back. Still, she didn't turn away. He wanted to ask, *Do you know me*? At the same time, he didn't want to stir things up.

On the street and at work, Camilo had altered the tone of his voice. He spoke in a higher register, as far from his microphone voice as he could manage. But here at Clare's he spoke in his old voice. Would a four-year-old remember something like that? It was all guesswork, because he could remember almost nothing from when he was four himself. Alameda stared, and he didn't know what it meant.

After bowls of rice pudding, Clare gave her a bath. There was an armchair but Camilo didn't sit in it. He sat at the table and glanced at the *Herald*. He wasn't sure what he was supposed to do. Wait, apparently.

He went to the front door, opened it and stood watching the street. Miami wasn't as busy as Havana, the streets not nearly as dense with houses. There were lawns and alleyways and fewer people on the sidewalks. Right now, no one. Behind him he heard Clare and Ala padding into another room, then murmurs, then silence. He didn't know what he was doing here. He'd been trying to give up on Clare. He thought he'd never see her again. Then, in an instant, he'd been dropped into the ocean of their past, and now what was he going to do? This was not like going into battle with every sense alert and a hundred decisions to be made. He felt lost. He stood at the open door, breathing in the damp earth and the smell of oranges. He could walk away and not come back. How easy it was for him to imagine sneaking into Cuba, with all its obstacles and dangers, and how difficult to conceive of a life with Clare—who probably didn't want him anyway. To live in a little house, with electric and telephone bills, paying taxes and sending a child to school—no, he'd always wanted something else, something larger. For years he'd had it.

His scars were itching as they sometimes did, an itch that could escalate and drive him crazy, that was sometimes so bad he wished for pain instead. Behind him he heard Clare emerge from Ala's bedroom and walk across the floor, coming to a stop at his elbow.

"Yes," she said, "you could run."

How well she knew him. But turning toward her, what he wanted was to take her in his arms. She didn't look ready for that. Would they ever again have a night like those in Havana, nights when they talked and drank rum and danced to a mambo on the radio as he slowly removed her clothes?

"Come," she said. "Sit down."

Her kitchen table was Formica with a chrome border and four tubular legs. He sat across from her without coffee, without water, without anything.

"Tell me about Costa Rica and Don Pepe's farm, and his wife."

He told her about his small house on the cooperative farm, and the coffee trees, and how good Pepe and Karen had been to him. Clare was interested in Karen's story, he could see: the young American woman who'd married the president of a foreign country.

"And your scars," Clare said. "Do they hurt?"

They did, just then. Had she seen that in his face? "Sometimes they itch and sometimes they ache. It's all much easier than before, but—this is how they're going to look. They won't get any better."

Clare nodded. But what did she think? Camilo, when he looked at his scars, could not get used to them. Even worse was feeling them, running his fingertips over them, trying to accept that instead of smooth skin he now had this wasteland of crusty flesh.

"Tell me about your plan," Clare said. She drew her chair closer. "Will you try to go back to Cuba soon?"

"Yes."

They spoke in Spanish. "How are you going to get there?"

"By boat."

"Do you have a gun?"

"I know which one I'm going to buy." It was a 9mm Smith & Wesson, small and easy to hide. "There's a hardware store on Flagler that sells them."

"And you have money for all this?"

"I have enough."

She made him explain. He had saved some money, and before he left Costa Rica Pepe had given him four hundred dollars from the sale of the engine of his plane. The wings and fuselage had been destroyed, but the engine had been rescued and was now flying around in another Cessna. "I'm not sure if that's true," Camilo said, "or if he just wanted to give me the money."

"So here, why work in a restaurant?"

"To make sure I can pass as Armando. I'm around a lot of Cubans and I fool them every day."

Clare set her palms on the table. "Why don't you wait and see if Artime and his men can take care of this?"

"Because I hate Artime. He's the worst of all these *gusanos*. He wants to kill Fidel, when the real problem is Raúl. If you can't see the difference, you didn't listen to me in Cuba."

"What I see is that your dreams are no longer about Cuba at all. They're about you and your anger. I understand, everything has been taken from you. But I don't want to get used to you being alive, then have you go back to Cuba where they'll kill you all over again."

"Do you think you will talk me out of this? I cannot live with Raúl walking around in the world, doing what he wants. Later I'll make some life, but for now all this"—he swept his arm around the room—"means nothing to me. I am sorry, but that's how it is."

Clare stood up. "*All this*? All this is my daughter—*our* daughter—and a life I'm trying to make out of nothing. I have my own plans, which I'm sure you would scorn. But it's your plans that seem impoverished to me. Once you got to be a big shot, that was it. You're still like Fidel, like Raúl, like all of them."

He struggled with this, he fought to stay calm and speak plainly. "As you can see, I am no longer anyone. In Costa Rica I lived in a little wooden house, much simpler than this. Now I'm washing dishes in a restaurant. Even my name, I have lost it."

"Only because of this grandiose plan of yours."

He could not win an argument with Clare. She saw through him too easily. It was true that he lived a simple life—but not because he wanted to. He'd been run out of Cuba, and hated it. Going back would not only take care of Raúl, it would make him feel that he could still do something in the world, that he *was* someone.

"Tell me about your own life," he said.

Slow to warm up, she took a few steps across the room and back. "Sometimes I shoot for the *Herald*. Also, there's also going to be a book of photos by me and two other photographers. Black Star found a little press for us in New York. Some of mine will be the photos Fidel hated."

"A revenge in itself," Camilo said.

"But not a revenge in which someone dies."

He should never have told her about going to Cuba.

"I can take photos," she said. "I'm good at it. But for now it's just a way to make a living. I could probably survive here by shooting weddings and bar mitzvahs and portraits that make people look good. But I haven't told you what I was doing in Cuba. You remember Natalia? We started medical school together. We were taking classes, and when Fidel threw me out we were about to get our cadavers. That's what I miss most about Cuba now, my cadaver, which I never got to open up. Can you imagine? Here, they wouldn't let me apply to med school, they said I had to go to college first. So I've started, and I like it."

How easily she went from anger to enthusiasm. "After this," Camilo said, touching his neck, "I have a great respect for doctors."

"Good. We share that." She sat down again and they watched each other in silence, their knees almost touching. She inched forward. "Would you like to kiss me?"

He wanted to, but feared it.

"Just kissing," she said. "To see what it's like."

She leaned toward him, keeping her arms at her sides. How soft her lips were. He'd forgotten that. He'd forgotten everything. He let her lead, feeling her slow tongue on his lips. Her breath was still rice-pudding sweet and the inside of her mouth silky. For a minute, for five minutes, he didn't know who he was.

She stopped. She sat back in her chair and watched him. "The problem," she said, "is this suicidal plan of yours."

He had to resist her convictions, the engine of her will. He tried to keep his eyes off her chest, off her legs, off the skirt that covered her thighs.

"There's something I have to tell you," she said. "I ran into Domingo, and I slept with him."

Camilo stood up. The woman was going to kill him.

"Not like before. I went to his house three times. I never let him come here, and didn't let Ala see him."

"You kiss me, but you go to bed with him?"

"Not anymore. I stopped that already. I won't see him again, and I won't tell anyone that Camilo Cienfuegos is alive."

34

B UT she did tell someone. She told Engracia. Then, feeling guilty, she said, "You must not repeat that to anyone. Swear to me you won't. Swear on the Bible."

"On the Bible? Better on Oshun and her yellow robes. It is Oshun who brought you together again, and surely it was Oshun who saved Camilo."

"*Armando.*"

"Yes, Armando. Who saved him when he was on fire. Oshun lives in the rivers, you know. It is her husband, Changó, who rules fire and the skies. Changó set him on fire, and Oshun saved him. She has always protected the two of you."

"Can Oshun stop him from going back to Cuba?"

"She cannot bring sense to the demented. Still, she is powerful. You have to tell her what you want. You have to know it yourself."

"I don't want him to go to Cuba. He's Ala's father and nothing has changed."

"A lot has changed. His face, for one thing."

"And his chest, which is worse. But I still like kissing him."

"I'm glad to hear it. Will he love his daughter?"

"You know how selfish men are. It's their own lives they think of first."

"But other men don't matter. It's this one you want."

"Perhaps it is you who are my Oshun," Clare said, half-laughing.

"*Oye muchacha, no hablas así.* You never want to offend Oshun. Especially after all she has done for you. Tell me, did she find him for you? Twice now!"

"But this trip will get him killed."

"Then he must not go. We'll work on it, and Oshun will help."

Three days later, returning from work, Camilo found a note taped to his door. *Clare called. Please call her back.*

Not wanting to talk in the boarding house, he used the pay phone on Flagler. She answered on the second ring and went straight to the point. She had a favor to ask. The *Herald* had called for a Sunday meeting of all their photographers. "That's the day I was going to take Ala to the Monkey Jungle, so could you take her for me?"

"Would she go? With just me?"

"We've been talking about the trip for weeks. She loves monkeys."

"What is this jungle?'

"It's a kind of zoo. I'll draw you a map and you can take my car."

"I don't have a license."

"Don't speed and no one will know."

"Why does the paper have a meeting on Sunday?"

"Will you do it?"

He wasn't sure it was a good idea. But "Okay," he said, "I will."

On Sunday morning he found Ala sitting on the step outside, waiting for him. She wore sneakers and a blue dress, and held a small stuffed monkey to her chest.

"You see?" Clare said. "She sleeps with it every night. It came with us from Havana."

In the car the girl sat upright and watchful, still clasping her monkey. Clare's Volkswagen was a cramped little vehicle, and the two of them sat close together on the two front seats. Camilo drove south on Route 1 past palm trees and patchy grass, past mattress and auto parts stores. Some of the residential neighborhoods, with their low houses, sheds and orange trees, looked like the outskirts of Havana. Alameda, staring at the road ahead, announced, "Monkeys hang from their tails."

"Some of them, I think."

"I saw it in a book."

Though grave and mostly quiet, she didn't seem nervous to be driving around with a man she hardly knew. He thought about telling her, *I'm your father*, just to see what her response would be. He wasn't going to say it, but the fact seemed a kind of time bomb.

He puttered along below the speed limit, turned onto 216th Street, drove a couple of miles and there was the Monkey Jungle. Ala scrambled out, leaving her cloth monkey in favor of the real ones, gathering up the boxes of peanuts and raisins that Clare had sent along.

Camilo bought tickets and they entered a narrow walkway, a cage with the humans inside. Roaming freely all around them, monkeys squatted on the ground or jumped through the trees. One landed with a *thump* on the cage, and Ala cried out in surprise. Soon she relaxed, and wanted to see more. There were spider monkeys, chattering macaques and white-handed gibbons. Camilo read the signs as Ala sprinted forward over the earthen path, yelling back, "Come here! Look at this one!" Before he caught up to her she was already running ahead.

Dangled from above and jiggled by a monkey, a small cup hung on a chain. Ala had Camilo open the box of raisins, then took the box herself and poured half of it into the cup, which immediately rose skyward.

"Perhaps a few at a time," Camilo suggested.

"No, look, he's hungry."

"We don't have that many."

"We can get more."

Of course. This was America and there was always more—and Camilo's caution was evaporating at the sight of Ala's joy. There were more cups and more monkeys waiting to be fed, and he let her run through the raisins as fast as she liked, then opened the shelled peanuts. Above, a ruckus broke out, two monkeys pushing and shrieking. Ala stared up at them, looking hesitant at first, then curious. Finally she told them, *"Don't fight. We have more."* As if obedient to her command, they stopped squabbling and one of them scrambled away, passing lightly down the walls of the cage.

Ala sobered up with the peanuts. She had a job now and went from cup to cup, five peanuts allowed per serving. She was in charge of the monkeys' lunch. When the peanuts were finished she handed the empty box to Camilo and said, "Let's go. Let's see everything!"

They did, passing through all the walkways. Sometimes there was nothing, not a monkey in sight, just sunlight piercing the trees and a few birds flashing past. From a store at the entrance Camilo bought some sunflower seeds, and Ala found more monkeys to feed.

"I want to live here," she said.

"We could come again some day."

"No, live here." She wasn't complaining, just making it clear. As she put the last of the sunflower seeds in a cup it began to rain. Drops fell on the ground, on Camilo's shirt and head. He looked up—and a goddamn monkey was pissing on him! He jumped back, but the squirts were finished. Ala, untouched, began to laugh. She jumped up and down. "He peed on you! Because you didn't feed him!"

Camilo found a faucet and washed his hands, splashed water on his face, then his hair and shoulders. A tang remained, and Ala looked more sympathetic. She held out her palms, explaining it to him: "He had to pee and he didn't have a bathroom."

"But he didn't pee on *you*."

"No, only you!"

In a day of adventures this was the high point, and every few minutes she broke into laughter. An hour later it was still a topic as they sat in a diner on the road back into Miami. Ala sat across from him in their booth, her finger tracking the items on the menu. "This is for the monkey with no tail," she said, "and this is for the monkey with the furry face, and this is for the monkey that didn't have a bathroom." For a moment she was solemn, then a smile crept over her face.

Waiting for the food to come, he drank a bland cup of American coffee from a thick white cup. The diner was nearly empty. Some cakes and pies were elevated on chrome stands like prizes, each displayed under glass. It was warm, and the afternoon sun fell directly on their table. The waitress brought four Crayons in a cup and a piece of coloring paper with the outline of some palm trees and a leaping dolphin. Ala began to color in the scene, and Camilo sat back, glad she had something to do. How did anyone take care of a child all day, one day after the next? Ala was not very tidy with the Crayons and soon broke them all. After a long silence, with her drawing half finished, she looked at him and said, "I remember you."

"You do?"

"You told me a story about a rooster."

"You remember that? It's true." This made him happy, but he also worried. "Do you remember my name?"

"Armando," she said.

That relieved him. She said nothing more about it, their hamburgers came and they ate. Ala bent forward over her plate, careful not to spill anything. He'd heard her fuss and complain before, plenty of times, but so far today not a word of it. He thought, *She's like me before I got burned. She knows how to have fun.* All day, just running around and laughing and being herself, she had showed him how nervous and resentful he'd become.

"Alameda," he said, "you're a great girl."

"Yeah," she agreed, "my mom says that."

35

Things must have gone well, Clare thought. Camilo lay in Ala's bed, reading *Babar* in English, his voice barely audible as Clare dried and put away the dishes. She stacked the plates and turned the glasses upside down. She nestled the spoons. From the bedroom now, only silence. He was waiting for Ala to go to sleep, she thought—and Ala hadn't asked for her. It was a miracle, but it made her sad. There was never a day that didn't end with a hug between them.

Then, "*Mamá*, I want you."

When she came out twenty minutes later, Camilo was sitting at the table before an empty bowl of pudding. She asked him if he'd listened to the radio today.

"No, why?"

"The invasion is coming. Some say it's already begun. It's why the *Herald* called the meeting of photographers. They needed someone to fly to Havana tonight."

"But not you."

"They know I'd never get past the airport. Someone else is going, we shuffled assignments, and I'm going to cover the Cuban community here in Miami. I might show up at your boarding house tomorrow."

"*No.*"

"Camilo, I'm joking. Can't you see that?"

She used to be able to tease him. Now he leaned forward, still frowning. "What do they say about the invasion?"

"That Artime and his men are coming on boats from Nicaragua. All this secrecy about it, and Fidel must know everything except where they're going to land. He doesn't need any spies, he can read it in the *Herald*."

"I wanted to go before this happened," Camilo said. "Yesterday I talked to a man who owns a boat, and he said he could take me in another week or two. I don't know what he'll say now."

"You're still set on going."

"You see this?" Between two fingers he pinched the flesh of his neck. "Raúl did this, and I'm going to show him what it looks like."

Clare let his words settle. He'd just spent the day with Ala. He'd read her a book at bedtime, the sweetest job in all the world, and still he was talking about going to Cuba. Engracia had assured Clare that the more Camilo looked after his daughter, the more he'd love her. It was why she'd set up their trip to the Monkey Jungle. But his mania about Raúl seemed unstoppable. Clare knew Ala's heart, and knew that in her unspoken way she was on the lookout for a father. Clare didn't want her to get used to Camilo, then lose him all over again. She didn't want that herself.

"You don't like the Cuban exiles here," she said.

"Every one of them ran away from the Revolution."

"Yet you remind me of them."

"What are you talking about? I'm nothing like any of them."

"They all want to get back to Cuba. But do you think that's going to happen? They've been shut out of their own past, and so have you. So have I, in a way. In five minutes I was turned out of the country."

"Still, I am nothing like them."

"No, because you want a revolution and they don't. But you are no longer part of Fidel's."

Everything she said stung him, she could see. She stood up and put his bowl in the sink, giving them both some time to settle down. She said, more gently, "There are other revolutions, you know. There's one right in front of you."

"What?"

"Me and Alameda, in a world where no one is watching. But after being such a hero, someone looked up to by everyone, could you live a simple life?"

"If that's what I'm given, yes. But I'll always have some dreams of something bigger. Tell me, isn't it the same with you? You live simply now, but you liked Domingo and his money. You liked Fidel. You liked me when I was part of the Revolution."

He was right, she did. She liked him when Fidel turned to him and asked, *¿Voy bien, Camilo?* What if she could have married him then and become part of the Revolution? She would have loved that—and told him so now.

He smiled at her admission, but it was a new, more delicate smile. He'd been through such an ordeal, she thought, that he probably didn't know what he wanted in life. Still, she could not relax about his plan to kill Raúl. It was a madness that would end badly for everyone. "Aren't you afraid of going to Cuba?" she asked. "Afraid of being caught and killed?"

"No, I'm not. It's like planning an ambush."

"How did you get to be like this? Have you never been afraid?"

"In the hospital I was afraid every day. I shook when they came to clean my wounds. Also, when I was in the Cessna with a bomb on my lap."

"What was the bomb?"

"Sticks of dynamite and a clock, like you see in the movies." He put his hands on his thighs and rubbed them softly. "The little hand never stopped, and I thought I was going to shit in my pants. Of course I can be afraid."

"Where did it come from?"

"Raúl must have found someone to put it in the plane. It was in a suitcase, in a compartment in back. An expensive suitcase of soft red leather."

"A *red* suitcase?"

"Yes, *marrón*, with a handle the same color."

"You threw it out of the plane?"

"If I did not, I would not be alive."

"Camilo, I have to go to bed. And don't you start early tomorrow morning?"

"At six."

"Then it's time." She stood up, escorted him to the door and gave him a quick kiss. Through the window she watched him go, then checked on Ala and went to bed herself.

On Monday she worked all day, walking through Little Havana with her cameras, stopping at shops on Flagler and parks on Calle Ocho, talking to Cubans and taking pictures of impromptu gatherings, of people listening to the radio, their faces beaming and expectant. The invasion had come at dawn, but the news of it, reported by telephone from Havana, offered few details. Some said there were two invasions, at Playa Girón and at Niquero, where the *Granma* landed. The Cuban part of Miami felt like Havana in the first days of 1959. People honked their horns and waved Cuban flags, sure that victory was near.

Exhausted that night, Clare went to bed soon after reading to Ala. The following morning she would drive to the Tamiami Airport.

36

SHE stood outside Domingo's house with no purse, no camera, nothing but the guayabera she had borrowed two weeks ago after spilling the glass of wine. The shirt was white, freshly laundered and folded. She held it on one palm as she rang the doorbell.

Domingo was happy to see her. Though she hadn't returned his calls, now he thought she had changed her mind. She saw this on his face. She went inside, keeping the shirt between them to avoid an embrace. She said, "Make me a cup of coffee, would you?"

She wasn't going to touch him, and she wasn't going to drink a cup of coffee. But she followed him to the kitchen. As he took down his old burr grinder she said, "I'll hang this up where I found it."

"Clare, you don't need to. I can take it up later."

"Let me put it back," she said, and headed for the stairs.

She dropped the guayabera on his bed, walked into his closet and found the suitcase she had seen the last time she was here. It was maroon, with a handle the same color. The leather was soft. She picked it up, walked down the stairs and through the living room to the front door, where she set it down. She could hear the beans being ground. She called, "Domingo, I'm out here."

He appeared, wearing a small apron against the dust of the beans. He looked at her, then at the suitcase.

"I need this," she said.

"Are you taking a trip?"

"Tell me again what day you and Felipe flew into the Tamiami Airport."

"What do you mean?" By now his round face was growing longer.

"What day was it?"

"I already told you. It was late December, a year and a half ago."

"You're lying."

"Now you insult me. I have never lied to you."

Clare stood beside the door, the toe of one foot touching the suitcase. If she had to grab it and run, the keys were in the ignition of her car outside.

"I just came from the airport." From her pocket she withdrew a folded sheet of paper and opened it. "Your brother's plane landed there at one in the afternoon on October twenty-ninth."

Now he could not fail to understand. Camilo's plane, as all Cubans knew, had disappeared on the twenty-eighth. Yet Domingo said, "I'm sure there has been a mistake. We flew up after Christmas."

She folded the note and put it back in her pocket. Her voice was a gun, pointed at him. "I also know this suitcase had a mate."

A visible shudder passed through Domingo's body. There was only one person who could have told her about the other suitcase. "He's alive," Domingo said.

"Alive and angry. And he's going to be even angrier when he finds out that the bomb was in *your* suitcase."

Domingo rushed her. She grabbed the suitcase and tried to get out the door, but he caught her by the waist and dragged her back inside. He was stronger than he looked, and faster. She knew this and was furious. Furious at this *cabrón de mierda* and even more at herself, for letting him catch her. He stood between her and the door with the suitcase behind him. She had to have it. Without it, Camilo might think this was all just a story she'd made up.

"He's going to kill you," she said.

"Not if he never finds out about me."

They stood, both breathing hard. "It's too late for threats," Clare said. "Whatever happens here, he'll know the truth soon enough. I wrote him a letter and mailed it from the airport. In two days he'll know everything."

She had lied to Domingo before. She'd lied about who Ala's father was, she'd lied about why she went to Santa Clara, she'd lied about many things. Now, she could see, he didn't know if she was lying or not. And once started, the next lies came easily. "He has a gun. He bought it at that hardware store on Flagler. So you better work with me on this."

"What do you care?"

"I don't want him to kill you."

"Why not?"

"Too messy."

This was so cold that Domingo's head snapped back. She watched him sag, but not so much that he forgot about the suitcase. It was still behind him, as dark and red as the floor tiles. Keeping her eyes off it, Clare sat down at the far end of the sofa. "Sit down, Domingo. Think it through, because I have."

He was slow to move, and when he did sit down he pinned the suitcase between his knees.

"How many people do you think Camilo has killed?"

"I don't know."

"Dozens, and he'll have no compunctions about you. Now tell me what happened."

"His plane disappeared. Everyone knows that."

"Tell me what happened before the plane took off."

Domingo shook his head.

"Then I will tell Camilo where you live so he can ask you himself. You can find out that way how angry he is. Or you can tell me now what you know about the bomb."

"I don't know anything."

"It was in your suitcase. How did it get on the plane?"

Again he shook his head.

Clare waited a full minute, letting the silence mount in the still room. "I guarantee he's going to kill you. He'll shoot you, or he'll break your neck."

Domingo couldn't miss the reference to their fight at El Panchín. He grew smaller and hunched, his eyes flicking around the room. Finally they settled on the floor in front of him. "Two men came to see me."

"Who?"

"They didn't say. To me they looked like Ministry of the Interior, and they had a bomb all prepared."

"Did Fidel send them?"

"I don't know."

"Raúl?"

"Do you think they would tell me something like that?"

"Why do you say Ministry of the Interior?"

"Because they knew all about you and me, and all about you and him. They also told me where he was going to be, and when. They said if Felipe and I put the bomb on his plane, we could leave Cuba the next day. So we flew to Camagüey. Felipe paid a guard five hundred pesos to wait in the hanger, and I put the suitcase in the plane."

"They made you do it," Clare said.

"No. I wanted to do it. After you left me I wanted to kill him."

Honesty, she thought, was all she wanted from anyone. She stood up. "You better get out of town. Take Felipe and go up to Silver Springs. Go to Saint Augustine and stay for a week."

"What are you going to tell him?"

"*You* don't ask *me* anything. If you don't want to leave, fine, stay here. You can lie here all night and listen to every sound outside and never know if it's him."

His knees did not resist when she pulled the suitcase from between them. Holding it tight, she walked out the door.

37

CAMILO was washing dishes, wondering still why Clare had acted so strangely at her house. One minute she'd been full of questions, the next she sent him away. Now, in the restaurant kitchen, all talk was about the invasion, which had entered its second day. Over the noise of the dishwasher and the sizzle of fried plantains, a radio gave what information was known: that a thousand brigade members, maybe more, had landed at Playa Girón—the Americans were calling it the Bay of Pigs—and were now advancing toward Havana. There were battles in the air, and a half dozen U.S. destroyers waited in international waters to the south of the island. The Cuban people, too long oppressed by a new dictator, were going to rise up against him and sweep him from power.

Camilo rinsed dishes from the lunch crowd, the remains of *ropa vieja* and red bean soup. Everyone else in the kitchen was electrified—but how could they believe that the people of Cuba would turn against Fidel? They would not, and the invasion would fail. This, Camilo thought, might be good for him. In the aftermath he might have a better chance of sneaking into the country. No one would be thinking about Camilo Cienfuegos. This afternoon he'd go over to the hardware store on Flagler and buy the little Smith & Wesson.

Behind him a stir, and he turned to find Clare walking toward him, accompanied by Antonio, the restaurant's owner. *El coño Antonio*, as everyone in the kitchen called him, was a tyrant about punctuality, yet now he was saying, "Of course, of course. Armando, what luck for you. This woman, who speaks like a Cuban, has an emergency and needs you. And I don't have any problems in this case."

The guy had never looked so congenial. His eyebrows were wiggling, his big hips were rolling, and he seemed actually happy to let Camilo off work. "On a day like this," he added, "we must celebrate." He was so happy to have met Miss Miller, such a delightful señorita, and he hoped to have the pleasure again soon.

Camilo looked her over on the way to her car. No makeup, a pair of dark slacks and a white blouse open at the throat. Not sexy, exactly, but of course she looked good. "What did you tell that guy? He's never been so nice to anyone."

"I told him that a very important, very personal matter had come up that simply could not wait. I told him I was sure he would understand."

"You played the coquette."

"But for a good reason."

"Which is?"

"I will tell you at my house."

Once there, she led him inside and asked him to sit down. Then she walked back to her car, opened the little hood in front, picked up the suitcase and carried it inside.

Camilo stared at it. He stood up but came no closer. He looked afraid. "What is in it?"

"It's empty."

When she set it on the floor and pushed it toward him, he recoiled. Slowly, he put a hand on it, then both hands, running them over the leather. He picked it up by the handle, set it on the sofa, then softly unhooked the two brass latches. It was empty, but he still looked hesitant. The blood, at least, had returned to his face.

"Where did you get this?"

"I think you know." She took the note out of her pocket and passed it to him. "This morning I found out that Domingo and his brother flew out of Cuba on the twenty-ninth of October."

He stared at the note, then at her. The logic was inescapable. He pushed the suitcase onto the floor, then picked it up and flung it across the room. It bounced off the legs of the dining room table and smacked into the wall. Camilo stood shaking. *"He will die."*

"You can't do that. This is the United States, not Cuba. They'll put you in prison forever."

"Tell me where he is."

She told him, instead, everything Domingo had told her about himself, Felipe and the two men. She said nothing about Fidel and nothing about Raúl. "I'm sure you could find Domingo's house, but he won't be there. I told him to leave town."

"He can't escape me." But now he was sinking. He sat down on the sofa, leaned back and stared at the ceiling. Clare crouched on the sofa beside him, and when she put her arms around him he began to weep.

An hour later he lay on the floor like a saint on a sarcophagus, rigid, naked to the waist, his arms folded across his chest and his head raised on a pillow It hadn't been easy to get him this far, to take off his shirt, then stretch him out on a rug on her living room floor.

Engracia had brought her a stoppered bottle of oil infused by herbs from Cuba, *sábila y lavanda*. They were good for Changó's wounds, she said, the best thing for burns. Clare explained this to Camilo, who stared at the ceiling. With the soft pad of a finger she closed his eyes. Then she dribbled some oil into one of her palms and rubbed them gently across his forehead, his eyebrows, his temples, down onto the burn on his left cheek. Here the scars were not too bad, only a rippled red skin that might go unnoticed in low light.

"Relax," she said. "I'm hardly going to touch your jaw."

He winced anyway as she passed her smooth oiled fingertips over the scars beneath his cheek. The small of his back arched off the ground and stayed that way, until she slipped a hand beneath him and pressed down on his pelvis with her other palm, a steady gentle pressure until his hips unclenched. She returned to his neck, to his *clavícula*, his *escapula*, his *acromion*. These she knew from her anatomy class.

His chest was the most difficult. She poured more oil in her hand, then hesitated—at which his eyes blinked open. Promptly she went back to rubbing his shoulders, the pads of her fingers circling down toward his stiff corded flesh. She closed her own eyes, massaging him steadily, softly, over and over, trying to get used to the washboard texture of his skin. She kept to her gentle rhythm until she felt him quiver beneath her hands. He was going to sleep. She opened her eyes and watched his face. His chest rose and fell. He made no sound. He slept. Finally she took a close look at the skin she was still rubbing, and cringed. It looked like the skin of a reptile. She would have stopped massaging him, but feared he would wake and see her aversion. With some oil poured directly on the burn, she kept rubbing. It was hard to believe this was his skin, after so many grafts. His smooth chest, that she had loved, was now a tumult of ridges and valleys, the colors a blotched red and pink. His nipples, always small, had almost disappeared. She bent closer, so close that she no longer saw his body, just the textures and colors. It was better with the oil, which softened the ribbed and horny feel of the scars. Still, she would have to live with this. This would be the chest she would feel above her, or beneath her, when they made love. This was the skin that would make other people skittish, that would sometimes make *her* skittish. Ala, too, would have to live with it.

He was far away now, fully asleep. Clare stood up, washed her hands, then took out her silent Leica with the macro lens she used at the morgue. She threaded in a roll of color film, crouched above him and began to shoot, bracketing her exposures because the color was so subtle. Through the viewfinder, his chest might have been a painting on canvas, full of swirls and trailing red lines. She came in close, then shot at different angles, from different heights, moving slowly from his ribs to his face. Many had photographed him in Cuba, but never in color and never when he slept. She shot his face from the good side and the bad. He lay still, and the longer he slept the more relaxed he looked.

She took three rolls of film, then sat back. She loved photography. She thought about the years when all she wanted was to take pictures and be famous, to be as admired as Margaret Bourke-White or Henri Cartier-Bresson. She had failed at that. Of course, some things had been easier for those two, who had been unencumbered by young children. They traveled everywhere, they came and went as they chose, photography was all they knew.

No, it was not just that. Better to admit the truth. They were braver than she was, and more inventive.

Camilo was the famous one. But then, what good did it do him, living as Armando? He'd lost so much he could no longer imagine the future. His foolish dream of revenge had been crushed. She hoped he would recover, but there was a chance he might not. For herself, she had decided. She would always take photographs, but that would not be her job. She wanted to study medicine and become a doctor. She wanted to get up every day and do something she loved, and be paid for it.

The front door opened to Ala and Engracia. Clare whipped her finger to her lips and both went silent. Engracia closed the door with a gentle click, and Ala looked at Camilo on the floor, lying there without his shirt. She came closer. She stared. Engracia, too, bent forward for a look, as Clare stood up with her camera. Ala paid no attention to them. She tiptoed even closer, putting a finger to her lips as if telling herself to stay silent. She squatted down beside her father like a beggar, at ease on her haunches, staring at his chest and neck. For five minutes she didn't move. Maybe the very young, Clare thought, could look at a burn like this without imagining all the torment that came with it.

No one said anything until Camilo stirred. He opened his eyes, sat up slowly, then reached around for his shirt and put it on. Ala stared at him, and he stared back. He said, "What a beautiful face I woke up to."

38

H E went along with everything. He had no idea what else to do.
Clare told him, gently, to stand up. She asked Engracia to stay with
Ala. She went outside and he followed. They walked in silence along
the shaded Miami streets, past orange trees and grapefruits, palms and
tamarinds. She took him into a café on Flagler, where they sat with a pair
of untouched sandwiches in front of them as a television, on a table in one
corner of the room, blared the unhappy news. The invasion wasn't going
well. Of course not, he thought—though he took no pleasure in being
right. A ship had been sunk, another damaged, and the brigade was no
longer advancing, perhaps had never advanced, was in fact pinned down
on the beach and in the swamps. Cries and groans flew across the room,
yet people kept eating. An invasion gone awry didn't get in the way of
that, Camilo thought. The room was a carnival of pork sandwiches, black
coffee and bad news.

"Say something," Clare said.

"Like what?"

"I don't know." She quoted Martí, *"Yo soy un hombre sincero, de donde
crece la palma."*

"That's what's so sad. I don't know where I'm from any more." He
bent forward and continued in English, not as loud, "Listen to these fools.
How could they believe that the Cuban people would rise up against Fidel?
In two days it will all be over."

"But the news isn't making you happy."

His face felt strange, as if his flesh were sagging. He touched his fingertips to the burns on his left cheek, but they hadn't changed. "It's because
I'm here, not there. And even there I'd be a stranger to the Revolution."

He wanted to show her that nothing could cheer him up, that all happiness was an insult to him. She was trying to hide her own happiness, but he saw it anyway. She was proud of her detective work, for now he had Domingo to blame, not Raúl. And the men from the Ministry of the Interior—what did they prove? Raúl could have sent them, or it might have been Fidel, or Ramiro Valdés. He would never know.

On the television, Fidel appeared in stock footage from one of his rallies in the Plaza de la Revolución. A wave of hisses rolled through the café, and when it died down Camilo told Clare what he'd told himself a few days before, "I cannot live in this city. I cannot be surrounded by all these people who only want to hear that the Revolution is dead."

"Where *could* you live?"

"Nowhere."

"And who with?"

"Nobody."

She stared at him, saddened. He looked away, he glanced at Fidel, still gesticulating on the television. "I'm sorry Clare, that isn't true. Later I'll want to be with you. With Ala as well."

"How do you know?"

"Because through all of this I have never stopped thinking of you."

"I thought about you—but I thought you were dead. This time I was sure of it."

"But this time you didn't marry someone else."

"No, I'd had enough of that."

"Perhaps it's because you couldn't find anyone as wonderful as Domingo." She stared at him, surprised.

"What?" he asked.

"You just made a joke."

"I can still make jokes."

"Do you think that one day we'll drink some rum and go dancing?"

He didn't know what to say. *One day*. When would that be? He could not imagine dancing. From the day his plane crashed he had drunk no rum.

"If we can't live in Miami," Clare said, "then where?"

She was like Fidel, he thought. She got on a topic and did not let up. "We were happy in New York," he said.

Clare pushed the plate with her sandwich aside. "No, I'm sorry. I cannot raise Alameda there. The city is too big. It has none of the grace of Havana, and I think it would crush us."

Havana was the city they would all have loved—but to them Havana was closed.

"What about Costa Rica?" she asked.

He'd always thought he would leave Costa Rica and go somewhere else. But he had nowhere else to suggest. "My house is tiny," he said.

"There must be other houses. The Figueres farm—it's not that far from San José, is it? San José must have a medical school."

"It does. But what about Ala? How would she feel about yet another country?"

"If everyone loves her, she'll be happy."

39

T HAT night they slept in Clare's narrow bed, the two of them touching but not kissing. Clare, used to sleeping alone when Ala didn't join her, woke up a half dozen times, surprised always to find Camilo there. She rolled over, turned toward him or away, then drifted off again.

In the morning she was dressed by the time he woke. "Feed Alameda," she told him. "Look after her, and I'll be back soon."

She drove to the same café on Flagler, ate breakfast rolls and drank two cups of coffee. The place was nearly empty and the waiters looked depressed. Not Clare. She was waiting for her bank to open, and when it did she withdrew her miniature savings of $257. From there she drove to a used car lot on 27th, the same place where she'd bought her Volkswagen, and sold it back to them for half the price, $300. That would be enough to take to the travel agency. She walked there, all the way to Calle Ocho through the sunlit morning. She liked Miami and could have stayed—but goodbye to the city and all the Cuban exiles, because Camilo couldn't bear how they hated the Revolution.

Later, in a small park, Clare sat on a concrete bench. Three one-way tickets to San José were in her purse for this afternoon's flight on Lacsa. Also, because Ala was going to miss her *abuelita*, there was a round-trip ticket for Engracia, undated, so she could come and visit.

On the sidewalk, men and women passed by with their eyes averted. As Camilo had predicted, they were coming to their senses. Their sons and nephews, instead of driving Castro from power, were pinned down on the beaches of Playa Girón, and dying.

It was a good day to leave Miami. She would get on a plane with the two people she loved most and fly to a country she knew little about. Camilo, after his time there, still did not think of it as home, but he had no other. In San José they'd find someone to drive them out to Pepe and Karen's farm. Camilo's small house would be there with its bed, a table, a kitchen, his few books and clothes. They'd go up to the Figueres house and she would meet Karen, an American like her. Later, with Ala stretched out between them, she and Camilo would sit outside in the warm still air and listen to the sounds of the night. She would learn to live with his scars, and with his new reserve. Sometimes, as Natalia had assured her, he would drive her crazy—and sometimes, she knew, it would be the other way around. So be it, Clare thought. If Camilo could make a joke, she was sure they would soon be dancing.

For Max and Harper, who love to read.
For April Eberhardt, agent extraordinaire.
And for my many readers and critics:

Michelle Ajamian
Dianne Arman
Ann Barr
Mary Ann Borch
Barry Campbell
Ted Conover
Will Dewees
Biddle Duke
Kathy Galt
Lois Gilbert
Isabel Graziani
Granville Greene
Cricket Jones
Paul Kafka-Gibbons
Beth Kaufman
Eddie Lewis
Tom Miller
Ann Moneypenny
Lisa Nelson
Art Norton
Raúl Ramos y Sanchez
Henry Shukman
Alan Thorndike
Ellen Thorndike
Janir Thorndike
LL Thorndike
Sandy Weymouth
Juliet Wittman
Mary B. Wood
…and surely some others, *desgraciado que soy*, whom I have forgotten.

John Thorndike grew up in New England, graduated from Harvard, took an MA from Columbia, then lit out for Latin America. He spent two years in the Peace Corps in El Salvador, and two on a backcountry farm in Chile. Eventually he settled with his son in Athens, Ohio, where for ten years his day job was farming. Then it was construction, but always he wrote. His first two books were novels, followed by a pair of memoirs. *A Hundred Fires in Cuba* is his latest novel, and he's at work on the next one, a half-fictional evocation of his mother's life.

Also by John Thorndike

The Last of His Mind

A Best Book of 2009
    —*The Washington Post*
Indie Top 20
    —*Publishers Weekly*
2009 GOLD Winner for Autobiography and Memoir
    —*Foreword Reviews*

"An engrossing memoir...a beautiful book."
    —*Publishers Weekly* (Starred review)

"A brave, moving story.... Thorndike's prose is serenely beautiful.... An affecting work of emotional honesty and forgiveness."
    —*Kirkus Reviews*

Another Way Home

"The directness, the honesty, the terrible plain chant of the narrative stunned me."
    —Doris Grumbach, author of *Fifty Days of Solitude*

"The prose is shapely and elegant, polished to a shine, with never a word out of place or a phrase too many."
    —*The Chicago Tribune*

"This book sings. It's a burning, beautiful memoir, rich in anecdote and character. And elegantly written. We need to see fathers in this light—tender, caring, committed."
    —Natalie Goldberg, author of *Writing Down the Bones*, *Wild Mind* and *Let The Whole Thundering World Come Home*.

The Potato Baron

"Thorndike offers an unabashed good read: exotic travels and love affairs, earthy sex and heart-twisting passages about Austin and Fay's devotion to their gaptoothed son, Blake. Their feelings shift as they are pulled in different directions, revealing Mr. Thorndike's sensitivity to the tortuous process of making and unmaking decisions. The novel unfolds with a finely calculated momentum. *The Potato Baron* is an intelligent and high-spirited story. In contrast to much of contemporary fiction, it explores characters who have never lost their connection to their work or to each other—and who, when these essential ties are threatened, are willing to fight to get them back."
—*The New York Times*

Anna Delaney's Child

"An affecting first novel" written in "lyrically powerful prose."
—*The New York Times*

"Ambitious and daring."
—*Los Angeles Book Review*

"A novel of grace and style."
—*The Columbus Dispatch*

"A terrific novel."
—*The Cleveland Plain Dealer*

CPSIA information can be obtained
at www.ICGtesting.com
Printed in the USA
LVHW09s1106200918
590669LV00007B/237/P